FADE into you

L.A. FERRO

Fade Into You: by L.A. FERRO Published by Pine Hollow Publishing

Cover by K.B. Barrett Designs

Proofreading & Editing: Lawrence Editing

Published by Pine Hollow Publishing

Cataloging-in-Publication data is on file with the Library of Congress.

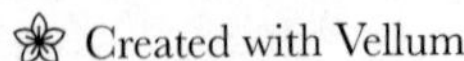

NOTE TO READERS

For anyone who has ever longed to see their love reflected in the eyes of the person they want. Here's your happily ever after.

Sometimes, unspoken love really does move mountains.

CHAPTER 1
CONNOR

"Fuck, you can't be serious right now," shouts the guy who just stumbled out of the stadium with a beer in hand. His shirt is soaked from bumping into me. "You owe me a shirt, ass—"

"I wouldn't finish that sentence if I were you." The guy can't be over twenty-one and has had one too many drinks.

"And why is that…" The kid's voice dies off a little as his attention snaps away from his soaked shirt and toward me. I've got at least six inches on his height, and I don't miss a day at the gym, compared to this kid who clearly spent one too many nights playing beer pong in college rather than doing anything physical.

I'm not trying to get into a fight right now. I have somewhere I need to be. "Look, kid, you're clearly inebriated, and this isn't a fight you're going to win."

"Who do you think you are?" he questions, puffing out his chest in a pathetic attempt to appear macho in front of his girlfriend, who seems to be just as trashed. Fucking newbie drinkers.

"Not the guy you want to mess with," I say as I step around him to continue on my way.

"You owe me a shirt," he demands as I attempt to brush off the entire encounter.

I stretch my neck and take a deep breath so I don't do something I'll regret and point to the exit he just stepped out of before saying, "That camera and the prohibited drink you walked out of the stadium with say different." As his eyes follow my pointed direction, I start walking away. The conversation is over, and I'm done allowing his nonsense to take up any more of my time.

Downtown is flooded in a sea of red. As I cross the street with the throngs of baseball fans heading toward Paddy O's to watch the game, I internally curse myself. The bar is going to be crowded as hell tonight. It didn't even occur to me to check the baseball schedule to see if there was a home game playing when I set up this meet two nights ago on Tinder. The bar we are meeting at is right across from the stadium. But I haven't been thinking clearly lately, which is another reason I need this hookup tonight. I need a release, badly.

Finding a place to park took a little longer than usual, considering the crowds and the drunken idiot who ran into me took up even more time. However, I'm still thirty minutes early, and that's more than enough time to have a drink and settle my nerves before my date arrives. Pushing through the front doors, I find the place is jam-packed. The inside temperature is just barely cooler than the ninety-degree air outside. As I make my way through the horde of bodies drinking and celebrating another win, I consider leaving. This is not the scene I signed up for. Downtown St. Louis is typically quiet, and it's far enough from my hometown that I don't risk running into anyone I might know. But just as I'm about to turn around and call it a night, a pair of tan legs in a baby blue summer dress standing at the bar catches my eye.

I'm tempted to pull out my phone to double-check the last message in the app just to ensure I'm remembering the text correctly because there is no way the girl from the app is this sexy. The girls on these dating apps are typically catfish extraordinaries, choosing pics with the best angles or using filters that alter their appearance. Men do it, too, but I'm currently pleasantly surprised. Technically, I haven't seen this girl, but in our last message, she said, "I'll be the blonde at the bar wearing a blue dress."

We matched strictly because of our interests: one-night stands with no strings attached. I'll admit her having no profile picture made me hesitant, but something about it intrigued me nonetheless, and I messaged her. On her profile, she goes by Blu. From what I gathered, she's a traveling nurse with no plans of settling down in the foreseeable future. Undoubtedly, months like this past one make me wish I had someone closer, but I'm not the settling type, and the few times I tried the whole friends-with-benefits relationship, it never panned out. I've yet to meet a woman I can sleep with multiple times without it turning into them wanting more. They always want more, and I can't fault them. It's a natural progression for most people, but I'm not most people. I don't just have myself to worry about.

Before I give my nonexistent love life any further thought, I'm squeezing in next to Blu at the bar. I can't help but get into her personal space. Everyone in here tonight is elbow-to-elbow, packed in like a bunch of fucking sardines. No sooner my palm hits the bar top than she peers over her shoulder at me. Her piercing blue eyes make my breath catch in my throat and throw me off my game.

"Hey," is all I manage as I internally cringe at my pathetic pickup line—if you could even call it that because technically, we are not on a date, for all intents and purposes.

"Hey," she answers somewhat skittishly as she bites the corner of her lip before returning her focus to the bartender mixing drinks.

Her demureness has me second-guessing if she is indeed my girl or if this is just a case of mistaken identity. Even if the latter were true, I'd probably jump ship and stay right here. However, this isn't my first rodeo. Some women like to play the shy, timid card on these hookups, and I have no problem putting in the work. If she wants to take it slow tonight and have a few drinks, I'm game, as long as it ends with her and a room.

Leaning in to ensure she hears me over the roar of music and voices in the bar, I ask, "Are you waiting for someone?"

She tucks a strand of her long blond hair behind her ear before giving me those gorgeous eyes again. They're beyond words. They're hypnotic, is what they are.

"Yes," is all she supplies. But this time, her eyes linger. She's checking me out.

When she doesn't shy away, I ask, "Just passing through?" It's the phrase she used in our messages a few days ago.

Her eyes narrow, and she rolls her perfect pink lips as if debating her response, but there's nothing to debate. The longer she hesitates, the more confident I am that the attraction is more than mutual.

"I am." Another short response but confirmation all the same.

"Let me buy you a drink."

She throws her head over her shoulder as if searching for someone, probably unconvinced, just like me, that we are, in fact, Blu and Cal from the app and that sometimes the universe does get it right.

"Yeah, okay."

"What do you like? Wait—don't tell me. Let me guess." Guessing will give me a reason to thoroughly check her out from head to toe.

"Anything with Red Bull feels too obvious, and I can tell you're anything but predictable. If I had to guess, you run off Starbucks Coldbrew Sweet Cream and not energy drinks."

That earns me a slight eyebrow raise but no balk, which means I'm probably right.

"While you can definitely afford to drink beer, I get the impression you don't."

Her lips pull to the side. "Oh yeah, and why is that?"

"Just a hunch. Those legs look like they've seen the gym, and most girls don't drink beer because of the carbs. I'm going to go with wine spritzer."

Before she can confirm or deny my claims, the bartender asks, "What'll it be?"

I motion for her to order. "Ladies first."

"I'll have a margarita."

The bartender looks at me, and I say, "I'll have an IPA—whatever is on tap is fine." St. Louis is known for beer, and they have some local microbreweries on tap.

"Margarita. I'll admit, I didn't see that one coming, but I guess I should have."

Her brow furrows. "And why exactly is that?"

"Easy: tequila makes her clothes fall off."

"So I went from a mature coffee-drinking fitness enthusiast to a ho. I must hand it to you. You really know how to impress the ladies."

"Wait, no, that was supposed to be a joke."

Her eyebrows rise, and I can see my comment leaves her thoroughly unimpressed.

"It's a country song. 'Tequila Makes Her Clothes Fall Off.'"

I haven't been on an actual date in years. They are too much work, and I can't risk more than one night. My life hasn't been my own for quite some time, and everything will change again in a year. No woman would want my baggage, and I'm not asking them to carry the weight. There was a time when I thought settling down and finding a woman to share my life with was a possibility. But I no longer believe that to be the case, which is why I'm here in this bar now, trying to give this woman all I have to offer, but fuck if my life choices aren't shooting me in the foot. My lack of actual dates is starting to affect my game.

Luckily, the bartender returns with our drinks and saves me from inserting my foot in my mouth once more. I know I'm older than her, but according to her profile, it's only by two years. Now that she's here in person, her age may have been a stretch. Hell, the entire profile was probably fake, but I can't really complain. It's not like I'm being honest on mine either. After all, we aren't here for the long game.

"Margarita for the lady and a Hazy Punch IPA."

I don't miss the bartender's flirt or his subtle dismissal of me. Hey, I get it. If I were him, I'd be flirting, too, but when he passes her the check tab, I can't help but get aggravated.

"Hey, bro, I'll take that. Do you really think I'd let her pay?"

I grab the little black book from in front of her, but she places her hand on top and says, "This isn't the nineties. Women can pay the tab."

Fuck, how old does she think I am? I wasn't drinking in the nineties. I'm only thirty.

"That might be true, but you'll have to excuse me for wanting to be a gentleman and buy my date a drink."

"Date?" she questions before picking up her drink and adding, "I think you're getting a little ahead of yourself."

The bartender quirks a half smile before fucking off and helping other customers.

"Does that mean you're not interested?"

I'm all about playing hard to get and even a little foreplay, but hell, the woman isn't even throwing me a bone here. I know she's interested. She can barely look me in the eye without blushing, and the way she's fidgeting with the silver pendant around her neck leans into nerves.

I've been so focused on the flush in her cheeks and the goose bumps on her arm every time I lean in to speak that I overlooked she has already hammered half of her glass.

That's a good sign. She's trying to calm her nerves. I get it: casual hookups and one-night stands have a stigma of being certified bad decisions, so making the sober choice to have one undoubtedly requires some amount of liquid courage.

She bites that pouty bottom lip again before running her hand through her hair and saying, "I didn't say that, but—"

Whatever comment she was about to make dies when I snatch the check holder. "Hey," she screeches as she tries to grab it back.

"Relax, Blu. I'm not letting you pay. Call me old-school all you want. I don't care. Where I come from, the guy pays the bill."

She reaches for it again, and I hold it up high. I have more than a foot on her in height. There is no way she will get the book, but I'm all about her trying, especially when her soft body presses against my front in her feeble attempts to grab something clearly out of her reach.

Those baby blues that could send nations to war land on mine while her hands lie on my chest. "Please give it back," she pleads, and damn if I don't want to give it to her, but I hold my ground.

"This is one battle you're not going to win, Blu. I rather enjoy hearing you beg."

Her eyes dart between mine as if she's thinking about another line, but rather than give me any more words, she shocks the fucking hell out of me and cups my dick. I was already getting a semi from her body rubbing against mine, and I'll be damned if he's not ready now.

"If you wanted to sample the goods before you made a decision, all you had to do was ask."

I move to snake my free hand around her waist, and in my lust-filled haze, my grip on the check holder loosens, and a black envelope slips out, falling onto the bar top. Her hand swipes out faster than my mind has time to process, and she pulls out of my hold. I instantly miss her warmth but quickly try to shove down the loss so that I can focus on what just happened.

"I thought you said you were just passing through?" I ask as she quickly shoves the envelope into her bag. *Because that's not suspicious at all.*

"I am," she says matter-of-factly, as if black envelopes falling out of check holders is nothing new.

"Then what was that you just shoved in your purse? Your plans with the bartender for later tonight?"

I don't miss the slight tremble of her fingers as she secures the straps of her satchel bag, ensuring all her snaps are tightly closed. Again, she gives me zero time to analyze what the hell is going on before she pins me with a glare and says, "You sure do ask a lot of questions for someone who's just buying me a drink."

I step into her. "I think we both know I want to do more than just buy you a drink."

Her eyelids flutter shut ever so slightly as her cheeks tinge with my new favorite shade of pink. I know I affect her. She's not wearing a bra under that sundress. Her nipples were rock-hard as she fought me for the check holder.

She pulls in a stuttered breath. "I'll be right back. I just need to use the restroom."

I throw my arm around her waist and pull her into me. "Are you trying to walk out on me?"

Her eyes briefly catch mine before she pins them on my chest, which could mean one of two things: I'm about to get a lie or I make her nervous.

"No. You bought me a drink. I plan to finish it."

I tip her chin up so her beautiful eyes are on mine when I say, "How do I know you're not lying?"

"I guess you don't."

Reluctantly, I let her go as I consider my next move. I'm pretty sure she's into me. I felt it. It's been a while since I got laid or even went on a date. It's part of the reason I let her go.

I need to make sure I'm not thinking with my dick and forcing myself on the girl. Just because I'm into her and ready to get a room doesn't mean she's on the same page. I reach for the check holder to try and bring the blood flow back to other regions of my body and refocus my brain, but when I open the holder, it's empty. There's no fucking bill.

My eyes immediately shoot up to the bartender who handed her the holder instead of me. I instantly assume he swooped in and stole my date for the night before I got to the bar. Well, screw that. Challenge accepted.

I take off toward the bathrooms in search of my date. She needs to know she has options. One of them being me. That's what the envelope was. It had to be. When I reach the women's restroom, I pace outside the entrance for a beat before deciding fuck it. I'm not even convinced she's in there, and I'm sure as hell not going to waste time waiting for her to come out if she did indeed ghost me.

The second I push open the door, a woman coming out says, "Hey, wrong door," as she squeezes by, but that doesn't stop me even though it should. The old me would have turned around and maybe considered that I'm being irrational. So what if the girl I never planned on seeing again stands me up? However, right now, I can't think past taking something for myself, even if I'm going about it the wrong way. It's something I haven't been able to do lately, and when I look up and my eyes lock with hers as she reapplies her lip gloss in the mirror, I know there will be no turning back.

Her eyes widen as she sees me cross the space to her. "What are you doing in here?" she questions in the mirror before turning around.

"You were about to stand me up."

"What?"

"Hey, you can't be in here," another woman exiting the stall says, distracting me from the task at hand.

Grabbing Blu by the hand, I pull her into the handicap stall and close the door, ensuring I have her full attention.

"The envelope. Those are your plans. It's why you wouldn't commit to more than a drink," I say as I back her against the wall. "There was no check in the holder. The bartender passed you an envelope and nothing more." I dip my head, my mouth mere inches away from hers. I'm so close I can smell the lime from the margarita on her breath. Her tongue darts out and I move in to taste her, but she turns her head right before our mouths connect, my lips landing on her jaw instead. I gently pepper kisses along her jawline and down her neck before saying, "Tell me I read this wrong. Tell me you're not interested."

Her breathing is ragged, the rise and fall of her chest clearly defined. "Does it matter if I'm just passing through?"

That's what this is. She feels it too. We could be more. Sometimes, there's chemistry on these hookups, which can easily overshadow the night if you let yourself get in your head. There's a reason we only wanted one night. It's clear, like me, she's single by choice, and when you have chemistry, it's easy to question all those choices. It's easy to run.

"So am I. That's the point, Blu. No commitments, no strings attached. Just this once."

"That sounds great, but I am really just passing through, and I have somewhere I need to be."

I remove my head from the crook of her neck and rest my forehead against hers. "Let me show you how good it can be, and if you still have to go, I'll let you go."

"What?" she questions breathlessly, clearly worked up from my mouth on her neck and my hard cock pressed into her stomach.

Once again, I try to take her mouth, but she turns away. I kiss the corner once before quickly moving down to her chest. My hands cup her breasts through her sundress, and I squeeze them hard. They're fucking perfect. I want to pull them out and suck on them, but I don't. I'm heading straight for heaven and ensuring there's no question of whose bed she'll be warming for the night. Dropping to my knees in front of her, I run my hands up her thighs.

"What are you doing?" she asks, her voice unsteady as I lift one of her legs and drape it over my shoulder.

"Blu, you can be shy all you want. I don't mind working for it." I kiss her inner thigh and feel her leg slightly tremble, and I can't help but smile.

When I start to trail my finger up her leg toward the apex of her thighs, she attempts to object. "Wait, I, this—"

I cut her off and loop my finger through the lace of her thong, pulling it to the side. I'm on my knees for this girl. I realize coming in here might be brash, but she's the one in control in this position. She could easily kick me in the balls. Hell, she could open that pretty mouth and tell me to stop right now, and I would, but she won't. I know she feels it. She wants this as much as I do. "I promise I'll be quick, and then you can decide."

"But that's not—"

Any further objections she had quickly die when she feels me run my tongue through her folds. "Aah, fuck," she hisses out on a breathy moan.

I can't help but growl as I sink my tongue into her tight hole. Knowing I'm making her feel good makes me hard. My dick is so fucking jealous of the swollen pussy my lips are currently pressed against. Fuck, I want to do so many things right now. I want to savor the taste of her on my tongue, and more than that, I want to open her up wide, spear her on my cock, and make her see stars, but I told her I'd be quick.

The second I slip a digit in, her hungry pussy clenches around it as her hand slides into my hair, sending a delicious trail of goose bumps down my back. When I slip in the second digit, she pulls my hair, and that's when I know I have her. This pussy is going to be wrapped around my dick tonight.

She starts to rock against my face as I pump into her harder. I know she's close, and damn it if I don't want to catch a glimpse of that pretty face flushed with ecstasy as I bring her to orgasm. Her pussy starts to clench hard, on the edge of letting go. I can feel it. Curling my fingers, I greedily hum against her pussy, my tongue working her slit, thoroughly stimulating her as I tilt my head up to see her face, but the second my eyes look up, they collide with hers, and fuck me if my dick doesn't drip with desire. I'm more than turned on that she's watching me pleasure her. I love it when women watch. When they don't, I demand it.

I know she was already on edge, but our eyes locking sends her spiraling, and she pulls my hair hard. *Fuck.* I growl hungrily against her pussy as I pump her through her orgasm, lapping up all her juices until her grip loosens. When her hand leaves the back of my head, I release her thong, adjusting it so it covers her before kissing her thigh once more and removing her leg from my shoulder.

As I stand, I press my body against hers, ensuring she feels every inch of my arousal. "So what's it going to be? Are you going to let me do more than buy you a drink?"

Her chest is still heaving, her arousal evident, but where I thought I had a for sure yes, she says, "I told you. I'm just passing through. I can't. I really do have to—"

"Montana!" a male voice calls out. "Are you in there? Let's go."

Her eyes close, and she presses her head against the wall. "Yeah, I'll be out in just a sec.

"Look, I'm sorry, but I have to go." She pushes past me, my head now reeling.

What the hell is going on?

I follow after her, but right as I throw the bathroom door open and step into the hallway, a man about my height wearing a ballcap is escorting her out of the bar. I push through a few patrons crowding my way to storm after her, but she's too far ahead.

"What the hell?" I growl out, thoroughly displeased.

I give up on chasing her. I don't chase women, but I make my way toward the exit anyway. I'm done with the city. Hell, part of me is done with this whole scene. I'm getting too old for this shit, but for now, this is the hand I've been dealt. I can either accept that every date won't end with a happy ending or choose celibacy. The latter has my chest tightening because fuck if that doesn't sound like hell. But as it would turn out, fate is a fickle bitch.

Just as I pull the door open, a pretty blonde wearing none other than a pale blue mini-bandage dress that hugs her curves in all the right places waltzes in.

"Thank you," she singsongs as she enters and heads straight to the bar. I grab my phone from my back pocket and check the time: 7:01 p.m.

"You've got to be kidding me," I mutter. She's clearly the girl I was supposed to meet tonight. We said 7:00 p.m., and here she is.

Fuck. I just went down on the wrong girl.

CHAPTER 2
MACKENZIE

"Did you not read the note Dax handed you?" the man, who could double as a Harry Styles look-alike, with dark brown locks and dreamy green eyes, asks as he places his hand on my back and escorts me out of the bar. If I weren't post-orgasm right now, my mind wouldn't be fuzzy. I have no clue who Dax is, but I will go out on a limb and assume Dax is the bartender.

"No, I haven't had a chance to open it."

I don't bother telling him a hot-as-sin bystander who may have given me one of the best orgasms I've ever had—and it wasn't even with his cock—somewhat distracted me. I'm one hundred percent positive getting a hotel room with him would have been a certified good decision. Where I'm from, they don't make men like him. He was hitting on me, and while he was forward and potentially borderline unhinged, some chivalry was sprinkled in. I mean, yes, he may have forced himself on me in the bathroom, but to his credit, I didn't really push him away, and even then, I still felt like I had a choice. I felt like I could say no, and he would have stopped, but there was no way I was saying no. Snapping myself out of my sex-induced fog and into the now, which is incredibly crucial, I clear my throat and prepare to leave my mystery man—whose name I never caught—and this night in my past. I wasn't lying when I said I was just passing through.

"I'm assuming since you know about the envelope, then there's a chance you know what the note says. Care to enlighten me?"

He adjusts his ballcap and looks over his shoulder before answering, "Not here. Come on."

The second we push out the front doors, the sticky, humid Midwest air has my nylon dress clinging to my already overheated skin. Montana definitely doesn't have humidity like this.

The hand that was on my back now skims down my arm before it wraps around my wrist. "Sorry, we need to be quick." He pulls me by my hand across the street. "I'm illegally parked."

He picks up his pace to a slow jog, and I follow suit as we head toward what I assume is his black Ford Explorer, parked with emergency lights flashing in a fire lane. Shit, now I feel bad I didn't immediately open the damn envelope. Reaching the car, he says, "This is me. Get in," as he rushes to the driver's side door. I oblige and quickly round the SUV and climb inside.

The door closes with a snick. "I'm so sorry. I'm assuming the envelope had instructions to meet you out here."

His eyes briefly flash to mine as if to say, 'You think,' before he shuts off the emergency lights and pulls out into traffic.

"It did. I circled the place a few times, and when you didn't come out, I assumed something might have happened. I didn't have another parking choice, considering it's game day and the lots are packed. I would have had to park a few blocks over, and given the situation, I didn't want to risk the time."

I'm about to ask what situation he's referring to until I remember. *Oh yeah, that's me. I'm the situation.* A flutter of unease sparks to life in my stomach, and I close my eyes to find my center and remind myself why I'm here.

He must pick up on my turmoil because he adds, "Hey, it's cool. Don't worry about it. I didn't get a ticket, and you're here. Trust me, you're in good hands. I'm Elijah, by the way."

"Mac." I reach for my satchel to grab the envelope passed to me.

"Mac, is that short for anything?"

"Yeah, Mackenzie."

"Did you have to travel far to get here?"

"It wasn't too bad. Only about eighteen hours on a Greyhound from Montana."

I've just pulled the envelope out when Elijah says, "You definitely need to read that note, but don't do it here. I'm taking you to where you'll be staying, and once you're settled in, you can read it then."

"So you do know what the note says?"

"I know it had instructions to meet me outside. As for the rest, I'm sure there are details, a few dos and don'ts, which you have already failed."

"Hey, I said I was sorry about not getting the message."

He glances my way and shakes his head. "That's not what I was referring to." His hands twist around the steering wheel as if considering his next words. "Look, I'm just the gopher here, if you will, but I asked you two questions that you answered without pause. Those questions have become second nature for you to answer without hesitation your entire life, but here, your answers aren't the same. You need to remember that."

"Who said I didn't?"

His big green eyes connect with mine once more and narrow as if to call my bluff before he smirks and rubs his chin. "Well played, but you still fail. I do, in fact, know your real name and where you're from. It's how I called you out of the bathroom, but that aside, you gave me all those details for a second time just now."

Damn. He's right. I already suck at hiding.

"This is the main living area. As you can see, there is a small, fully stocked kitchenette to your left, and down the hall to your right is a full bath and your bedroom." Elijah stands at the front door, seemingly unwilling to move farther into the space, which I suppose is polite and customary given the circumstances of why I'm here.

But I know no one here, and he seems nice enough, not to mention he's not hard to look at. "You don't have to stand at the door. You are welcome to come in."

I place my bag down on the oversized beige lounge chair that sits with a sofa and another matching chair opposite it in a semicircle in front of a stone fireplace with a stack that runs up the A-frame structure's entirety. This place seems too opulent for me, and I feel more than a little out of place, like he's the wrong guy and this is definitely the wrong house.

"Are you sure you brought me to the right place?" I ask Elijah as I continue to take in the space.

It's not that the place is huge by any means. Walking up, it looked like a quaint A-frame cottage, but inside is like stepping into a five-star rental cabin with top-of-the-line appliances and furnishings. It's a far cry from the double-wide I grew up in.

Heading toward the kitchen, I rub my hand along the white granite countertop before stopping in front of the refrigerator and opening it up. I'm not hungry, not even thirsty, just curious. That's when Elijah decides to speak again.

"It should be fully stocked with anything you could possibly want. Same with your bedroom. There should be clothes for you to change into. If you don't find what you need, arrangements can be made to take you shopping in town."

He's not wrong. The fridge has anything and everything. I'm not sure I've ever seen one so completely stocked in my life, and not with store brands. No Great Value Purified here. Perrier and Evian for the win. As I close the door, I hear him open another.

"Wait, you're leaving?" I anxiously run the jump ring of my pendant along the chain around my neck, not ready to be left alone.

Holding the key between his index finger and thumb, he says, "I'm just going to leave the key here," then places it on the shelf next to the front door. "Open that letter, read it over, and in the morning, I'm sure Everett can fill you in."

"But you never answered my question."

With half his body out the door, he pauses. "You're in the right place. Of that, I am sure."

I rush out with another question before he leaves. "Do I have this place all to myself, or should I be expecting a roommate?"

He gives me a small smile as if my ignorance and surprise have finally registered. This is more than anything I'm used to and different from what I expected.

"This is the pool house. You are not technically alone, but you have privacy in this house. The property is under surveillance. You have nothing to worry about. You are safe."

"Wait. I have one more question, and I promise I'll leave you alone."

His lips quirk to the side, and his green eyes meld into mine even across the span of the pool house. *Damn country boys.*

"Will I be seeing you around?"

He throws me a nod and pats the door. "Yeah, I'll be around. Have a good night, Mac."

Without another word, he shuts the door, and I'm left alone in what apparently is a pool house, though I saw no pool as we walked up. It is, however, very dark outside. I'm used to semi-rural living. The trailer park I grew up in was on the outskirts of Billings, Montana. You could still hear the hum of cars on the highway at night, and my surroundings were never drenched in complete darkness. We had streetlights, which they apparently don't have in rural Illinois. After we got off the main highway, there were a few, but the longer we drove, the less I saw until finally, there were none.

Tapping my fingers on the countertop, I take one more look around the place before deciding to head down the hall Elijah said led back to the bed and bath. A shower sounds fucking fantastic right now. The past two days have been more than stressful with travel. However, the tension that's riddled my body for the past three months leading up to this decision can't hold a flame to that discomfort.

I thought I knew what I was signing up for when I agreed to all of this, but now that I'm here, nothing is as I thought it would be, and I need a reset. Nothing a scalding hot shower can't fix. Opening the first door, I come to the main bath, which is more like a master bath. There's a walk-in shower and a soaker tub. I've never been in a soaker tub. Screw the shower. I'm taking a bath. There are even jets.

I waste zero time crossing the room to fill the bath and sample the oils neatly displayed in a basket on the ledge. It's like a damn hotel spa in here. After removing my dress and slipping off my thong, I step into the bath. My feet hit the piping hot water, and I hiss out my discomfort as my ass quickly finds the ledge to pull my feet out and turn the tap to cold. Damn, that's some good-ass hot water. The heat of it is worlds hotter than what I grew up with. Back home, I could fill my tub on the hot setting and still wish it were hotter.

I give it a moment then dip my foot back in and swish the water back and forth to cool the tub so I can get in. Once it's just right, I lower myself in and lean back against the ledge, letting the warm water lap at my sides as it fills around me. For a few moments, my mind is free, and everything is perfect. I'm not stressing about leaving home or worrying about my mother or the risk I took in coming here. It's just me in this ritzy bath with a house all to myself for the first time in my life. As I bask in the warmth of a steaming tub with notes of jasmine dancing over my body from the oils I poured in, my chest can't help but tighten as guilt quickly steals my peace.

I hate that I can never keep a happy moment without guilt trickling in. Without fail, my mind always chooses to see only the negative, even though I know the fact that I'm here in this house is already a small victory. A necessary hurdle on what feels like an endless journey to get my family back and maybe even my life. The past eight years have felt like a lie, and somewhere in the recesses of my mind, I wanted to come here for me, even if that meant everything falling apart. At least if it all fell apart, it would be honest and on my terms. It hurt to leave the way I did, for more reasons than one, but it hurt worse to be in the dark. My brother Josh knew I'd show up at the warehouse. *How could I not?* He went missing years ago, and suddenly, a random letter from him appears in my room detailing a place and time. There was no way I wasn't going to show up. In his letter, he told me the choice was mine, but he knew there would be no going back. It's another reason I shouldn't feel bad about taking these fleeting moments for myself. I have no clue what's in store for me tomorrow, and for now, this is where I am supposed to be.

D*ing-dong*. My mind slowly processes the ringing in my ears, but I can't be sure that I didn't just hallucinate the sound and that I'm not still in a dream state. The trailer doesn't have a doorbell, my mind reasons as I stretch and make myself comfortable and content with not moving. But then it sounds again: *ding-dong*. The second ring forces me to open my eyes, and when I do, my limbs instantly go stiff as I take in my surroundings. Panic briefly ensues before I remember where I am and why. *Shit. Pull yourself together, Mac.*

Sitting up in bed, I realize I never put any clothes on last night after my bath. I had thoroughly planned on checking out every nook and cranny, going through all drawers, and rummaging through whatever wardrobe they have for me, but none of that happened. It took every last bit of energy I had left to make it to the bed. My body felt like Jell-o, and I was blissed out. I was asleep seconds after I lay on the bed, and it was by far one of the best nights of sleep I've ever had, but in true Mackenzie fashion, all my wins are short-lived because now there is a stranger at my front door and I am completely naked.

Wrapping the blanket around myself, ensuring nothing is on display, I hop off the bed and scurry across the room to the door and peer into the hallway to make sure there are no windows for anyone to see me in my state of undress. There is an aggressive knock before I even have one foot out the door. *Sheesh, have these people not learned patience?*

"I'll be out in just a second," I shout down the short hallway loud enough that I know whoever is on the other side of that door can hear me. The vaulted ceilings more than amplify my voice. I'm positive my visitor got the message. I pause for a second, waiting to see if they'll respond, and when they don't, I storm back into the room and head straight for the closet.

Opening the six-panel single door, I expect your average closet, but it turns out I have a mini walk-in. Nice. I don't waste any time scoping out the selection or trying to determine the best outfit for this situation. Instead, I grab the first things I see in front of me, which happen to be a T-shirt and shorts. I'm assuming they fit. Heading back into the bedroom, I rush over to the dresser and start opening every drawer, looking for undergarments, which I find in spades. I now have more underwear, thongs, and bras than there are days in a week.

I'd like to fix my face and hair, but I also don't want to keep my guest waiting, so I head straight for the front door after my clothes are on. Throwing the door open, I see no one. *What the hell? Did I just imagine the doorbell and the knocking?* The knock and my visitor are quickly forgotten when I catch sight of the oasis in front of me. Holy shit. The pool in the backyard rivals any pictures I've ever seen of the Playboy mansion. Hell, this pool lagoon puts that place to shame. The water is the perfect shade of blue that flows in lighter shades along the entryways. Lush greenery cascades over the rocks and hugs every perfectly placed boulder and stone. There's even a damn waterfall covering what looks to be the entrance to a damn grotto. A throat clearing to my right pulls my attention away from the perfection.

"Good morning, Mackenzie."

When I fully turn to face the direction of my visitor, I find an older man likely in his mid-forties. If his deep, sultry voice doesn't do things to your lady parts, his looks will. *Damn. What the hell is it with these Midwest country men?* There must be something in the water. His hair is dark brown, almost borderline black, but his full, short-length beard gives away his age as specs of gray pepper his sides. As I subtly inspect the rest of him, I'm suddenly insecure. I look the epitome of the trailer park I crawled out of, even with the expensive shorts and T-shirt I threw on out of the closet. The man looks like he just walked out of a business meeting, wearing a full charcoal suit and black suede loafers.

Clearing his throat, he draws my attention back to his face, and when his dark, molten eyes meet mine, I can't help but wrap my arms around my front, wishing myself invisible.

He gestures toward the door. "Are you going to ask me to come inside?"

My eyebrows rise, and my mouth opens, but no words come out. *What am I? A fucking fish? Get your shit together, Mac.*

"Well, it is your house. I suppose you don't really need to ask." I move toward the front door and pull it open. "After you."

He doesn't immediately move. Instead, he eyes me from head to toe the same way I did him moments ago before placing his hands in his pockets and walking my way, but rather than enter the house, he stops at my front. "While you are staying in this pool house, I will never enter it without first being welcomed in, nor will any other man who sets foot on this property. Are we clear?"

"Yes," I answer, my voice barely audible. *Why does he make me so nervous?*

"What was that?" he questions in a tone that makes his intent clear.

"Yes," I answer, forcing confidence into my reply. "No one enters without my permission."

His eyes hold mine for a beat as if he's assessing that I did indeed understand. "Good."

Entering the pool house, he heads to my kitchenette and opens one of the cabinets to retrieve a jar of coffee pods. As he pops one into the Keurig, I sit on one of the oversized couches and tuck a pillow against my front as I fold my legs underneath me.

"Would you like a coffee? Tea? Water, perhaps?"

"I'm fine, thank you."

He stops what he's doing and his eyes lock on mine. "I didn't ask if you were fine. I asked if you'd like something to drink. Since it took you ten minutes to answer the front door, I'm assuming you just woke up, which means you've had nothing to eat or drink, and that doesn't work for me. There is no room to be shy here, Mackenzie. You will be here for a while. If you don't like what is stocked in this kitchen, I expect a list of what you want to see in this refrigerator on my desk by sunset."

From how he's leaning on the counter, his eye contact unwavering, it's clear he wants a response.

"Understood," I respond.

"Good, then what can I get you to drink?" he questions as he grabs his coffee.

I briefly run through the bottled drinks I saw when I opened the refrigerator last night. "An orange juice would be great."

After collecting our drinks, he joins me in the living room, sitting on the oversized chair adjacent to mine. Passing me my juice, he asks, "How did everything go last night with Elijah?"

"Fine. He was a gentleman."

Everett's words about no man entering this house without my explicit consent explain Elijah's peculiar behavior last night.

"Was he not clear on instructions?"

I purse my lips, unsure of what he's getting at. Elijah didn't really tell me much of anything. I was hoping he'd stick around so I could question him, but he seemed eager to leave. However, I don't want to get him in trouble. "No, he was clear."

He takes a sip of his coffee and holds my eyes. "You're either lying to me or deliberately disobeying my requests. Would you like to fill me in on which one is true?"

My eyes widen. "I'm not lying. Elijah was nice. He dropped me off, told me I could leave a list of whatever food or essentials I needed, and even said someone could take me into town to shop if I needed anything. Then he left the keys by the door and took off." My response does nothing to prove my innocence or clear Elijah's name, so I add, "And he didn't come in past the door."

He smirks at my addition. "Were you not given directions to read a letter handed to you?"

Shit. That damn letter. First, there was the hottie at the bar, then Elijah, and finally, a bubble bath that turned me into mush. The distractions were many, and I completely forgot about the letter.

"I'm sorry. I never opened the letter. Elijah was clear that I needed to. It's not his fault. I got distracted."

He's quiet as he considers my words and takes another drink of his coffee, his dark eyes never straying from mine. I have so many questions, but my situation is unique, and all of this is worlds different from anything I expected when I decided to come here.

"I'm going to need you to do two things." He sets his coffee on the table and crosses his leg over his knee. His hand rubs his short beard on his jaw. "First, I'm going to need you to drink that juice, and then I'm going to need that letter back."

We both sit unmoving for long seconds as my mind runs through everything that has happened in the past twenty-four hours. I'm not scared of Everett, but he's different from any man I've ever known in my life. I never knew my father. He took off when I was a baby, and my older brother, well, it appeared he took off the second he was old enough to do so. We were both young when he disappeared, so I can't be sure of the man he is today. Then there are my mother's boyfriends. They were definitely nothing to write home about. Most were shit. However, I always felt like my mother intentionally picked the losers, and they were her willing victims. Though we lived in a trailer park, we had the nicest double-wide on the lot, and my mother was the living embodiment of a diamond in the rough. Tish is intelligent, but her life choices contradict her circumstances. She chose the losers because she was smarter than them. She held the upper hand and she never wanted to be tied down. The men she chose were expendable. Sitting here now under Everett's calculating stare, I have a little more understanding of why she made some of those choices.

He subtly starts tapping his index finger on the armchair as though he's waiting for my response. I quickly sputter out, "Oh, you mean like right now."

I move to stand and grab my bag that is still lying on the chair across the room where I set it when I walked in, and I can feel his eyes following my every move. It's unnerving, but I have to attempt to put it out of my mind. This man is supposed to be the good guy. He's helping me. I mean, hell, look where I'm currently staying. That last thought really has me wishing I had opened this damn letter. *Why does he want it back?*

As I open my satchel and pull out the black envelope, I say, "I can read it now if you'd like."

This stupid envelope now feels like it might burn a hole through my hand as my curiosity and regret practically eat me alive. *How did I manage to mess up on night one with something so important on the line?* I can't believe I let some hot guy distract me from this. I should have stopped him. I should have known I was not the type of woman capable of letting a man have me for just one night. From the moment I fled the bar with Elijah, my mystery man consumed every other thought.

I stop just a few feet out of arm's reach from Everett as I wait for his response, hoping it might change and that I get a second chance to make amends with whatever fate lies within this envelope. But I have no such luck.

He motions with his finger for me to hand it over, and I take a few small steps to reach him before he takes it from my hand. "The contents of this envelope no longer apply to your situation. They became null and void the second you gave Elijah your real name and where you were from."

Damn it.

"Elijah doesn't count. You sent him to extract me, and it was obvious he knew who I was and enough about my story."

Not that being a good liar is anything to write home about, but I will say I have a decent track record of being pretty damn good at it. After all, it's partly why I'm here, but maybe Everett believing the opposite to be true isn't such a bad thing.

"Yes, well, given the circumstances of why you are here, you can see how that is a conflict of interest. You are here for protection. You can't very well be walking around giving people your legal name and telling them where you are from unless you are looking to be found."

I reclaim my seat on the couch, and his eyes lock onto the orange juice I set down earlier to fetch the envelope. Without words, I know he is waiting for me to drink it, so I swipe it off the table and snap it open, making sure I drink half the contents as I watch him take whatever fate that black envelope held for me and put it in the pocket of his suit coat.

His lips quirk up into what could be the formation of a half-smile, but it's gone almost as fast as it came. "Maybe there's hope for you yet."

Who would have thought drinking juice would earn me brownie points with this man? These thoughts running through my head right now speak volumes and snap me out of whatever alternate universe this man has managed to plunge me into. It's not just the guy from the bar. It's all of it. I've never left home, and none of this is what I expected. The past seventy-two hours have me out of sorts, but that ends now.

My self-confidence has taken a major hit over the past few weeks, but I'm not the girl who just accepts things because someone says it's so. With that in mind, I challenge him. "I'd like to know what was in that envelope and why it no longer applies."

"This letter was your new identity. It detailed the name you would be using during your stay, the job you would take, and the home you would be placed in. But as I said before, everything became void the second you gave someone your real name. This is a small town. People talk, and we can't afford rumors."

"Clearly, you trust Elijah, or you wouldn't have sent him to pick me up. Can't you just ask him not to say anything? I'm an excellent actress. I can be Tiffany, Mazie, or Christina. I can be whoever you want me to be."

He strokes his beard before pulling in a breath and standing. As he towers over me from where I sit on the couch, I can see his resolve before his chest deflates.

"I'm sure you can be. In fact, I'm counting on it, but for now, you're Mackenzie. You're an exchange student planning to attend Southwestern in the fall. You'll be working the concession stand at Hayes Fields." He pauses and pulls a cell phone out of his pocket. "This is your phone. My number, Elijah's, and Parker's, who you have yet to meet, are all programmed into that phone. Do not contact anyone back home. No social media, not even fake accounts. People searching for you will already be checking every new follow of every one of your family members and friends. It wouldn't be hard to piece together that a new account is suddenly following friends and family, even if you are just looking."

He places the phone on the table before looking at his watch. "You have twenty minutes to get ready. The shorts you are wearing are fine. It's the beginning of June in the Midwest, and you'll be working at a baseball field. They'll give you a Hayes Fields shirt once you get there. I'll be driving you down there today."

Fuck my life. It would have to be baseball. It couldn't be any other damn sport. I stand and ask a question I'm sure I don't want to know the answer to, but I ask it anyway because I'm nothing if not a glutton for punishment.

"What would my job be had I opened the envelope?"

"Camp counselor."

Honestly, I'm not as butthurt as I thought I'd be. Being a

camp counselor would have meant hanging out with kids all day. That would not help me with reconnaissance and discovering why Waterloo is significant to helping my brother come home. With that in mind, I dutifully swipe my orange juice off the table before he has another second to analyze my reactions or change his mind, and take off toward my room to find shoes and to fix my hair and face.

I may not have expected this preferential treatment when I entered this witness protection of sorts, but I'm also not naïve enough to think what is happening here is standard protocol. I might be young, but I'm not dumb. I know you catch more flies with honey than vinegar, and playing by the rules will do nothing but behoove me in this game of cat and mouse. He may have the upper hand for now, but that's because I just got here. I'm not the typical person in need of protection.

CHAPTER 3
MACKENZIE

It's been a week since I arrived in Waterloo, and I've learned nothing new about Everett Callahan or why, of all places, this is where I need to be. Coming was a choice. It's the destination I didn't have a say in, and that's the part that has me stumped. That's why, today, I'm determined to start getting some answers. I've kept my head down and played the part of the quiet, timid, new girl who is trying to blend in and lie low, but the reality is I am none of those things.

I've seen very little of Everett over the past week, mainly because he left for a business trip the day after I arrived. The first day I worked the Fields, Everett drove me to work and made a point of picking me up. On the way back to his house that night, he drove me around town, and honestly, there's not much to it. Downtown has a few restaurants, bars, local shops, and convenience stores, and outside of that, there's nothing but flat farmland—and when I say flat, I mean it. I Googled it. It's the second flattest state in the US. There are some wooded areas like where Everett's property is located, but for the most part, it's corn fields for as far as the eye can see. If someone needs to disappear, this isn't a bad place to hide. There is nothing here. Who the hell would want to live here? There is literally nothing to do outside of local sports.

Initially, when Everett told me my fuckup landed me a job at the Fields as opposed to a summer camp with a bunch of kids, I was grateful. But that was before I knew how damn busy the Fields would be. I'm on my feet for eight hours straight. I work the concession stands from 3:00 p.m. to 11:00 p.m., except on weekends. We open early on the weekends. However, the day of the week doesn't matter. The place is always busy because there is nothing else to do around here, so everyone comes here. Technically, it is baseball season. It runs until mid-July, but after that, beer leagues and senior leagues fill in the schedules. Apparently, the owner of the Fields draws big crowds because he's a local kid who actually made it to the major leagues. Holden Hayes was born and raised here and has been the number-one pitcher for St. Louis's team for the past three years. People hang out at the Fields just on the off-chance they might run into him.

Let's just say learning the job and keeping up with the demand in the stifling heat of the summer has kept me more than busy. By the time I return to the pool house, shower, and eat, I'm dead. It's why I'm now running late to the Fields today. Last night, Parker, my boss, asked me to come in at 8:00 a.m. to teach me how to open. The concession stands open at 3:00 p.m. every day, but every morning, they have someone come around and unlock the facilities for teams that practice here, and on Fridays, which is today, they get inventory delivered for the weekends, so I'll be learning that as well.

Parker said I wouldn't be here all day and could go home for a few hours before my scheduled shift, so I didn't wear my uniform shirt. No, today I threw on a pair of black Lululemon spandex shorts, a white tank, and a black baseball cap from the fully-stocked closet of name-brand clothes Everett had brought in before I arrived. He told me if anything wasn't to my liking, he would make arrangements for me to go shopping or I could order more things. However, what he has in that closet is more than I needed and, oddly, everything I would choose for myself. But I don't think he stocked that closet himself. He had to have hired a personal shopper. I don't get the impression my current outfit is anything he would approve of me wearing. The majority of the clothes are conservative. This is clearly meant for working out. There is a gym at the main house that he said I could use whenever I liked, but he's not here, and this outfit is meant to tease.

Those thoughts, coupled with the fact that I'm running late, have me stepping on the gas to get to the Fields. On Tuesday, before he left for his business trip, Everett handed me the keys to an old truck and said, "This is to get you to and from work." I had to remind myself to mentally school my expression, and for the first time, I think I finally affected him because he felt the need to add, "This is all I could get you. You know, impressions and all."

Inside, I was screaming. I've never had my own car, but I think he believed I felt he was being cheap, considering it is obvious he has more than enough money to afford a nicer car than this. Still, he's not my sugar daddy, and buying the exchange student—or lending said student—one from his collection could give off the wrong impression.

Pulling into the parking lot, I'm twenty minutes late. A beer truck is already pulled in, and there are about ten pickup trucks here as well. My ride is starting to make more sense. Everyone around here seems to own a truck. It's probably how I ended up with this one. I'd bet my first paycheck that this truck belonged to one of these guys once upon a time. I pull into the first empty spot I come across, only to slam on the brakes as a man in front of me hits his hands on the hood of my truck and falls to the ground.

"Fuck!" My heart is practically beating out of my chest. I throw the truck in park and rush out, fully expecting blood and broken bones, only to find my victim picking up balls from the bucket I knocked over.

"Oh my God, I am so sorry." I quickly bend down to help collect the balls that are now rolling between cars and through the lot.

"You need to pay attention when you're driving. You're lucky this was a bucket of balls and not a kid, for fuck's sake."

My hands shake as I retrieve the balls and attempt to toss them in the bucket. "I know. I'm sorry. I was running late. I didn't think anyone would be here this early."

"You didn't think. That's the problem."

I pick up another ball, and when I miss the bucket this time, I stand and rub my sweaty palms down my shorts. This guy, whose face I've yet to see, is okay. I don't need to listen to him berate me. I apologized. There's nothing more I can do.

"Look, I said I was sorry. I promise I'll be more careful next time."

"You're lucky you even get a next time."

I'm clearly not going to get anywhere with this guy. He can't even look at me. Stepping off the curb, I move toward my driver's side door to shut off the car and attempt to calm my racing heart, but I don't make it more than two paces before his voice rings out loudly at my back, his proximity more than evident.

"We're not done here."

When I turn, my eyes meet his chest. He easily has a foot on me at full height, but I don't give a shit. *Who does this asshole think he is?* However, no sooner I steel my spine and find my words than they are stolen when my eyes collide with his. They are the same obsidian orbs that have played a starring role in all my dreams over the past week.

My mind barely gets a chance to process his reaction to me before a voice calls out behind me. "Mac, what's going on? Is there a problem here?" Parker asks as he steps up to my back.

Those dark, inky eyes that were full of want and desire just days ago now hold mine with contempt, and for a second, I question if he recognizes me—but I know he does. I might be dressed down, wearing a hat with my hair pulled back, but there's no way he doesn't remember me. I can feel it. It's why he hasn't moved or said a word.

"I asked a question. Is there a problem here?" Parker asks again.

My mystery man thins his lips with a scowl before breaking our stare. "Yeah, we have a problem. This girl shouldn't work here. She nearly ran me over just now."

God, why do his words sting so damn much? I get that I fucked up, but I don't understand why he's being so cold. What happened to the man I met at the bar? I push the hurt down. "I said I was sorry—"

"'Sorry,' doesn't cut it when it's someone's kid."

I can't help but cut him off this time, finding my nerve. "But it wasn't a kid. It was just your balls." I don't understand why he's being so difficult.

His eyes hold mine, and the coldness I felt before is nothing compared to the ire I see now. He then pins Parker with a no-nonsense glare. "You can handle this, or I will. Either way, she's out."

"You're right. I will handle this, seeing as how she's my employee. Mac, get your keys and go inside. I'll be there in a second to start training."

I waste zero seconds taking the two steps toward my door, cutting the ignition, and grabbing my bag. I don't care to stand here for a stranger to scold me. One who has had me intimately, nonetheless, and apparently couldn't care less that I exist.

"You really want me to go to Hayes over this?" my mystery man asks wholeheartedly, appalled by Parker's defense.

As I close my truck and exit the aisle toward the rear so

that I don't have to pass him, I hear Parker say, "Con, let it go. She said she was sorry. Besides, Hayes has nothing to do with hiring her."

"Look, just because you're clearly fucking doesn't mean she gets a pass."

I want to march back there and give him a piece of my mind, but I don't. Whatever we might have had is clearly gone, and that's for the best. I don't need a distraction while I'm here. I've been here almost a whole week, so I'm hopeful that since this is our first run-in, staying off his radar shouldn't be too difficult. The problem is, he told Parker he'd go to Hayes, and it's easy to conclude that he's friends with the owner or knows him. That might sway things in his favor, and I don't need to make a scene when I'm supposed to be lying low.

Pulling open the door to the concession stand, I bypass the men unloading the trucks into the freezers and walk straight back to the office, determined to get out of sight. When I came to work, making a scene was on the agenda, just not this one. Today, I planned on making waves but clearly hit the wrong target, figuratively and literally. I need a second to collect myself and get out of my head.

After hanging my satchel on the back of the door, I pace the small space. While I may have wished for it, I never in a million years thought I'd see that man again or run into him here, of all places. The night at the bar, I was utterly hypnotized by him. Those dark, inky eyes framed by thick eyelashes made it look as though I was his sole focus when they were trained on me, and fuck me if that stare isn't what set me off and gave me the best fucking orgasm of my life when it locked with mine. I anxiously rub my thumb over the 'M' on my necklace before giving myself a pep talk. *Damn it, Mackenzie, sack up. It was clearly a one-time deal for him, and now you need to run reconnaissance. He clearly has it out for you and you need to know who you're dealing with and determine if this is something you can make go away before Everett finds out.*

"Mac, are you okay?" Parker throws open the door to the office, startling me. My hand immediately flies to my chest from being caught off guard. "Fuck, I'm sorry. I didn't mean to scare you."

"No, it's fine. You're fine. I'm just rattled, is all. It's not your fault."

He rubs the back of his neck sheepishly. "Do you need a minute, or do you want to get at it?"

"No, I think I'm good, but can I ask…" I pause, trying to find the right words. I don't want to give away that I know the guy from the parking lot, and I also don't want to sound overly interested because if I had never met him, my reaction to him would look different. "Is he always like that?"

Parker holds open the door for me to exit the office. "As much as I'd like to talk smack right now, I can't. Connor isn't a bad guy. His problem is with me, not you. He wants to flex, but you working here isn't a choice he gets a say in."

I exit the office, but I don't miss the reflection in the beverage cooler as I do. Parker is totally checking out my ass. So I use the opportunity to my advantage. If I've learned one thing this week, it's that he is selective with his words. Honestly, I didn't expect anything less since he's one of the only three numbers programmed in my phone. I understand that he's my boss here at the field, but I've also learned that he is Elijah's brother, which means both of them are loosely in the loop about why I am here. I'm unsure how much they know, but it's clear Everett trusts them, which means I need to crack them.

"Does Connor frequent the Fields often?"

"Yes, you'll probably see more of him than you'll care to, especially since his daughter just left for summer camp."

Daughter! What the fuck? My stomach instantly knots, and I rack my brain and try to recall our night at the bar. Surely, he wouldn't have worn a wedding ring, but was there an indentation? A tan line? *Damn, why did I even ask?* I didn't set out to be a homewrecker. I now have a million more questions to add to my already lengthy list, and none of them can be asked subtly.

So I decide to take the focus off me and turn it on him, hoping that might shed a little light on my mystery man, who I now know is Connor. "Why does he have a problem with you?"

Parker picks up a clipboard off the counter and hands it to me. "Why are you fishing?"

"Seriously, I can't ask you any questions? You don't think I've noticed how you keep everything strictly business? What's wrong with being friends, or is that against the rules?"

I'm done acting like it's not evident that Everett has him watching me, but I don't understand the strictly business piece. *Why am I not allowed to have a friend?* I've only run into Elijah once this past week when he came in to grab keys for the equipment storage around the back. He acted cordial like Parker, just casually passing pleasantries, no sustenance.

He eyes me suspiciously and quirks a brow. "Is that your 'just friends' outfit?" His comment only slightly catches me off guard, but before I can snap back, he adds, "Don't get me wrong. Those tits and that ass are what wet dreams are made of, but you, Mackenzie, are off-limits."

As he reaches for another clipboard, I say, "Says who?"

He doesn't give me his eyes as he turns to walk away. "We both know who. Now, come on."

I take that comment as a solid win. Parker acknowledges that I'm not wrong in my theory that Everett is having me thoroughly watched. Nothing about being here is standard. You don't just hand over a cell phone, truck keys, and a pool house stocked with food and clothes to a girl you've never met in exchange for protection.

Knowing I have Parker somewhat rattled, I apply pressure. "I just assumed you were good at keeping secrets."

He stops outside the freezer door and hangs his head, releasing an irritated breath. "I am." Then he reaches for a coat hanging next to the door. "Here, put this on."

Slipping the clipboard between my thighs, I take the coat, push my arms through, and ask my next question. "Does that mean there are cameras in the office?"

Once the coat is on, he looks me in the eye. "No."

That's when I know I've got him. He's an intelligent man. I'm sure he knows what I'm suggesting, but I'm not about to leave it open for interpretation. "Then how will he know if I give you a blowjob under the desk?"

He bites his lip on a groan as he adjusts himself. "Stop. This conversation is over." Throwing open the door to the freezer, he gestures. "Get in. Now."

I pass by, and as I do, I ask, "Have I been reading this wrong all week, and you're not interested?"

Entering behind me, he says, "Start on the ice cream and work your way to the bomb pops. Make sure the physical counts match what's on that sheet, and when they don't, highlight the row and correct the quantity."

I'm just about to tell him I don't have a highlighter when he steps up behind me, his front just barely grazing my back. "As for the rest, I think we both know I'm interested, but I enjoy having my balls attached to my body." Reaching around, he places a highlighter through the clip of my board, his heat just barely enough to tease and mingle with mine. "But it's more than that." His mouth is dangerously close to my ear. Then, before my body can react to his warmth and proximity, he pulls away, crossing the freezer and throwing over his shoulder as he does, "I can't give you what you want. I'm not a short-term kind of guy."

My heart stumbles in my chest from his words. It figures I would find a good guy here and be unable to keep him. I wish

I could say, 'I'm not a short-term kind of girl,' but I can't, and he's right, and because I need to ensure this ends here, I ask, "Does Elijah feel the same way?"

His head snaps in my direction as he side-eyes me, searching for a tell—one I know he won't find. It's then that I see his posture change ever so subtly and I know regardless of whether he wants to feel it or not, my words wounded.

Returning his gaze to the stack of frozen meat, he says, "No. My brother…" Pausing, his jaw ticks as he bites back annoyance. "Doesn't mix business with pleasure either."

Without another word, he exits the walk-in freezer, and I'm left cold and alone. But at least my cruelty wasn't for nothing. I now know my keepers are related.

CHAPTER 4
CONNOR

It's Saturday, and I officially had yet another sleepless night. Sleep never comes easy for me, but it's been practically impossible after running into my mystery girl from the bar, who I now know is Mac. My brain never once shut off. I couldn't get comfortable even in the meat locker of a basement I sleep in. That woman has consumed my every other thought since I met her that night, for more reasons than one.

Last weekend, after she ran out of the bar, I watched another blond-haired woman wearing a blue dress enter. My interest was piqued. I had to know if the girl whose pussy was just in my mouth truly rejected me or if it was indeed a case of mistaken identity. I'll admit it. My ego took a hit when she shot me down. It's why I didn't leave as planned. I headed toward the bar for two reasons. One, to make sure I still had game, but secondly, and maybe most importantly, to see if I just fucked up and went after the wrong girl.

Turns out I had. The girl who deliciously came all over my tongue in the bathroom was not the one from Tinder. Coincidentally, she just happened to have a matching profile with the girl I was supposed to meet. My date from the app was a knockout, and there was definitely chemistry. She was ready to get the check and head back to the hotel after one drink, but I couldn't do it. I couldn't pull the fucking trigger, not with another girl's juices still on my face. Mac's soft sandalwood scent has been embedded into my skin for days, threatening to steal what little sanity remains. I'm already teetering on the edge with everything that's been going on lately between the divide in my family and Summer. I can't be held liable for my actions when she's around.

She's fucked with my head every night since the first. It's why she has to go. She can't be here in my town.

That's why I called Holden and had him meet me at the Fields the second I knew his plane landed. This is a small town. People talk. Usually, I would have heard about the new girl working at the Fields, but I was in Alabama with my team all week for an out-of-town tourney. I don't understand why she's suddenly here, but I can guarantee she won't be staying.

"What the hell is so important that I had to come down here right away? You realize I haven't been home in over a week? I would like to see my wife and son, not to mention you live in my damn basement. Could we not have had this conversation at home?"

"I need you to fire a concession stand worker."

Holden places his hands on his hips and blankly stares at me as though I've suddenly grown another head. "You can't be serious right now. Have you lost your damn mind? Con, my name might be on the field, but you know I pay people to manage the staff."

I take the ball cap off my head and run my fingers through my hair, thoroughly aggravated. Have I lost my mind? Perhaps, but isn't that what friends are supposed to be there for? To have your back when shit gets hard. This girl cannot be here, in my hometown, let alone at the Fields. It's not an option. "She ran me over with her truck. That could have been a kid."

"Did this happen just now or…" He looks around as if to emphasize his point that I look just fine. "Con, talk to me, man. This isn't you. What's going on? Does this have anything to do with Summer leaving for camp?"

I put my cap back on, sit on the bleachers, and shake my head but give him no words.

"Con, look, you know I'd do anything for you, but you have to give me something."

I put my head in my hands as a whirlwind of mixed emotions washes over me. "Then make her leave."

"Her?" he questions. "So this concession stand worker I had to rush down here and fire is female."

He paces back and forth and curses. "Man, something has to give. Summer is gone for eight weeks. You need to take this time for yourself. Date some fucking women, and I don't mean 'fuck and run' like you do now. I mean, date them, get to know someone, and actually let them in. You can have your pick of half the damn town. Stop being selfish—"

I cut him off. "Selfish. You think me not having a girl is selfish? More like it's selfless. Why would I bring a girl into Summer's life who won't stay? No one wants to sign up to be a mom at our age. Not to mention, Holly isn't exactly out of the picture. You know me, Holden. You, of all people, should know I don't get a say."

"No, Connor, you have a say. Blaming Summer, Holly, or anything else is a fucking excuse, and you know it. Hell, I don't care if you want to be single forever, but we both know that's a cop-out. This isn't the life you want. We both know you want an Aria. It's why you haven't moved out of my damn basement."

He's not wrong on the Aria part, but he couldn't possibly understand the rest. Holden has never been a single dad, let alone one with my baggage.

"You know you're welcome to stay at my place as long as you want. Aria and River love having you around, and I don't hate knowing that you're home with them when I'm out of town for games, but you need to start thinking about what comes next."

I practically fly off the bleacher. The longer I sit here and listen, the more pissed off I get. "So that's it then, we're done. After everything we've been through."

"Con, that's not what I'm saying, man, and you fucking know it—"

I cut him off. The person I thought would have my back through thick and thin apparently doesn't. I ask him to do one fucking thing, and he can't even do it without turning his back on me. "Isn't it, though? We both know that shit you just spewed was a bunch of specially curated words. They wouldn't have come out of your mouth if they weren't on your mind. You know what, Holden, just forget it. I hear you loud and clear, bro. You want me out. Well, wish granted. I'm out."

I don't wait for some bullshit excuse that I'm sure he'll give, like, 'You're overreacting. That's not what I meant.' It is what he meant, and so what if I'm overreacting? I'm well overdue. I've been the nice guy. I had my role and played my part.

"Con, stop," he yells after me. "Come on, really? This is how it's going to be?"

I don't let up as I storm back to my truck, but I can feel him hot on my heels. When I throw open the driver-side door, I catch him standing on the curb in front of my truck and decide to give him one more piece of my mind.

"I asked you for one damn thing. One. Name a time I've ever asked anything of you, Holden?"

He's quiet, and I know it's because he has nothing. I don't live in his basement because I can't afford my own place. I live there because it's the way that made sense for all of us. We've been best friends for the past ten years. We played college ball together. We were roommates, and that carried over even after he made it big and got married. But right now, I feel duped. I was convenient for him, and now I'm not because suddenly I need something. Well, fuck that.

"Fine, I'll have her fired. I'll figure it out. Just fucking calm down and talk to me."

"Do what you want, Hayes. I'm out anyway."

Without another word, I slam the door, throw my truck in reverse, and head to the one place I haven't been in months: my father's house.

Driving down the tree-lined path that leads to my family home, I'm furious and bitter, but, more than anything, hurt. Holden was the last person I expected not to have my back. We know each other's darkest secrets, and lately, he's been more blood to me than my own family. Just as the tree line breaks, the English Country-inspired estate comes into view.

My mother always wanted to move to Europe. It was her dream, though my father's business kept us here. So, instead, he built her this place. A sprawling ten-thousand-square-foot home nestled on over one hundred acres of prime Illinois real estate, and I say prime because it has everything. This state is flat as far as the eye can see, but our family home is nestled in a wooded area with manicured gardens that my mom used to plant, greenhouses, and a ten-acre lake.

Growing up here was any kid's dream, but now all I see are lies, and all because my father couldn't walk a straight line. It's not that hard: love a woman and love her with all your heart, but I guess some men are just made differently. Hell, I'm one of them, but that's also why I'm alone. I can't fuck around and break someone's heart.

Pulling into the driveway, I see Cameron's car, and I can't help but roll my eyes. Cameron is the daughter of one of my father's partners, who died tragically in a car accident coming home from a gala with his wife a few years ago. She was in her senior year of high school when it happened, and rather than go back to Maine to live with her mother's family, she stayed here when my father offered her our home so she could finish her senior year. Well, her senior year ended almost four years ago, and she's still here.

Before I can give Cameron and her questionable room and board at my father's house any more thought, my phone pings with a text.

Holden: I looked into your girl. You need to talk to your father.

What the fuck does my father have to do with Mac? Cutting the engine, I hop out and hastily walk inside. I didn't come here for a fight, but it seems fitting. My old man has done a bang-up job of giving me reasons to hate him lately. Walking into the house, I head back to his office, only to hear laughter from the pool outside. I veer off toward the kitchen and head straight to the window to see who's at the pool. My dad has never been one to use the pool, but hey, for the past thirty years, I thought he was a different man. Maybe swimming is suddenly in his repertoire.

When I reach the window, I see it's just Cameron out there having a drink with another one of her friends. I guess she's home for the summer. When I don't see my father, I take off down the hallway to his office. I want to catch him off guard before he knows I'm here, so when I reach the door, I waste no time knocking and let myself in, only to find my girl from the bar standing in front of his desk wearing nothing but a bikini.

"What the hell is going on in here?" I demand as I try to get a grip on my outrage.

There is no fucking way this girl is here in my father's

house, half naked, nonetheless. My blood instantly starts to boil for multiple reasons. First of them being that she's here at all, and secondly, I hate that I'm once again affected by her presence. Having my father see her in this state of undress only adds fuel to the fire. Her big blue eyes land on mine and widen in surprise. She's clearly just as shocked to see me as I am to see her.

"Connor, good you're here. I couldn't have planned this more perfectly if I tried," my father says in a calm tone that grates my nerves.

My eyes quickly scour the office, finding a throw blanket on a love seat across the room. It only takes me three long strides to reach it before I toss it at her. "Please cover yourself."

Her forehead pinches slightly as though the action was offensive, but whatever offense I thought I may have seen is quickly replaced with a scowl when she wraps the blanket around her body.

"Please, have a seat. We have things we need to discuss," my father requests.

"I don't plan on staying, so there's no need." It's then that movers entering the pool house catch my attention and Holden's text to talk to my dad about Mac circles back. My teeth grind of their own accord. "Don't tell me she's moving in? What the hell are you doing? You get rid of Mom and start letting twenty-somethings move in?"

"You'll watch your tone speaking to me, Connor. She's not moving in. In fact, it's the opposite. She's moving out."

"What?" we both say in tandem.

"After today, you can't live here anymore. A marriage commissioner will be here in two hours to perform your ceremony."

"What do you mean, 'my ceremony?'" I demand.

My heart is about to pound out of my chest, and my mind is racing to stay present and not completely zone out.

This can't fucking be happening. There is no way he is for real.

"You and Mackenzie are getting married."

So, Mac is a nickname. Hmmm, I like Mackenzie better, but that's neither here nor there. The girl looks like she's in shock as she stands glued to her spot, tightly gripping the chain around her neck, but she has no need to worry. I'm not marrying her. I have a list a mile long of all the reasons why I can't and won't, but I'll start with the biggest and my dad's favorite. Summer.

"What about Summer? You expect me to just marry someone she's never met. When she returns from camp, I'm supposed to pick her up and say what?" I pause for effect as I hold his eyes. "Meet your new mom?"

Summer's real mother, Holly, hasn't been in the picture since birth. We've mostly been vague when she asks about her mom, but the older she gets, the harder it becomes. Semantics aside, she has a mom, and it's not the woman standing before me. I don't think my father has honestly considered the impact this will have on Summer.

"You can't live in Holden's basement with Summer forever. Summer needs her own house, and so does your new wife."

With my hands on my hips, I drop my head and bite my tongue so I don't spew more offensive words at the girl than I already have, though I'm sure she has her own for me. She can't be happy with how I've treated her or this new arrangement, but what do I know? Maybe all her silence is acceptance. So I continue this battle on my own.

"What will the town think when they find out I'm married to the new girl I clearly detest?"

Her blue eyes find mine again, and suddenly, the words I just said feel vile, and that pisses me off because they need to stick.

"Yeah, well, lucky for you, Parker is the only one who saw

that little temper tantrum you threw in the parking lot the other day."

"Parker *fucking* Michaelson. Why am I not surprised he's involved? You know what, why don't you have him marry her? Apparently, giving Mom away to Kipp wasn't enough. Now you want—"

"Enough," he booms as he slams his hands down on his desk, making Mackenzie jump. "This is happening."

For some reason, she chooses that moment to find her voice, which shocks the hell out of me. My father has a very commanding presence. It's why he's such a damn good lawyer. He can intimidate with his looks alone, but apparently, she's not on board with his plans either because she stands and says, "You can't force me to marry someone. That's not part of the deal."

"Deal? What fucking deal?"

My father doesn't even acknowledge that I've spoken. Instead, he holds her gaze in challenge. "Wrong. I can, and I will. We both know you haven't been exactly transparent in coming here."

Neither of them moves, and I know I'm missing half of the story, a story I want no involvement in. "You know what, fuck it, I'm out."

I turn to head out of the room. My father can take his demands and shove them up his ass. If he insists on being chummy with the Michaelsons, he can have one of Kipp's sons marry her.

"Don't even think about walking out that door. I've about had all the disrespect I can handle from you to last a lifetime."

"Yeah, well, you haven't given me a reason to respect you."

"Mackenzie, can you please leave us? You'll find an outfit in your room fit for the ceremony."

She quietly gets up and does as my father asks, which only piques my interest. What does he have on her? If I stay, it's for that reason alone, but I know that whatever it might be isn't reason enough to give her my last name, so when she passes by to exit, I say, "Don't bother. I will never marry you."

She doesn't cower or give me any words. Instead, she keeps walking as if my words meant nothing, and maybe they didn't, but her lack of reaction only makes me feel worse. I'd rather have her snap back. Her anger I can take. Her silence, I cannot.

No sooner the door is closed than I say, "What the hell is going on? Why do you think you can force me to marry some girl I don't know?"

"Sit down, Con. You act as though you don't know the world we are involved in."

My legs suddenly feel heavy as his words sink in. I stand firmly planted in place as I watch him reach for his bottle of Remy Martin Cognac on the bar tray at the corner of his desk. When he goes for a second glass, I know he means business. All his business deals are done over a glass of cognac. But I'm his son. I'm not a business transaction, and while I know the family business and play my role, this is not anything I ever saw happening.

"Connor, my patience is waning. Please sit. We don't have much time before the marriage commissioner arrives."

I can't help but clench my jaw and shake my head in annoyance, but I do as he asks nonetheless because although I will not be going through with his demands, I'm curious. *How the hell is Mac tied into all of this? What's her story?*

"It better be one hell of a story. Any threats of pulling my trust fund will fall on deaf ears when it comes to this. You can fucking keep it. I get a say in who I marry," I snap as I throw myself into the leather winged-back chair that flanks his desk.

"I won't need to bribe you. You'll do it," he says as he pushes a glass of cognac across his desk. I take it because fuck if I don't need a drink to calm my nerves to prepare for whatever tale he's about to spin in an attempt to make me heel.

After taking a pull off his glass, he says, "You'll marry her because it's what will bring Holly back."

I immediately regret my decision to take a drink when the cognac threatens to fly out of my nose in shock. I choke on the burn as I swallow it down. "How the hell is that girl linked to Holly?"

Holly gave birth to Summer while in prison and was recently moved to another facility. My father has no ties to the warden or any of the correctional staff, which I know he doesn't like. I visit Holly once a year, but my father monitors her weekly, if not more. I'm sure he's been working tirelessly to get her transferred. However, I know she doesn't have that much time left on her sentence.

Years ago, around the same time we met, she ran with the wrong crowd. She dated a guy named Trent Wells for a few months. He was a shady motherfucker. When he wasn't quiet or lurking, he was making snide comments. I swear he would push people's buttons just to get a reaction out of them. Holden almost kicked his ass on more than one occasion for fucking around when it came to Aria. I gave him the benefit of the doubt for a while, assuming he was just socially awkward. This is a small town, and he wasn't from the area. Moving into a small town where everyone knows your name is difficult. But, as it turns out, first impressions are never wrong. Trent was indeed dubious. He was visiting small towns to target women for sex trafficking and exploitation, and Holly was one of them.

My father and his brothers are lawyers. Garrett and Colton, my uncles, deal in corporate and civil law, while my father runs a family law office out of St. Louis. Our family also started the Macbeth Foundation as a consistent way to support charities that directly benefit organizations that help shelter and rehabilitate victims of sexual violence. My father started that organization for my mother. Moira was a survivor herself. Her maiden name was Macbeth. The foundation was established to leave a legacy, but it also came with many other benefits. Aside from tax incentives, it's also how our family plays an active role in fighting against sexual violence.

"As you know, we've already had to move Holly twice due to targeted attacks. I thought those hits would pull him out, but they haven't, and that's because he has someone on the inside. I wouldn't be surprised if he wasn't behind them altogether. Runners are doing his bidding. At this rate, we won't see him coming until it's too late. However, Mackenzie is a different story."

"How so? Why is she different?"

"Besides being young and beautiful, she's important to him."

I try hard to ignore my father commenting on her looks, but I can't help but be perturbed. I don't like that he's noticed her looks, but what's more: I hate that I care. I shouldn't give a flying fuck. My father is young. He had me right out of high school, so he's only forty-eight and I know some women are all about older men, and while I wouldn't put it past him to look, I don't believe he would touch.

To get my mind back on the topic at hand, I say, "Okay, you want to lure him out. Why does that require giving Mackenzie my last name?"

Setting his glass down with a little more force than necessary, it is clear he's annoyed that I'm not one hundred percent on board with his plan. He thought after his explanation, this arrangement would be a done deal, but I'm still shocked that he's even proposing it. Sure, we get our hands dirty, but not like this.

"Because it needs to look like you are taking what's his, laying claim. Mackenzie is important to him. Therefore, she is important to us."

Well, I guess that clears up my other question. She was

screwing Trent Wells, that's why she's important. The thought has me clenching my fists, and my father notices.

"Hell, Con, you're acting as though I'm asking you to marry the Hunchback of Notre Dame."

For my father, her appearance is supposed to somehow make up for the fact that this isn't my choice or that I'm giving up something I can never get back. When I thought about getting married, I planned on staying that way. He's now taking that away from me.

"I don't like it. You're not thinking about when Summer comes home—"

He slams his hands down on the desk, silencing my objections. "Damn it, Con. I'm doing this for Summer. You don't think I'm doing this for her? The end goal is, she gets her family back, and you get your life back."

Before we can discuss the matter further, there's a knock on the door and the marriage commissioner enters with Mackenzie by his side.

"Sorry to interrupt. He rang the doorbell, and no one answered, but I didn't know he—"

"Yes-yes-yes, dear, you didn't know I would see myself in. Everett and I go back many years."

"Morgan," my father greets the peculiar white-haired old man as he walks around to shake his hand. "It's been a while. I swear, you never age." My father playfully jeers.

Which I find odd. I can't help but look on, entirely bemused. The man walked in as though he knew my father and our house well, yet I haven't met him a day in my life.

"Yes, well, what goes up never comes down. You'd be wise to note that, given your new single status. Before you know it, your hair will be as white as mine."

The old man doesn't miss a step, setting his briefcase down on my father's desk and making himself at home, spreading documents out across the front of the desk.

"I pulled some strings and got the marriage license for

you. However, I will need to see some ID to ensure the paperwork matches the identities of the individuals listed."

"I don't have my ID on me," Mackenzie says, drawing my eyes away from the piles of officiality laid out on my father's desk.

My annoyance has been set to a slow simmer since I pulled up in the driveway, but it now feels like it might boil over. She's wearing the same damn dress she wore the night we met, and fuck me if she doesn't look fucking edible. But I'll be damned if she didn't put it on to taunt me.

"Don't worry. I'm nothing if not efficient. I have it," my father says.

Her eyes narrow on the ID he tosses down on the desk, and I don't miss how she subtly tucks her thumb into her fist. *Good.* At least I know she has a tell. Her acceptance of all of this has felt somewhat rehearsed, and I was undecided if that was because she and my father had spoken about this before I arrived or if all of this was sprung on her as well. Don't get me wrong. Mackenzie did put up a fight, but given the severity of the circumstance, her opposition seemed lacking, as though she saw it coming. But the fidgeting she's doing now tells me she's nothing, if not just as annoyed with all of this as I am. I was right to be bothered by her silence earlier. It's always the quiet ones you must worry about, for they have the loudest minds.

"Connor, give Morgan your ID, please," my father asks, pulling my focus away from the mystery girl I'm about to marry.

As I reach into my back pocket to pull out my wallet, Morgan says, "Mackenzie, would you be a dear and come review these documents and verify that this is your full legal name?"

Without missing a beat, she takes a few steps from the door to meet Morgan at the desk.

"Please confirm your full name, date of birth, social

security number, and place of birth are all accurate on each form, and then sign where I have them highlighted with yellow flags."

My eyes never leave her form as I watch her every move and try to place her nerves or lack thereof. I didn't get to question my father as thoroughly as I would have liked because we were interrupted. While I know my father's intentions, hers are still unclear. He may want her as bait, but no one up and volunteers for this. Something happened. It's the only thing that makes sense.

The flexing of her fingers before she runs her hands down the sides of her hips snaps my attention away from her motives and back to the now. I can't help but clench my jaw in irritation when the movement from her hands pulls the fabric of her dress tight against her plump ass. Fuck. I'm no prude. I couldn't tell you how many women I've had. I'm thirty, and I like sex. What man doesn't? But no woman I've ever had has stuck with me like she has, and the worst part is, I didn't even sleep with her. Nothing good can come from this. I feel it in my bones.

"Connor, it's your turn," Morgan says as Mackenzie steps to the side.

But just as I hand him my ID, her birth year catches my eye, and I snatch it back out of his hand.

"Connor," my father scolds, "what is your problem?"

"She's just barely twenty-one! Are you fucking kidding me? I can't marry her. She's a kid."

I'm about to lose my ever-loving mind. My father has officially fucked up this time. It's then that my thoughts this past week and today make me feel like shit. Hell, fuck the thoughts. I had her damn pussy wrapped around my fingers while she came on my tongue. I throw my hands into my hair and bite my tongue to hold back the hate I want to spew at my father.

"You need to calm down. Are you forgetting I was only eighteen when your mother gave birth to you?"

"That's not even an accurate comparison. You and Mom were both eighteen. I am almost ten years older than her."

"For fuck's sake, I'm not asking you to sleep with her. I'm asking you to give her your damn last name and make this shit look real."

"Yeah, and I'm not offering," Mackenzie sardonically replies as she reaches around me to grab her ID off the desk.

The comment already caught me off guard, considering the borderline submissive attitude she's sported since I arrived. Still, every hair on my body stands on end as her arm brushes against mine, which has me losing my objections. It's electric, and I know she feels it too because her pouty lips part as a small gasp escapes her mouth. Those baby blue eyes connect with the pebbled skin on her arm from where our bodies touched and she sees it. Without so much as another glance, she pulls away, but I saw what I needed to. I affect her.

"Sign the papers, Con. Stop making this into more than it is," my father says, his voice rising an octave in annoyance. Well, fuck that. I'm annoyed, too.

"If it's not a big deal, then you marry her. Like you said, you don't have to fuck her."

"That's enough. Sign the papers, Con. We both know her age doesn't change anything."

I hold my father's eyes as I glare at him with enough hateful sentiments that he would turn to a pile of ash were they tangible. Over the past two years, my father and I have grown apart. For the most part, a lot of the respect I once had for him is long gone, but it's those years of him being my rock that keeps my mouth closed now. I swallow my ire and tell myself I'm not doing this for him because, ultimately, I'm not. That thought has me stepping toward the desk and reaching for the pen.

"Where do I sign?" I grind out.

The white-haired man, who's remained silent and seemingly unfazed through this entire spectacle, says, "Next to every blue tab."

As I sign the documents, which I now see include a prenup, I ask, "We're not saying vows and all that shit, right? I sign, and I'm done?"

"Technically, no specific words are legally required on your behalf. However, you are required to make a declaration of intent, and then I make a pronouncement. It's clear neither of you has words to share, so I can read a traditional script, and all you have to say is, 'I do.'"

I never thought I'd see the day I learned my wife's full name by signing a piece of paper. As I put my signature on our marriage certificate, I read her full name: Mackenzie Marie Mercer.

No sooner I've set the pen down than Morgan says, "How about we move over to the fireplace for the vows?"

I turn toward the fireplace, and it's then that my eyes collide with hers. She was watching me, but the look in her eye now is far away. It's easy to see reticence. That's a normal reaction, but there's a more insidious intent lurking behind those pale blue eyes, one I intend to unearth. My father might be a calculated man, but from just one look, I already know he has underestimated the woman standing before me. With one blink and the roll of her lips, she turns on her heel, drops my gaze, and heads toward the fireplace.

"Okay, dear, if you'll stand here. I'll have Connor stand opposite. I can recite the script, and I'll gesture toward each of you in prompt when I need you to repeat after me and say, 'I do.' As for the traditional exchanging of rings—"

"Wait," my father interjects from where he's stood, posted up against the front of his desk. "I have rings." Reaching into his pocket, he comes forward and pulls out two matching white gold bands. He places the bigger one in her hand before handing me the other.

"You really did think of everything, didn't you?" I can't help but make a snide comment, given the circumstances.

"Every bride deserves a ring on her wedding day, even the fake ones."

Morgan clears his throat. "I can assure you, Everett, this is anything but fake. These two will be married under Illinois law once these vows are recited."

"Yeah, yeah, you know what I mean." He waves off Morgan's very real assertion. I shake my head in annoyance at my father's dismissal, only to turn and direct my anger toward her.

"Is there a reason you wore this dress today?" I question, my voice clearly laden with disdain. Then it appears again, that small flare of what looks like hurt, but that can't be it. How could it be when she clearly has her own motives in all of this, none of which are love and adoration for me? The look I saw in her eyes moments ago, coupled with this dress, screams suspect. She's not just being the dutiful fake bride coerced by my father into marrying me. She's cunning, sly, and devious.

Her spine straightens as her eyes narrow on mine, and her lips pull up into the slightest of mischievous smiles. "Something borrowed." She snaps the hair tie around her wrist. "Something old." Her fingers slide over the silver pendant around her neck. "Something new." She clicks her sandals before picking up the skirt of her dress and letting it cascade back down to her sides. "Something blue."

Morgan clears his throat to begin after her little show. I'm unsure if the other two men in the room bought her crap. All I know is that I did not. As Morgan starts the ceremony, my eyes never leave hers. She knows damn well everything she just said was bullshit. She wore that dress for me, out of spite. But I can't blame her. I know I've been more than unkind. The man standing before her is not the same one she met at the bar, but the man she met at the bar doesn't exist here. He can't.

As the last vow is spoken and I slip the gold band my father handed me onto her finger, I can't help but feel the enormity of what just happened. For better or worse, quite literally, she is mine. Now, I just need to figure out what to do with her.

"While I'd love to stick around and toast to the happy couple, I must be going. Donna hasn't been doing well lately," Morgan says as he hastily packs up all the documents we signed moments ago.

My father shakes his hand. "Thanks for coming on such short notice. I appreciate your time and discretion. Do you mind showing yourself out, Morgan? I have a few more things to discuss with my son and his new bride."

"Of course. I know the way. I'll see you next week at the gala."

My father sees Morgan to the study door as I leave Mackenzie beside the fireplace. Standing next to her and putting any more weight into the words 'mine' and 'my wife' is not healthy. This is not forever. This is temporary. Allowing my mind to use words that suggest otherwise will only end in pain.

Walking around his desk, my father opens the top drawer and pulls out a set of keys, tossing them to me.

"What are these?" I ask as I run my fingers over the smooth metal.

"Keys to your house, of course. You can't be married and live in Holden's basement, nor will you live in mine. That house has been yours for ten years, Connor. It's time you used it. Movers are packing up Mackenzie's things as we speak. They will be delivered within the hour."

"Why—" I start, only for him to cut me off.

"I expect full cooperation from both of you on this. There

is no room for mistakes. You both have something at stake. Keep that in mind when you consider breaking the rules."

"I was going to say, 'why can't we get an apartment?' Why that place?"

"It's not up for discussion, Connor. Every decision made here today was made with the utmost care and consideration. Now, if the two of you wouldn't mind vacating my office, I have business to tend to, and what appears to be the start of a pool party to shut down."

Fucking Cameron. Apparently, everyone around here is more important than his own blood today. I turn on my heel and head out of his office, thoroughly annoyed, but just as I reach for the knob, he says, "Don't forget your wife."

CHAPTER 5
MACKENZIE

What in the ever-loving fuck did I just do? I spin the gold band around my ring finger as I sit in the driveway of what I suppose will be my new home for the foreseeable future. I wordlessly followed Connor here after he stormed out of Everett's house. I can't say I blame him for being upset. Being forced to marry someone I didn't know wasn't in my cards either, but if it means I get my brother back, I'm in. It's evident from Everett's words back at the house that, like me, Connor needs something out of this marriage the same as I do, and I'd be lying if I said I wasn't curious. *What does his father have on him that could convince him to up and marry me on the spot?*

I will say I've learned more in the past two hours marrying this man than I did the entire week I lived here. It's one of the reasons I kept my mouth shut. The less I said, the more they forgot I was there listening to every detail and studying every unspoken word through their mannerisms. Everett and Connor are clearly at odds, but I don't think it has always been that way. Connor bit his tongue more than anyone with a deep-seated hate ever would. But I now know that Everett's ex-wife remarried Parker and Elijah's father. I find it peculiar that Everett seems to trust those boys as though they are his own while Connor clearly despises them. I could hear the condescension in his voice when he told his father to marry me off to Parker instead, and if that tension wasn't enough, the altercation between him and Parker at the Fields the other day was. Connor clearly carries some kind of grudge.

Connor exiting his car catches my attention. We've been sitting in front of this house for at least five minutes now. He could have been on a call or responding to a text all this time, but I don't believe that's it. It was apparent back at his father's house that this is the last place he wants to be. I can't say I currently understand why. The house looks like a fancy dollhouse, complete with a princess tower and gabled window dormers that I can only imagine have fancy pillow-topped seating nooks tucked into them. I'm not sure why he would choose to live with his daughter in someone's basement over this place. The front porch alone is any little girl's dream. I don't know how old his daughter is, but she can't be too old. Connor is only nine years older than me, and I don't get the impression he was a teen dad. The wraparound deck boasts two porch swings, and on the right, there's even an attached gazebo. I could have played with dolls or colored pictures on a deck like this for hours as a girl.

The surrounding property is much like Everett's house but a little more open. Whereas trees surround Everett's house, the tree line here is set a good couple hundred feet back from the house, but there are a few clusters of redbuds and white oaks around the property, perfect for spreading out a picnic blanket and basking in the shade with a good book. All things I've never done but dreamed about. Maybe one day.

Exiting his truck, Connor doesn't bother coming to mine or throwing me a wave. He simply looks back at where I'm parked behind him and stares blankly in my direction, his eyes void of emotion, before he walks toward the house. I guess that was his way of saying, 'I'm going in. Are you coming or not?'

Pulling air through my nose, I take one last cleansing breath and rub my necklace for good luck before I exit the truck and step into this new, temporary life. I have no idea what the next few weeks or months hold, but I'm sure with Connor, they will be anything but easy. He may have liked me once, or hell, maybe even 'like' is too strong of a word. The man was looking to get laid, and I was easy prey. One look at those dark brown eyes and that boyish dimple he has when his mouth quirks up into the start of a smile, and I was putty in his hands. But that's in the past. The man I met at the bar is not the same one walking into that house, and I need to remember that.

After grabbing my satchel off the passenger's seat, I close the door and make my way toward the house. Sitting in the car looking at the place, it felt majestic, but the closer I get, it feels cold. As I draw near, I can tell things haven't been maintained, which isn't something I expected from Everett, but he did say this was Connor's home when he tossed him the keys, which means I'm sure no one has been here in a long time. I take my time approaching the house. After all, there is no need to rush. Connor has already let himself in, and I'm not sure I care to be next to him when he steps foot into whatever awaits behind those doors. He doesn't have fond memories of this place, and I'm sure my presence only worsens it.

I take my time running my hands along the white rails of the front porch while looking out over the property. The floorboards creek underfoot, which gives me pause. It's too quiet. No shuffling or movement come from inside the house. Part of me wants to post up on the porch swing until the sun sets, but I know that's just me prolonging the inevitable. At some point, I will have to speak to my husband. Turning on my heel, I leave the gazebo connected to the main deck and steel my spine in preparation for the dirty looks and snide comments I know are in store.

But, of course, this old house wouldn't allow me to sneak in. As I open the screen door, the screech of old metal feels loud enough to wake the dead. No sooner it slams behind me than I'm greeted with an unexpected scene. The entire house is covered with drop cloths. *What the hell did I get myself into?* I clench my fist and find the nerve to continue walking farther into the house. I'm not scared of Connor. I doubt a man who told me he wouldn't allow any man to enter my pool house without my explicit permission would marry me off to his unhinged son, but a creaky old house, now that's a different story.

Come on, Mackenzie, get your shit together. I crack my neck and shake off my nerves, only to take one step and practically jump out of my skin with a yelp of surprise when there's a knock on the door behind me. My hand flies to my chest, my heart pounding as I turn around.

"Sorry, ma'am. I didn't mean to scare you," the man at the door says, "We just have a few items to deliver."

"What the hell was that?" Connor suddenly appears in the office right off the foyer. For a second, the look on his face is one of concern, but it's gone almost as fast as it came after he eyes me from head to toe and sees that I'm fine.

"I just gave her a fright when I knocked on the door. I apologize. Would you like to show us to the room where we should deliver the boxes?" When Connor doesn't immediately answer the man, instead choosing to let his disapproving scowl linger on me, he adds, "Or we can just leave them on the porch."

Connor's jaw clenches, his lips thin, but he eventually answers, "You can take them to the master down the hall to the right."

The delivery man pulls on the screen door and props it open as four men carrying boxes file in and head down the hall as Connor instructed. I watch as they take boxes that seem too big to hold just the contents of the closet Everett had for me back at his house. They must contain more than just my stuff. That thought has me closing my eyes with a groan. *Connor couldn't possibly want to sleep in the same room together, could he?*

Intent on clearing the air between us, I ask, "Are we going to talk about the elephant in the room?"

He quirks a brow and crosses his arm as he leans against the doorway to the office. "And which elephant would that be?"

Before I can respond, the mover, whose name I didn't catch, returns from dropping off his box. "That's it. There wasn't very much. If you guys want, we can stay and help uncover the house. The move was slotted to take four hours, which included packing and delivering. It took us less than an hour to pack up the contents, and we still have three hours of paid time—"

Connor cuts him off. "That won't be necessary. Thanks for the offer, but we are good here. Claim the time and call it a day."

"Okay." He shrugs before outstretching his hand to Connor. "Thanks, and here's our card if you change your mind."

Then, without another word, he and his overstaffed crew leave. Everett hired five guys to do the job of one. I guess that just means he wanted to ensure I was out. When the door closes, I look back at Connor, who has already started down the hall.

"Hey." I follow after him. "I thought we were going to talk."

When I finally catch up to him, he's in the kitchen opening cabinet after cabinet, looking for what, I'm unsure. He stops, vexed that he can't find what he's searching for. With his hands on his hips, he looks right. As I follow his line of sight, I notice a glass door. Behind it are rows stacked high with wine bottles. Fancy. Can't say I've ever been in a house with its own wine room.

As he enters the room, I uncover one of the bar stools tucked under the kitchen island and make myself comfortable. He doesn't have to like me, but I'd at least like to know why he hates me. After running into him at the Fields, I considered the possibility that maybe he was miffed after I abruptly left the bar. However, I feel like it's more than that, but if we are going to be forced to endure each other's company, I'd like some answers.

Exiting the wine room with a bottle in hand, he pulls open drawers in search of a wine opener. That's when I notice the cabinets beneath the island I'm sitting at have glasses hanging underneath and more drawers. Reaching down, I grab a glass and place it atop the island before trying one of the drawers on my side.

"Looking for this?" I say as I slide the opener across the counter toward him. It's clear that he's not only annoyed I found it, but that I'm here. *Well, fucking ditto.* This isn't what I signed up for, either. "Getting back to the elephant in the room. I know you recognize me from the bar. Are we just going to keep pretending that didn't happen or…"

His eyebrows shoot up, and he swallows his wine, his expression cross as he swipes his thumb over his lips. "You think the elephant in the room is that I ate your pussy."

My eyes widen before I drop them to the island, my cheeks no doubt flushed from his brazen choice of words. Yes, technically, that is what happened, but I've never been on the receiving end of such vulgarity, and considering I more than enjoyed what he did, I need a second to get my bearings. I won't let him win this one. I did nothing wrong. He initiated it, and I allowed it.

"Is it not?" I ask as I straighten my shoulders and dare to meet his disarming gaze once more. I don't know what it is about this man, but the look those deep-set dark eyes give me is unnerving. As much as it is sexy as fuck.

"No, it's not. I don't care much for liars. You failed to tell me your age, and you let me believe you were someone else," he says before he takes another drink of his wine.

"You can't be serious right now. I don't recall you asking my name, and I told you I was just passing through. I even explained in the bathroom that I had somewhere to be. Whatever mistaken identity happened at that bar is solely your problem, not mine."

He slams his glass down. "Bullshit. I called you Blu, and you never once corrected me."

I can't help but stifle a sarcastic laugh. "Really, that's what you're going with? I have blue eyes. I was wearing a blue dress. Excuse me for thinking you were hitting on me and trying to come up with some cute pet name for the girl who was just passing through." Tongue in cheek with his arms crossed across his chest, he stares me down hard, my comments doing nothing to rein in his obvious disdain. "This can't seriously be about my age. I'm twenty-one, not sixteen. You're acting as if you defiled a child. I've been drinking since I was a teenager, and I can promise you I'm not a virgin."

He just finished refilling his glass and sets the bottle down harder than necessary before hitting below the belt. "My mistake. So you're not just a liar, you're a slut."

"You know what? Screw you. I'm not the one who went to the bar looking to hook up with someone named Blu. Glad I had somewhere to be that night, so I didn't waste my time on a subpar performance."

Without another word, I turn on my heel and exit the kitchen in search of the room I saw the movers deliver my boxes to. At least I know tonight I won't go to bed dreaming about him.

A buzzing beneath my pillow stirs me awake, and my arm tingles as the blood rushes back through my veins when I reach for my phone. Fuck, that hurts. I force my eyes open when I feel the unfamiliar clash of metal against the glass face of my phone as I wrap my fingers around the sides to silence my alarm. "Why couldn't that just have been a bad dream?" I say out loud to no one as I stare at the beams of light cascading through the sheer white curtains in the master bedroom. Mental note: Buy blackout curtains with your first paycheck.

My phone starts to buzz again, and this time, I hold it up to shut off the alarm, only to find it's not my alarm at all. It's Parker. *What the hell? Why is Parker calling me?*

Clearing my throat, I try my best not to sound like an eighty-year-old grandma who just woke up. "Hello," I answer, forcing fake glee into my voice.

"Where are you? You're an hour late." Shit. I sit straight up and pull the phone away from my face to check the time. "Mac, answer me." I hear him say as I bring the phone back to my ear.

"Umm," I start.

"Did something happen?" His voice lowers, and I hear his concern.

Does he know what happened yesterday?

"No-no, I overslept. I'll be there in thirty minutes."

"Mac," he starts again, but I hang up the phone. The last thing I need right now is another man telling me what to do. I can't believe I overslept. Better yet, what the hell happened to my alarm? I set one for every day I worked when I was in the office earlier this week. It's 9:00 a.m., so I only slept roughly five hours.

After everything that went down last night, I couldn't sleep, so I spent the night occupying my mind and getting this room in order. It still needs some work, but at least I got everything uncovered and all my things put away. I was relieved that all the boxes were indeed just my things. Nothing of Connor's was in them, and since he never came knocking on my door last night, I think it's safe to assume we will not be sharing a room.

In the en suite, I switch on the shower, dig my toothpaste out of the travel bag it was packed into, and start opening the cabinets in search of a towel. After opening them all, I come up empty. Fuck it. I grab the hand towel off the wall and head toward the shower as I finish brushing my teeth. I need this job. I don't have time to waste searching for towels, but I need a shower after all the moving and dust I stirred up last night.

Once I've thoroughly scoured my body with hot water and the men's bodywash that happened to be in the shower, I use the hand towel to pat myself dry before wrapping the towel around my head and running naked to the closet. After I've slipped into my clothes and a pair of Converse, I run back to the bathroom, brush my damp hair, and grab my compact bag that has my ChapStick, mascara, and scrunchies. I need to get on the road. I can throw this stuff on at a stoplight. Exiting the bathroom, I take one last look around the room, ensuring I have everything before I quietly turn the lock on my door and open it.

I'm not hiding from Connor, but I don't care to see him. His comments last night were the final straw. We may have once thoroughly enjoyed each other's company, but that day has come and gone. He's determined to be my enemy, and the last thing I need is a distraction.

"Hey, you're here. I need you on the snack window. Apparently, everyone needed to be reminded they had a job today."

"Yeah, yeah, I'm sorry," I rush out as I put my hat on and rush over to the snack window to roll up the counter door.

As I place my hands on the counter and lean forward to call out, "I can help the next customer down here," I catch sight of Parker glaring at the ring that now rests on my left hand. The muscles in his arms flex, and his jaw ticks as though my new status bothers him. However, he was the one who said I was off-limits when I tried to make a move. We are too busy for me to pay him or my fake marriage any more thought. As the first person steps up to place their order, another ten file in behind.

"Can I have two black coffees and a pack of white-powered donuts?"

Looking behind me, I check to see that we have the donuts in stock before pressing the keys on the register and ringing up the order. "That will be six dollars even," I say as I turn around to fill the coffee order.

"When Cameron gets here, we can call out orders to her," Parker says as I return to the window with the coffees and hand them to the customer.

"Who is Cameron again? Is she the one with the short brown hair?"

He shakes his head and mumbles something under his breath that I can't hear over the hum of the machines and the crowd.

"I'll take a Bud Light, tall," the next customer orders.

Before I can respond, Parker says, "You'll have to order that down at the beer window. These windows are snacks and soft drinks only."

"You're telling me I just stood in this line for ten minutes, and now I need to stand in another line when the beer is right behind you?" the old man claps back. He's clearly agitated, which I can sympathize with. Parker nods at me to switch sides, and I take his window as he takes mine to handle the old man.

While I help the next customer, I overhear him point out the sign that hangs above the windows in bold that says no beer sold at these windows, and he even gives him a little extra lip service that I sure as hell wouldn't have supplied. He can read up on state laws on his own time. We have a shit ton of paying customers to tend to.

"Oh my God, Parker, I am so sorry I'm late," a voice chirps up behind us, her sincerity clearly missing. When I turn to see her face, I immediately recognize her from Everett's. We briefly crossed paths at the pool the other day. She introduced herself and asked me if I had a swimsuit and to come join her by the pool, but no sooner I sat in a pool chair to hang out than Everett was escorting me inside. No wonder Parker was mumbling under his breath.

I have a ring on my finger that says I'm married to a man I clearly don't know. Otherwise, I would know precisely who Cameron is. Damn it. As much as I don't want to, I need to talk to Connor. We need to come up with a story if we expect this small town to buy our marriage.

"Sure you are. Seriously, Cameron, I'm not doing this with you this summer. If you can't get here on time, then you need to find another job."

"Sheesh, Parker, relax. What has your panties in a wad today?" He doesn't respond, instead choosing to refocus his attention on the customers. His snub has her eyes snapping to mine, and a big smile spreads across her face. "Oh hey, Mackenzie, right? Looks like we were meant to be besties. First the pool and now work."

"That's enough chitchat. Make us orders as we call them out," Parker snaps back at us, his annoyance piqued.

After the morning crowd started to wane, I escaped to the back office for a short break to shove some food in my mouth; since I didn't have breakfast or dinner last night, I was starting to feel faint. I grabbed a hot dog, blue Doritos, a Diet Coke to wash it down, and a bag of M&M's for some added sugar. I'm running on fumes from the lack of sleep I got last night, and just as I shove the hotdog in my mouth for a second bite, the office door swings open.

"Want to hang out after your shift?" Cameron says as she comes bouncing in, throwing herself into the only other chair in the room with a bottle of water in hand. She's taller than me by at least three inches, has long, lean legs like a ballet dancer, a flat stomach, and perfect-sized breasts. My breasts have always been too big, getting in the way of any sport I played, and don't even get me started on my thighs. They've always been on the thicker side. It didn't matter that I was physically active. My stomach has always been softer. I like food.

As I swallow the colossal bite I took, I rinse it down with soda before saying, "I'm not sure, I—"

She cuts me off. "I'm not going to take no for an answer. You owe me pool time."

It's not that I want to say no, but the new jewelry addition to my left hand has me feeling somewhat insecure. Because Cameron was at Everett's yesterday and Parker all but growled when I asked who she was, I feel unprepared for girl talk, especially if she starts to question me about Connor. Obviously, they know each other, and anyone who talks to me for five seconds could see that I do not know shit about Connor. But I need a friend, and considering she's opening the door and can probably give me deets these men refuse to spill, I say, "I wasn't going to say no. I was going to ask for a raincheck. I just moved into my new place last night, and there is so much work that needs to be done."

That's not a lie. When I snuck out of the house this morning, not one cloth had been removed from a single piece of furniture.

"I bet. I'm sure that place needs a lot of TLC. No one has lived there for years. That's perfect. I'll follow you home and help you get the place in shape."

Well, that was a loaded statement. Just like I assumed, she knows something about me. I never mentioned where I lived. The question is, how much and what. Before I get a chance to object, she's out of her chair as if it's settled, and Parker walks in. "Break time is up. Let's go."

Shit. I didn't even finish my hot dog.

CHAPTER 6
CONNOR

Fuck, my back is killing me. I barely slept a wink, and what little sleep I did get was shit, considering I spent it propped up against the door to Mackenzie's room. There was no way I could sleep after the disgusting words that came out of my mouth last night. After I downed one bottle of wine and started another in hopes I would pass out, I ended up outside her door instead. I listened to her walk around the room for hours, playing music and organizing shit. My hand gripped the knob multiple times, tempted to turn it, but I knew an apology was the last thing I would give. It's better this way, even if it's not what I want. I'm not the asshole she believes me to be. I don't hate Mackenzie. I hate that I want her.

After I woke up on the floor beside her door, I went straight upstairs to shower and searched for something to cure my pounding headache. By the time I came back down, she was gone. I've been sitting on the front porch for the past hour, debating what to do next. I want to go get my shit from Holden's place, but I also don't care to run into him or Aria. I should visit my father and pump him for more information on Mackenzie's background. He was very vague with what he gave me last night. The problem is that my father is also the last person I care to see.

Luckily, or unlucky, I'm still undecided when the sight of her old blue Ford pickup comes kicking up dust down the gravel road that leads up to the house. My head is a completely fucked-up mess of emotions because I'm mad that she's been gone all day, yet I don't want her here. However, as she draws near, all I can think is while I may not want her here, here is also the only place I'll allow her to be. There's some kind of misplaced peace that comes from knowing she's in the house even though I'm mad at her. At least I know where she is and where she's not. Whatever small grip I was gaining in the sanity department quickly slips away when I see a silver BMW break the tree line behind her. You've got to be kidding me.

Pinching the bridge of my nose, I try to find some small amount of composure that keeps my tongue in check, so I don't do a repeat of last night. As she pulls into the driveway, I can't help but stare. There's a reason I got on my knees after knowing her for a handful of minutes. She's perfect even when she's not trying to be. Her long blond hair is in a ponytail, and she's wearing a Hayes Fields ballcap. My annoyance slightly spikes, but I attempt to shake it off as I walk down the front steps. I'm sure she didn't have a say in working there, but she does now. She's supposed to be my wife. The mere thought of that title, the reference to her being mine, gives me anxiety. It fuels my hate and desire all at once. *Fuck.*

When she steps out of the truck, I can't help but bite my lip. She's wearing spandex shorts that show every fucking curve of her ass. Even sporting an oversized work polo, she's sexy as fuck. I know she's not jailbait, but damn, this is not what I need right now. The scowl she's wearing pulls my head out of the gutter and reminds me there is no space for the direction my thoughts were headed. She walks around to the back of the truck to grab a few bags just as Cameron climbs out of her car.

"This isn't a good time, Cameron," I say as she walks toward the back of Mackenzie's truck to help with the bags.

"Is there ever a good time with you, Con?"

"I have things to discuss with my wife." I try to keep the annoyance out of my response, but when Cameron pops one of her perfectly manicured brows at me, I know I've failed.

Her eyes flick between Mackenzie and me. "Shouldn't you two still be in the honeymoon phase of this marriage? Go bang it out in the bathroom." She starts up the path to my house with bags in hand before adding, "Don't mind me. I'm sure I can find the kitchen and the liquor cabinet."

So much for keeping my temper in check. "Cam, you realize this is my house, right?"

"Yeah, yeah. Well, your wife invited me, so I'm staying."

What the fuck? When I turn back to Mackenzie in question, she's staring after Cameron the same as me.

"What exactly does she know?" I grit out as Mackenzie rolls her eyes.

"I have nothing to say to you. We live under the same roof. We don't have to like each other, and I refuse to let someone who doesn't even know me degrade me or make me feel inferior because I did something I wanted to do."

She adjusts the bags she's holding and moves to step around me, but I reach for her wrist.

"That didn't answer my question."

Her eyes lock where my hand is wrapped around her wrist before flashing up to mine, and for the moment, I'm grateful they are hidden behind her sunglasses. I don't need to see the venom I know is there.

"Yeah, well, you haven't been the most forthcoming yourself. You haven't shown me an ounce of decency since I arrived. Why should I extend any toward you?"

"For starters, we are married, but more importantly, we need to talk."

She yanks her wrist out of my grip. "You're right. We should talk, but you lost that chance last night. Don't worry. I don't care to taste your name on my lips. Whatever this bullshit is will stay between us."

Her legs start to move before my mind can catch up with her words. I deserve everything she said, and fuck if it doesn't make me want her more. I saw it in my dad's office. There is more to Mackenzie Mercer than meets the eye, or I guess it's Callahan now. Either way, my new wife is not innocent. She plays the timid, reserved, submissive card well. Too well, almost as if she's been trained for the part. My fists clench in annoyance. I fucked myself here. I need her story, and while she may not see it now, we need our story. Mackenzie may have yielded to my father, but it's clear she will not be doing the same for me.

CHAPTER 7

MACKENZIE

"Seriously, this place feels like a haunted house. The first item of business to get to is uncovering all this crap. Well, shit, I take that back. The first thing is making a drink. The second is tackling this house," Cameron says as she unpacks the few things we picked up at the convenience store on the way home from work.

I wasn't lying earlier when I told Connor I wouldn't talk about us. I'm not trying to blow up our fake marriage. Technically, I need it, but I don't need to talk about us to get helpful information out of people. Hell, I know Cameron will give me a treasure trove of useful nuggets to be tucked away for later just by being here. The fact that she's here has already told me a few things. One: she clearly knew where I was living and with whom. Two: her knowledge did not come from me or Connor. He made that more than evident with the question he asked me outside, and lastly: Connor isn't a big Cameron fan, which just bumped her to the top of my 'people I'd like to be friends with' list.

Unpacking one of the bags, Cameron asks, "Why did you buy such a big bag of M&M's?"

I reach across the island to snag it from her since I never got to eat my bag earlier. Instead, it was left on the desk.

"What do you mean? Aren't big bags sold to be eaten?"

She laughs. "Good point. I'm not really a sweet girl. I crave salty stuff."

I shrug. "Yeah, I suppose I'm the stereotypical female who craves chocolate, especially if it's that time of the month. Don't get me wrong. I won't eat this bag in a day. I mean, unless it's a bad day. I like to have them around to quench my sweet tooth. They've more or less become a comfort food."

"What sounds good? I bought stuff for margaritas..." she trails off as she opens the refrigerator. "And oh, hey, it looks like Everett stocked the refrigerator."

Another nugget earned. She called him Everett, not Dad. I assumed she was Connor's sister because she clearly lives with Everett, not to mention Parker's reaction when I acted as though I didn't know who she was. His scowl immediately screamed, 'You're married to the guy, and you don't know who his sister is?' Relation aside, she's also familiar with Everett's idiosyncrasies, which means she's been around for a while.

"There's beer in here. I mean, it's the kind Connor likes, but beer all the same."

I can't help but lean over to look past her, curious as to what the brand is. I said I didn't care to talk about him, but it doesn't mean I don't want every morsel of information I can gather on Connor Callahan.

Closing the door, she gestures toward the wine room. "Or wine?"

"I'm easy. I'll have whatever you're having."

As soon as the words leave my mouth, Connor walks into the kitchen, and I don't miss the way his eyes flick to mine. I'm half waiting for a jab related to the easy comment, but instead, his lips slightly pinch as if he knows the direction of my thoughts, and for a second, I sense the tiniest of regrets, but the moment quickly passes.

"You missed one," he says, setting the bag on the countertop.

I didn't miss that one. I didn't care to bring it in with everything else. It's a bag of toiletries that I planned on grabbing later. I wanted some feminine bodywash, and it's getting close to that time of the month, so I figured I'd grab the necessities in case my period comes earlier, though the amount of stress I've felt lately will likely have the opposite effect on my cycle.

He slices Cameron with a vexed glare she doesn't see as she ignores his presence and rummages through the cabinets. "Ah-ha, found it," she says as she holds a drink mixer. I guess we're having margaritas.

Turning around, she asks Connor, "Should I make three? It's going to be a long night getting this place in order."

He gives her no words and turns his back on her, giving me one last look from head to toe before saying, "Don't even bother. We won't be in this house long enough for it to matter."

And then he's gone.

"God, I wish he'd get over his shit and stop being such a prickly motherfucker." Cameron sighs as she pours tequila into the cocktail shaker.

No sooner he's gone than my chest deflates. I can't help but instinctively hold my breath around him. He makes me tense. I mentally prepare for battle whenever our eyes collide, and I hate it.

"Sorry, I shouldn't be such an ass. You married him. Please tell me he gives you his fun side." Her eyes optimistically search mine, and I give her a half smile that hopefully lies more than the words I can't give, considering I have no idea who the man I am married to is. "I honestly thought you two would take me up on my offer and go bang it out. A good fuck in this place is what he needs to replace the hurt."

As I watch her pour our margaritas, I process everything she's given me. Whatever Cameron knows about Connor and me is fabricated to some extent. She doesn't know that our marriage is arranged. Connor's shit attitude is a new development. Cameron and Parker have all but vouched for him, confirming that he hasn't always been an ass, not to mention I myself met a different man at the bar. I want to directly ask what changed him, but I can't. After all, his wife should know. So I'll use the house.

"How about you pass me a glass? This place could use some attention. I need to see what I'm working with under all these sheets."

I'm sure that Cameron is an intelligent girl. I have no doubt she doesn't miss how I don't comment on my relationship with Connor, sexual or otherwise, but I also get the impression, similarly to me, she just wants a friend, and I can use an ally. She doesn't care what we talk about or what I say, just that we are talking.

She's just taken a sip of her drink and set down the glass when she says, "Damn, that's good. Where should we start? I mean, it's been ten years since Everett and Moira gave him this place. I think every room could use more than a little TLC, but—"

"How about we start uncovering things and see what shape everything is in? I uncovered the master last night, and it's actually very nice. I'd like to change a few things out to my taste, but otherwise it's well preserved."

I take a sip of my margarita, and she's right. It's excellent. She made them stiff, and I'm thankful. The warmth from the tequila slowly works its magic and releases the tension built up in my neck, and the weight that's been sitting on my chest since I arrived here in Waterloo feels less like an anchor and more like the choice it was.

"Let's start in the living room and try to knock out the first floor tonight," she says as she kicks off her tennis shoes and heads out of the kitchen, drink in hand. I grab mine and follow after her.

As the first few sheets are pulled off, huge gray couches are revealed. Oak side tables that match the exposed beams of the ceiling and fireplace balance the dark furniture. The place looks as though it was professionally decorated. It's beautiful. The design is timeless. There's not a bunch of knickknacks, though I wonder if that is by design or happenstance. It doesn't seem like Connor has lived here since it became his. Maybe it was meant to be lacking so that he could fill it, personalize it, and make it his own.

Cameron pulls off the last cloth draped over the bench seat of the bay window in the front of the house. It's the perfect spot to lounge the day away.

"I can't believe the shape everything is in. I suppose since Everett left the electricity on and paid to cool this place in the summer, it preserved what has been sitting here. I've never been inside this house. I've only seen the outside and heard the stories. I mean, I get it; Connor didn't think he'd be living here alone, but this place is picturesque."

My heart slightly pinches at her last comment as I think about what the last part implies. I know Connor has a daughter. Did her mom die? Was this supposed to be their family home? My stomach slowly churns, and I know I'm overthinking all this. I should give zero shits about this man. This stupid beating organ inside my chest shouldn't care that maybe he's jaded and spiteful because he's a single dad who got dealt a shit hand.

Pushing the thoughts away, I pick up my now-empty drink and shake it so the ice clinks against the glass. "I think it's time for a refill."

CHAPTER 8

CONNOR

Sleep evaded me yet again last night. I don't care to be in this house. I have my reasons. Most of them, nothing anyone could really understand. Most of the time, I don't understand them myself. This is the house I grew up in. I have fond memories of it. As a kid, this was where all my buddies wanted to hang out. We have a small lake on the property that my father used to keep stocked for fishing. I spent countless summers hanging out there on the dock, skipping stones, swimming, jumping off the tree swing into the lake, and when I wasn't down there, I was forging trails on my ATV through the woods and on the fields. Even now, as I sit in the breakfast nook, drinking my coffee and staring out at the backyard, I can see the treehouse my father and I built when I was ten. I never wanted to leave that place. I loved it so much that we built two more throughout the property. But I can't find the space in my chest to feel anymore. It all feels like another life because, in the end, it was all a lie.

My parents built a life here. I thought they were happy here. At least at first, anyway. Growing up, my father told me everything he did was for my mother. If she wanted it, he made it happen. This place was her dream.

I vaguely remember being six years old and sitting with my mother on the living room floor. She had a bunch of magazines spread out, and she was cutting pages out and putting them into another book. When I asked her what she was doing, she told me she was manifesting her dreams. Of course, I had no idea what that meant, but she handed me a pair of scissors and said, "If you could make your room look like whatever you wanted, what would it look like?" She flipped through a few pages, showed me how she had cut out images of things she liked, and filled up pages with room after room of ideas. We spent the entire afternoon doing that.

When my father came home later that day, I was so excited to show him our book, but I couldn't find it, and my mother was in the shower. I tore the living room apart, looking for it, only to find it under the couch. My father was mad that I had made a mess until I showed him the book. We were flipping through the pages when my mother walked in. Looking back on the memory now, I can see signs I missed then. She was hiding the book from my father. He looked up from the book and asked her, "Is this what you want?"

I remember her being so nervous. She was twisting her fingers when she said, "No, Everett. Connor and I were just having fun."

The book was clearly so much more than just fun. It was well thought out and distinctly labeled. My father's expression was pinched briefly as he returned his focus to the pages. My father and his brothers were just getting their company off the ground at that time. They were barely making ends meet. He was finishing up his last year of law school and was hardly home. I thought that was why my mother was nervous. She didn't want to put any pressure on him for more. My father closed the book, got up from the couch, went over to my mother, kissed her forehead, and said, "It's done." In hindsight, I know she was hiding it because it was her dream, but not one she wanted with him. Being back in this house in a marriage I didn't ask for… I can't help but feel like I'm being forced to endure the same fate my parents had.

A cabinet closing pulls me out of my memories and draws my attention back toward the kitchen and away from the yard. It is obvious Mackenzie hasn't noticed me sitting here in the alcove of the breakfast nook because she looks relaxed, and every time she's around me, she's anything but. She pulls out a coffee mug and starts the Keurig before searching through the refrigerator for creamer. My father stocked the kitchen before he sent us here. I'm sure he did that for her benefit, not mine. When she walks over to the pantry, my blood pressure rises. She's wearing those damn spandex shorts again and a tank top that shows way too much cleavage.

I clear my throat, announcing my presence, and she startles, throwing her hand over her chest as she whirls toward me. "It's time to have that talk."

Her breathing is erratic, but she still manages to force venom into her tone. "A conversation is a two-way street and something I don't care to have with you."

I stand from the booth and approach the island, where I set my mug down with enough force to let her know I mean business. "Sit down. I gave you my name. The least you can do is listen to my words."

She turns her back to me, grabs the granola bar she was after and lets out a huff of frustration before tossing it on the counter and picking up her coffee.

I can't help but study her as she moves. The woman is testing my patience, and she knows it. "Problem? Am I not allowed to grab my coffee before I sit?"

I cross my arms over my chest. "I didn't peg you as a petty grudge holder. Your skin seemed thicker than that."

Everything this woman does riles me up. I'm not sure there's a sentence she could say that I wouldn't react poorly to at this point. Is she allowed to grab her breakfast for a conversation? Yes, we are adults, for fuck's sake. I realize I'm asking her to try and be civil when I've acted the opposite. I deserve her sharp tongue, but she could try to meet me halfway so we can get off this damned rat wheel. Instead, she is choosing to draw this out.

"Who said I'm holding a grudge? Your existence annoys me. Every other word that comes out of your mouth is barbed. What you're picking up is my overall disdain for all things related to you."

She brings her coffee to her mouth and raises a brow at me. Those damn eyes make my heart skip a beat. They've haunted my dreams since they locked on mine while she came all over my tongue. *Fuck.* My cock twitches, and I grind my teeth. It makes sense that I would be put into an impossible situation with this woman. Nothing in the past decade has gone in my favor. I feel as though I've been cursed by the gods and ordered to pay reparations for crimes I'm unaware I committed.

I ignore her antics, instead choosing to take the high ground and keep my mouth shut rather than hurl more insults her way. "You shouldn't have brought Cameron here."

"And why not? She's close to your family and one of the only people outside of Parker who talks to me."

"We're talking now."

She waves her hand as she swallows her coffee. "This isn't talking. This is a threat, an order."

"Because you're making it so with your obstinance. You said last night we don't have to like each other. It's time to get over yourself and play the part."

Her eyes narrow as she reaches for her granola bar. "I could say the same thing to you after the shit you pulled last night with your, 'We won't be staying here,' comment and then burning out. I didn't see you jumping at the bit to play the role of a dutiful husband helping his new wife get the house in order. Instead, you took off."

Swiping my mug off the counter, I head toward the Keurig to brew another cup.

"I didn't leave. I was upstairs." It's not a lie, and I know she can't refute my claim because neither of them came up.

"Whatever," she says as she rises from her stool. "Look, I need to get to work. I was late yesterday—"

I cut her off before she can continue. "My wife doesn't work at the local ballpark."

"Yes, she does." Her voice rises a few decibels as she crosses her arms in defiance, only further pissing me off.

"Also, you aren't leaving the house like that. Your breasts are practically falling out. It's not appropriate for a married woman."

"God, you're infuriating. I planned on putting my work shirt on over this, but now I'm leaving it as is just to spite you. You don't get a say in how I dress, and I'm keeping the job. It's not up for debate."

"Like hell you are. I can and will dictate where and if you work, and those breasts are for my eyes only." *Fuck. Did I really just say that?* I know why I care about where she works, but as for the rest, I know I'm out of line. It can't be helped. She's here in my house with my name attached to hers. I was attracted to her before this arrangement was sprung on me. That hasn't changed. Her eyes widen in surprise at my comment, catching her off guard. I wave my hand and turn toward the coffee pot in an attempt to dismiss my faux pas. "You know what I mean, Mackenzie."

"What exactly does Connor Callahan's wife do?" Her voice is gruff.

I can tell I've pushed a button, but who in their right mind gets upset about being told they don't have to work?

"You don't. My wife doesn't need to work. I make enough money to support my family."

She slams the drawer to the pullout trash can after tossing her untouched granola bar. "No. That's a deal breaker for me.

I refuse to be a kept woman while I am here. We both know this arrangement has an expiration date, and I need to make my own money."

Damn it. She knows she has me by the balls. We both need each other for reasons neither of us has yet to share, but whatever they are, they are of enough consequence that each of us thought this arrangement was worth it.

"Then we'll find you something else. My family has money. You working there doesn't fit the narrative," I offer in compromise.

"Wrong, try again. Parker and Cameron both work there. If it's good enough—"

"No, let me stop you right there. Parker Michaelson and Cameron Salt are not Callahans, regardless of how far up my dad's ass they like to be."

"Noted," she sneers. "As for the rest, it all sounds like a personal problem, one you can work out alone because I need to leave before I'm late."

She doesn't wait around for a response. Instead, she stomps off toward the master, leaving me holding my proverbial dick, so to speak. *This woman.*

Just as I'm about to give chase and follow after her, my phone vibrates in my pocket. Pulling it out to see who the hell is calling rather than texting, the number on the screen instantly makes my heart skip a beat.

"Hey, sunshine. How's camp going?"

"Coach, did you know Marne was coming here too?"

I can't help but smile when I hear the excitement in her voice. It's apparent she's having a good time.

"Yes, I knew Marne was going to be there. Uncle Garrett thought it would be a fun surprise if we kept it secret from you guys."

Before the words even finish leaving my mouth, a wave of realization sweeps over me, and I'm instantly pissed again. I hear her talking to someone in the background. "Yeah, I'm on the phone now. Is that all we need?" She pauses. "Hey, Coach, I need our address. I only remember the street and numbers. I don't know the stuff that comes after that."

Crap.

Summer doesn't know I'm not staying at Holden's anymore, which means she's not staying at Holden's anymore.

"What do you need the address for?"

"One of the things we do every Saturday is write a letter home talking about everything that happened that week. Since we aren't supposed to use the phone to call home, the counselors said it's a way to stay in touch with our parents and help us remember everything we did once camp is over."

Shit. I want her letters. I don't want those going to Holden and Aria's.

"It's 10 Maple Drive, Waterloo, Illi—"

"Aria and Holden live on Beech Creek. Did you move?"

I run my hands through my hair and let out a stuttered, "Yeah, Sunshine, I—"

She cuts me off, "Is it close? Can we still go see River whenever I want?"

We lived with Aria and Holden for the past three years. She and River are as close as it gets.

"Yeah, of course, don't worry about that while you're at camp. Try to have fun while you're there. Only seven more weeks until you're back home."

"I'm not worried, Coach, but I need those numbers I was asking for."

"62298."

I barely get the last digit out before she says, "Thanks, got to run. Make sure you read my letters, and whatever you do, don't throw them away."

I want to tell her I'd never throw them away, but she hangs up before I get the chance. The sound of the screen door closing as Mackenzie leaves for work snaps me out of my thoughts of Summer and back to the epiphany I had while she was on the phone. Garrett Callahan knows something. It's not a coincidence that he suggested this eight-week-long camp for Summer and Marne, only for Mackenzie to show up a week later. Summer's absence was orchestrated, and I want details.

Scrolling through my email, I click out of my personal account and into the Callahan and Associates email, where I'm still technically on staff, and pull up the shared calendars for my uncles. Garrett lives in the St. Louis area but frequently travels to the East Coast to manage clients at our Boston location as needed. Perfect. He's in St. Louis for the next two days, and his morning doesn't appear to have anything scheduled. Looks like I'm going to the city.

But first, I need to call off work. Calling off today, of all days, pains me. After Mackenzie's show about quitting her job this morning, I was looking forward to showing up. I can't wait to see the look on her face when she discovers we are colleagues.

"Connor, I don't think Garrett was expecting you. I'll let him know you're here."

"Sheila, that won't be necessary. Garrett will be seeing me whether he wants to or not. Please hold his calls."

"Well, I, you know you can't…" she starts, but whatever arguments she has for me die when she sees I don't give a shit, and I continue past her desk and down the hall to Garrett's office.

This isn't a client issue, it's a family issue, one that involves my daughter, and I'll be damned if I don't know every fucking detail. Pushing through the frosted door to his office, he's sitting behind his desk on a conference call. Garrett's a few years older than my dad, but he didn't get married until later in life, so his youngest is the same age as

Summer. He's only now just starting to show his age. The genetics on the Callahan side are strong. There is no denying that my dad and uncles are brothers. They all have jet-black hair and dark eyes, just like me, aside from the hair. My hair is more a dark brown than black. But Garrett appears to be getting gray in his beard and around his face, which only makes the fucker somehow look all the more intimidating.

I don't interrupt his call. Instead, I walk over to the cabinet I know holds his bourbon and pour myself a drink. The sound of him snapping his fingers means I better pour him one. I showed up unannounced. He knows I'm here to talk, and if I had to guess, he already knows exactly what's on my agenda, which is why he wanted a drink as well.

"I have another meeting to get to, gentlemen. If there are any more questions regarding the contract, Austin can help you." I hear his legal assistant pick up right where he left off before he clicks off the call.

"And to what do I owe the pleasure of seeing my favorite nephew in the office?"

I hand him his bourbon before taking one long pull off my own and making myself comfortable in one of the leather chairs in front of his desk.

"Cut the crap, Garrett. You've always been straight with me, and I don't expect anything less from you now."

My family has always been close. Family cookouts on the weekends, vacations to the lake every summer, on top of running the family business—one that I was supposed to take over eventually. I had the chance to go onto the minor leagues after college but chose to get my hands dirty instead. The work my family does behind the scenes to take down sex trafficking rings and operate safe houses for victims is honorable and close to my heart. However, the last role I took on has kept me from getting my hands dirty since, and the older I get, the more I realize that's probably for the best, especially with how things have played out recently between my parents.

I didn't know it growing up—I suppose it's not something that you just up and tell your kids—but my mother was a victim of sexual assault in high school before she met my father. It's one of the many reasons my father started charities to benefit victims of assault, but over the years, through those charity events, he met people and, being in law, some of the stories led to more. He realized he could go after some abusers and make a difference. That said, I don't think he or his brothers ever saw it getting this involved.

With the hand holding my bourbon, I clink my new accessory against the glass. "I think we both know why I'm here."

My uncle's one tell is that he has no tell at all. He can wear a mask of indifference like nobody's business. But that's also how I know I was right in coming here. He'll talk. I just have to ask the right questions.

"What exactly do you want from me that you can't get from your father?"

He knows damn well that my father and I haven't been on speaking terms for the past two years, apart from where Summer is concerned. I left the company when he and my mother divorced.

"I know sending the girls away this summer was intentional. What I need to know is, what are the other moving pieces. Why was I pulled in at the last minute? I feel like a fucking pawn, and someone better start talking before I blow this shit up."

"Fucking relax, Con. You're not a damn pawn. You've known for years all of this was temporary, Holly's situation, Summer, Trent, all of it. I wouldn't put Marne or Summer in harm's way, which is why they aren't here. Holly was released last month—"

I shoot out of my chair. "Are you kidding me? You're just

going to casually sit there and act like you didn't just drop a fucking grenade. What do you mean, 'Holly was released last month?' She has a year left on her sentence."

I'm fucking livid that neither my father nor Garrett thought to tell me this information. It's been seven fucking years since I've seen Holly. For that time, Summer has been mine. Holly got mixed up with the wrong crowd and started turning tricks, among other things. Weeks after we hooked up, one night at the Fields, she tried picking up the wrong guy. Turns out he played into her hand, let her take him back to her place, only to arrest her when she tried to slip him a roofie and steal his wallet. That night, they found a box full of stolen credit cards stashed behind the return air vent in her apartment.

Holly was taken to jail and ended up serving seven of the last eight years there for charges related to petty theft and grand larceny. The entire town knew she was working with Trent—if not *for* Trent—but the pathetic piece of shit took off, and we haven't been able to find him since. But this information changes everything.

"Where is she? I can't believe you would keep this from me, knowing what this means." Holly gave birth to Summer while she was locked up. They let her have the baby for a few hours before she was taken away and handed over to me. We never planned on keeping Summer away from her mother, but I haven't had a chance to discuss Holly coming back into the picture with her. Summer is not aware that her mother has been in jail for almost eight years. As I pace the room, something else hits me. "If Holly is out, why aren't we using her as bait to draw Trent out?"

"Sit down, Con, and I'll catch you up, but if you're going to keep flying off the handle, by all means, go ask your father."

He drinks his bourbon and loosens the tie around his neck before giving me a look that says I better take my seat if I expect to get any answers. I do as asked because I'd rather have this conversation with Garrett than my father. At the moment, I don't trust my father's decision-making abilities, considering he just forced me into a marriage with someone I've never met.

"Let's start with your first question. The second Holly got out, she took off to Montana."

His eyes hold mine for a beat to see if I'm at least connecting the dots between her release and where she is headed, and I am. Mackenzie is from Montana. I saw it listed on the legal paperwork that was laid out beside the marriage license. When I don't say anything, he takes my silence as acceptance and continues.

"In regard to her being bait, she is. It's why we've stayed out of the picture. We're watching to see what her next move is going to be. Your father and I currently don't see eye to eye regarding Holly's release."

Now, that is news to me. Garrett and my father have always been the closest. In fact, I've always felt they share a brain, so it begs the question: *what the hell don't they agree on?*

"Do you care to enlighten me on why that is?"

His eyes zero in on the ring on my finger, and I know without words my new marriage is one of those things. "Your father believes Mackenzie is a target, and I believe it's Holly. I think he's trying to stack the odds in his favor, which is why you are now sporting that new ring."

I can't help it. I throw my drink back and lose my temper. "Are you fucking kidding me? I'm married to a girl just so that my father can, what? Prove his rightness?"

I'm again out of my chair, pacing the room, trying to calm my nerves that I know are blocking my ability to reason and analyze the words Garrett is giving, compared to those he's not. Because at the end of the day, while Garrett might give me more details than my father, I know he's not giving me everything, no matter how much he might lead me to believe that he is.

"That's why we sent Summer away. We don't know what move Holly will make, but it's not lost on me that she didn't come straight for you. You'd think a mother would want to see her daughter. Which, again, is why I think she's the one we need to watch."

I run my hands through my hair as I try to calm the rage inside and think his words through. Nothing can ever be black and white in this family. I know I'm getting half-truths.

"You don't think Holly is the pawn. You think she's the rook working with the enemy."

"It's a hunch. Obviously, I can't prove too much since she's been in jail for the past seven years. Your father may have jumped the gun with your nuptials, but if he's right, all of this will end a lot sooner, and you can get your life back, Con. You have every reason to be bitter. No one blames you, but you shouldn't stop living your life."

Is he kidding right now?

"How the fuck am I supposed to do that, Garrett? Please tell me. I didn't ask for any of this."

He finishes what's left in his glass and stands. "You may not have asked for any of it, but you didn't say no, either. You had choices, Con. No one took those from you, and while you might hate Everett right now, you're his whole world. Just because the two of you aren't currently seeing eye to eye doesn't make it any less true. He doesn't stop being your father because you've chosen to cut him out. And as for the girl, stop making this into a death sentence. It's not. I saw a picture. It can't be that hard to have her around. If handed the same opportunity to hit my enemy where it hurts, I'd be making the most of every minute. You want to hurt him. You want to make him pay." Standing at the liquor cabinet, bourbon in hand, he says, "Steal his girl."

CHAPTER 9
MACKENZIE

I have yet to speak to Connor since I stormed out of the house yesterday after our conversation about my decision to stay on at the Fields. I may have entered this arrangement willingly, but I refuse to be a doormat. He doesn't get to tell me who I can see or where I can or can't work. Everything that's happened over the past week and a half that I've been in Waterloo seems surreal. I'm still trying to piece together what it all means, and I can't help but question if this isn't all some big case of mistaken identity. Sure, Everett knows who I am, and I met the criteria "for protection," but if I'm honest, even that feels like a stretch.

I'm starting to learn more about this family and the dynamic, but I still need to figure out how I play into it. What reason could Everett possibly have to go to such lengths as to arrange a marriage between his son and me? When we were in his office, he insinuated that he knew I lied or forged my way into this witness protection program. Those words are the only reason I said yes. I said yes because I needed to know what he knows. I need to get Josh back, and Everett might be the key.

"Mac, let's head out back. I'm going to show you the storage shed."

"Because that doesn't sound suspicious at all. I'm not going to lie. That might have been the worst sales pitch ever," I say as I turn to find Parker standing in the doorway, sweaty and glistening from doing shit around the Fields. We might work together, but ever since I showed up wearing a ring two days ago, he hasn't said more than two words to me, which kind of pisses me off. I didn't have much of a choice, and out of anyone, he should know, but looking at him now sporting cut-off sleeves with his bulky, exposed muscles on display, I should have pushed the issue when Connor nominated Parker for the part. If anything, I think he'd treat me nicer.

He raises a brow playfully, and his lips quirk up to one side. "You're not looking at me like someone who doesn't want to go to the shed with me."

His flirtatious jest isn't lost on me. I'm hopeful it's an olive branch to make up for the awkwardness that's existed between us for the past few days. "Let's go. Condiment orders can wait."

As I follow him out the door, he says, "For the record, married women shouldn't look at their bosses like that."

"You think married people don't look?"

I catch his reaction out of the corner of my eye, and by the way his brow furrows and his lips press together, I can tell he doesn't like it. What I don't know is, why. *Did he expect me to flirt back? Was my acknowledgment of the fact that I'm legitimately married not what he was expecting?* In the end, the answers to those questions don't matter. They aren't why I'm here. Parker is talking to me for the moment, and I need to work to repair whatever got bent between us so that I can stay on task and get something out of him. So I change the subject.

"What's in this shed, anyway? Am I finally being brought into the fold on whatever it is you guys really do around here?"

He side-eyes me as we walk and shakes his head. "I seriously can't figure you out, Mackenzie."

"Ditto," I say as I kick a random rock off the pathway leading to the shed.

When we finally reach the shed, he slides the big door open, and I realize the shed is more like a barn. This is where they keep the lawnmowers, UTVs, and, apparently, golf carts.

"What are these for?" I tap the wheel of one of the lifted carts with my foot.

He grabs two coolers under the tool bench toward the back of the barn. "That's your job this weekend. The field is hosting a major tri-state tournament. It's going to be all hands on deck. You'll be out in one of the carts selling soda, water, and snacks."

"Sweet." I hop into one of the carts. "I've never driven a golf cart."

Throwing the two coolers on the back bench of the four-seater cart, he says, "Seriously, how have you never driven a golf cart?"

I shrug my shoulders, suddenly feeling a little self-conscious. I realize Parker has some kind of preconceived ideas about the life I came from. My presence here would make it seem as though I didn't have the best life back home. Which I was okay with initially, but the more I get to know the people here, the less settled I am with the idea. The words leaving my lips wouldn't be a lie, but coupled with me being here, they will make it sound wretched, and I'm not ashamed of my roots. We can't change where we come from. It is what it is. All we can do is push forward.

"Where I grew up, there weren't any golf courses nearby, for starters, and my dad left before I was born, so I didn't really have any male figures around who would facilitate such an outing."

He pauses for a minute, and while I'm not looking him in the eye, I'm sure he feels like shit for asking. Coming around the cart and sliding into the driver's side, he nudges his knee against mine. "You trying to tell me you never had a boyfriend?"

I smile, thankful for the downplay. "Yeah, Zane wasn't a golfer."

"Zane?" he questions, his voice rising a few octaves. "Seriously? You dated a guy named Zane."

"Why is that so weird?"

He shakes his head and throws the cart in drive, and we make our way out of the barn. "I guess it's not, considering you grew up in a trailer park."

"Wow," I say in surprise, causing him to hit the brakes, and as I careen forward, he throws his arm out to stop me.

"Shit. Mac, I didn't mean it that way. I don't think any less of you. Fuck, I don't even see you that way. Maybe we should just go back to not talking. No good can come from us talking anyway."

I hold his eyes for a beat, disappointment more than evident on both our faces. He can tell me all he wants that he doesn't see me as the girl who grew up in the trailer park, but here's the thing: I know that's one lie we can never make true. First impressions are a bitch. He knew me and some part of my story before I knew him. There's no changing that. I don't care to be the girl he pities.

"Don't worry about it. I get it. You're not the short-term kind of guy." I parrot the words he gave me last week when we were in the walk-in freezer, and for good measure, I add, "And I'm taken, so you shouldn't worry about hurting my feelings."

His lips thin, and he turns forward slowly, stepping on the gas. *Good.* I thought I wanted to talk to Parker, but I'm learning there's not much room in the gray with him. As I focus my eyes on the path in front of us, they collide with a scowl. One that seems to be permanently etched onto Connor's perfect fucking face just for me.

"Great," Parker echoes my sentiment when he notices Connor looking straight at us.

Pulling around to the back door, Connor storms toward the cart, and Parker jumps out. Parker doesn't back down, though he probably should because it only spurs Connor on. He pushes him. "You were reckless back there. That's my wife," he yells as he points toward me.

"Oh, she's your wife now? That's strange. The guy demanding I fire her last week didn't give off husband vibes."

"I couldn't care less about whatever vibe you think I did or didn't give. We both know she is mine. Mine to love, mine to protect. MINE."

My eyebrows practically shoot off my forehead. *Did he really just use the word 'love' in reference to me?* That's what I get for missing breakfast. I'm getting delusional.

Parker stares him down hard, almost like he's waiting for him to crack, but it never comes. He shakes his head. "Whatever. You teach her how to drive a golf cart, then. She'll be driving one this weekend for the tournament." He walks toward the back of the cart, grabs the coolers, and heads inside.

Once he's out of sight, Connor turns to me, slowly raking his eyes up my body before finally meeting my eyes. "Don't worry, wife. Obviously, I don't love you."

"Shocker. I'm sorry, I didn't realize I gave you the impression I care."

When I move out of the cart and away from him, he asks, "Where do you think you're going? As I heard, we have a golf-cart lesson."

I can't help but roll my eyes. "It's a fucking golf cart, not rocket science. I drive the truck just fine. I think I can manage a golf cart. Besides, don't you have somewhere you need to be?"

"And where exactly is it you think I should be?"

I fold my arms over my chest, annoyed by his antics. "I

don't know, work? Anywhere but here patronizing me. Is it not enough that you get to do it at home, now you have to come here?"

Slapping his hands onto the roof of the cart, he leans in with the sexiest shit-eating grin I've ever seen. "Seeing as how I work here, no, I don't have anywhere else to be."

"What do you mean, you work here? Is this some kind of sick joke because I stood my ground and refused to quit yesterday? You're insane, Connor—"

"Let me stop you there, wife. You can be as pissed as you want about the circumstances, but it doesn't change what they are. You didn't do your research. If you had, you may have put together that I work here. Now get in the cart."

"You're not the boss of me."

Geeze, I internally cringe at my own petty response. *Really, Mackenzie, that's all you can come up with?*

He gives me a knowing look that reflects my thoughts. "You're right. I'm not your boss. I'm your husband. Now stop making a scene and get in the cart, wife."

I narrow my eyes and consider telling him to fuck off but think better of it. He's right. I didn't do my research because where he's concerned, I have a blind spot. I can't look at him without thinking of the man I met at the bar. The one who saw straight to my soul. I constantly tried to focus on anything and everything that wasn't him so he wouldn't see my truth. I was instantly enamored by him. Now, when I look at those eyes, I see nothing. I feel somehow duped, even though it was only ever going to be one night. That's what he was there for. Any feelings would have been irrelevant. Connor wasn't looking for a girlfriend. He was looking for a hookup. If only I had a dick. I could chase away these stupid childish affections with a bottle of whiskey and perhaps an actual one-night stand.

Regardless of how it's done, it needs to be done. My anger is proving to be my weakness. If I had thought things through rationally, I may have looked closer at the chain of events that transpired, like how I practically ran him over on my first day. He was clearly here for a reason, and if that weren't reason enough, try him attempting to get me fired and then telling me I couldn't work at the Fields. All the warning signs were there, practically screaming, 'stop.' 'Do not advance.' 'Take your money and cut your losses.'

"Since this isn't rocket science or anything, how about you show me how to put it in reverse."

I eye the dashboard and what few buttons there are, and see nothing apart from a light switch. *Great. How fucking pathetic am I?* I let out an exasperated sigh. "I don't know." The corner of his mouth quirks with amusement, and that damn dimple makes an appearance. My eyes can't help but lock onto his lips as his tongue slowly grazes over his bottom lip before he gently bites it. *Asshole.*

His eyes find mine. "Want to pull the lever?"

Is he flirting with me? That can't possibly be right. He's made it clear that while he was once interested, that is no longer true. So I can't help but be leery of his sudden decency. Being in the same room with him has been a task in itself, and now he wants to share a golf cart and make small talk. As much as I'd like to be, I'm not immune to his charms, devious or not.

"Sure…" I drawl pensively.

I assumed he'd just direct me to the lever, but no. His rough, calloused hand is suddenly dwarfing mine, and damn if it doesn't do things to my insides. For the briefest of seconds, I can't help but believe the contact has the same effect on him. His hand lingers longer than it needs to while his mouth remains closed, giving no further instruction.

Clearing his throat, he takes my hand and pulls me forward, then places it on the lever between our legs in the middle of the cart. "Right is reverse, left is forward."

With his hand still on mine, I get nervous and pull away. "Got it. Right is reverse, left is forward. Is that it?" I tuck my hair behind my ear. "The rest seems self-explanatory. Brake, gas, lights." I wave my hand at the lackluster dashboard. I mean, seriously, there's nothing there, and I would have eventually found the reverse lever.

He purses his lips, and the smallest of glowers briefly appears before he throws the cart in reverse. "Yeah, that's about it for the cart, but now it's time to tour the grounds."

"I mean, am I not seeing everything right now? These are wide-open fields, Connor. What exactly do I need to tour on the cart that I can't already see with my eyes?"

"You really hate me that much, or is my wife just ready to get back to her boyfriend?"

I put my feet up on the dash as he drives down the path toward the back fields. "If anyone hates anyone here, it's you. You're clearly looking for an argument because we both know Parker and I aren't hooking up."

"Doesn't mean you don't want to."

"You don't have to worry about Parker. Two days ago, maybe. Not now."

"You expect me to believe that ring changed your mind? We both know this isn't forever. He could be."

That snaps my attention away from the fields and back to him. My neck is five seconds away from needing a brace from the whiplash.

"What are you playing at here, Connor? No less than five minutes ago, you jumped in Parker's shit for giving me a ride, all but pissing on me to claim me as yours, and now you're over here trying to tell me that he can be my forever."

Tongue in cheek, he grips the wheel harder than necessary. "I didn't say he should be."

Because that's not fucking cryptic.

"Well, believe it or not, I have choices, and he's not one I care to make."

My eyes haven't left the side of his head as I mindlessly run the bale of my pendant along its chain and watch his every move. This is the closest we've been since the wedding, where I watched and banked as many idiosyncrasies as possible. Everett Callahan set out to help, but so far, his son has set out to make me the enemy. I can't help but wonder if that's not what this is now: the old adage of keeping your friends close and keeping your enemies closer. Either way, sharing my feelings about Parker doesn't give away some big secret. If anything, it keeps him talking and gives me the opportunity to continue my research.

"Care to elaborate on that?" he asks, his eyes trained forward.

"Depends. You going to tell me why you don't like him?"

He shrugs. "His dad married my mom. I don't need another reason."

Okay, I was expecting a different response. "Well, my reason is a little less juvenile than—"

"It's not juvenile at all," he cuts me off, his tone terse. "Kipp Michaelson took advantage of my mother while she was still trying to pick up the pieces of her life after my father left her. He proposed marriage within less than two months of the divorce being finalized, ensuring there would be no reconciling with my father."

My brows slightly rise from not only his passion but his confessions. I can see why that would be upsetting for him. As I understand it, his parents have only been divorced for two years. Who doesn't want their parents to get back together? However, the haste in remarrying seems somewhat suspect as an outsider looking in.

"Maybe 'juvenile' was the wrong word for what I'm trying to say. Perhaps I should have said fundamental. Parker doesn't see me. He sees my circumstance, my past, and whether he wants it to be true or not, he'll always judge me for it."

"I get that. Growing up in a small town, you can't outrun your mistakes. Everyone knows your business."

He stops the cart. "This is the end of fields one through

six, but that little clearing of trees up ahead with the bridge leads to two more fields."

"You're not going to drive me back there?"

"No. Believe it or not, I really do have a job here." He tosses his head to the side. "My team has started to arrive, and they are playing in the tournament this weekend, so I need to get back." Then, stepping out of the cart, he says, "Drive us back."

I slide over to his vacant seat, somewhat peeved that he thinks I am incapable of driving a cart, and though I try to bite my tongue, the words come out anyway. "You really don't think I can operate this thing?"

Swinging into the side, he takes my spot. "I'm sure you can, but it's only fair that I get to stare at you the entire drive back."

CHAPTER 10
CONNOR

I've been sitting in the kitchen for an hour or so, waiting for Mackenzie to come out of the bedroom. I know she's awake. I can hear her in the master getting ready. She likes to play music on her phone while doing so. She did it the first night we stayed in the house when she locked herself in there and spent the night setting up the room exactly how she wanted it. I've been contemplating knocking on the door for hours, but I think better of it every time. We never got the chance to talk last night, and that's on me. After working with my team all afternoon, I met my cousin Cayden at a bar in the city to discuss digging into Mackenzie's background. While I don't believe my father or uncle are acting with malicious intent, I also know I'm in the dark, and that just won't do.

By the time I came home last night, it was midnight. I could tell she had to have just gone to sleep because her scent was still fresh in the air, and when I climbed the stairs to the room I've been sleeping in, it was apparent why. She uncovered the upstairs. Every room had the drop cloths removed. Her wish to uncover the downstairs made sense, even though her time here is limited. I can see how living in the state the house was in could be unsettling. It felt cold, even to me. But the upstairs floor, she didn't have to see, so her desire to tackle it was somewhat confounding. That, coupled with the fact that the house was completely dark, didn't sit right with me.

The idea of her being on this property alone was unsettling for reasons I've yet to fully accept myself. I've already called a security company to come out this weekend and install security cameras as well as a few strategically placed surveillance cameras. I want to protect her, but on the other hand, I don't know her. Having cameras she is unaware exist can't hurt. It's also how I'll know if her cleaning is sheer curiosity or snooping.

Staring out the window at the barn down the hill, I can't help but think about our time spent together on the golf cart. It was intense. I hadn't planned on touching her, but there was no going back once I did. Though I should have been, I wasn't prepared for the rush of emotions that would hit me from simply putting my hand on top of hers. Every moment after that was insanely charged with a pent-up burning need for more. I couldn't explain it if I tried. All I know is I needed more. I can't stand how this woman makes me feel, but here we are, and I'm getting more than a little aggravated that I live with her, yet never see her. We gained some ground yesterday. We both shared something with each other, and while it wasn't anything crazy profound, it was more words than we ever shared before, and I'm hoping to piggyback on that energy today when I discuss some of my own limits. Mackenzie has hers, and I'm entitled to mine.

That's it. Mind made. I set down my energy drink and exit the kitchen, intent on knocking on her door.

I'm just rounding the corner when I run straight into her, causing her to drop her drink tumbler and knocking her back enough that I have to catch her to keep her from falling. "Shit, I'm sorry." I was so consumed in my thoughts, I didn't even notice that the music stopped, nor did I hear the door open. *Damn it.* "Are you okay?"

Her brow furrows as her eyes find mine, and the displeasure written all over her face suddenly registers. My tone was all wrong, and my grip was too tight. I close my eyes and release her. I can't even apologize without taking two steps back. *This woman…*

"I'm fine," she says, but her voice is strained, and I know she's not. That's when I look down and notice one foot is rubbing the other. Without question, I pick her up by the waist and toss her over my shoulder. The move catches her by surprise, and she yelps. "Connor, put me down. I'm fine."

Fuck. If I thought grabbing her arms was too much, that's nothing compared to having this ass next to my face.

"Seriously—"

Entering the kitchen, I place her on the large granite island before walking straight to the freezer and grabbing an ice pack.

Dropping to one knee before her, I say, "Let me see it."

"I'm fine. It's fine, really, Connor—"

I take the foot she is currently using to cover the other. "Stop arguing with me. This is my fault, and I'm not giving you an option." When I finally see it, my heart rate kicks up an unreasonable amount for someone who shouldn't care. It's already red and inflamed. "Did I step on it?"

"Maybe a little. I dropped my tumbler on it, and then you stepped into me. The damage was already done. The source of the pain doesn't matter. It's probably just bruised."

"I'll be the judge of that."

"And what makes you qualified to do so?"

I pull both feet toward me and rest them on my knee, comparing their size. "For starters, I'm a coach. I've seen my fair share of jammed, broken, and sprained ligaments my entire life."

Gently, I prod the sides to see if I can feel any difference, and she flinches, yanking her foot back. "Ouch, that's enough. I can go to urgent care after my shift if it still hurts. I'll get an X-ray."

"You're not going to work today."

"You can't be serious. You're just looking for reasons to keep me from going there. It's a bruised toe."

I pull her foot back to my knee. "Wrong. I changed my mind…" I look up and find her watching me intently, which has my breath catching in my throat briefly. I fully expected her eyes to be trained on her foot, not me. But I deliver my next words all the same. "You working there is rather ideal. It ensures I know where you are and allows me to keep an eye on you. Works out great for carpooling, too."

"We are not carpooling."

"Wrong again. This is your right foot. How do you expect to drive?"

"It's just bruised, sprained at best. Give me the ice pack. It'll be fine in a few minutes."

I lightly run my finger up the bottom of her foot and watch as she flexes her foot in response. All her toes curl, including her big toe.

"Ow, why would you do that?" She winces.

I place the ice pack on top of her foot before bringing her legs up and resting them on the island. "I don't think it's broken. All your toes moved. Working on it isn't going to help. You need to take some ibuprofen to help with pain and inflammation. If you are still in pain later, we can get it X-rayed."

When I stand, her eyes hold mine, and surprisingly, I don't see her stubbornness. What I see on her face is indifference. She is no doubt trying to decide how she feels about this entire interaction, and that's fine because I don't need her to decide. She is mine. It doesn't matter how much I don't want it to be true.

"I'll drive you to work. We're both going to the same

place, and I don't like you driving that truck." She rolls her eyes, and I can't help but crack my neck in irritation.

"I drive that truck just fine. I'll allow the ride today, but it's otherwise not necessary."

"It's not your driving I'm worried about. It's that truck. It needs to go."

"That truck isn't going anywhere. Your father is letting me keep it when our deal is over."

As my anger builds, I walk over to the sink and away from her. "Even more reason for it to go. You are my wife. You will drive a car of my choosing."

The icepack hit the ground and I turn around to find her hopping off the counter. "The truck is staying, Connor. This is a hard limit for me," she says as she slowly limps off. I grip the countertop hard, willing myself to not pop off.

When she turns the corner, I start after her. "Mackenzie, you don't get to call everything a hard limit just because you don't get your way." She doesn't stop or respond before she slams the bedroom door. A door won't keep me from her, but the sound of a truck door closing out front will. *Who the fuck even knows I'm here?* I want to go after Mackenzie and hash this shit out, but I also don't need an audience.

My steps are heavier than necessary as I walk down the hallway toward the front door, my annoyance evident in every thud my boots make against the hardwood floors. When I reach the door, I see Holden walking up the path. Great. Pushing open the door, I meet him outside. I don't need him coming in.

"What do you want, Hayes?" I jog down the front steps to cut him off.

"What the hell do you think I want? You've been MIA for the past five days. The first night, I assumed you were out blowing off steam, maybe getting laid like you needed to. But then I went down to the Fields this morning and found out, not only are you now living here, you're fucking married. What the hell, Con?"

I rake my hands through my hair. "Look, Holden, this isn't the time or the place, and you don't need to concern yourself with my problems. You wanted me out. I'm out. I'll send movers over this weekend to clean out the basement and remove our things."

He pushes me back, catching me off guard. "Stop being a dick. This isn't you."

I step toward him, ready to swing, but stop when I hear, "Connor Callahan, you better not punch my husband in front of his son."

Climbing out of Holden's blacked-out Suburban is Aria, Holden's wife.

"You brought the family."

"I brought reinforcements. I figured you might continue taking whatever's fucking you up out on me, but not them."

Just as Aria finishes walking around the car to pull River out of his seat, the screen door behind us slams, and I cringe. Not only because that door is hella loud and screeches like nails on a chalkboard, but because I know that means Mackenzie has walked out. Holden's gaze immediately zeros in on her, and considering I hear no footsteps, her eyes must be locked on our visitors.

Clearing her throat, she announces, "I'm running late for work."

I glance at my watch and see that she isn't. She's using this opportunity to get her way.

I hear her come down the stairs, and her step is too slow. I don't even have to turn to know she's limping. "Mackenzie…" I warn, but she brushes me off.

"I know you wanted to drive me in, but you have company. I'll see you when I get home."

Aria walks up through the yard with River on her hip and gives Mackenzie a small wave. We all silently watch as she starts the old truck my father bought her and pulls down the gravel drive leading off the property.

When her truck disappears behind the tree line, Holden says, "Start talking. Who the hell is that?"

"Language," Aria scolds.

"Why don't you take River inside while we talk?" Holden suggests.

"No, you guys aren't staying—" I begin.

"Bullshit, Callahan. You can walk out on Holden all you want, but not me, and definitely not River. You're family to him. Now, you're going to walk your ass back in that house, find my son a juice box, and tell us what the hell is going on."

Holden and I both stare at her in surprise. Aria is not one to lose her temper. Holden bumps her shoulder. "How come you get to curse, but I don't?"

"Inside. Now," she demands as she extends her arm, pointing her finger toward the house.

I shake my head, wholly peeved with the timing of all of this, but do as she asks because it's Aria, and I'd do anything for her.

After getting River hooked up with a cup of juice and some cheese puffs, Aria returns to the kitchen and helps herself to a sparkling water. "Spill."

"Where would you like me to start?"

"How about with the new accessory? Who is she, Con? Is this one of your one-night stand girls from that app you use? Did you forget to wrap it up, and now she's carrying your baby?"

I press my palms into my eyes. "Yes and no. It's hard to explain."

"She's pregnant!" Aria gasps as Holden walks to the refrigerator and pulls out two beers, sliding one my way.

"No, she's not pregnant. I kind of met her through the app. She happened to be at the bar I was at the night I was meeting up with another girl. I took her to the bathroom, messed around, and found out it was a case of mistaken identity." I shrug, twist off the top of my beer, and take a long pull.

"Okay, and… how the hell did you end up married to her?"

"My father."

Holden and Aria are familiar with the underbelly of what my family does. It's not like we are some big underground organization. We make moves that make sense. Aria was one of those moves years ago. She was a target and had no clue. That's how most of our business goes. We watch the players and their targets. We are not a crime family. We don't kill people to right a wrong. We use the law where applicable, provide sanctuary, and make calls when we need people to disappear. The best way to describe it is we are one piece of an extensive interconnected web that operates discreetly. Discreet being the critical word. To act any other way would put a target on our backs, and we wouldn't be able to help.

"I'm still not connecting the dots, Con. You said you met her at the bar. Was your father there? We know you didn't meet her at a local bar."

"It's an arranged marriage," Holden cuts in. "But why?"

"Trenton Wells," I answer before I take another drink of my beer. I hate even saying his name. It's not only an admission that the piece of shit exists, but that I'm now married to his girl. The thought of them being intimate makes me want to punch something.

"What's the connection?"

Holden knows enough about Trent from our past. This is a small town, and people talk. It was no secret that Trent was a conniving prick, but no one knew the true extent. Similar to how no one in this town knows what my family does on the side. To everyone in Waterloo, Trent disappeared years ago and moved on when his girlfriend got locked up for theft. Sometimes, I wish I could go back to a time when that was my ignorance, too. I didn't find out that my family had their hands in any type of crime ring until eight years ago when I chose to open Pandora's box.

"Con, I thought you said you didn't want any part of that world?" Holden questions.

"I don't. Aria's case was my last. You know I got out when Summer was born, but pretending something doesn't exist doesn't make it so." My shoulders tense up, and I feel the need to defend my family. "Besides, it's not like we're out there killing people. We just help people get the resources they need. We make connections happen for those who wouldn't otherwise be able to help themselves."

"If that's all true, how have you suddenly ended up in a marriage your father forced upon you?" Holden questions, his eyes trained on my every move. He's waiting for a sign. For me to act like this is all some prank.

"We've wanted to find Trent since he disappeared after Holly got locked up for crimes he helped commit, but he's fallen off the grid. We haven't been able to find him until now. Mackenzie is important to him." I parrot my father's words rather than say what she was to him because it's my name she has, not his. The relationship is implied.

"So he thinks attaching your name to hers will lure him out?"

"Pretty much," I offer as I finish off my beer and toss it in the trash.

Aria has been quietly assessing me from her stool for the entirety of this exchange, no doubt dissecting everything I'm not saying with her counseling background. Her eyes narrow briefly. "That's your side. What's hers?"

I know what she's asking because it's the same question that's kept me awake at night for the past week. *What does my father have on her? Why did she agree?*

"I don't know."

"I'm sure your piss-poor fucking attitude has been great

for getting her to talk," Holden adds as if I'm not already more than aware I've been a dick lately.

"Yeah, Con. What's up? Your shit attitude can't all be attributed to your new wife. You haven't been yourself for some time now. You know you can talk to us. Is it because this is the first time Summer has been away for an extended amount of time?"

I grip the countertop hard and close my eyes. All of this is because of Summer, but they couldn't possibly understand. I'm alone in this, and it fucking sucks, but this is my mess, not theirs.

"Can you guys just understand this is something I must navigate on my own for now?"

"Sure, as long as you stop pushing us out. You're family, Callahan. You're my son's godfather, for crying out loud."

I can't do emotions, not right now. It's the last thing I need. Hell, it's why I'm where I'm at. When I care, it's deep. When I fall, it's hard. That's why I choose to stay single. I can't get hurt, and neither can Summer. I don't need a girl who thinks she can handle me, who wants to play house only to find out I'm not what she wants—or, should I say, *we* aren't want she wants. It's not just my heart on the line.

I rap my knuckles on the counter. "You guys can show yourselves out. I need to get to the Fields."

It's not a lie. I do have practice. My assistant coach can technically handle the team if I don't show up, but there's no way Mackenzie is getting away with her little stunt. She's about to learn firsthand what being a Callahan is like.

After the slight delay back at the house from my surprise visitors, I finally made it to the Fields thirty minutes late. I texted Bret, one of my assistant coaches, on the way here that not only would I be late, but I had something to take care of before I got to practice. Practice is only two hours long, meaning I'm missing half, but my team is looking good this year. Our coaching staff is top-notch, and I'm confident they will place first this weekend. However, I'm pissed that I'm missing practice. I've never missed one, and I've worked my ass off to build this organization over the past four years.

In college, I played ball and studied law. Making it big like Holden is rare. Every athlete knows that. In our last year, Holden was drafted straight to the major leagues. I was offered a spot on a feeder team but ultimately turned it down for more reasons than one. A lot happened in that last year of ball. Summer came along, and I learned a lot about the family business. Law felt like a natural progression for me, considering my father and uncles were all lawyers. It is the family business. I grew up around it and respected my family's work. I just never knew the extent they went to for some clients. I made the ultimate sacrifice eight years ago and never looked back until I needed more, and that was this team.

I had Summer, my family, and my job, but I had nothing for me. The Bulldogs Collegiate Baseball League is mine. I own it, and I get to do something that makes me happy. Sure, I never planned on quitting law. This started as a side job, a hobby, giving back to the community, and staying involved in the sport I loved, but when my parents divorced, I felt I no longer had a reason to stay at Callahan Brothers. What was the point, when he left the woman he started the company for?

That's when I threw everything into this franchise, and now, here I am, coaching the sport I love for a team I own. Hayes technically owns the Fields, but we have a five-year contract that makes these fields home until the stadium is finished in two years. These boys don't have to play summer ball, but we keep them warm and offer them the opportunity to be seen by professional scouts outside of the NCAA season. Playing collegiate also gives players the ability to adjust to using wood bats. There are a lot of perks to playing summer ball when you have the right franchise behind you, which was lacking in this region.

Holden and I played beer league in the summers when we were in college to stay warm because there weren't other options, but Waterloo's geography is perfect. We're less than an hour outside of St. Louis, which has a major airport and is home to one of the biggest MLB teams around, and seeing as how Holden is the team's number one pitcher, a partnership with him only made sense for drawing donors and bringing attention to the franchise. It's been a lot of fucking work and is a big reason Summer calls me 'coach.' She's eight and has practically grown up on the Fields. With all that said, it's not lost on me that I'm now deprioritizing something I've poured my fucking heart and soul into for a woman I've just met.

I park my truck beside hers and head straight for the concession stand. I've gone over all the words I wanted to give her upon arrival multiple times, but now that I'm here, the only thing that comes to mind is throwing her over my shoulder like I did this morning and hauling her out. I don't care if I have to do it with her kicking and screaming. A fucked-up part of me wants people to see. Then they'll know who she belongs to, at least for the time being. But none of that matters because I don't see her when I walk into the stand. I also don't see Parker.

My fists clench, and I head for the office, pissed about what I might find when I open the door. When I reach the door, I pause and try to ground myself so that I don't completely lose my shit when I catch Parker with Mackenzie, but then think better of it and say fuck it. If he overstepped, then he deserves every blow I dish out. But the scene before me is nothing but anticlimactic.

"What do you want, Callahan?" Parker says as he looks up from eating his sandwich.

"Where's Mackenzie?"

He tosses his sandwich down and leans back in his chair. "Are you asking me to keep tabs on your wife now?"

"Cut the shit, Parker. You're her damn boss."

His eyes narrow on mine, and I can tell he's mad, but he can get in line because so am I.

"She shouldn't have come in today, something I'd think her *husband*," he accentuates the word 'husband' with sheer disdain that doesn't faze me in the least—Parker can hate it all he wants, but it doesn't change the fact that it's true, "would have put his foot down on."

"You'd do good to keep your nose out of my marriage. I don't care what task my father assigned. Consider it null and void. He lost the privilege of having a say the second he handed her over to me. It's my name on the marriage certificate, not his, and certainly not yours. Now, where the hell is my wife?"

"I tried to send her home after she dropped her first soda and I noticed her limp, but she refused to go." He stands from his chair and throws the remaining bits of his sandwich in the trash. Then, coming around the desk, he grabs his Gatorade. "Now she's down at field five with a cooler of water that I told her to hand out to the team for water breaks."

"We don't do that."

"I know." He quirks a brow. "Now, if you'll excuse me, I have staff to check on."

Walking down to field five, my eyes immediately find Mackenzie sitting on the bleachers watching my team practice, and the irritation that has existed since I left the house slowly subsides. For one, she's sitting, which calms my inner beast that demanded she stay off her foot, but also, she doesn't see me coming, and for a few seconds, I get to see her without a mask on. Right now, she's just a girl watching a team practice. She's not the wife of a man she was forced to marry or a girl with a hidden agenda. She's just Mackenzie, and she's fucking breathtaking. Even from here, I can see my players stealing glances.

I pick up my pace, ensuring I make it to the bleachers before she sees me or a player calls me out. Walking up behind her, she startles when my hands slide down both sides of her thighs. Fuck, she's so soft. Her bare skin pressed against mine makes my cock twitch.

"What are you doing?" she snaps discreetly as I slowly drag my arms back up her thighs and wrap them around her waist.

"You like to play games, but so do I." I let my hands roam up the soft curve of her hips as they trail up her waist.

"What are you talking about? I'm not playing any games, Connor."

I tsk. "I told you I didn't want you to drive in to work with your foot injured, yet you went anyway and lied to our guests."

My hands stop right under the weight of her breasts, just barely skimming the bottom, but they are close enough that I can feel her heart racing. She's not pulling away, and I can't help but believe it is because she likes my hands on her, just like the night we met. Mackenzie didn't stop me because she wanted it, but I need her to stop me. Neither of us entered this marriage willingly. I can't be what she needs, and she's not supposed to be what I want. It's easy to feel forever. Seeing it reflected in the person you want to spend it with is harder. Letting myself see this for anything short of an arrangement with an expiration date would be foolish.

"Parker told you to go home. Why are you still here?" I pull back and release her.

She draws in a stuttered breath that's all too telling as she pulls at the chain around her neck, something I've noticed is somewhat of a nervous tic for her. I affect her, and I'll be damned if that doesn't make me happy. I didn't miss the subtle look of disappointment that tugs at her mouth when I pulled away, but my words quickly turn her frown into a scowl.

"Same reason I'm not getting rid of the truck. I need the money—"

"Do my eyes deceive me, or are the rumors really true? Connor Callahan landed himself a wife." Bret walks up behind me and squeezes my shoulder before stepping around me and extending his hand to Mackenzie. "Bret Schwartz. It's nice to meet the woman who finally made an honest man out of this lone wolf."

"Mackenzie. It's nice to meet you."

"Are you going to stick around for the rest of practice? See what your man here built."

That's when I cut in. The last thing I need is her on the bench being a distraction for all these players, who are closer in age to her than I am. "Actually—"

"Yes!" she cuts in over me. "That's exactly why I headed down here. I've been wanting to see Connor in action."

I fold my arms over my chest and bite my lower lip. If I didn't know better, I'd think she's taunting me, and when those ice-blue eyes land on mine, I see it. She knows exactly what she's doing. Mackenzie is playing a game of tit for tat, but that's not how I play. I play to win. There is no outcome here in which she will be the victor.

"Bret, do you mind giving us a minute? I'll be down in a second."

"Yeah, but hurry up. You've already missed the first half, and Chavez needs some pointers on his changeup going into this weekend. He can't get out of his head, and that's your department."

I nod, and he heads toward the field as I step up next to Mackenzie. "Now I know you are testing me. Specifically going against my word twice in one day. Do you realize your disobedience is a crime, one that I vow to seek punishment for?"

"Punishment doesn't make me less inclined to commit the crime. If anything, it teaches me how to avoid it."

"Then you suck at avoiding it."

"Maybe I don't want to." Then, turning on the bleacher, she asks, "Do you mind helping me down?"

I move my hands to grip her hips as she places hers on my shoulders for leverage. She's tempting the enemy, and she knows it. As much as I want to believe she's flirting, I can't help but think that if it's anything, it's manipulation. *She didn't come here to be your wife.* This is Trent's influence. Now I just need to decide how I want to play my hand.

"I see what you're doing here." Once her feet are firmly planted on the ground, I add, "Go home, Mackenzie."

"I already told you—" she starts.

"Use personal time. Get off that foot. Parker said he won't let you back without a doctor's note." That last part is a lie, one I'm hoping she buys. If anything, it will get her home tonight, and I can take her to the doctor in the morning.

"Fine," she huffs as she hobbles to the golf cart. I'm unsure if I will pay for this later, but right now, I'm willing to pay the price for whatever wrath awaits me when I get home tonight just to know she's no longer here and, hopefully, off that damn foot.

CHAPTER 11
MACKENZIE

The past few days have had me feeling out of step. I'm not sure what's going on with Connor or us. I realize there's not technically an 'us,' but the hate I felt initially has been downgraded to what I consider a minor annoyance. When he ran into me in the hallway and I stubbed my toe, he immediately showed me an entirely different side of him. I saw that he could be caring, considerate, apologetic, and, dare I say, comforting. Once the initial shock of his reaction to my injury subsided, I thought I saw something more. Something akin to what I saw the first night I met him. I thought I saw what looked like affection and what I could have sworn was flirting.

When he showed up at the Fields later that afternoon and snuck up behind me, wrapping his arms around my waist, my entire body buzzed. He could do no wrong, and I would have given anything to keep his hands on me. I only snapped at him to play the part. I was attempting to seem as indifferent to him as he was to me because falling for my husband wasn't and isn't an option, but damn it, if he wasn't getting in my head and making me think it was a possibility. That night, when he came home, I heard him go straight up to his room. He didn't come to check on me once. It wasn't until the next morning, when I got up to make coffee, that we spoke, and it was only to tell me that we had an appointment at the urgent care center in town to see a doctor and get an X-ray. He mistook my silence for unease about my foot because he said, "Don't worry. I've been there plenty of times with Summer. I doubt it's broken, but I'd rather a doctor confirm that."

It was then that I realized his attentiveness and care were just a case of mistaken intimacy. He's a father. Which is easy to forget, since his daughter is away at camp and this house we live in has none of her things. Between being a coach and a father, his first-responder instincts are on point. I just got caught up in his bedside manner and allowed myself to consider an existence where we weren't at each other's throats.

Pulling up to the house, I notice men walking around the perimeter, which makes me uneasy. I reach for my phone out of habit, thinking I'll send a text to find out who's at the house, only to remember Connor's number is not in my phone. I proceed up the driveway cautiously, scanning the men to see if any look familiar. I park my truck along the side driveway instead of the circle drive out front. As I look around, I see a utility van parked behind the building. Curious, I look closer and notice the logo on the side of the truck, indicating that it belongs to a security company. On further inspection, I see a man on the roof, which leads me to believe that Connor is having a security system installed.

Now that I know what these men are doing, I'm less on edge, but a heads-up would have been nice. Considering why I'm here and what I still don't know about the Callahans, I feel justified in my unease. Yesterday, I stayed at home because the doctor wouldn't release me to work until Saturday, despite having only stubbed my toe. I now understand why Connor insisted on me going to that clinic. He knows the damn doctor. I'm positive that at the end of the appointment, when he left to quote, "Pull the car around," he was, in fact, speaking with the doctor about the details of my release.

I spent all of yesterday snooping around the house to no avail. This house might be old, but it doesn't hold any clues. That's when it dawned on me to Google Connor. That would feel like an obvious thing to do when thrown into an arranged marriage with someone you don't know, but it's not like Connor Callahan is a celebrity. I didn't think a Google search would show me anything of value, but after meeting his assistant coach and hearing him ask, "Did you come to see what he built for yourself?" I realized how much of an enigma Connor truly is. He's been nothing short of an asshole to me, but I'm learning that's not who he's always been. Hell, maybe it's not even who he is now. It could just be the side that is reserved for me. Either way, I now know the man; while he might be arrogant and sometimes downright demanding, he does not boast, and in this town, his name is respected, and not just because of Everett.

When I discovered Connor worked at the Fields, I assumed he was just a standard coach. Never did it cross my mind that he ran an organization that helped local college kids and gave back to the community. I mean, the man is building a stadium for his team. That's going to bring significant revenue to the area. I found a quote from him in a local newspaper that read, 'This town raised me. It's where my roots are, and I want the world to love it as much as I do.' Aside from his connections with the collegiate team and the stadium, the only other things I found were related to Everett and his mother, Moira.

Everett and Moira are big philanthropists. They've given hundreds of thousands of dollars to organizations and charities that work with and support victims of domestic violence. The way Everett, Parker, and Elijah all handled me now makes a lot more sense. I knew they were helping me. I just didn't know more than that. People always have some hidden agenda, and what might seem like good intentions could all be a ruse. I know there's more to the special treatment I've received since I got here. I just haven't figured out what I have that he would want. Now that I'm aware of the stories he's heard, considering his line of charity work, I feel like my situation is not as serious as others. It makes me feel like an impostor to be here because of it. What I went through was an accident, and it only happened once. I don't consider myself a real victim, but nonetheless, here I am.

Walking into the house, I'm startled once more. Seriously, Connor really should have given me a heads-up about this. The fact that he didn't grates me. There is a man in a black outfit with glasses holding an iPad in the foyer.

"I'm sorry. I didn't realize anyone would be here. I'm Murphy." The man extends his hand for me to shake, which I do politely.

"Connor and I went to high school together."

I nod, unsure of what to say.

Lucky for me, he's not the lingering type to stay and make small talk. "Well, I'm done inside. It was good to meet you, Mackenzie." He makes his way toward the front door.

Once he's out of sight, I walk down the hall toward my room. When I enter, I toss my bag onto the bed. It hits my pillow, and the sound of something falling to the floor catches my attention. Looking under the bed, I see nothing. So I walk around to the nightstand and see if whatever fell to the floor landed under there, and sure enough, there's a white envelope. When I pull it out, I see that it's addressed to M, and my stomach instantly knots as my palms get sweaty. I hold the letter close to my chest, closing my eyes as I try to calm my racing heart.

This could be one giant coincidence, but that's when my interaction with the man in the foyer resurfaces. I didn't give him my name, but he knew it anyway. *Stop, Mac, he said he went to high school with Connor. Connor probably told him you'd be here.*

With the letter in hand, I jolt up and head to my window, which has a driveway view. All the men outside have red Spyder Security shirts on. The guy who was inside the house did not. He was dressed in all black. *Crap.*

I head to the bathroom and into the toilet room. The last time I received one of these letters, I got my heart ripped out. My brother Josh left when I was twelve without a word. He literally just disappeared. My mother and I went to the police station to file a missing person report, but because he was twenty years old, there wasn't much they could do. There was no evidence of foul play to suggest he was taken against his will. He was just gone. At that age, he could have simply left of his own free will. It took two years for me to accept that maybe that was what had happened. Maybe my brother left our little Podunk town and the trailer park we grew up in for a better life. But we were close. He was the only steady male figure I had in my life. I never would have thought he would just up and leave and never look back.

Then, six months ago, I came home from visiting my mom at Sweetwater, the assisted living facility I had to place her in for early onset dementia, and found an envelope just like this on the counter in our trailer. It had the same 'M' on the front and everything. When we were younger, Josh used to joke that Mackenzie was too long of a name, and he didn't like calling me Mac because he thought it was a boy's name, so he called me M. I remember being so mad at him. In the beginning, I told him shortening my name to M made it sound like my name was Emily. Em is short for Emily, and I wasn't an Emily. Once he found out it annoyed me, it stayed for that reason. After a few months, it had grown on me, but there was no way I would tell him that and risk getting a worse nickname.

Closing the toilet lid, I take a seat and slowly lift the seal on the envelope and pray like hell this one isn't sending me anywhere like the last one did. Once I have the letter in my hand, I close my eyes and give myself a pep talk. *This is for Josh, for mom.* I exhale a breath of resolve and unfold the letter.

> *You are right where you need to be. I'll be in touch soon.*
>
> *Josh*

Well, that was anticlimactic but also reassuring. Ever since I got here, I've felt like maybe I somehow ended up in the wrong place. Nothing about this town or these people makes sense. What connection could Josh possibly have to the Callahans? Folding up the letter, I stick it in my back pocket and walk back into the bedroom, only to get the shit scared out of me again.

"Holy crap!" I screech as I find Cameron sitting on my bed. "What the hell are you doing in here? Haven't you heard of knocking or, I don't know, using a phone?"

She shrugs casually like it's no big deal. "I did knock, you didn't answer, and I don't have your phone number. Otherwise, I would have just called and told you to drive over. I'm cashing in on the pool day raincheck you promised."

Walking over to the bed, I hold out my hand. "Give me your phone." She pops her pink bubblegum and hands it over. I dial my number and then press call. The phone in my back pocket rings once, and I hang up. "There, now you have my number. No more surprises. I'd rather not die of a heart attack before I reach thirty."

After I hand the phone back, I briefly think back to Everett's instructions about using this phone. He only had two numbers programmed when he gave it to me. He told me not to contact anyone back home or stalk their social media accounts, but he never said I couldn't give the number to people I meet here.

"Great, now pack a swimsuit and let's go."

For a second, I consider my foot and that I'm supposed to stay off it until tomorrow but then say fuck it. Connor and I are back to two ships passing in the night. He couldn't even think to remind me about the security company coming out today, and I'm tired of sitting in this empty house alone. Plus, he's been coming home late, so chances are I won't be missed.

It's settled. I'm going.

"Do you want a drink?" Cameron asks as she lays her pool towel on the lounge beside mine.

"Yeah, a drink sounds good. I'm fine with a beer. You don't have to make us margaritas again."

She walks over to the pool bar in her revealing white string bikini. I'm all for body positivity, but her prancing around here half-naked with Everett inside is somewhat confounding, to say the least. Cameron is out here in a thong bikini, and here I thought my blue swimsuit was revealing because the top is a little small for my breast size.

When she returns, she says, "So spill it. I want all the details."

I take my beer and nervously twist off the top. *What the hell was I thinking coming here to hang out with Cameron?* I'm still unclear on exactly what she knows about Connor and me. I could easily misstep and give away our entire ruse.

"What exactly do you want to know?"

"You know," she says as she waggles her eyebrows at me.

She wants spicy deets. Got it. But I want something too, so I try to play it off like I missed her meaning.

"Maybe the better question is, what exactly do you know?"

"Enough." She shrugs. "Everett doesn't tell me anything. I swear, that man can be so infuriating. All I know is your name and that you're married to Connor. As for the rest, I got nothing."

I don't buy the 'she doesn't know much' claim. How could she not know more and, better yet, if she lives in this house, surely she's had reason to question things. She was here when my things were moved out of the pool house. So I attempt to pry inconspicuously.

"You don't find it odd that Connor married me before I met any of you?"

She laughs as she takes a swig of her beer. "No, like father like son. Neither one of the Callahan men samples the local goods. Every woman in town would love to land either of those men, yet they couldn't care less."

"Everett was technically married for a long time before he and Moira divorced."

"Yes, but it's not lost on anyone that she remarried right away, and he's still single."

"Yeah, Connor doesn't talk much about his parents."

"That doesn't surprise me. Ever since the divorce, Connor stopped coming around. He drops Summer off for family dinners, but he doesn't stay. He took it hard, and he blames his father. He thinks his father cheated on Moira for years while away on business, but if there is one thing I know about Everett, he would never cheat."

I lie back on the lounger. "So what happened?"

"I couldn't say for sure. I can only speculate, but what I do know is that Kipp and Everett were best friends in high school, and rumor has it that Moira and Kipp had a fling before she and Everett were ever a couple. Some of the older women in town say she cheated on Kipp to make him jealous, and that's how she ended up pregnant. Everett did the right thing and put a ring on it. Only the three of them know the truth, but her marrying Kipp before the ink on her divorce papers was dry leans into that rumor. She must have held a flame for him for all these years."

"Why is Everett so friendly with Parker and Elijah? The entire situation baffles me, and Connor hates to mention either of their names."

"I honestly think Connor is just hurt. Moira and Everett were the local 'It Couple' for decades. The ideal marriage with the perfect life, until one day, they were suddenly divorced. They still operate a few charities together, and as an outsider looking in, Moira and Everett are friends but nothing more. The thing is, in Illinois, you have to be separated from your spouse for six months before you can legally divorce. The two of them knew what they were doing for a while, and neither told Connor. As for Connor's issue with the Michaelsons, I think it's the same. He is hurt. They are suddenly living his life. The two families get along, and everyone moved forward without missing a step, except him."

I swallow the sip I took, enthralled by all this information. "What about Elijah and Parker's mom? Is she still in the picture?"

She flips over on the sun lounger. "No, she died of a brain aneurysm a year before any of this ever went down."

That screams if anyone in this marriage cheated, it was Moira, but I digress. Apart from being one major soap opera, I'm not sure their marriage has anything to do with why I got that letter today. We lie in silence for a few minutes, just soaking up the sun, until the sound of a gate closing steals my attention.

Everett walks across the patio from the driveway to the back entrance, only to stop and say, "Cameron, a word?"

She pops up off the lounger, and I don't miss the extra sashay she adds to her step or the way she flips her long red hair over her shoulder as she crosses the cobblestone patio to meet him. Our loungers are laid out facing the back of the house near the zero-entry part of the pool, so I can't help but watch their entire exchange. Everett crosses his arms like he's displeased, but when he pushes his sunglasses on top of his head, I see a softness there, even from this distance. His eyes flash up to mine briefly before returning his attention to Cameron. She glances back at me and then throws her arms out wide before crossing them and storming off. His jaw clenches at her abrupt departure, but I also don't miss how his eyes glance at her ass before he turns on his heel and enters the house.

"What was that about?"

"You mean me getting in trouble, or did you, by chance, catch him looking at my ass?"

I cover my mouth to keep the beer I just took a swig of from flying out and instead choke on it. "What?" I gasp as I pull in air.

"Oh, don't act surprised. It's not like we're blood, and I've always been attracted to older men. I've had a crush on that man since I was sixteen."

I try to regain my composure and act like her admission isn't a shock. I mean, Connor mentioned that Cameron wasn't a Callahan, but I thought maybe she was adopted or a half-sibling.

"Are you guys fucking?"

My question makes her laugh. "Girl, no. Don't get me wrong. I've dreamed about fucking him on every surface in this house for years, but these Callahan men are hard at seeing what's good for them. Obviously, the past four years were spent being a secret admirer. I'm not a homewrecker. I was just a girl with a crush, but now that Moira is gone, I'd be lying if I said I don't make myself available. I don't have to stay here. I'm just not in a hurry to leave, either."

I don't press her for more, even though I want to. There are some questions I can't ask without feeling like they are something I should already know. So I leave it alone and instead address the other burning question. "Why are you in trouble?"

"As if you don't already know," she huffs and throws herself into her chair.

"I really don't." It's an honest answer. I am still determining what Everett has on me. It's the whole damn reason I'm here, trying to pull any morsels of information I can from Cameron.

"Apparently, you weren't supposed to leave the house, and now that's somehow my fault. Why didn't you tell me you were on house arrest?"

"Seriously, what am I, sixteen? I'm a grown-ass woman. I can leave the house whenever I damn please. I fucking bruised my toe, and I'm supposed to be resting so I can work the tournament tomorrow. What's the difference if I rest it on the couch or beside the pool?"

I take a long pull off my beer before getting up and waltzing over to the pool bar.

"Where are you going?"

"My beer got warm," I toss over my shoulder. Plus, I need to stomp out my frustration. Everett isn't talking to Connor. That much, I know. Connor does what he can to avoid him, so he must have another source, and I hate feeling like I'm under a microscope.

Cameron meets me at the bar. "Maybe we should do a shot. These Callahan men can be stubborn—"

"Arrogant," I toss in.

"Cocky," she adds.

"Bossy-as-fuck assholes!"

"Preach!" she exclaims as she pours a shot of peanut butter whiskey, then slides mine toward me. "To showing these men we refused to be caged."

After taking the shot, I chase it with a fresh beer. Probably not the best combo, but I have nowhere to be, so what the hell.

"Why weren't you at work today? It is a Friday. I know you

don't work during the week, but don't you typically work Friday through Sunday?"

I haven't been around long enough to know if she typically works anything. All I know is when I looked at the schedule hanging in the back office, I saw her name on the next few weekends.

"Yeah, I called off today. I don't need to work."

Wow. I didn't see that comment coming from her mouth. Cameron has never struck me as pretentious, but her tone and those words came off more than a little high-sounding. I take another drink as I try to hide the unsavory surprise I'm sure is written all over my face.

"Sorry," she blurts out. "This month is hard for me—has been for the past few years. It's the month my parents died, four years ago. I've grieved and learned to let go of the things I can't change. But it still hurts, and sometimes those feelings come out as anger. I have money because my parents died. That doesn't make me feel good. It just is what it is. Everett and Moira took me under their wing. I have family on the East Coast that I could go live with, but when the Callahans offered me a place to stay here, I took it. I've lived here most of my life, and finishing my senior year in a new state with a family I wasn't close to made my anxiety spiral. I went into a dark place the week after their accident. The Callahans' offer was light in the dark, so to speak. My parents were wealthy, and my brother and I were the sole beneficiaries of their assets. Everett helped me invest my money and develop a portfolio that would help me make money on my money. I don't need to live here, and I don't need to work at the Fields…"

Now I feel like an ass for being quick to judge. "Cameron, I'm sorry. I didn't know your story. That's not something that has come up between me and Connor."

She nods in understanding. "That makes sense. Connor is a good guy like that. He doesn't air other people's business. It's my story to share, not his, but now you know." Grabbing the whiskey bottle again, she lines up our glasses. "On that note, what do you say we get fucked-up?"

That is the absolute worst idea. I need to be in control of all facilities, especially my mouth, but after the past month and the stress of the unknown and all I went through to get here right now, all I want to do is forget. Once my shot is poured, I clink it against hers and say, "Hell yeah we are!"

CHAPTER 12
CONNOR

I've been sitting in the living room in the dark with a bottle of Jack for the past two hours, trying to tame the rage building inside of me that wants to burn everything to the ground. When I held her at the Fields, she didn't push me away. If anything, she wanted it, which caught me off guard. I was teasing her, touching her the way I wanted, believing it was the last thing she wanted after the words and grief she'd been giving me. Add on the fact that she was forced into this marriage. I expected her sharp tongue. The day she got hurt changed things for me, even though I'm still not convinced I know her true colors. Every day with her changes how I see her and how I look at our arrangement. She may have belonged to the one man I despise, but our one night at the bar before either of us knew each other—that wasn't fake, and she wasn't his then, and she's not his now. She's mine.

The silence between us has been deafening, but it's also felt heavily charged with tension, sexual and otherwise. I haven't missed her stolen glances, and I know she's caught mine. That's why I'm pissed now. I thought we were past this. I know exactly where she is, and I debated multiple times whether I would go pick her up before I started drinking, but ultimately decided to let this play out. She's testing me, I can fucking feel it, and you better believe I'm going to push back. Lights pulling down the gravel road shine through the front windows, temporarily lighting the otherwise dark house. I finish my drink as the tension that had finally started to ebb returns when I hear the telltale sounds of a diesel truck I'm all too familiar with. Parker drove her home. *You've got to be kidding me.*

As soon as his truck parks in the front circle drive, I hear a door open, which should settle my nerves but somehow doesn't. I should be glad that Mackenzie isn't hanging out in the cab of his truck, but she's not stupid. She was here when the security system was installed. My friend Caleb called to let me know once everything was complete and asked who the girl was. Apparently, the entire town hasn't yet learned about my marriage.

The front door opens, she turns around to wave, and Parker's truck take off. She doesn't make it more than two steps before I switch on the light setting on the table next to me. Her head snaps up, and she drops her purse.

"Fuck, Connor. You scared the shit out of me. Why are you sitting in the dark?"

"Waiting for my wife to come home."

"Since when do you sit up waiting for me or care where I am? You come home every night and go straight to your room."

"That might be true, but I know exactly where my wife is when I do so. When I got home today, her truck was in the driveway, yet she was nowhere to be found."

She throws her arms out. "You can't keep me cooped up in this house, Connor. It's not like I was out on the town. I was at your father's house with Cameron."

I stand and rub my chin, reminding myself not to say words I'll regret later as I did the first night we spent in this house. When I'm around her, I can't help myself. I'm not even the kind of guy who says those things to women, yet she pulled them out of me. I didn't understand initially, but the longer she's here, the clearer it gets. She's making me feel, and that's something I've refused to do for a long time.

"What kind of idiot do you take me for? That was not Cameron who dropped you off."

She shakes her head and starts to walk away as if this conversation is over. Fuck that. I jump over the couch and cut her off before she can make it to the hallway, and her eyes widen as she pulls her hands to her chest, something I don't like. I would never lay a finger on her, but right now, my concern is her lies, not her fear.

"Explain it to me. Explain why Parker dropped you off."

Something in my words quickly takes away the fear I saw in her eyes, and that grit she's displayed from day one rises to the surface as she crosses her arms and snaps, "I didn't have my truck. Cameron had too much to drink. She couldn't drive me home, and the two other numbers programmed in my phone belong to your father and Elijah. Strangely, Daddy dearest didn't feel I would need my husband's number when he gave me a phone."

I hold my hand out, and her eyes narrow before she huffs and reaches for the phone in her satchel. Once she places it in my hand, I consider tossing it at the wall. I hate knowing who gave it to her. I hate knowing whose numbers are in it, but I can't let my anger win. I've done that enough, and fuck if it's not half the reason I'm here right now instead of in my own bed.

Opening her contacts, I angrily pound out my number and make sure there's no mistake that she finds it. Taking a page from her book, I tease her the same way she's thought to tease me over the last twenty-four hours and save my number as, first name: Connor, last name: AAH. I can't help the devilish grin that tugs at the corner of my mouth as I place the phone back in her hand. If she insists on poking the bear, I'll poke right back.

Her eyes narrow on the screen, and she quirks a brow. "AAH…" She shakes her head. "What the hell is this?"

Crossing my arms over my chest, I say, "Easy. Always Available Husband. It ensures my contact is always number one." My eyes drag down her body, raking in every inch of her exposed sun-kissed skin of their own accord before finally meeting her gaze again. "Plus, I don't recall you hating that word the last time it rolled off your lips." It was her delicious pant the second my tongue made contact with her sinful pussy.

She thins her lips and rolls her eyes. "Whatever, I don't have time for your whiplash tonight. I had too much to drink, and I'm ready for bed."

Shoving her phone in her purse, she attempts to dismiss me as per usual, but I throw my arm out.

"We're not done here. If you need a ride, you call me. If you're sick, you call me. When you're bored, it's me. You're mine, Mackenzie. It's my last name attached to yours, no one else's." I meet her eyes. "Have I made myself clear?"

"Fine," she grinds out. "But let's get one thing straight: I'm not yours. Not really. Out there, you like to talk a big talk, but behind closed doors, we both know I'm nobody to you—"

"You know that's not true," I grunt. There's no way the chemistry between us is a one-way street. I refuse to listen to her words tell me otherwise.

"Are you serious? Connor, you don't even talk to me."

"You run off whenever you don't like what I say," I argue.

"Then give me something real."

"What do you want?"

Those piercing blue eyes practically glow in the night as they reflect light from the moon coming through the transom window above the front door. "Tell me why I'm here. Tell me why you said yes?"

I clench my jaw in irritation. I want to give her words, but I can't. Not yet. It's half of why I pumped the brakes over the past few days. I wanted to come straight home after practice and push her buttons like I did at the field. I wanted to see how far she'd let me go, but on the way home, I got a text from my cousin. Cayden was vague, said he needed more time, and didn't want to give me anything until he was sure he had his facts straight. It reminded me that I can't be all-in with a girl I barely know. So when she walks past me to go to her room—my room—I don't stop her.

"That's what I thought. Don't forget I'm your temporary wife."

After I've showered to wake myself up after only roughly two hours of sleep, the smell of bacon wafts through the air and my stomach immediately growls. I can't tell you the last time I had home-cooked bacon. Living at Holden and Aria's meant I got home-cooked meals, but Aria is a bit of a health fanatic, which meant turkey bacon. I can assure you that what I smell now is not turkey bacon. I could use a big breakfast, and fuck if she doesn't owe me one. Mackenzie is the reason I got zero sleep last night. First, I stayed up waiting for her to come home, and then I tossed and turned in bed, lying awake, going over everything she said and all the things I should have said. I can't go on like this for the next few weeks, or however long it takes to get Trent Wells to mess up. I know what I can give her, and I know what I can't. I just have to keep my feelings out of it.

When I enter the kitchen, I find her standing at the stove, dancing around. Her phone is tucked in the pocket of her jean shorts, and a cord is running up her back. She's listening to music and has no idea I'm here. When I look past her at the stove as I pull out a bar stool under the island, I see a pan of scrambled eggs and at least a pound of bacon, but her snapping pulls my focus back to her ass as she shakes it, humming what sounds like, "Hit Me With Your Best Shot," and I can't help but roll my eyes. The night at the bar, she made me feel old when I referenced an older country song, yet here she is, busting a move to some '80s ballad.

She dances over to the cabinet to grab a plate, and I don't know which I hate more: her in cut-offs, or her in spandex. Both need about ten inches added to be acceptable for wearing outside the house. The bottom half of her full ass threatens to pop out with every step she takes, and my blood pressure rises. There is no way she's driving a cart around the fields today in those shorts. Temporary wife or not, I don't need a distraction. Men would be following her around and giving me shit left and right. It's not going to happen.

Right as I'm about to get up, she turns around, and the sight of me sitting at the island startles her, causing her to jump back. *Why the fuck is she so easily spooked?* I get zero time to process her reaction or ask the question because the next thing I know, she's grabbing her hand.

"Ouch." Her face contorts in pain. Shit, when she jumped back, her hand grazed the stove.

I rush over and grab her arm. The skin on her wrist is already red. I walk her to the sink and turn on the water. She moves to stick her hand under, but I pull it back. "Wait, you don't want cold water. It needs to be a little warm. The cold will make it burn."

She pulls out the earbud that didn't fall out when she jumped. "Stop acting like you care."

I reach around her, testing the water to ensure it's slightly warm before taking her wrist and placing it under the water. "I never said I didn't care." I have her caged in, my body pressed against hers, ensuring she doesn't pull away before the wound has had time to adapt. I don't want to fight. I'm tired of fighting, and I need to distract her. "Did you make me breakfast?"

She snorts a laugh. "No, I made me breakfast. I drank too much yesterday, and I'm starving."

"So you're going to eat a pound of bacon and a pan full of eggs all by yourself?"

"Connor, I thought we went over this last night."

"Breakfast?" I question, not following.

"No, blurring the lines. You're rubbing my shoulder. Holding my wrist and…" She pushes her ass into my groin, which has me stifling a groan. "You're too close."

And because I can't help myself, I push her hair over her shoulder and bring my mouth to her ear. "Are you saying you don't like it when I touch you?"

Her breath hitches, and her face turns slightly toward mine in search of more before she stiffens. "I think we both like things we know we shouldn't. It's best that we remember this isn't real. It's temporary."

My cock started stiffening the second she pressed her ass into me, and I reciprocated, pushing into her more firmly, ensuring she felt what she did to me. For some reason, she seems to think I don't want her behind closed doors, and that couldn't be further from the truth. "Temporary or not, the title remains, and I like touching my wife."

My lips graze her ear, and she says my name in warning, "Connor," but the solemnity in her tone is false bravado.

"Do you want me to stop?" I press into her once more and pull her closer to my front with the hand that was on her shoulder.

She allows it for the briefest of seconds before abruptly shutting off the water and pushing off the sink, effectively shoving me back.

"Stop playing games and blurring the lines." Her eyes meet mine, and I see her desire, but I also see what looks like hurt, and that stings. I don't want to hurt her. "Sit down before I change my mind and eat all this food myself."

"What about your wrist?"

"It's fine. The gas was off. I only grazed the pan. I'll wrap it up before work."

Standing mere feet apart, neither of us moves. The tension in the air is still thick. We both want more, but reaching for it has consequences. So, for now, I'll take it. For now, I'll step back because I got more today than I did last night. We both have our walls built high, but there are cracks, and that's all I need. Stepping back, I move to reclaim my seat at the island. "I'm driving us to work."

She gives me her back and walks toward the stove, her dismissal grating my nerves until she adds, "Fine."

"Yo, Coach, Harrison is hitting on your girl over there."

I look over to find our number one hitter, who has three scouts coming out tonight just to watch him play, hanging all over Mackenzie's golf cart. This weekend will be the death of me before it's over. It's half of what kept me up last night. I knew I'd be pulled between her and my team. Today's game is huge, not just for my players but for the organization. It's our biggest tournament of the summer season, and we need to show out. We have some big donors backing us to help fund the stadium currently being built on the other side of town. The team needs to show up, but so do I.

"Harrison," I call out as I approach the cart.

He glances over his shoulder, doing a double take when he sees it's me. Unfortunately for him, he missed practice the day I made a showing of who she belonged to. As I step up to the cart, I put my hands on the roof next to him and casually lean in.

"Are you hitting on my wife, Harrison?"

"What?" He looks between her and me, and she rolls her eyes.

"Go warm up. The game starts in twenty minutes, and I need a minute with my wife."

"Oh, you're serious." He backs up from the cart just as a bunch of guys from the bench start laughing and hollering. The fuckers set him up.

"Get your head in the game, Harrison."

He straightens his ball cap. "Got it, Coach."

"Was all that really necessary?" Mackenzie huffs out, her voice riddled with annoyance.

"Was he hitting on you?"

"No, he was asking what snacks I had in the back."

"So that would be a yes. It's concerning that you can't tell when someone is trying to pick you up."

"But—" she starts.

"Mackenzie, I don't have time to argue semantics. His body language, coupled with the fact there's a damn sign on the side that says what snacks are on the back, means he was indeed trying to get your number. His head needs to be in the game and not on you tonight. I did him a favor, and in case you need a reminder, you're not on the damn menu."

My eyes slowly rake down her body and the outfit they stuck her in for the tournament. She's wearing those damn black spandex Lululemon shorts that show off every delicious curve she has. Curves I've been fiending to touch and claim, especially today because today, rather than wearing one of the oversized staff shirts, they gave her a tournament tank top. Everything is on display, including her full, perfect breasts. I can't help but scowl with annoyance, and she notices.

"Is there something wrong with my outfit?" she questions as she looks down at her attire.

When she's convinced it's fine, her eyes find mine. "No, you're like treasure wrapped in sin, same as always." She visibly pulls in a stuttered breath, my words catching her off guard. I drop my gaze and shake my head to clear the fog before opening the cooler on the back seat and grabbing a Gatorade. "Look, I need you to stay away from this field tonight. I can't afford the distraction."

She whips her head back, seemingly affronted.

"Don't look at me like that. This right now is exactly why. I can't be worried about you while I need to focus on my team." I twist the top off the Gatorade and take a drink, mentally preparing myself for an argument I seriously don't have time for, but it doesn't come.

"Okay."

"Okay?" I question, but she steps on the gas pedal, making me jump back. "Mackenzie," I warn.

In the kitchen this morning, she was in my shit for playing games, but that devilish glint in her eye now tells me that's what this is. Once I'm off the cart, she takes off, and I shake my head as I watch her go. I adjust my hat, feeling sweat pooling around the rim as I walk back to the field. This woman has seeped into my pores and infected my soul. The challenge now will be quieting my mind.

The entire team is lined up against the gate of the dugout as Harrison gets ready to take his final swing. The other team is good. I'll admit I didn't think they would be this good. My boys were prepared, and they've shown up all night. We have been evenly matched the entire game, but it's the bottom of the ninth, and we have a guy on second, and the other team is up by one. We need to bring Menotti in, or we are out.

For me, coaching is no different than playing. Every at-bat, every pitch, every base stolen resonates. I feel it more than I ever did playing. As a player, I had my role. I could only do so much, but as a coach, I train, direct, demonstrate, and lead by example for every player out there, so I feel every mistake for them. I question if their failure is a result of my own ability to be what they need. But tonight is more than the team for me. It's the town. It's my reputation. It's my future. This is where I was always meant to be. I know it's just a game, and we can't win them all, but fuck if I don't need this win tonight.

So, my heart starts to soar when the opposing team's pitcher throws his curveball. Every curveball follows its own parabolic path. It's not going to break or drop the same every time, but for some reason, this kid's pitch has the same slight drop right every other pitch, and in the last inning, I pointed it out to Harrison. The crack of the ball against Harrison's wood bat is the best fucking sound I've heard all night, and the ball climbs higher. The entire team scales the fence with a roar as Menotti rounds third, and their center fielder misses Harrison's ball as he leaps and crashes into the wall, the ball dropping behind, only missing his glove by mere centimeters.

The team rushes the field in excitement. They all know Harrison had three scouts here tonight. This win doesn't mean we've won the tournament, but we've seated tomorrow and made a hell of a showing tonight. I walk out of the dugout, and the team starts chanting, but it's the sight of Mackenzie in her golf cart at the corner of the adjacent field with her feet kicked up on the dash, watching discreetly, that makes this win one I'll never forget. Players start slapping the back of my head, and by the time I look up again to steal a look at her, she's gone.

After ensuring everyone got all their shit out of the dugout, I return to the concession stand. Mackenzie's shift ended a half hour ago, but I drove, so I expected to find her in here since she wasn't out by my truck. The windows are closed, and no one is back here. That's when I turn the corner and find Elijah mopping the floor. Out of all the Michaelsons, he's the one I can stomach the most, but still someone I don't care to talk to. However, he's also my only option.

"Hey, have you seen Mackenzie?"

He looks up from the bucket before pushing it over to the side. "She took off with Cameron about twenty minutes ago. I think they were all headed up to JP's."

"Thanks." I don't stick around for small talk. It's not my style, but it's why I tolerate him. It's not his, either. We are the same age, and like me, I don't think he cares for our parents' arrangement, but he does bear it better. But fuck that. I don't care to win the award for best ass-kisser in the family. He and Parker can take it. Family isn't supposed to lie and hide shit from the people they love. These days, it feels like that's the story of my life. I'm just done ascribing to it.

Pulling up to JP's, I see that half my team is here tonight. These assholes have two games to play tomorrow. I realize I have six years on all these fuckers, and hangovers hit differently when you're younger, but no athlete should be out drinking the night before a game, not at this level when they're so close to making their dreams come true.

When I step into the bar, my eyes immediately find Mackenzie on the dance floor in a short boho dress and black cowboy boots. I know she didn't have that shit with her when she left the house, which means this entire night has Cameron written all over it. I'm positive she planned all of this. She latched onto Mackenzie the second she learned she was important to my dad. Something about Cameron living at my father's house without my mother doesn't sit right with me. I get that her family died, and my parents took her in, but she's in college, and I know she has her own money. The Salts weren't paupers.

I'm watching Cameron teach her one of the line dances playing when Bret calls out, "Callahan, get your ass over here."

What the hell? My assistant coach is up here drinking with the players. I didn't think I needed to discuss discretionary acts of conduct with these guys, but apparently, I do.

"What are you doing up here?"

He flags the bartender down and orders me a beer. "Jeff and I came up for a few beers. We had no idea the team was coming up here, but hey, I figure they'll keep their shit in line and maybe wrap it up early knowing the coaches are sitting over at the bar."

I'm glad my earlier assumption that he came up to celebrate the win with them was incorrect, and hell, I can't talk too much now that I'm here myself. He just doesn't know I'm here chasing my wife.

"So what's the story with you and her anyway?" He nods toward where Mackenzie is on the dance floor with Cameron.

I shrug as I watch her shake her hips and slap her heels. "I saw something I couldn't let slip away."

"And that's it? You just asked her to marry you, and she said yes?" he questions, clearly amused.

"That's it." It's not a lie. In fact, it's the God's honest truth. I pursued her the first night we met. It didn't matter if she was the girl I was supposed to meet. I had to have her then, just like now.

"You're a lucky son of a bitch. Shit like that doesn't just happen to guys like us."

I turn to him and take a long pull off my beer. "And what the hell is that supposed to mean, guys like us? You think I can't land a girl like her?"

"You know exactly what I mean. Small-town country guys like us. We end up with a girl from high school or a friend of a friend, not a fucking Halley's comet."

I can't help but snort out a laugh at his antics. "Halley's comet?"

"Yeah, don't kick my ass for saying this, but you landed yourself fresh meat, untouched by anyone we know, and she's hot as fuck to boot. Anomalies like that only come around so often, and you, sir, won the lottery."

He's right. I don't like knowing he's noticed my girl, but I'm unsure what upsets me more: that he noticed her, or that I just admitted she's my girl without trepidation, only further solidifying that my mind is the only thing keeping me from her.

"Hey, I've been meaning to ask since I found out about the two of you. Has your relationship with the Michaelsons changed?"

"What do you mean?" I ask, somewhat perplexed by the direction he's going.

"Well, I know you guys are technically stepbrothers now, but he seems to be a little more than brotherly out there with your wife."

My head snaps back toward the dance floor. Rooster Crow is pounding through the speakers, and while it is not a couples dance at all, Parker has his hands on Mackenzie's hips. Fuck that. Now he's crossing the line.

CHAPTER 13

MACKENZIE

We've been at the bar for maybe an hour, and Cameron and I've been laughing harder than I've laughed in months as Cameron tries to teach me line dances. I knew the cupid shuffle, and that's where it ended. I've never heard of the watermelon crawl, and while I've listened to the country song "Good Time," I didn't know it had a line dance. I'm so glad I let Cameron talk me into coming out tonight. I was hesitant. I actually wanted to wait for Connor. He asked me to stay away from his field today while his game was being played, and I did—until the end, anyway. His game was the last one going on, and I'd be lying if I said I didn't want to see him in action. Heck, part of me needed to. I wanted to catch a glimpse of the man everyone else sees. It's why I was so quick to say "okay." I knew I'd be on a spy mission. I just didn't realize I'd pick up a new weight in my chest in a place where my heart should feel nothing.

All I managed to witness tonight was the man I've thought to be cold and uncaring is anything but. He cares about every player on that team, and more than half the town knows him. Word that I'm his wife has spread like wildfire. Every other guy who bought snacks from me congratulated me. Don't get me wrong, the women did as well, but it was definitely the fake side-eye type of compliment. The kind where you tell your opponent good game, even though you lost. Connor is an attractive man. Every time our eyes connect, even when I'm pissed at him, he gives me butterflies, and while I know his family has money, after tonight, it's obvious that his appeal is more than just those superficial things. It's because he's the whole package, which is another reason I said yes tonight.

I didn't need to sit around and let my stupid heart develop more feelings for a man who runs hot and cold for me. Take the past twenty-four hours, for example. Connor stayed up waiting for me to come home, only to yell at me. He takes and gives nothing in return. I asked him for a truth, the one that brought us together, and he couldn't give it to me. Then, this morning in the kitchen, he wanted me. I felt it, and God, I wanted to let him take it so bad, but I couldn't forget about the night before or the other times he's pushed me away or given me the cold shoulder. If he would come out and say, 'I want to fuck,' that's one thing, but he doesn't. He toes this line that makes it seem as though he'd like more than just a quick fuck. At least if he'd say what he means and mean what he says, I'd know where we stand. Hell, I'd risk my heart to have him one time.

"Shots!" Cameron announces as a tray is brought to the table next to the dance floor.

"Cam, have you thought about how we'll get home?"

"Did you just give me a nickname?" Her voice rises into a screech of excitement as she comes around the table and throws her arms around my neck. "I knew we were going to be the best of friends."

I hug her back and smile. It feels good to have a girlfriend. I've never really had many of those. The girls at school were more like acquaintances. They were nice enough. I wasn't a loser or anything. I just never had any authentic relationships with anyone outside of Zane, but looking back now, I can't help but feel like that was by his design. I'm just angry that I wasted so many years not seeing him for who he really was. I was the epitome of the girl with abandonment issues who latched onto her boyfriend because he was a man who gave her attention. He was the man who stayed, and I was the stupid girl who ignored all the signs that, in hindsight, feel like fucking billboards.

"Has no one ever called you Cam?" I question, a little surprised by her reaction. Cam seems like an obvious nickname for Cameron.

"Well, yeah, but not you. I think this moment calls for double shots," she says, releasing me to pass me our first shot.

"Who the hell is going to drive us home?"

"We do have Ubers here, ya know, but I think you'll be just fine. Your man is sitting at the bar."

I look over my shoulder, and sure enough, Connor is sitting at the bar, and my heart skips a beat for two reasons. He's here, and she called him my man. While behind closed doors, there are holes in that statement, here there aren't. Here in this bar, he's mine. In public, he stakes his claim, and damn it if I'm not going to put a little extra shake in my ass when the next song plays.

"To best friends." Cameron holds her shot up and clinks it against mine.

"To best friends," I cheer before throwing it back. It goes down too smoothly, and I have a feeling I will quickly find myself more than drunk if I don't watch it.

A new song starts playing, and Cameron squeals, "Ah, I love this one. Hurry up, take this one too." She passes me another shot. This time it's blue, and I know it's a bad decision before I take it, but I do it anyway. Cameron's energy is contagious, and I'm here for it. The next thing I know, she's pulling me back to the dance floor. "Let's go. It's Rooster Crow. I love this one."

Almost every girl in the place comes out for this song, and

suddenly, I don't feel so out of place. While they might know the moves, at least I don't stick out like a sore thumb. However, out of all the songs we've danced to thus far, this one is easy, apart from the jumps to change position, which only irritates my toe a little. I've never worn cowboy boots, but it was these or heels, and heels were not going to work with my foot. Luckily, we are the same size shoe. The back of Cameron's trunk had at least ten pairs of shoes and countless outfits. You'd think she lived out of the back of her car. When I asked her why she had so many outfits in her trunk, she said she likes to be prepared for any situation, which, the more I get to know Cameron, that statement isn't far-fetched. She likes her fashion. The dress I picked out was the longest in her trunk, and on her, it probably covered everything, but my ass hikes it up a little higher, and I was nervous it was too slutty. However, these girls are wearing booty shorts that may as well be underwear.

I'm just getting the hang of the turns when I feel someone's hands on my hips, but the touch is wrong. Connor wouldn't hesitate. I turn around, and my eyes widen.

"Parker, what are you doing?"

He steps in closer. "Look, I've thought about it, and we both know this thing between you two isn't real, but we could be."

"Parker, I'm sorry, but I don't feel the same way."

"You're lying. I know you felt something for me."

The next thing I know, familiar hands wrap around my waist and pull me close. "You heard my wife. Walk away, Parker, or I won't hesitate to make a scene in front of this entire bar the way you just thought to."

Parker's fists clench before his hands find his hips. "You don't even like her," he grinds out in a hushed tone.

Connor takes a step forward, but not before Cameron interrupts. "Parker, dance with me." He doesn't immediately move, and for a second, I think he's considering making a scene, but then he drops his eyes to me and shakes his head, and there it is again, that passive pity as if I don't make my own choices.

Cameron pulls at his hand, and begrudgingly or not, he walks away, which says something else. He doesn't want me enough. He literally just backed down. A man who knew what he wanted wouldn't let anything stand in his way.

As they move away, Connor leans in. "How's your foot?"

"My foot? After all that, you're asking me about my foot?"

He grinds his erection into my ass, "I thought maybe talking about feet would help me with my other problem. Right now, I want to take my wife in the bathroom and consummate our marriage." I teasingly press my ass back into him. "Mackenzie, stop. This isn't a game."

"Who said I was playing games?"

His lips skim the shell of my ear as his arms wrap more firmly around me. We're in the middle of the dance floor, people line dancing all around us, and I just want to let go. I want to let my guard down. I don't want to think about the consequences. I just want to be reckless and stay caught up in the moment. His hands slowly wrap around my waist, taking their time to explore while his lips finally connect with my neck the way they did the first night we met, and I swear I'm fading in and out. I have one foot in the now, and the other is far away, high on the way he's making me feel. For the moment, it's me and him back at the bar again, and the night is full of promise. Nothing is broken, and he's only mine. As his lips trail down my neck, I lean away, giving him more access, and he takes it. His teeth graze the vein I know is pulsating to the wild beat of my heart, and I just want to disappear.

I lose myself fading into him, and the feel of him pressed tightly against my body. Taking his hand, I move it higher, forcing him to cup my breast as I push back against his hard length. He groans loudly, and it vibrates through his chest, and

I swear I feel it resound in mine. I could stand in this moment for the rest of the night, but then he says, "Let's go."

The next thing I know, he's pulling me off the dance floor and leading me out of the bar, but something doesn't feel right. On the dance floor, it was me and him. I felt connected to him, and there's no way he didn't feel it, too. Suddenly, he shut it all off. In the bar, I could barely tell where he started and I began, but now it's blatantly obvious. Once again, it was all for show. He opens the door to his truck, and I climb in. He slams the door behind me, and I try not to cry. I can't help it. I don't want to cry. I'm just one of those people who can't help but cry when they're mad.

I should have seen it coming. Just like at the ball fields when he wanted to make sure everyone knew I was his, he put his hands on me, and tonight, after Parker's stunt, he wanted to ensure there was no mistake. His team, colleagues, Parker, Cameron, and the entire town were there to see him claim his wife.

He climbs in the truck, sees my tears, and asks, "Why are you crying?"

"Don't worry about it. Just take me home."

"I'm not going anywhere until you tell me what the hell this is."

I wipe the damn tear that can't help but fall and further piss me off. "Parker was right. You don't like me. Now take me home."

He hits the steering wheel hard, and it makes me jump. "Damn it, Mackenzie. Are you serious right now? That's what this is about? You think I don't want to fuck you?"

"You did it at the Fields the other day, too. In public, you act like you want me, and then when no one else is around, I'm back to being the inconvenience you've been forced to endure. It's fine. Just don't touch me anymore. I think we've given the town enough PDA."

"Let's get one thing straight: nothing that happened back

there was fake. I wanted every fucking second. I'm not sure when you started making shit up in your mind that I wasn't one hundred percent attracted to you. I thought I made that more than clear the first night we met. If I recall correctly, you're the one that ran out on me, not the other way around."

I wipe another tear, and he growls in annoyance as he reaches across the console. Instinctively, I jump back.

"What is that? Why do you do that?" he asks as he hands me a napkin from the glovebox.

"Do what?"

"Why did you flinch?"

I startle easy. Always have, but recently, it's been more. At first, I thought it was the entire situation. I know I'm being watched to some extent, which is unsettling in its own right, but I know what Connor's asking.

When I don't immediately answer, he slaps the console between us. "Who hurt you? I want a name, Mackenzie."

"It doesn't matter. He's part of my past. We broke up."

"An ex hurt you? Is that why you're here?"

Isn't that obvious? I hesitate because I never thought I'd be that girl who said yes. I never thought I'd say I dated a man who put his hands on me. It was only once, and then I was gone, but it happened all the same.

"Damn it, Mackenzie, I'm not mad at you. I fucking swear it. I would never lay a finger on you, but I need you to answer the question before I lose my mind."

"Yes," I stutter as I wipe one last tear. I refuse to cry any more tears out of anger. I'm not this girl. I left home to help my brother, to bring him home. To help Mom. That's been the worst part of all of this: not seeing her, not being able to check in on how she's doing.

All my thoughts of home and the guy who helped land me here are quickly forgotten as Connor throws the truck in reverse. *Shit.*

"What are you doing?"

"Put your seat belt on. I'm taking you home."

"Connor, I'm not from around here. It's not like you can go kick his ass. Stop acting like a crazy person. I'm fine—"

"Don't fucking say 'fine.' It's never fine. It's never okay for a man to touch you in any way you don't explicitly allow."

"You don't understand. It was an accident. It only happened once."

"This isn't up for interpretation. Stop talking. You're not helping your case. If anything, you're making it worse."

The rest of the ride home is spent in silence. When he pulls into the driveway, he doesn't pull up alongside my truck. Instead, he pulls into the circle drive. "Go inside, go to sleep, and please, for once, stay put. Don't leave."

"Connor—"

"Mackenzie, I'm asking nicely once. Can you please do this for me?"

His eyes hold mine, and while I still see his anger, he somehow looks less reckless than he did twenty minutes ago. Tomorrow is the championship game, and I'm confident Connor wouldn't do something stupid like drive to Montana to hunt down some ex-boyfriend of mine.

"Yeah…" I trail off slowly, reaching for the door before climbing out. "I'll see you in the morning."

His lips pinch together. "Close the door, Mackenzie."

And just like that, the certainty I felt vanishes. *Damn it.*

I slept like shit last night, or better yet, I didn't sleep at all. I'm pretty sure all I accomplished was tossing and turning. All I could do was replay our night on the dance floor and his words, "You think I don't want to fuck you? Nothing that happened back there was fake." Those were all great, but what that has left me in knots is, "If I recall the night we met, you ran out on me, not the other way around."

That line is the one I've lost sleep over. For hours, I pointed the finger at myself as though I'm the one to blame for where we are and why we can't find a way to coexist. But I know that's not fair. He's shut me out, too. First, with the utter look of disgust when he saw me at the Fields for the first time, then on our wedding day, when he acted like marrying me was a fucking death sentence. I know he has a daughter, which means he has an ex, and I've considered that maybe she's not an ex by choice. There are too many variables to consider. The biggest is why he agreed to all this in the first place, and apparently, neither of us is in a place to share.

When I received Josh's first letter. I fell to my knees and cried. I couldn't believe I'd finally heard from him after five years. It felt like prayers had finally started to come true. I never believed he would leave without saying goodbye or take off to start a new life without me and Mom, but I also didn't have any proof to refute those notions until his letter. It was an apology, a hello, an I love you, and a riddle all in one. I read it over a hundred times, ensuring I didn't miss anything and that I wasn't reading into something that wasn't there before I did as instructed and burned it.

M,

I'm so damn sorry I left you and Mom. You have to believe me when I say I wouldn't have done it if I thought there was another way. Looking back, maybe there was. Hindsight is always twenty-twenty. I can't change what happened or how I got to the here and now, but I would if I could. I've kept an eye on you. You've grown into a beautiful young woman. You look just like Mom, same grit, too. I know you're busting your ass to work and help pay her medical bills. I promise I will help you, but I need your help first. What I need is a big ask, M, and I wouldn't ask it of you if I didn't think it would truly make everything better. I have an address where I need you to be in four weeks, at 10:30 p.m. on the dot. You can't be late. M, it's going to hurt. There's no way around it unless, of course, you say no. If you say no, nothing has to happen. I promise I won't be mad. I'll always love you. You'll always be my baby sister, and I swear I'm trying to come back, but I need your help, M. Whatever you choose, choose it for you, not for me and not for Mom, but whatever you decide, you can't tell a soul. No one can know you received this letter. It must be burned.

Josh

Of course, the first thing I wanted to do was tell my mom. I'd avoided talking about Josh with Mom, not for her sake but mine. Alzheimer's and dementia patients tend to do fairly well talking about things and people from the past, but I couldn't be sure what she'd remember and what impact it might have on her. Tish had children late in life. She didn't have me until she was forty. Both my brother and I were accidents, so to speak. Not that she didn't want us once she found out, but we were not planned. When she found out she was pregnant with Josh, she was unmarried. Tish never married, though she had five engagement rings from suitors over the years. My mother was a free spirit. The woman was all about peace and love. She was a hippie through and through.

Never wanted to be tied down, never wanted to answer to anyone. Men were a part of her world when she allowed it, and the woman ensured she was always the smartest person at the table. It's why I never saw what we had by living in a trailer park as less than. Living there was a choice. It didn't make for the best school life growing up. I was judged for being one of the kids from the trailer park, but it taught me not to care what other people thought from a young age. The people who are quick to judge you before they take the time to know you are never going to be your people. They would inevitably be fair-weather friends hanging on as it suited them. When you no longer had anything to offer, they, too, would be gone.

Thoughts of my mom and Josh are what have me tossing the blankets off and climbing out of bed for a shower, though I still have another hour before my alarm is scheduled to go off. I can't sleep. Trying is pointless. I may as well get up and try to busy my mind, not to mention ever since I found that letter on my bed, I haven't been able to shake the eerie feeling of someone watching me. Even if it is my brother, I don't like it. Knowing someone might be watching me through the windows is creepy.

Entering the bathroom, I turn on the shower and let the water heat up as I brush my teeth. This house is quiet—too quiet. That's how I know I didn't hear Connor come home last night. Even if I dozed off for ten or twenty minutes, I know it was not deep enough that the squeaky-ass front door opening wouldn't have woken me. I spit and rinse the toothpaste out in the sink before pulling off my nightie and testing the water. Scorching. Fucking fabulous. The hot water pelting my body is precisely what I needed.

I'm just getting my hair wet when hands wrap around me from behind, and I scream.

CHAPTER 14
CONNOR

After dropping Mackenzie off last night, I tore out of the driveway with one destination: Montana. I wanted to drive straight through the night to whatever backwater town she came from. If Trent came out for her, chances are he's still in hiding nearby. It's not a coincidence that it's also the first place Holly went. She hasn't called from prison once since Summer has been in my custody, and the first thing she does when she gets out is go straight to Montana. The exact last place Mackenzie was linked to Trent.

The last communication I had with my cousin, Cayden, regarding the dirt I asked him to dig up on Mackenzie, he said he was going dark, which meant one thing: it's not all as it seems. *Fucking story of my life.* Add in that my father and Garrett don't see eye to eye on all of this means the truth lies somewhere in the middle, and I'll be damned if I don't want to find it first. I got Garrett's side of the story, and while he didn't give me all the details, I know it's because he doesn't have them, which means this hunch he's working off is new. Something tipped him off to make him think Holly isn't as innocent as we initially believed. The narrative has always been that she fell into the wrong crowd. She was the fall girl.

Holly herself even said she was set up, claiming they never kept the physical wallets. That's evidence linking them to a crime and bad business. But before I start allowing myself to go down a rabbit hole where she is indeed the villain and not the damsel in distress, I need to talk to my dad. I need his story, and something tells me he knew I would all along. He set me up.

My father is an intelligent man. Everything he does is calculated and well thought out. I do not doubt that when he set all this in motion, Mackenzie's safety and well-being weren't his only motivations. Yes, Summer is number one. That little girl means the world to him, but there's always another way. There's more to this marriage than just giving this woman my last name. I feel it in my bones, and I want answers.

When I pulled into my father's driveway last night, it was 10:00 p.m. I knew he'd be up. He stays up working later than any person should. He's been that way my entire life. The man lives his work. However, when I keyed in the garage code, I noticed his car was gone. I pulled out my phone and checked his calendar, only to find out he was on the East Coast. Figures the one time in two years that I needed to talk to him he'd be gone.

I considered going in and making a drink until I remembered Cameron may or may not be home, and I didn't care to run into her or anyone else. After I closed the garage door, I climbed back in my truck and pulled out of the driveway, but only after checking the security system I had just installed and ensuring Mackenzie did, in fact, do as I asked and stayed in. Flipping through the cameras, I found it dark, but it's always dark. Like me, she doesn't leave a light on. My thumb hovered over the camera I had installed in her room. I didn't take the decision to install one there lightly. Installing a camera in there is an invasion of privacy, but she's a stranger living in my house. It's not just myself I have to consider, but Summer.

When I clicked the button that showed me the footage of her room, my heart skipped a beat for two reasons. One: she listened, and two: she's fucking perfect. Her long blond hair was sprawled out on the pillow behind her as she lay on her side in bed in her deliciously short silk nightgown, her back to the camera, scrolling through her phone. It made me want to climb in behind her so I could see exactly what she was looking at. That's when I tossed my phone in the passenger seat. I had to stop looking before I did something reckless like drive straight home and take her the way I've wanted to since day one.

After driving around town for a few hours, I finally came home, but I didn't go inside. I got out and sat in the truck bed for hours, not trusting myself to go inside, but now that the sun is starting to rise, I'm sure she's asleep. I can go upstairs and maybe catch an hour or two of sleep before I need to head to the Fields. Games start at 9:00 a.m. today, and while our team plays at noon, you better believe I will be up there scouting the competition.

When I open the front door, the house isn't as quiet as I thought it would be, and the door that's always closed when she's inside isn't. It's open. Setting my keys on the credenza next to the front door, my feet move of their own accord and take me straight down the hallway to the very back of the house and the first-floor master where the girl I've lost countless hours of sleep thinking about should still be sleeping. She shouldn't be up. She shouldn't be tempting me with this open door. Last night on the dance floor, I lost myself in her. I couldn't tell you where I stopped, and she began. She felt like part of me. I've never felt so wholly drawn to someone in my life. People talk about love at first sight and finding the one, and I've never ascribed to any of that—but now I know why. I hadn't met my person.

This woman has had me wrapped around her finger like the ring I've been wearing for her since I met her, and I'll be damned if she doesn't make me weak. I should turn around and go upstairs. I shouldn't take one step, let alone two, into the room, but I do, and it's then that I know there's no turning back. The scent of her bodywash wafting out with the shower's steam wraps around me, and I have to see her. I need her. Last night I told her I wanted to take her to the bathroom and consummate our marriage, and she didn't pull away. She tempted me, and then she fucking cried. I wanted to pull her onto my lap and take her right there just to prove every inch of me wanted every part of her, but then she flinched, and I saw red.

For now, there's nothing I can do about the man who hurt her, the man who stands between us, but I know one thing for sure: if I have anything to say about it, he won't be getting her back. I didn't miss how last night she wouldn't give me a name. She's protecting him, and I haven't decided if that's out of fear or because she wants him back. As much as I hate her choice in men, I can't hate that I'm one of them, even if I know I'm no better than Trent in some ways. I see her silhouette in the glass door, and my cock is instantly hard. She's a goddess standing before me.

I'm done denying I want her. This is probably one huge fucking mistake, but she's one mistake I know I can't live without making at least once. I haven't gotten laid in months, and I'll be damned if I'm not going to make a move on the woman living under my roof, using my last name for her own. Last night, she wanted me. I hope like fuck that's still true now.

Figures she's one of those women who takes her showers scalding hot, but even the threat of third-degree burns doesn't thwart the ache in my cock. I kick off my shoes and unfasten my belt before pulling my shirt over my head. I stack all my shit by the door to grab it quickly on my way out. I know I won't be hanging around after. I can't, not with her. It would be too easy to blur the lines of what this really is. Before I drop my jeans, I grab a condom out of my wallet.

I wait until I see her run her hands through her hair to rinse out the soap before I make my move, opening the door and wrapping my arms around her from behind.

She lets out a blood-curdling scream, but I tuck my head into her neck, shushing her into submission.

"Shhh, shhh, shhh. It's just your husband making good on his word to fuck his wife."

She gives me no words, her heart racing under my palm as I grab her full breasts with both hands and pull her tight against my front. My God, she feels too good. All the curves I've been staring at for days are softer than I could have imagined, and I fucking love it.

I nip and suck my way up the side of her neck, and she still doesn't try to pull away, but then she asks, "What is this, Connor? Is this real?"

I pull back and pinch her nipples before asking, "What's real to you, Mackenzie?"

Her head lulls back onto my shoulder, and she moans just a little, and my heart clenches as I look down at her wet body with me wrapped around it. I haven't even had her once, and I want a repeat.

"You want this? This isn't another one of your games?"

A part of me hates that I have given her any reason to doubt my feelings, but no sooner the thought crosses my mind than I push it out, remembering this can't be more.

"If you're asking me if I want to fuck my wife, the answer is yes. If you're asking me if this is more than a quick fuck, the answer is no. This isn't a bed. It's a shower. Beds are for lovers. That's not what we are."

She straightens in my hold as if reminding herself that this can't be more. "What if I don't want this?"

"Then you can walk out of this shower, and I'll let you go. I won't touch you again."

I use her words. The same ones that played on repeat in my mind all night, coupled with those damn tears. I never want to be the reason for her tears. I hated that, though she despised my touch. She wanted it. Craved it. I hated that it couldn't and can't be the touch she deserves. The forever kind, but I can give her now. The kind that feels good and takes the edge off. Maybe this is what we both need to survive our time together. Release.

When she doesn't move, I try to keep it light. To play the role I've somehow built for myself when it comes to her. I'm not her Prince Charming. I'm the bad guy. The one she can't predict. The guy who makes her feel everything before ripping it away. I bite the lobe of her ear. "Be a good little wife and put your hands on the wall and spread those pretty legs."

I don't for a second believe she doesn't want this. She has fought me on everything since day one except this. Even at the bar, before we meant anything to each other, she gave me this. She trusted me with her body. My right hand leaves her breast and trails down her stomach until I reach her pubic bone, where I firmly press the heel of my palm against her clit before running my middle finger through her folds and whispering in her ear, "I'm going to need you to leave now if that's what you want because I'm one slip away from not being able to stop myself." I run my finger dangerously close to her entrance, making those perfect lips I long to kiss part with a gasp.

For a moment, she's still as I slowly run my thick digit up and down her center, just barely teasing her entrance one more time before she answers by leaning forward, placing her hands on the wall, and spreading her legs. My hands immediately find her cheeks, and I grab them hard like I've wanted to for days and squeeze, spreading them wide as I run my bare cock through her crack. Her puckered hole is so tempting, and when she slightly pulls away, I know no one has ever been there. *Fuck.*

"Don't worry. That's not the hole I want right now." I pull back and line up my erect cock with her entrance, pushing it in just enough to taunt her. "I have to make it fit here first." I run my tip through her folds a few times before reaching for the condom I placed on the ledge when I walked in.

Once I'm wrapped up, I waste no time aligning my cock with her entrance, anxious to feel her around my throbbing length. She looks like heaven with her back arched and that fine ass in the air, ready to give me what I've craved since meeting her. But fuck me if she's not too damn tight. I grit my teeth, borderline pissed that I have to ask a question I don't want an answer to.

"How long has it been since you let someone have you?" I just want to fuck. I'm usually all about foreplay, but I know with her, keeping my feelings out of it will be next to impossible.

"That's none of your business."

"Wrong. The second you became my wife, it became my business."

"Just shove it in. I can take it."

Is she fucking kidding me right now? Don't get me wrong. I love the idea of fucking her hard, and I have every intention of doing just that, but I already know she will be sore tomorrow without me forcing myself in.

"I'm sure you believe you could, but I don't want to hurt you."

I abandon an answer, intent on fixing the problem, and reach for the handheld showerhead. After switching it to the pulsating massage setting, I reach around and hold it a few inches away from her clit. The hot water and the pulse of the spray instantly make her react, and she pushes back away from the water and into me. Her soft ass presses up against my groin as my dick slips in a little farther, drawing out a gasp that is more surprise than euphoric enjoyment.

"What was that you were saying about a poor performance? I assure you there will be nothing poor about what I give you." I echo the words she spewed at me, and rightfully so, as I push in some more while bringing the showerhead closer. Her head drops, and she must like the view because she starts to loosen and let me in. It takes everything I have not to come. She feels too damn good, and I'm not even all the way in. "Fuck, why are you so damn tight?" I mumble under my breath more to myself, but she answers anyway.

"Because I'm not the slut you think I am, that's why."

I don't know where all this aggression is coming from. We've played the enemy card well, and I can't help but think that's what this is now. I told her this was just fucking. Maybe this is her way of keeping her walls up. I could apologize for those comments, and while I know I should, I won't. I can't. Not here in this moment, when emotions are already high. It would be too easy to lead her on, to make this feel like more than it is. Right now is about a release, one I know she wants just as much as I do. Nothing else. Words only fuck shit up. They come with feelings, and this isn't about affection. It's about lust. It's about getting what I've wanted since the first night I laid eyes on her. Part of me wonders if this is the cure. This may be what I need to get over her and leave things alone.

"Spread your legs wider and push up on your toes." She does what I ask without question, and at the new angle, I slide home.

"Oh, fuck," she pants as her walls already start to spasm.

"Are you all right?" I ask as I press my lips against her shoulder and try to rein in my own desire so I don't blow my load in one fucking pump. It's been too long since I've hooked up with anyone, and Mackenzie is by far the hottest fuck I've ever had.

"Yesss," she says as a subtle tremor runs through her legs. "You're just so deep. Can you go slow?"

"Was that just grandstanding earlier? 'Shove it in. I can take it.'" I throw her words back at her as I slowly pull back.

"I can. Just shut up and fuck me."

I slap her ass hard, making her cry out and drop the handheld. "You're going to be sorry you said that, wife."

I won't hurt her, but she will remember I was here. With both hands on her cheeks, I grip them hard and spread so that I can watch my cock disappear inside the tightest pussy I've ever had. My God, she's fucking perfect. Her blond hair is wet as it lies against her delicately arched back. If only I could see those tits. I've dreamed about sucking them into my mouth more than once. On the third slow thrust, she loosens, and I start to pick up my pace.

A tremble runs down her leg, and that's when I remember her toe. "Fuck, Mackenzie." I pull out, and she whimpers from the loss. I slap her ass. "Don't worry, that pretty pussy will come on my cock. Turn around."

Those hypnotic blues find mine and I brush a strand of wet hair back. "But first you're going to come all over my tongue and give that foot a rest. For once, you shouldn't have listened to me." Now that those perfect tits are dripping and on display for my eyes to see, I bend down and take a nipple into my mouth as my hand cups its weight. I love breasts. I've always been a breast man. What I wouldn't give to watch these bounce while she rode my cock. I bite her nipple a little too hard from the mere thought, and she hisses.

Backing her against the wall, I release her breast before sliding down her body and dropping to my knees. I let my hands feel every inch, memorizing every dip, every curve. Damn, I love a woman with curves. I take her right leg, the one with the injured toe, and drape it over my shoulder just as I did the first night, but unlike that night, I also pull her other leg over.

"Connor, it's too much. I'm too heavy and—"

"Stop," I warn, my voice somewhat terse. "I'm on my knees right where I want to be, and you're not too heavy. You're fucking perfect. Now let me have you."

My eyes hold hers as I dip my tongue and run it up her center, and she whimpers. "Show me how good it can be."

When she uses my words from the bar, I dive in. My hands grab her ass and my tongue finds her sweet hole, spearing her as hard and deep as I can. I've always been a giver, but I can tell with her it is different. If I let myself, I guarantee I could come hard just from making her come. I knead her ass gently, squeezing and spreading her wider because even though she's sitting on my face, I can't get close enough. *Fuck.* Her thighs start to clench around my head as she slowly rocks, and I know she's close, but she asked me to show her how good it could be, and I'll be damned if I'm not going to show her the stars.

Spreading her cheeks, I spear her pussy one more time before tilting her just enough to run my tongue over her puckered hole. Her hand comes down and tangles in my hair before pulling. "What are you—" she starts, only to be silenced when my mouth once again covers her sweet pussy as my pinky pushes into her ass, and I suck her clit into my mouth. "Connor," she screams my name as her orgasm hits hard and her legs tighten around my head. Fuck if her screaming my name isn't the best sound I've ever heard. I dip my tongue into her pussy, stealing one last taste before rising with her still tightly wrapped around my shoulders.

"Con…" she pants in question.

"Shhh, I got you," I say, using the wall to steady her weight and slowly lift her legs off my shoulders as I let her soft body slide down mine until that perfect pussy is right where I need it. My tip nudges her entrance. "Are you ready for my cock, wife?" Her head sways from side to side, her eyes closed. "No?" I question as I press in just a little.

"No, I want it. I want you, Connor."

Those were all the right words, yet so wrong. She's not supposed to want more, but they don't stop me. I bury myself deep in one thrust, unable to hide my desire. "Fuck, you feel good," I grind out into the crook of her neck as I reluctantly pull back, too scared to stay still and overthink how she makes me feel. Right now, I want to give her everything. With every thrust, my heart pounds harder in my chest. With every pump, the barriers I set for myself begin to crumble as my heart and soul seek to claim her.

Damn it. My hands grip her ass harder as I try to ground myself and start to let go. Pounding all my resentment, all my frustration, all my desire into this woman I can't fucking keep. But the harder I go, the more her delicious moans reverberate throughout my chest. She's loving every fucking second. The harder I go, the wetter she gets. Her desire for how I'm making her feel is evident.

"Con, I can't last. I'm going to come."

My nickname on her lips as I bring her to orgasm sends me spiraling. My guard fucking slips, and I let go as she milks my cock and owns the best fucking orgasm I've ever had. I couldn't come down from the high she's wrung out of me if I wanted to. Her tits pressed against my chest, her ass in my hands, her pussy squeezing my dick as her scent wraps around me. I'm so high on her that I'm not convinced there's her or me. All I feel is us. As the high of my release fades and I come down from a place I've never been, I slowly pull out of the only woman I ever want to be inside of for the rest of my damn life and set her down. I knew this moment was coming. I knew I'd have no words. It's why I left my things piled by the door.

My eyes can't help but find hers, and I see it. What was supposed to be a quick fuck was more. She lost herself just now. It was as good for her as it was for me. I feel it in every fiber of my being. My brows pinch together as regret and apology grip me hard, but the words don't come. Standing before her now, I don't know what to say. I don't want to make it worse. I can't be sure she sees my pain. If our past says anything, it's that she doesn't. She doesn't see how hard this is for me, but that's not her problem. It's mine. With that in mind, I drop my gaze and walk out of the shower. It's better if I'm the asshole than the guy who breaks her heart, and giving in to any of those emotions I felt back there would inevitably lead to a world of hurt.

CHAPTER 15
MACKENZIE

I suppose you could say I brought this on myself. I said yes. I let Connor have me. Who am I kidding? I knew before it was ever an option that I had to have him at least once. I had to know what it was like. No man has ever made me feel the way Connor does, even when he's mad. Even when his eyes are filled with disdain, they somehow say 'it's only you,' and I would know because my hate loves his. It's been a week since we've seen each other or talked. We fucked, and then he disappeared. I'll admit I didn't see that coming, and in fairness, he warned me that it meant nothing. It was just sex. It's not his fault it felt like more for me.

On Sunday, when he walked out of the shower, I wasn't hurt. I wasn't even upset. It was that, coupled with everything else, that stung. Sometimes, being left with your own thoughts is the worst place to be. There's nowhere to hide, and your doubt and insecurity can easily take root and steal your solitude. The wrong thoughts can eat you alive, and that's precisely what they've done to me since the moment I walked out of my bedroom after our time in the shower. It's been one hit after the next. The first came when he didn't just leave the shower. He left the damn house, and not in his truck but mine.

I showed up to work an hour late once I decided to take his. He clearly went into my purse to get the keys because they were gone. It's not like I left them laid out and he accidentally took the wrong set and decided fuck it, I'll take hers. No, he deliberately took them, and I know that for a fact because after his team played Sunday, he left the Fields in my truck, not his. He didn't come to the concession stand to swap, and I know he saw his truck. It was parked five spots over from mine. I expected him to be there when I got home, though I'm unsure why. Since I've been here, he's never beat me home. Connor always comes strolling in late at night and heads straight upstairs. But this week, he hadn't come home at all until Thursday.

Thursday night, I finally heard him walking around upstairs. I didn't get up, even though every ounce of my being wanted to go upstairs and yell at him. I wanted to call him every name in the book because while, yes, I knew it was just sex and nothing more, leaving me here alone all week following our tryst was a dick move. He knows I have no one here. No family or friends. I couldn't even go hang out with Cameron. When I texted her, she said she was out of town and wouldn't be home until Friday, and I can't help but feel like he knew that. But I bit my tongue. I swallowed my anger because I didn't want to be that girl. I didn't want to let him see that he got to me, that he affected me. So I stayed in my room, but when I woke the following day, once again, he was gone. However, when I walked outside to take his truck for work, it was gone too, and in its place was a brand-new white BMW X7 with the damn keys sitting on the roof.

He knew I wanted to keep that truck. He knew it was important to me. It was going to be my way home when all this was over, a car I could drive to see my mom whenever I wanted. I could stay however long I needed instead of relying on the damn bus schedule because Uber was too expensive. When my mom fell at work a little over a year ago, it was due to a stroke. Her side of the family is predisposed to early-onset Alzheimer's, but her stroke triggered it for some reason. It didn't help that Tish was a smoker most of her life. It's the one ugly habit that beautiful woman had. She loved her nicotine. After the stroke, it wasn't the forgetfulness or inability to keep up with ordinary conversation that made me look into senior living. It was the hallucinations. She truly believed she was seeing people. At first, it wasn't anything too crazy. Here and there, she'd ask me who someone was, and when I'd ask who she meant, she pointed out the back window to the yard, but there was never anyone there. It wasn't until she started seeing people in the house that things got bad, not to mention creepy. I don't care who you are. When someone says they see people, my mind automatically goes to fucked-up scary movie mode, but what tipped the scales was when those people started talking to her.

Unfortunately, I could no longer trust her to stay in the trailer without burning it down because she left something on and forgot or someone told her to do something—not to mention I couldn't trust that she wouldn't leave. So I sold her car, the same one I had used since the stroke to get groceries, go to work, and take her to appointments. I sold it for the down payment to put her in assisted living that, coupled with a small pension I discovered she had from a job she worked before I was born, helped me ensure I had somewhere I knew she'd be taken care of while I went to work and tried to make ends meet.

It's part of why accepting Josh's request to come here was so damn hard. He had to have known where Mom was when he asked this of me. I put a lot of faith in the man I used to know, and I've been praying like crazy that this wasn't all for nothing. I want to help my brother, but I have priorities, too. I need to get back to my mom, not because she's dying but because I don't know how much time I have left where she'll even remember me… and then there's the bills. Thirty states still require children to take care of their elderly parents' basic needs. Montana is one of them. I would have helped anyway, but in the scheme of things, it's not an option. It's a requirement. The requirement aspect of my obligation to my mother is why I find it hard to stay mad at Connor. Our marriage was a demand, not a choice. Ultimately, I can't fault him for his asinine behavior. After all, he's doing me a favor. I don't think my heart could withstand a kind version of Connor Callahan.

The door to the back office opens, startling me out of my thoughts as Parker appears in the doorway with a bouquet of flowers.

"Hey, do you think we could talk?"

"Um, sure." I wrap up my half-eaten sub sandwich. My stomach has been in knots for days. It wasn't going to get eaten anyway.

He sets the flowers on the desk. "These are for you."

My eyes widen in surprise before I lightheartedly say, "Apology flowers really weren't necessary."

Putting his hands in his pockets, he shrugs. "They're not from me, and I'm not here to apologize."

"Oh…" I trail off, a little embarrassed. "Sorry, I just assumed."

"You're misunderstanding. That's a leading theme in our relationship. It's all a big misunderstanding. I would buy you flowers in a heartbeat if I thought that would fix things, but I know it won't, and I'm not here to apologize for what I said. I meant it. I just need to know. I need to hear from you. Is he really what you want?"

I pull in a deep breath and look up, only to find his dark blue eyes locked on mine, almost pleading for a response different from the one I gave him days ago.

"Parker," I start, but he holds up his hand.

"Don't start like that. Starting like that never bodes well for anyone. Hear me out, Mac. You can tell me things. We can be real with each other. I know things about you. We can figure this out."

"And I can't do that with Connor?"

With his hands on his hips and his voice a little more sure than it was just seconds ago, he says, "Something tells me you haven't."

My eyes narrow on his. "What is it you think you know?"

I watch for any signs that he's lying: turning away, delay in response time, or body movement that might suggest he's not being truthful, but there's none. Instead, he answers without missing a beat.

"I know someone hurt you, and that's enough. In my eyes, nothing else matters."

I consider his words and his offer. I already know Parker and I have no future, but why couldn't he be my guy? Why does it have to be Connor when he clearly hates me? As if he heard my internal dilemma, he adds, "It wouldn't be the first time a Michaelson stole a Callahan."

Wow, that was a solid low blow. Parker and Connor clearly have a deep feud, but even as someone with no horse in the race, that felt harsh.

The door behind him pushes open, and my breath hitches slightly until I see Elijah peek around the corner. "Park, get out here and help me with the keg delivery."

"Yeah, I'm right behind you." He turns to me and rubs the back of his neck, clearly upset about the interruption. "I don't want you to say anything now. Just think about it."

"Park, let's go," Elijah calls out.

"All right, I'm coming." And then he's gone, and I'm left alone with my thoughts yet again, but at least this time I have flowers.

Getting up from the desk, I spin the bouquet, looking for a note. Parker said they weren't from him, and my heart can't help but beat out of sync as I consider the only other person they could be from. *Why am I getting excited?* I just told myself his silence was a blessing to be thankful for, and now I can't find the damn card fast enough.

Finally, shoved down in the middle, I see a white envelope and pull it out, only for my heart to drop for an entirely different reason. They're from Josh. On the front of the envelope is a single letter:

M.

My hands shake as I consider opening the letter now or saving it for later, until I am reminded of how keeping important notes hasn't worked well for me lately. I hastily nudge my finger under the corner, searching for real estate to tear this baby open. Flipping the card open, it reads:

M,

I'm sorry. I thought the hard part was behind you. However, I'd be lying if I told you I didn't expect them to play hardball, but I need you to play nice with Callahan.

Josh

"What the hell, Josh?" I mumble as I put my head in my hands. How the hell am I supposed to interpret the meaning of this card? When I received his first note saying I was exactly where I needed to be, I took that figuratively, as in I'm in the right town, with the right people looking after me. I didn't think it was his way of saying you are living with the man I need you to get close to. I mean, how else am I supposed to interpret this? The question is why.

My phone vibrates in my back pocket, and I pull it out to find a text from Cameron.

Cameron: Are you coming for a swim or what?

I look at the time and see it's just after 4:00 p.m. My shift technically ended fifteen minutes ago. I worked through my lunch until Elijah forced me to take a break. It's Friday, and while Josh might want me to play nice with Connor, I can't very well do that while he's ignoring me, and I refuse to sit at home by myself for one more night.

Me: Yeah, I'll be there.

It's a strange way to ask me over for a pool day, but beggars can't be choosers. I have zero friends, and an invite is an invite. I fold up my letter from Josh and stick it in my bag before grabbing my half-eaten sandwich and soda and heading out.

When I pull into the driveway, it's packed with cars. I didn't realize hanging out by the pool with Cameron meant I would be coming to a party. I was expecting another girls' day. I don't love crowds, so I shoot her a quick text.

Mac: Can you meet me out front?

Cameron: Sure. Text me when you get here.

Mac: I am here.

Cameron: Oh, okay. Coming now.

Climbing out of the car, I lean on the hood and wait for her to come out. From where I stand, I hear laughter coming from the backyard and my anxiety spikes. I have no idea who is back there, but I hated meeting new people and being put on the spot back home, and nothing on that front has changed since moving here. If anything, it's worse knowing I have secrets.

The privacy gate to the backyard opens, and Cameron comes out wearing an emerald green bikini with a matching sarong, looking like a fucking runway model as always. She is the definition of a girl's girl. The woman loves fashion, her makeup is always on point, and I swear she must go to the gym daily. She is toned and lean everywhere a woman wants to be. I cringe, knowing I will have to stand next to her, though maybe I shouldn't. Standing next to her could be a good thing. All eyes will be on her and not me.

"What's up? Why didn't you walk back?"

I gesture toward the driveway full of cars. "What is all this? When you texted me 'get your ass to the pool,' I assumed you meant for girl time."

Her brow furrows as if my words have somehow confused her. "The family is here for a BBQ." She tosses her thumb over her shoulder. "Were you not already planning on being here?"

Shit. That's when I notice Connor's truck parked near the front of the row. How do I say, 'No, my husband didn't invite me to this evening's family dinner?' *Crap, think fast, Mac.*

I slap my palm to my forehead. "Oh my God, I completely forgot that was today. I wasn't feeling good earlier, and when I texted Connor, he said to go home after work and relax. You know how protective he is when it comes to my health. First, it was bed rest for a stubbed toe, now this." I roll my eyes for added effect.

She stares at me with a hint of suspicion for two seconds. "Well, grab your shit, get changed, and meet us at the pool."

"Any chance you can sneak me in the front door and point out everyone first?"

"I keep forgetting that you haven't had the chance to meet

Evan yet. He and Hannah just got back from their month-long honeymoon in Spain."

Stepping into me, she links her arm through mine. "Come on, I'll give you all the deets on Evan and his friends."

I swipe my bag off the hood and let her lead, hoping she'll pull a classic Cameron move and do all the talking so I don't have to ask flat-out who the hell Evan is. I can already tell he's someone I should know, seeing as how I'm married to Connor. *Fuck my life.*

When we enter the house, I hear more voices down the hall coming from the kitchen, but she quickly pulls me over to the side staircase. "Let's get you changed in my room. It has a pool view, and I can point everyone out."

Entering her room, it's typical Cameron. It's decorated like it could be in a *Homes & Garden* magazine layout. The entire wall behind her bed is a deep royal blue with ornate 3D circular scroll designs running the entirety of the wall. Her tufted headboard is a light gray tweed that is carried through into the throw pillows set atop fluffy off-white and dark blue blankets. The room is dark and light, with walnut furniture grounding the space and white-and-gold accents balancing the heavy elements. I could sleep comfortably in here.

Tossing my bag on the bed, she pulls me to the window. My eyes immediately find Connor posted up on a stool at the swim-up bar. But where I thought he'd be relaxed, he's not. I can tell from up here he seems tense, which does nothing to settle my nerves. He didn't tell me about tonight for a reason. While I may technically be his wife, it is not by choice, so I can understand why he didn't. Scanning the crowd, I see faces I know. I would think not having me on his arm tonight would raise more questions, but I also know two of the men out there know this marriage isn't exactly real.

"Okay, obviously, there's Parker and Elijah."

They got here fast. When I left, they were still unloading

kegs, but maybe they didn't have to run home before heading here like I did.

"The brunette standing next to Elijah is Bree. She's been trying to get Elijah to put a ring on it for years."

"Why hasn't he?"

"I'm not sure. Elijah is not a player, and he plans on marrying her. If anything, she shot herself in the foot by dropping too many hints. I see him as a big proposal type of guy, and Bree always talks as though he's already asked. That's taken the element of surprise out of it for him, and now he's unmotivated."

"I get that. Dropping down on one knee is a big deal. When you do it, you want to be sure the person will say yes, but at the same time, you don't want them to see it coming. When you offer someone forever, you want it to be genuine, not rehearsed or expected."

"Exactly. Luke and Miles are the two tall drinks of water standing on the other side of Bree. They are best friends with Evan. And as for those girls, I have no idea who they are. They showed up with the twins. And that's everyone…" She trails off in her perusal, only to smack my arm and say, "Oh wait, there's Hannah. I hate her. Do you hate her? Never mind, that's a stupid question. Of course you hate her. She royally screwed over your man and broke his heart, but what I don't get is how Evan could do that to Connor. Not to mention, why would you even date a girl like that? What brother marries his younger brother's girlfriend? Talk about fucked-up."

Letting the sheer drape fall back over the window, she heads over to the bed and flops herself down as if she didn't just drop a bomb. Now, I have to play dumb like all that isn't news to me. First of all, I didn't realize Connor had siblings, but add in the shit about his girlfriend. Looking down at him now, I can't help but feel sympathetic to his discomfort. Talk about being dealt a shit hand.

"As for everyone in the kitchen… There's Kipp, Moira, Everett, and his two brothers, Garrett and Colton. Colton is unmarried, and Garrett's wife is home with their middle child who just had their tonsils out."

Pulling my gaze away from the window and back to her, I say, "Thanks."

"No worries. I got your back. Now put your suit on so we can go down to the pool. I'm ready for a drink."

"Is there an en suite or something?" I look around. She can't really expect me to change right in front of her.

Rolling her eyes, she says, "I'll wait for you downstairs. In the living room."

"Thanks."

When I found out that Connor was here and didn't invite me, I was immediately peeved. I thought we were past some of this shit. Yes, he's ignored me for the past week since we hooked up, but the one thing he's always seemed adamant about is appearances, though I guess they don't matter around his family. I realize we are both in this marriage for reasons we haven't been fully transparent about, but I don't understand why he doesn't even want to try to get along. Why does our time spent together have to be toxic? It only makes what Parker said ring true. *He doesn't even like you.* There's nothing else that explains his behavior. Sure, he said he wanted to fuck me, but I'm not stupid. You don't have to like someone to get off.

Rummaging through my bag, I find the blue bikini I threw in here from the last time we hung out and undress. My stomach is in knots thinking about what Connor's reaction to seeing me here tonight will be. I know he won't say anything rude aloud in front of people because of appearances, but his silence is just as loud. I only wish I knew what was going through that head of his. His eyes speak a different language than his words. More times than I can count, I feel like I've seen my feelings reflected in them, but then he'll turn around and do something that tells me I was coloring his eyes with shades of fondness that were never really there.

After my swimsuit is on, I fold my clothes and stack them in a pile next to my bag before digging through and looking for a hair tie. Once I know I've thoroughly scoured the bag only to come up empty, I take my clothes and shove them in before looking around Cameron's room. Surely, there is a hair tie around here somewhere. The girl's hair goes halfway down her back, like mine. When I turn around, I see two doors. One must be an en suite.

I head over to the bathroom and open the door, only to find a closet. Damn. I try the next, and bingo. Forgoing the light, I head straight toward the vanity and start opening drawers. There's enough light from the window that I can see just fine. After pulling open every drawer on the left side, I head over to the right but stop dead in my tracks when I hear, "This is the last time."

What the hell? I stay frozen in my spot, straining my ears to listen. The voices aren't familiar, but how am I hearing them? It's quiet for a minute until I hear, "Mmm," rumbled in a low, throaty moan that makes my skin pebble.

"Be quiet, or we're going to get caught."

"You like it when I'm loud," a female voice chides in response.

The pace of my heart instantly picks up, and my palms begin to sweat as I take a shaky step to peer around the corner. When I do, a guy has a girl pinned against the wall, his hand trailing up her thigh as he crushes his mouth to hers. *Shit. This is a fucking Jack and Jill bathroom.*

I quickly snap my head back before I get caught, and that's when the guy breaks away to say, "Correction: liked it. We can't do this anymore, Hannah. You're married, and I have a girl downstairs waiting."

My eyes widen into saucers. I just found out this woman married Connor's brother after being with Connor, and now she's up here making out with another man. Hell no. The direction of their rendezvous is clear, and I've heard enough. I ditch my efforts of finding a hair tie and pad out of the bathroom and grab my bag before flying back downstairs. When Cameron sees me coming down the steps, her eyes widen as she gets off the couch and meets me at the bottom.

"Why are you flushed? Is everything okay? Oh my God, did you get sick?" Her hand meets my forehead.

"What?" I swipe her hand away. "No, I'm fine." I try to recover from what I saw upstairs. While I like Cameron, and I believe she knows more about everyone and everything that goes on in this place than she lets on, I'm not in a place to cause family drama.

"Are you sure? We can go downstairs, play pool, or watch a movie."

All of those options sound a lot better than walking outside, but after the letter I got from Josh, it feels like saying yes to them is counterproductive to why I'm here.

"No, I'm good." I fidget with my swimsuit top, trying to pass my anxiousness off as nerves instead. "Is this top too revealing?"

"Hell yes, it's why I love it. If you don't want revealing, you need to buy a size up from your bra so these babies don't accidentally pop out," she adds as she pushes my breasts together.

Wow, that was not the response I was expecting. One, I didn't think my top was too revealing, though I've always had big breasts, so maybe I'm used to a certain level of exposure. *Now, I am self-conscious. Great.* I've bought three swimsuits for myself in the past five years, so the bigger top size is solid advice. It's on the tip of my tongue to say Daddy Everett bought me these tops to poke fun at her crush, but I don't. It's too telling of my situation. I'm still trying to figure out how much she knows.

"Let's grab a drink before we head outside." She links her arm through mine and leads me through the house.

"Um, I'd rather not meet Everett's brothers in my bikini."

"Fine." She veers right hard and opens a door. "We'll go downstairs and grab a drink."

"Geeze, give a girl a warning next time. You practically pulled my arm out of its socket," I say as we head down the steps. She huffs a breath of annoyance, and I realize what just happened.

"Wait a minute." I pull my arm out of hers. "I see what this is. You're pissed you didn't get a chance to shimmy that ass in front of Everett. Look, I'm down if you need a wingman, but maybe offer me a towel first."

"Haha, very funny," she says as she rounds the bar.

"Where were you this past week, anyway? It looked like you were on schedule for Sunday with me, and then you didn't show up."

Her back is to me as she pulls out salt, glasses, and what looks like pre-sliced jalapenos. "It was sort of an impromptu trip." Standing, she brushes her hair over her shoulder. "Do you like spicy margaritas?"

I don't miss how she didn't answer my question, but since I'm the queen of sidestepping questions myself, I let it go.

"I've never had a spicy margarita, but I like regular ones, so why not."

While she makes our drinks, I spin on my chair and look around the basement. Seriously, this place is enormous. Who needs this much space? There's a full-on bar, pool, shuffleboard tables, and what looks like thick black velvet curtains at the far end. They must lead to a movie theater since Cameron asked if I wanted to watch a movie.

"There must have been a lot of house parties here back in the day."

"Yes, there were always kids here. That pool and this basement made this the place to be in the summertime."

The mention of the pool has me getting up and heading to the windows. When we were lying out the other day, you couldn't see in these windows from outside. My eyes zero in on the man whose back I've only seen from a distance in the fields all week. Damn, even when I'm mad, it's hard to stay that way, especially when I see his ex saddle up to his brother. Even if she didn't fuck Evan's friend upstairs, she's still a cheater, and their conversation confirmed their affairs. It's evident from here that Connor is uncomfortable, and it makes me want to go out there and put on a show. He should be thankful she broke up with him, and instead, it seems he's somewhat dejected.

"Hey." Cameron hip-bumps me before handing me my drink. "Oh, yeah, and fair warning: don't take it personally if Hannah's a bitch. She's a bitch to everyone, and I'm pretty sure she's already put Connor in a mood."

"What happened?"

"Evan commented how Connor finally moved into the house, and she said, 'Yeah, it's not like I ever minded.' I only caught a little because Elijah and Parker showed up."

"Wait, why would she have any say, to begin with?"

"Well, because they dated throughout high school, and the house was gifted—"

I cut her off, "Don't tell me they were engaged."

Her eyes narrow on mine, and I realize I'm giving too much away. Shit.

"What?"

I think quickly and backpedal. "Connor told me about her, but with where you were going, it was starting to feel like maybe he left some things out."

She quirks one of her perfectly manicured brows as if she is debating if she believes me. "Men, even when you marry, you can't trust them. I was going to say that Moira and Everett gifted him that house for his eighteenth birthday. It seemed like a natural progression that he would move into it with Hannah because they were high school sweethearts and Everett and Moira married at the same age, but a month after graduation, before they ever moved in, she broke up with him. Two weeks later, she was with Evan."

Damn, who the hell gets a house for a graduation gift? That's wild. Now, I can't help but wonder if that's why he never moved in. That could also be why he didn't invite me tonight. He still has feelings for her. I'm sympathetic to the whole first love thing. For some reason, you can't just let them go even when they break your heart. That first love changes you forever, no matter what.

"Yeah, well, I'm no stranger to stuck-up bitches. I dealt with them my whole life. Let's go."

May as well get this shit over. The second we step out the door, Parker stares me down hard. *Great.* The last thing I need right now is another complication. Hannah, moving to stand on Evan's left side, closest to Connor, steals my attention, and I'm instantly annoyed. It's not enough that she's fucking one of her husband's friends, but now she wants to traipse around and try to make mine jealous. I may still be trying to figure out my shit, but I refuse to let this slut at the bar take up any space in Connor's mind. She doesn't deserve it.

The more information I collect on him from everyone else, the more I'm convinced he hasn't always been the asshole he is now. He's tired and worn out from the shitty fucking cards he's been dealt. His fuck off attitude is starting to make a hell of a lot more sense. While it doesn't excuse some of the hurtful words or shit I've endured from him, it explains a few things. I see him in a different light. I understand a little more why he doesn't date. He's been burned, and not just once. The man has some baggage, and I'm not just referring to his exes, but his family.

I'm still unsure of what the Callahans have going on behind the scenes, but I imagine it's not an easy lifestyle to explain to a potential partner. I only understand because I've now lived it, and I fucking hate that because I'm not that girl. I'm not the girl who lets a man beat on her, but all it takes is once to believe that about yourself. To make you question everything you thought you knew about your character, judgment, and overall sanity.

As I enter the zero-entry pool, the cold water has every hair on my body standing on end. Once I'm deep enough that the cool water laps at my sides, my nipples immediately harden, and this blue bikini suddenly has me showing a lot more than I bargained for. I'm unsure how Connor will react when I reach him, but I hope he'll let me in, at least with this.

Running my hand up his insanely defined back, I stop when I reach his shoulder and squeeze in greeting, "Hey, sorry I'm late."

All eyes at the swim-up bar are suddenly on me as everyone goes quiet.

CHAPTER 16
CONNOR

Fuck, this past week has been absolute hell, and the hand gliding up my back right now feels like pure heaven. God, I've missed her, but right now is the last place I want her to be. Hell, I don't even want to be here. I barely get a chance to process that she's here, touching me after how I acted this past week before Evan's busting my balls.

"Well, it's about damn time. When Connor showed up alone, I was convinced the rumors about him getting hitched were just that. Small-town gossip with no merit."

"Oh, she's very real. Royal pain in my ass on the daily," Elijah chimes in beside him, throwing a wink at Mackenzie that kicks my jealousy up a notch. He's been with Bree for years, and even now, his arm is slung over her shoulder as she's tucked into his side, but I don't like feeling like he has a relationship with Mackenzie that I don't.

"What can we get you? A beer, some kind of fruity drink." Evan pauses, his eyes doing a slow perusal of her body that has me clenching my fist. "Or are you more of a shot girl?"

I swear to fuck I'm not in the mood for him or his shit tonight. I've been on the edge of kicking his ass since I arrived, and he's not helping his case now, especially considering he's clearly only looking at her tits. Otherwise, he'd notice she already has a drink.

"She has a drink, dumbass," I can't help but grind out.

He ignores my dig. "Then a shot it is. Who else is in? We have to do a round for the newlyweds."

I'm about to spout off with another dick comment when Mackenzie steps up to the bar and slowly slides between me and the ledge. *What the hell is she doing?* I mean, fuck, I'm not complaining. I've been thinking about nothing but putting my hands back on her body since I left her in the shower Sunday, but this move is out of character.

Evan claps. "Rowan, line up ten tequila shots, fine sir."

As everyone watches the barback my father hired for the night line up shots, I take the opportunity to lean in. "What do you think you're doing?"

My mouth next to her ear has her skin instantly pebbling. She slightly dips her head toward me. "Just follow my lead and pretend that you don't mind me sitting on your lap."

I let my hands slowly glide up her thighs until they settle on her hips, fueling the heat that sparked to life the second I felt her hand touch my back. Fuck, who am I kidding? She doesn't even have to be touching me for my dick to notice her. "Oh, there's no pretending required," I say as I lift her by the waist. "But if you're going to sit, then sit."

"How much have you had to drink?" Her pitch is a little too high, and I know exactly why.

My cock was hard the second her ass rubbed across my knee to squeeze between me and the bar, so I know she's not missing an inch of it now, with only the thin layers of nylon separating us.

She grinds against my length, and I bite my lip hard to hold back my groan. "This has to be because you're drunk. We both know you don't like me."

My hands circle her waist as I pull her against my chest, my mouth finding the crook of her neck where my lips graze the shell of her ear. "Turns out even when I'm drunk, you're my only type," I tease her right back, pressing my rock-hard cock against her center.

She lets out the smallest of whimpers that I know only I can hear, and it fucking wrecks me. I want to throw her over my shoulder and take her away so I can bury myself deep inside her, but I can't. I came here tonight for a reason, and I'm not leaving until I've accomplished it. I'm not enduring this shit company for nothing. I came here to talk to my dad since he just got back into town today, but he hadn't yet returned from the airport when I arrived. Instead, I walked into this shit show of a reunion.

"All right, all right, all right, everyone grab a shot," Evan calls out. "Circle up. I don't want anyone to miss this." Once everyone has a shot in hand and has gathered around, he says, "I know none of us thought this guy would ever settle down—you know, once bitten, twice shy, or however that shit goes." He pulls Hannah into him as if to drive home his point.

Such a fucking dick. I seriously don't know why I put up with his shit. Scratch that. I know why, but my sympathy for him has just about run out.

"Well, fuck, I don't know what I was trying to say." He laughs as if that's sincere. He knows exactly what he just did. He wanted to point out that he stole my girlfriend and married her. It's pathetic, really. I couldn't care less that he has Hannah. Apparently, he's the only one who hasn't got a clue that she's been fucking his best friend for years.

"What he was trying to say is you landed yourself a good one, so don't fuck it up, you lucky son of a bitch," Elijah chimes in, his eyes holding mine with a geniality that feels sincere even though I know he's aware that this marriage is anything but genuine. Everyone shouts cheers, and I quickly take my shot, though I need ten of them to take the edge off.

"Hey, we have enough for pool volleyball. Evan, where's the net?" his friend Luke calls out. I'm pretty sure he's the one fucking Hannah. Interestingly, he's been hanging on some other girl he brought with him tonight. I haven't hung around Evan, Hannah, or the twins in years, so I couldn't tell you what the dynamic is, but even as an outsider, I can feel the tension. Hannah and Luke are clearly trying to make each other jealous. What I don't understand is why she married Evan to begin with.

Everyone sets their shot glass back down on the bar before swimming toward the volleyball area, but I don't miss the glare Parker serves Mackenzie as he sets his glass down.

"Do we have a problem, Michaelson?" I say, irritated that he hasn't let whatever this shit he has with our marriage go.

"Yeah, your wife has the wrong last name."

I start to rise out of instinct, but Mackenzie pushes herself down on my groin, stilling my movement. Tongue in cheek, I simmer, knowing I'll never let my rage get the best of me with her near. "She has the name she was always meant to have, and the exact one she wants." I hold his eyes, and I know he sees it. I caught him, but he doesn't know how. "She's told you no twice now. Ask again, and I'll—"

"Connor, leave it alone. He knows this isn't—"

I cut Mackenzie off, pulling her flat against my front as I grab a delicious handful of her breast and bring my lips to her ear, my eyes never leaving Parker's as I whisper, "Say this isn't real. I dare you." With her breast in my hand and her ass against my groin, I abandon any fucks I gave about taunting Parker. I want my girl. I pull her lobe into my mouth and suck on it, only for her to tilt her head ever so slightly, granting me more access.

"Whatever. Don't come crying to me when he breaks your heart," Parker says before joining the others to play volleyball.

However, before he gets too far, she surprises me and says, "Who said I had one to break?" And fuck, if that doesn't make me want her more. I hold her tighter as my lips trail her neck, and my mind wanders back to our night at the bar on the dance floor where she and I ceased to exist, but this time, she doesn't float away with me.

"Stop, Connor. I'm not in the mood. You know I like your hands on me, but—" She attempts to push out of my arms, but I don't let her go. Instead, she turns, and her eyes widen as she sees my face for the first time in a week.

"Connor, what happened to your face?" Her hand reaches up to cup my cheek, and damn if I don't want to lean into her touch, but I don't. I pull back.

"It's nothing. Don't worry about it."

"You've ignored me all week, and now your face looks like that. It's not nothing. What happened? Connor, look, we don't have to like this shit, but we're in this together. We need to stop pushing each other away. This thing between us has an expiration date. So what? We both know that. I've felt like you made me your enemy from the start, and I don't understand it. Can't we just…" She trails off and breaks eye contact, looking across the pool toward no one. "I don't know, never mind. Forget it." Her eyes come back to mine. "Let me go."

"No, say it," I softly demand as I pull her tightly against my body and move away from the bar.

"Say what?" she asks as I walk her into deeper water.

"I want to know what you think it is that I don't want to hear."

My hands move from her waist to her ass as I drop lower into the water. She bites her plump bottom lip, the one I've wanted to claim for my own since we met, but she refuses to give me.

Pressing my forehead to hers, I say, "Tell me."

"No, I've given you more than you gave me. If you want it, you have to give me something."

I groan and squeeze her ass before pressing my erection firmly against her center. "What do you want?"

She pulls back, unwrapping one of her hands from around my neck to touch the stitches over my right eyebrow. "I want to know a lot of things, but I will start with this. Tell me how you got this."

I close my eyes, knowing she won't be happy when she hears what I'm about to say, but I own it anyway. It was always going to happen. I just hadn't planned on fucking my face up in the process.

"I crashed the truck."

"What? How… Why?" she starts rambling in confusion.

Now I know she will be mad, but she asked for it. "You weren't going to give it up. It was a hard limit for you. You refused to discuss it."

Her hands drop to my chest, and she shakes her head. "You don't understand. I could afford that truck. I need it when this is over—"

"I do. It's you who doesn't understand, and I'm not asking you to. The car is yours. You don't owe me anything."

Knowing she's driving a safe, reliable vehicle with or without me brings me peace. I know it shouldn't. I'm not supposed to care, but I can't change that. I do.

"But why?"

"Does it matter if we both get what we want?"

"It shouldn't, but like you said, I want to hear it."

I can't help but groan and pull her close. Fuck, I just want to make her mine. Consequences be damned. But I don't trust her, not when I know who she dated. However, the more I'm around, the more I get to know her, the noise that surrounds us and complicates things fades out, and all that's left is me and her. I squeeze her ass hard, and her lips part with a gasp that I want to swallow.

"The list is endless, but let's start with, it was junk, then add that my father gave it to you. I said it once, but I'll say it again because, clearly, it needs repeating. It's my last name attached to yours that makes you mine to protect and mine to fuck." I grind my hard cock against her pussy, which I'm sure is more than ready to be filled. Even in this cool water, I can feel her heat.

Her hands glide up my chest and back around my neck, blazing a trail of heat in their wake before she teases, "That last part wasn't on the table the night we said our vows."

There's only one reason for her coyness now. Like me, she's not ready to admit that this could be more, but that's okay. I'm not asking for forever. I'm asking for now. I want to know that, at this moment, she's mine. However, I won't push, not now anyway. I can't ask something of her that I'm not ready to give myself, even though I want to demand it.

So I tease her right back, knowing damn well what she was suggesting earlier. I squeeze her ass and dip my head so that my lips are on her shoulder. "So, just to be clear, this is off the table." I grind my cock against her pussy. "And my wife wasn't suggesting that we be friends with benefits?"

The sexiest little moan escapes her throat as my mouth makes its way up her neck, but our moment is cut short when a volleyball bounces off my shoulder.

"What the fuck?" I grind out as I turn with a glare to find Evan laughing.

"Sorry. Come on, toss it back. Let's play."

"Fuck off. I'm busy."

I don't toss the ball back. Instead, I take a few more steps in the direction I was heading and enter the grotto.

"Your brother is a douche."

"He's not my brother."

"But I thought Cameron said—"

"I'm an only child. Cameron and Evan are charity cases. That's not me trying to be an ass. That's just facts. Cameron lost her parents in a tragic car accident, and Evan's mom was a drug addict who couldn't get her shit together. His mother was working with mine on a charity event when she confided to my mom that she was going to check herself into a rehab facility. She had no family to help with Evan, so my mom agreed to be his legal guardian while she got treatment. The day after the paperwork was signed, she disappeared. It's why I don't push back when he makes his snide remarks. I've always felt bad for him, but the older we get, the more I see it differently. When we were younger, I thought his snarky comments were how he dealt with abandonment issues, but now I only see jealousy and resentment. Hannah is not worth stealing, but he pursued her because she was mine. It might sound arrogant as fuck, but I think he wants to live my life. My name, my money, my family—it's my legacy, and he wants it."

Her eyes search mine, and I can't tell what she's thinking, but she's clearly deep in thought. "Is she the reason you never moved into the house?"

Cameron must have been in her ear, giving her the details of who Hannah was before they came outside. I don't like feeling like someone else has told my story and tinted how she sees me or what she thinks she knows. However, I can't blame that all on Cameron. I have yet to be forthcoming with anything. I walk her into the circular seating area at the back of the grotto and set her on the ledge.

"In the beginning, yes. I was hurt. I didn't want to move into a house that I'd expected to share with someone else, but she wasn't 'the reason.' She was just an easy excuse, an easy lie." I slowly drag my hands up her thighs until I reach the strings on her bikini. "Did I give you enough?" I kiss her thigh. "Can I fuck my wife now?"

"Connor," she screeches as I pull at the strings. "Someone will see us."

If that is her only reason to say no, I'm in. "No one will see. It's an unspoken rule. When two people come in here, you stay the fuck out." I pull her to the edge so that my chest is at her stomach, place a kiss between her breasts, and pull the strings at her back. Her perfect tits easily fall out. The thin piece of fabric was barely supporting them as it was. Her arm immediately moves to cover herself, and she turns to look behind her. "Hey, look at me." I grab her arms and pull them away. Those fucking eyes threaten to puncture a hole in the thick armor I've built around the place my heart used to be, and for a moment, I stumble. "Let me see you…" There's no way this woman doesn't feel what I'm saying right now. I'm not looking at her breasts. I'm looking straight into her soul. There is no way she doesn't feel the weight of my words.

She lets her arms fall, and I hold her eyes as I reach up and untie the last string around her neck so she's fully bared to me. "My God, you're so damn beautiful."

My mouth covers one of her nipples before she starts overthinking this. I need her to stay with me. I don't want her to think about who might walk in or what happens next. I just need her to be in the here and now. As my tongue swirls and sucks her nipple until it's stiff, I tug and twist the other before pushing them together and enjoying their weight in my hands. They're more than a handful and fucking perfect. "I love your tits, but tell me: did this pussy miss my mouth as much as my tongue missed its taste?"

I release her breasts and kiss a trail of open-mouthed kisses down her stomach before reaching the one place I've dreamed of endlessly since night one. I pull her forward slightly and kiss her thigh before bringing my mouth to her center, ready to take what I want. Her fingers run through my hair, making my scalp tingle, and then she pulls my hair in protest. "Connor, I-I can't…"

CHAPTER 17
MACKENZIE

What am I doing? This is crazy. He's just given me so many words without actually saying anything at all. My brain has had zero time to process any of it. When his hands are on me, everything else fades away, and I feel like what we have is so much more, but I need more. I thought I could handle having him once. I had to know what having him felt like, and fuck if it wasn't everything, but a second will surely wreck me. It's slowly breaking me now, and we haven't even fucked.

"Connor, I-I can't…"

His big hands grip my ass as he peers up at me. Those dark eyes hooded with sheer desire have me clenching before he licks me straight up my center. *Shit.* I know he felt that, which doesn't help my plea for him to stop.

"Whatever it is you're thinking, stop. I already told you no one is going to see you. I want this." He licks me once more, sending a shiver straight down my spine. "And you want this. Let it happen."

Why does that not make it better? Why can't that be enough? Why am I asking myself questions I already know the answers to? It's not enough because I had one taste and want more. It's not enough because I don't want to be just another girl he fucked in the grotto, and while I need to be close to him, I don't have to lose whatever pieces of me I've slowly stitched back together over the past few months. God, now I'm picturing him bringing other girls in here.

I close my eyes and try to swallow down the hurt. He's a one-night-stand type of guy. I've known that from day one, and just because his name is currently attached to mine doesn't change that.

"Hey, don't do that. I know whatever this is, it's not normal." He rests his chin on my stomach, and his eyes soften. "I have no right to ask this of you, but I'm going to anyway because this, right now, you and me like this—it's never been like this. Don't push me out." His voice is tender. I bite the corner of my mouth and close my eyes. I want this. I do, but… "I promise no one will see you, but you should know, if there was any question of if this was real before, there's not now. You coming in here with me made it crystal fucking clear you belong to me. If you want me to stop, I will, but it doesn't change anyone's perception."

What he doesn't see is, I don't care about anyone else's perception but his. His thumbs brush over my hips in a manner meant to soothe as I try to decide if I can do this. That perfect mouth, the one that makes me feel everything every time it touches my skin, kisses my ribcage right beneath my breast before he repeats the movement on the other side, and I go weak. This version of him, the one that wants all of me, is the one I not only crave but need.

When I don't give him any more words and instead watch as he worships my body, his eyes flash up to mine, and I know he sees it. He has me, and for now, I have him, too.

He slowly descends, returning to where I want him most, his hands finding my knees as he gently pushes my legs open once more. The vulnerability I feel in this position is too much. Sure, I've had sex, and he's not the first man to go down on me, but he is the first to put me on display, and I've never seen a man look at me with the intensity and hunger I see in those impossibly dark eyes. I quickly snap my legs closed, and he growls. *Damn, Mac, you want this. Let him have it.*

"Connor—" I start in but am quickly cut off when he rises out of the water, his arms planted on either side of me, and his mouth finds my neck.

"What does my wife need? Do you need more words? Would it help if I told you you're the first?" he says, biting my lobe.

My head quickly spins as I try to focus on what he's saying. I feel like there are a bunch of words I somehow missed. "What?" I breathlessly question as he peppers my collarbone with kisses.

"You think I've fucked other girls right here. But I haven't, and I didn't mean what I said that first night at the house. I don't think you're a slut. That's not what this is."

That's not where I was going, but fuck if I don't love hearing it. Why is he doing this? *Stop it, you stupid fucking heart. He didn't even invite you here today. You're just his fake wife. There's an expiration date on this marriage. He's thinking with his dick. STOP.*

I quickly change the subject away from me, needing the distraction to separate my heart from my desire. "You expect me to believe you had this grotto growing up and never fucked in here?"

"You met my high school girlfriend out there. We never fucked," he says as his lips kiss their way across my jaw, coming too close for comfort to my mouth.

I dip my head away and ask another question. "Why?"

"She told me she was waiting for marriage. Turns out she was just waiting for Evan."

Damn, that relationship had to have taken a toll on him. He's a man. He can sit here and try to spin whatever bullshit he wants about how she wasn't the only reason he didn't move into that house, but I guarantee, based on everything I've learned, it was a bigger one than he's making it. Everyone knows a young heart is raw and exposed. It hasn't lived enough to know how to protect itself. His heart has long since been hardened. She was clearly just the first, because there's at least one more that undoubtedly took a toll on this man, and that's the mother of his daughter. Knowing these things shouldn't change anything for me, but it does. It makes this hardened heart before me more human. It gives me hope that his hate isn't because of me, or for me, but because of his past—one I can't change. But maybe, even if only for a little while, I can show him he's worthy of someone who would treat his heart right.

"Are you going to let me put that pretty pussy in my mouth now?" My thighs clench of their own accord, and he notices. "I'm going to take that as a yes." His teeth graze my nipple as he makes his descent, leaving a trail of open-mouthed kisses down my torso until he reaches my pubic bone, where, this time, I spread my legs wide for him. He pulls me forward, positions me where he wants me, and I let him.

I've always been attracted to him. That was never the issue. He's disgustingly beautiful for a man, and now he's somehow managed to say all the right words, and I can't think of why I even closed my legs to begin with. He positions his mouth centimeters away from my lips, his hot breath enough to make me clench, and then those dark, velvety eyes land on mine as his tongue darts out and licks me straight up my center.

"Fuck." I hiss as I throw my head back in pleasure. I'm so fucking wound up. I've needed more of him since the first night, and I'm done not taking it. Our time together is limited. We're already using each other. *Why can't I use him for this?*

I know he must echo the same sentiments because a throaty, deep moan of appreciation rumbles up from his chest and vibrates against my center as his tongue dips inside me. I mercilessly start to rock against his face in search of more, and that's when he slides in a thick digit. I feel myself clench around it, wishing it were more.

"You have a greedy pussy, wife," he says as he adds another finger and pumps into me a little harder on the next thrust while sucking my bundle of nerves into his mouth.

"Oh fuck." My vision blurs, and I'm about to come. I clench hard, only for him to pull back. His mouth, his fingers. Gone. My eyes pop open to see why he stopped, only to find him staring at me with a look of indifference on his face. "What are you doing?"

"While I'm more than willing to do the work, I'm not convinced you want it. If you want to come, you're going to take it."

He pops out of the water and sits on the smooth stone beside me. My chest is still heaving, my breathing erratic from being on the cusp of orgasm, but I manage to find my words all the same.

"Is that a challenge?"

He shrugs. "No. I just need to know I'm not taking something you don't want to give."

The night in the shower, I said, "What if I don't want this?" I never verbally gave him an answer, and tonight, I hesitated more than once. It clearly affected him, not to mention there's a woman outside who never took it. I get it now. He needs reassurance, too. I can't help but wonder if that's what kept him from making another move this week. If that's why he didn't come home. Yes, I didn't stop him. I wanted it, but in his mind, he forced himself on me. He took something I wasn't offering. This must be the Connor the world used to see: sweet, compassionate, and thoughtful. Without pause, I'm throwing my leg over his lap and straddling him.

His lips quirk up into the smallest of satisfied smiles. "Is my wife going to take me bare?"

"Are you clean?" I ask as I dip my fingers into his shorts

and wrap my hand around his length, giving him a stroke as I await his response.

"Yes, you're the first person I've been with in months, and I get tested regularly," he answers as I flip the band of his shorts down and push up on my knees to rub his tip through my folds. "Fuuuck…" he draws out as I bring him to my entrance, only to pull back and grind against him. "Don't tease me, wife. Take it or get off."

I can't help but tease him, though. It feels too good, and I don't want this moment to end too soon. When we are intimate, he gives me more. We cease to be Connor and Mackenzie, the two people forced into marriage, and we fall back into the two people who met at the bar. The two people who had instant chemistry, and when it's like this, it feels like in some alternate universe, he could really be mine. I run his tip through my heated flesh one more time before putting him at my entrance and slowly taking him in. I brace myself on his shoulders and start to lower myself, watching every inch disappear inside me as I slowly push down and pull up to get acclimated. He's only the second person I've been with, and compared to my ex, he's enormous. I never thought Zane was small, but he's definitely on the smaller side compared to Connor.

His hands glide up my hips as I find what feels right, and his touch melts me. Those hands on my body were the missing piece. I'm right where I need to be as long as I'm there with him. I bottom out deliciously full, with every inch of him inside me. When I bring my eyes up, they clash with his as I find him watching me, mouth slack, eyes dark and packed with all the words I'd imagine he'd say if I were his girl. If I could be his forever.

"You're fucking perfect, Mackenzie. Every inch of you." He squeezes my hips, and his eyes search mine. "Do you understand me? Perfect."

I nod because I can't talk. Talking will only ruin this. I

know what he's saying, or at least I think I do. Same as me. If all this shit wasn't between us, if we had met under different circumstances, if we weren't both puppets in some bigger game, there's a chance this could be so much more. That's when I remind myself: be happy with what you have. Love every second now and take it home with you, knowing that it's what you want from whoever comes next, to feel so utterly and wholly desired, wanted, beautiful, and maybe even loved.

His big hands glide up my ribs and cup my breasts, pushing them together before flicking his tongue over my erect nipples. There's nowhere this man can touch me that my body doesn't light up inside. I feel heat everywhere, and it spurs me on. It gives me confidence to take what I want from him, and he's so fucking deep, hitting a spot I didn't even know existed until him. I pull up just to throw myself back down hard, and when I do, I can't help but let out a delicious moan of pure ecstasy. It's never felt so damn good.

"My little wife is driving me crazy. Do you know how sexy it is when you watch yourself take my cock?" His hands squeeze my ass hard, and I whimper as he slams me down and pushes up into me simultaneously. His words and vigor make me pick up my pace as I mercilessly chase my orgasm.

"Fuck, listen to how wet you are for me. The sound of this pussy slapping against my balls and echoing off these walls is intoxicating. It's my second favorite sound."

I'm so damn close. I slow my pace, not wanting this to end. He feels too damn good, and we fit so well. My walls start to clench, and he closes his eyes with a groan.

"You need to get there."

And I will, but only after I get something else. "What's your first favorite sound?"

"The sexy little mewls and whimpers you make with my cock inside you."

Those words, coupled with the way my nipples are rubbing against his chest as he holds me close, send me spiraling. I expected him to lie down and watch me ride him, but he didn't. His hands never left my body. He held me close the entire time like I was something that should be cherished. As though this was more than sex.

"Fuck, fuck, fuck," he hisses as he loses himself, holding my hips still as he shoots his load deep. I can feel him coating my walls, the force making my pussy spasm and crave more. His cock is still buried deep when his mouth seeks mine, but I turn away. "I want to kiss my wife," he growls.

I shake my head. "No, you can put your mouth anywhere on my body, just not on my lips."

"They're mine." He grabs my jaw firmly, forcing me to meet his gaze. "You're mine."

And then he's bringing his mouth closer. "Please don't," I beg as I close my eyes.

"Why?" he questions, his tone gentler but confused.

"Because you don't plan on keeping me. Let's not make this more than it is."

I open my eyes, and I see it. Our moment is over. We're back to the here and now, where there's this bottomless void between us that neither of us dares to cross, for the stakes are too high. The risk is too great. It's clear whatever we have is something, but we also have something more precious hanging in the balance.

As I move to get off him, he lets me go, but when I reach for my top, his hand covers mine.

"It doesn't mean I don't want to."

I'm just toweling off after getting out of the pool, and my head is a straight mess. *Why the fuck did he have to give me those parting words?* Not to mention the 'these are mine—you're mine' comments. I can't figure out where his head is at. It's the theme of our relationship. I wordlessly put my swimsuit back on and exited the cave without him. There wasn't going to be any other way. We couldn't very well walk out the same way we walked in. Going into the grotto, our heads were full of lust. Our judgment was clouded. After our release, we both came down and remembered our precarious situation.

But, as I waded out, I decided I'm done. He can have my secrets. I'm not going to figure this out on my own. I was thrown into all this. A blindfold was removed from my eyes, but I still have no idea what I'm dealing with or why I'm here. Josh said to get closer to Connor. He hasn't told me not to say anything, which could very well be implied, but what do I have to lose? The more I hear about the Callahans from other people and what I witness, they are good people. Guarded, yes, but callous, no.

I've just wrapped a towel around me when Hannah approaches, her arms crossed and her face smug.

"I can see right through your little façade. You think I don't know what you tried to do back there?"

"I'm not sure what you're talking about."

"Connor was mine first, and everyone knows he never got over me. You don't know Connor like I do and—"

I cut her off with a wave of my hand when I see where this is going. "Jealousy doesn't look good on you. You had the boy, but I got the man. Get over it."

Connor walks up behind her. "Wrong. She never had the boy. He's been right here waiting for you." He walks over and puts his arm around my shoulders. "If you and your husband want to continue coming around, I better not catch either of you disrespecting my wife."

An hour ago, I would have told you those words were all part of an act, but I can't be sure after what we shared in the grotto. I told him where I stood. I made it clear why I didn't want to kiss him because this wasn't going to be anything more, and then he walks up with that. Those words could have been for appearances, or a scorned ex getting in his dig, but they felt like more. Just like all his words, today felt like more.

"Come on, let's go home."

He grabs my hand and laces our fingers together, and my stomach twists into knots. I'm caught between allowing it and pulling back, but our moment is cut short because a woman bearing a striking resemblance to Connor walks out the back door and pins me with a glare full of intrigue and careful wariness.

"Con, I was wondering when I would meet your wife. I've been back in town for two days. I thought I'd at least get a call for dinner."

She walks toward me and extends her hand. "Moira Michaelson."

"Mackenzie—" I start as I move to shake her hand, only to be rudely cut off.

Connor reaches across my body and halts my arm. "She knows who you are."

"That might be true, but we haven't met."

A tall man appears in the doorway behind her, his features a stark contrast to hers. Moira has long dark hair, charcoal eyes like Connor's, and porcelain skin. The man behind her is tall, though not as tall as Everett, and bears a striking resemblance to Matthew McConaughey, curly locks, beard, and all.

"There's no need to disrespect your mother, Connor."

"She might have your last name, but she's my mother, and I'll speak to her as I see fit, with the same respect she's given me."

"That's enough, Connor." Everett appears.

Moira holds her hands up. "Stop, we're making a scene. Connor, please come inside. I think it's time we talk."

She steps to the side and holds her arm out for both of us. I don't take more than one step before Connor pulls me back.

"Can I talk to you for a second?"

I furrow my brow and search his eyes, but he drops his gaze before I can gauge what he wants. Pulling me to the side, he says, "I need you to go home. This is something I need to do alone."

I yank my hand out of his. "Connor, I deserve to be a part of that conversation."

He shakes his head. "You're not wrong, but I came here tonight to talk to my father alone. It's why I didn't invite you to begin with. I never planned on staying, but then you showed up and…" He looks toward the pool and his face contorts with annoyance. "Go home, Mackenzie." His eyes return to mine and soften just enough for me to believe the problem isn't with me but everything else. "I promise I'll come home after."

I should push back, but something tells me I wouldn't get the answers I'm looking for going into that conversation. I'm sure whatever topics they discuss would be censored for my benefit anyway, and honestly, everything I learned here today already has my brain on information overload. Time alone with my thoughts would be good. I need to get away, so I can pick through all of it and decide what's real.

"I'm going to hold you to that promise. I'd like to talk."

His eyes lock onto mine. "Okay, we'll talk."

CHAPTER 18
CONNOR

"The way you talked to your mother out there was out of line. I raised you better than that."

I throw myself into the chair in my father's office, perturbed with all these comments on my attitude. "You're one to talk. You have no room—"

"Connor, that's enough. I've watched you berate your father and paint him into a light he doesn't deserve since the divorce, and I'm done. He doesn't deserve your hate. He's done nothing but be a supportive husband and loving father. The divorce was not his idea. I asked for this. It was always going to end like this."

"What the hell is that supposed to mean?"

I can't help but put my head in my hands as my stomach churns. I know I'm about to get the confirmation I've felt in my bones since the day I heard about the divorce. It was all a lie. We were never a big, happy family. Their marriage was a sham, just like mine.

"Connor, are you ready to listen, or will you continue to fight us?" My father's voice is terse, which only further pisses me off.

"Why do you guys think I don't deserve to be upset? I've

never understood that. You think I don't know you're about to tell me everything was a lie? I spent my entire life believing we had a happy family, but more than that, I made life-altering choices that supported the values the two of you instilled in me. I poured myself into this family, into something I thought we stood for, and then you guys pulled the rug out from under me on top of everything else that's been put on my plate. So excuse me if my reaction doesn't fit the mold you expected me to fill. Neither of you has room to comment on behavior. It's not like you have led by example yourselves recently."

I bite my tongue before I say things I can't unsay. They know exactly what I'm saying without the words. My mother married a man two months after her divorce from my father was finalized. That move alone screams infidelity. Regardless of which one of them committed the sin, they both walk away with the stain of a failed marriage. However, their sins only scratch the surface of the anger that has settled over me since they announced their split. Out of everyone in my life, they know the depth of the sacrifice I made and why I made it all those years ago. It's why I thought I'd at least earned their damn respect.

"Connor, that's unfair. Your life was not fake. Our family was happy, and we were happy. Your father and I were just never in love."

"Great, you married each other because you fucked around and got knocked up. That makes it so much better. I'm sorry if hearing that I was one of those kids with parents who stayed together for my sake doesn't give me warm fuzzies inside. Everyone knows that is bullshit."

My father sets his cognac down on the desk with enough force to draw my attention away from my mother and to him. "We didn't marry because of you, and we didn't stay married for you. While we love you, Connor, not everything is about you. Though I understand how you could come to that conclusion."

I flick my wrist. "Care to elaborate on that?"

My parents share a knowing look before my mother says, "You've always known that our family donated money to charities that supported victims of sexual violence and assault, and when you were in high school, you learned that it was because of me. You never asked what happened, and I always assumed you didn't want to know. I reasoned that knowing it existed was enough for you. But I think it's time you heard the story. Our marriage was arranged like yours. Your father married me to protect me."

My mother moves to sit in the upholstered wingback chair adjacent to mine, and my father pushes her a glass of cognac across his desk. She quickly takes a drink before clearing her throat.

"You know Aunt Janey raised me after my mother died when I was in middle school, but what you didn't know is that Uncle Craig was my abuser."

My mother's hand trembles ever so slightly before she takes another sip of liquid courage. I remember meeting Uncle Craig a handful of times. For the most part, he didn't come around. Aunt Janey would visit occasionally, but she was always alone. Her excuse for coming alone, without fail: Uncle Craig had to work. Because he was on the police force, I never thought anything of it, but now the pieces are slowly starting to fit together.

"It wasn't until high school that he tried anything, and at first, I couldn't be sure that I didn't imagine it. I remember waking up on the couch one night after falling asleep watching a movie. The room was pitch-black aside from the glow of the TV in front of me, and I immediately felt that sixth sense of being watched. I knew I wasn't alone in that room, but I didn't dare move because I could feel it in my bones if I moved, someone else was going to move. The blanket I had used to cover up had fallen to the floor, and I knew my night shorts had ridden up. The tiniest of shivers ran up my spine, and I knew Uncle Craig was behind me. I kept my eyes closed, determined to make it a dream and wish it away, and at least for that night, I had. I wasn't so lucky a few months later."

My father interrupts. "Moira, I'm not asking you to do this. You don't have to relive these memories."

She shakes her head. "No, our son apparently needs a reminder of the kind, selfless man his father is. Plus, he deserves the truth. I'm done hiding. If I want to move on, I have to let it hurt and let it go."

Another swig, another shot of courage, and she's back. "I'll spare you the details, but two months later, Craig made his move in the middle of the night, and I was taken against my will. The next day at school, I was clearly upset and distraught. I had no one to turn to. I couldn't tell Aunt Janey. I didn't think she'd believe me, and then, even if she did, what could she do when her husband was the chief of police? There was no escape. It was our word against his. I was convinced I'd have to bottle it up and keep it to myself, but my boyfriend knew without words what had happened. Kipp was furious—"

I cut her off. "Wait, Kipp was your high school boyfriend?"

I'd heard rumors of that, but rumors are a dime a dozen in a small town like ours. Hell, just being friendly with someone of the opposite sex in the same grade could start rumors of wedding bells.

"Yes, Kipp was my high school boyfriend and one of your dad's best friends until…"

My mother puts her hand on her stomach as though she might be sick, and my father says, "Moira, he doesn't need the details. Please let me finish it."

She nods her agreement before sitting deeper into the chair with her drink, a void expression on her face, and it's then I know I don't need the details. I never needed them, but I'd be lying if I said I didn't want to know how my mother and father came to be. They were teen parents, so I always assumed that meant they were high school sweethearts. That's what I get for assuming.

"Kipp did his best to be around, but he couldn't protect her at night until finally, one night, he stayed. He knew he'd get caught, but he also knew that meant so would Craig. For a while, it was quiet, and his method seemed to have worked. Craig wasn't sneaking into her room anymore, knowing someone else could catch him, but that's when he set us up. Kipp and I were varsity captains and top of our class. One night, we went to the Fields, as high school kids do, for a bonfire and beer, and he showed up to break up the party. He slapped everyone with MIPs and a few other bullshit charges, and it was clear why. He wanted to make us look like a bunch of punk kids, should we come forward with allegations.

"That night, he threw your mother in the back of his car, and Kipp went after him. All the other cops had left. The party had been broken up. It was just the three of us and him. Kipp had confided in me, and I wasn't going to step in, but when he busted out his baton, I couldn't do anything, and that's when it dawned on me to use my dad. Your grandfather had just been elected as the new District Attorney. Kipp must have had the same idea when he saw me step in to break up the fight because when Craig told me to stay out of it, Kipp said, 'You won't put another finger on Moira. Do you know who his father is?' But Craig didn't back down. He was out for blood. He knew I wasn't dating your mother. He wasn't about to be put in his place by three teenagers, so he hit back. Kipp insisted that he and Moira were just friends and I was your mother's boyfriend, hoping that Craig would back off because of my family connections, and that's when Craig played his filthy perverted hand and made us prove it."

I scrub my hand up my face and pinch the bridge of my nose, trying to hold back the raw emotions that threaten to steal what remaining sanity I have. "Are you telling me I was conceived that night? When some piece of shit made you two —" I can't even say the words. I never want to hear about my parents' sex life, let alone find out I'm a product of some messed up sexual assault.

My mother rushes out, "No, Connor. I swear on my life you were not conceived that night. It's just our story. This is how your father and I became a couple. After that night, Craig never laid a finger on me again because I belonged to Everett, and his family had more power than him."

"Why didn't you guys just go to Grandpa? He would have helped."

"Things were very different back then, and Craig wasn't a hated police chief. It wouldn't have been easy for your grandfather to go after him. For one, there was no proof. It was our word against his. We had to sit and wait for him to mess up again so that we could build a case."

A lot of things have changed in the past thirty years, that's for sure. If those same things had happened today, the likelihood of someone believing my mother would be greater, but all that aside, it doesn't explain the rest. "Why didn't you just fake it?"

My father's eyes lock on mine, and I see it. He didn't fake it because he loved her, but there was nothing he could do about not being the one, and fuck if that doesn't resonate with me now. It's how I feel when I look at Mackenzie, believing Trent still means something to her.

"Your father and I did and do care for each other deeply, Connor. You were conceived out of love. In the beginning, even though circumstances pushed us together, we felt like it was love. When you go through a traumatic circumstance like that, you lean on the person who was there with you more. When we got pregnant, it was love. It just wasn't the right kind of love. You can love someone and not be in love. There's a difference."

This time, when I look at my father, his gaze is on his glass of cognac, and I know it's because his thoughts differ from my mother's. When it comes to emotions and feelings, my father has always been a man of few words. Knowing the truth about my parents should change things. I should have sympathy for their trials and tribulations, and maybe I would if they hadn't forced the same fate on me.

It's that thought that has me asking, "Why would you force this marriage to Mackenzie on me? Why would you want me to endure the same trauma?"

"It was never going to be you, Connor. It was going to be Parker. However, you changed it. You both changed it."

That explains why Parker continues to pursue her even though she's turned him down multiple times.

"How the fuck did I change it?"

"You saw her first. Call it fate, destiny, kismet, whatever you want, but you hit on the wrong girl—or maybe the right girl. Elijah was there to pick her up, and he saw you, and to top it off, she never opened the damn letter that was passed to her. There were many things in play that night, and none happened as they should have. I couldn't very well marry her off to Parker after you fucked her in the bathroom."

My fists clench of their own accord because I don't like the derogatory tone associated with his comment.

"I didn't fuck her in the bathroom."

"Either way, you wanted her, and she clearly wanted you. Elijah gave me a full account of the events that took place afterward. She was clearly affected or, as Elijah said, enamored. He told her to read the letter, and by the time I went to the pool house the next morning, she still hadn't read it. I can't say that's all because of you. I'd be lying if I told you I didn't believe she's well aware of this setup. It's why I gave her the letter. I laid the bait, and she didn't take it. She didn't fucking take it, Connor. That letter was a test."

"What was in the letter?"

"Her new name and summer job as a camp counselor at Twin Rivers."

My father's eyes hold mine, and I can tell I'm missing something. Her new name was no doubt Mackenzie Michaelson. He just said as much when he said she was always meant to be Parker's, but why the hell would he send her off to be a camp counselor at Summer's camp? What purpose would that have served?

I'm just about to question him when my phone rings. It's Cayden. He's been radio silent while visiting Mackenzie's old stomping grounds in Montana, and there's no way I'm missing this call for more of my parents' spin bullshit.

CHAPTER 19
MACKENZIE

I'm unsure why I believed Connor when he said he would come home last night. He's been nothing if not unreliable and unpredictable. Every time I've thought we made some type of connection, he proves me wrong, showing me that everything I thought was real was only a figment of my imagination.

I stayed up until 1:00 a.m. last night waiting for him. I spent hours replaying our time together, the note from Josh, my interaction with Everett, and all that I've learned since coming to Waterloo. Those things occupied my mind, but I genuinely thought I had at least earned a conversation. I felt, after everything, he wanted at least the same out of me. Even if he didn't care about my story, I assumed he'd at least want to pick my brain to figure out his father's angle. It was clear on our wedding day that all of this was sprung on him, and he didn't have all the pieces, but no, it's 2:00 p.m. on Saturday, and he still hasn't come home.

This is the first Saturday I've had off since arriving in Waterloo, and I needed something to occupy my mind and help pass the time. I woke up at the crack of dawn after a restless night's sleep and couldn't stay in bed any longer.

Despite being almost a mile long, the gravel driveway leading up to the house beckoned me. Now I understand why. It held my project at the end. Once I reached the main road, I spotted the mailbox, and out of instinct, I checked it. It clearly had been weeks since it was checked. Most of the mail was junk, but there were two postcards from his daughter, and I quickly read them both, soaking in every word, trying to get a glimpse of the man my heart can't stop yearning for no matter how much I fight it.

Coach,

Week one has been fun. We got our cabin assignments, met all the counselors, learned our stations, and I tried every activity they had just so I knew which ones I wanted to sign up for every week, but at night, I missed home. The nights make me want to come home. It's when I miss you the most. I know we moved, but when I return, I really want to do a sleepover at Holden and Aria's. When I think of home, it includes them. Have you started decorating the new house? Hopefully, Aria is helping. I'm excited to see my new room. I've been thinking about it, and I think purple could be a good color for a room.

Love you, Coach.
Your Sunshine

Why do I love this little girl already? Their nicknames pulled at my heart in ways they shouldn't. The first letter made me fall even harder than I already am. It's clear that little girl is his everything. They're all each other have. She is eight, and I can sense her moxie through her writing. Summer said she missed home, but she was obviously downplaying it for her dad's sake. Connor would probably jump on the first plane to Maine if he sensed one ounce of regret in this little girl's tone. She talked about missing home and quickly changed the subject to the new house. Her excitement for their next chapter and the following letter was even more revealing.

Coach,

Week two! Has it felt like a lot longer for you, too? I was thinking if you need something to pass the time, I've officially decided I like purple. Last week, I was still undecided, but I'm all in. My new friend Brook's favorite color is purple, too. Maybe you could paint my room while I'm away. I like light shades, not dark shades of purple. It would be too dark at night. This week, I started archery. When I get home, I was thinking maybe we could look at crossbows together. I still don't want to shoot a deer, but I'd like to walk the target-shooting trail you go on with Uncle H. I want to do that.

P.S. The nights aren't as hard, but I still miss you, Coach.

Your Sunshine

By the time I returned to the house from my jog, my mind was made on what I'd be doing today. I ran up to the local hardware store, picked out a purple shade that I thought would be perfect, and got all the supplies I needed to do the job. Back home, I worked at a local hardware store. When I thought about college, my mind always went to design, but there weren't any local colleges that specialized in interior design, and honestly, with the internet and social media, you can design and build your business and a brand without design school. You just have to find your niche. Working at the hardware store, I ended up painting murals in two nurseries. It's not a lot, but it was a start and side money that helped make ends meet. I loved painting those rooms. I turned on my music and escaped for hours while I was painting, and that's precisely what I plan to do now.

I found some old linens in the basement that I had already taken upstairs for drop cloths, and I pulled an old T-shirt out of the dresser in my room so I didn't ruin any of the designer clothes Everett purchased for me. While I may not have bought them, the thought of getting paint on a sixty-dollar athletic crop top hurts my poor girl soul. I grab my phone from the bedroom for music when I hear the front door open. Great, the asshole decided to come home after all. Maybe I'll get lucky, and he'll go straight to his room. The sound of boots approaching on the hardwood floors tells me I'm getting no such luck.

I steel my spine and school my face as I count to five before turning around. It doesn't matter that I'm mad at him. Connor affects me whether I want him to or not. I can't help it. Even now, my skin prickles with the awareness that he's currently staring at me, but I refuse to be weak or, better yet used, because that's what I feel like right now: fucking used. However, I realize I have no one to blame but myself. Connor hasn't forced himself on me once. Every time, I've let him in, but that's over.

Turning around, I find him standing in the doorway, and those damn stitches above his right eye remind me of what he did and why. His expression is partially dejected, only further making me doubt the resolve I'd found. I quickly break eye contact and head toward the door, determined not to let his face or presence once again blur my reason for being here. Josh said to get close, not fuck him and fall in love. He puts his arm out to block my exit when I reach the door.

"Can we talk?" His tone is dripping with what sounds like regret, but I pay it no mind and instead dip under his arm. "Seriously, you're going to give me the silent treatment now? How old are we, Mackenzie?" he says as he follows me down the hall.

I veer off into the kitchen to grab a water bottle, aware that he's on my heels, and grab a granola bar because I plan on locking myself in that room until he's asleep or gone again, and instead settle on taking the whole damn box. Exiting the kitchen, he follows again, which catches me by surprise. I'd thought by now he had lost interest. After all, in our past arguments, it didn't take much.

"Where do you think you're going? You have no shoes on and no pants."

I have shorts on, and the shirt I found to paint in is simply oversized, but I don't correct him. The vixen inside me doesn't mind raising a little hell at his expense. If he's taking a look, good, I hope he's hard. It just makes shutting him out all the better. He's tortured me endlessly. It's his turn to squirm.

I've just grasped the banister to go upstairs when he covers my hand.

"Is this because of last night? Mackenzie, it's not what you think, I swear. I got into it with my parents and then got a call…" He trails off.

"It's fine," I answer, pulling my hand away.

"No, it's not fine. Everyone knows 'fine' is bullshit." As I start up the stairs, he continues, "I didn't mean to hurt you. That's not why I stayed away. Staying away was never to hurt you. This past week, last night, it was always for you. It's always been for you."

His words give me pause because they're all the things I want to hear, but they also piss me off. "I can't do this right now, Connor. I need to clear my head, and you need to leave me alone."

His hand frustratedly runs through his hair before he yells, "Why can't you see I'm doing this for you? I went there to talk about you. The call was about you. I'm trying to figure this shit out."

I can't help but put the same passion into my own response. "Did it ever occur once to fucking ask me? You've gone to everyone but me. Why is that? This is my life. My mess, and last night I told you I wanted to stay. We could have figured shit out together, but you pushed me away."

His chest is heaving, reassuring me the conviction behind his words is genuine. He is trying to help me, or at least he believes he is, but right now, it's too little too late.

"I did ask you. I stood right here and asked you, but you refused to confide in me."

That's bullshit. I know he's referring to the night I came home from his father's house with Parker. He's also conveniently leaving out that he refused to share any of his stories with me, but whatever the fact is, I did share with him, just not that night. I'm done playing his game. I refuse to let him win this one, and I'm done allowing him to twist the narrative, so I give him a truth he can't refute.

"Did I? Your family helps abuse victims. My boyfriend hit me. Now, here I am. That's my story." I start back up the stairs.

"Mackenzie, please…" His voice is empathetic, which makes the words I gave all the more bitter on my tongue. I don't want his damn pity. I walk faster just to get away and slam the door to the room I picked for Summer behind me, and when I do, I hear a loud crash downstairs. As my back slides down the door and I twist the lock, I know exactly what happened: he shattered the huge mirror that hung in the entryway. Good, I'm glad I'm not the only one who hasn't been fond of their own reflection.

I've been up here for hours. There are three rooms upstairs, and the one at the front of the house is where Connor has been sleeping. I didn't go in there, but I knew it wouldn't be the room I'd choose for a little girl anyway. When I was up here uncovering furniture, I knew this would be the perfect kid's room. It has a view of the lake at the bottom of the hill, and you can see a treehouse off in the distance. Plus, just like the front of the house, the back has these beautiful bay windows with built-in bench seats. It's perfect for reading, drawing, or just dreaming. I would have loved to have a room like this.

Pulling the furniture away from the walls and taping off the molding took a while, but most of the walls have now been painted. There's only one wall left, and my hands and arms are tired from rolling, so I decided to change it up and start using a brush. I've found that the best way to paint along the ceiling is with a brush. Those silly pads on rollers we used to sell at the hardware store did not do the job for me and took more time than they were worth. If you have a steady hand, using an angled brush does the job best. Honestly, you get it done in half the time.

I've just propped the ladder against the wall when the door opens. *Damn it.* I locked it earlier when I came up, but the last time I used the bathroom, I didn't think about it. The music has been on all day, and the house has been quiet. I assumed Connor had left, but seeing as how he's now standing in the doorway, eyes wide as he enters the room, it's clear he did not leave. His eyes roam over the space before finally landing on me and raking in my disheveled appearance from head to toe.

I clear my throat when I feel he's had more than his fair share of looking. I don't need his judgment. While I might do a great job of keeping my canvas clean—in this case, the walls—the same cannot be said for myself. This old T-shirt quickly became my rag anytime paint got on my hands, and I know I have a few splashes on my ankles, and the cute messy bun I styled this morning is no longer worthy of the title. It's more like a rat's nest now.

"Ahem, is there a reason you're in here? Is the house burning down? If not, I asked you to leave me alone."

His forehead momentarily wrinkles before he gestures to his outfit. "No, I came up to help. I read the postcards you left out on the island. Summer is mine. I want to help. Just go back to ignoring me. You seem to be pretty good at it."

I press my lips together, annoyed that he's in here stealing the little peace I had found for myself, but ultimately agree. "Fine." I can't very well tell him *no, you can't paint your daughter's room in your own house.*

"Is this wall getting painted, or are you planning on doing an accent wall over here?" he asks as he points to the wall I've yet to touch.

"If I say yes, it's an accent wall that's not getting painted, will you go away?"

"Not a chance."

Without words, he knows it's not a damn accent wall. I already have it tapped off with the roller and there's paint lying in front of it. He licks his bottom lip and attempts to hold back the tiniest smirk before heading to the adjacent wall. I decide to move my ladder and position myself so that not only is he at my back, he's not in my damn peripheral. The ass had the nerve to wear an old shirt with the sleeves cut off, showing every vein and tendon in his biceps. He doesn't just coach his players. He trains alongside them, and it shows.

When I get to the top of my ladder, I glance behind me one last time just to ensure he is indeed painting and not just here to pester me and be a pain in the ass, and when I look, he's already started rolling. I relax a little as I try to get my head back in the zone, but it's useless. My mind is already on him and all my unanswered questions. The most significant is that he said he went to his father's house last night to discuss me. *What the hell did the two of them have to talk about that Connor thought I shouldn't be present for?* Connor's comment to Parker at the pool bar is the other detail I've been stewing over. He alluded that he knew Parker cornered me again the other day about choosing him, which has left me feeling restless. If he knows about our interaction in the office, surely he knows about the flowers, and he's nothing if not obsessed with appearances, so it begs the question: has Connor not said anything because he doesn't know, or could those flowers possibly be the reason he wanted to speak to his father alone? *Does he know that Josh sent them?* Josh clearly knows Connor.

That last thought, coupled with the reach I try to attempt instead of moving my ladder, has me shrieking as I quickly try to find my balance on the ladder, but it's no use. I lose my footing, but I don't hit the ground. Instead, strong arms catch me, and those damn obsidian eyes lock onto me and show every ounce of the storm brewing beneath the surface. Well, fuck that.

I beat him to it. "Put me down. Stop touching me."

"Don't provoke me, and I won't." The sternness in his voice and the firm grip he has around my thighs and back assure me I was correct in my assessment. He's perturbed.

"You're still touching." I raise a brow.

"You're still provoking me." He licks his lips, and my eyes trace his tongue's path across his perfect Cupid's bow, which he doesn't miss. The storm brewing behind those coal-black eyes tempers. "Can we please talk?"

"No." My answer comes quickly, and his grip tightens a

fraction more, reminding me to add the next part. "Not while you're touching me."

Connor has some of the fullest, darkest eyebrows I've ever seen, and paired with his dark eyes, his expression appears so studied, as though he's always listening intently to every word. Most of the time, they amplify the gravity of his anger, but right now, the slight crinkle I see as he sets me down shows me something else. Regret. Yesterday, his touch was welcomed, and now it's not.

Once I'm on my own two feet again without his hands on me, I say, "Look, maybe we call it a day up here. I'm a mess—"

His fingers reach out and graze my shirt. "You could never be a mess wearing my shirt."

My cheeks instantly heat. How could they not? The man looks like he stepped out of a Dolce & Gabbana commercial. I'm starting to understand why my old boss used to say she could never stay mad at her husband as his eyes were too pretty. All of Connor is too pretty.

I don't immediately respond, and he drops his hand.

"Hey, let's finish this. I promise I'll keep my hands to myself, and"—he looks around the room—"maybe we can start small, and I can tell you about Summer."

Our eyes lock for a brief second once more, and I give him a subtle nod. I would rather finish this all tonight than come back to it tomorrow. Seeing the walls painted and the furniture back in place will help me decide what else the space needs besides kid stuff. This room was clearly used as a guest bedroom, which makes sense. From what I understand, it was his childhood home, and he's made it clear that he was an only child.

Walking back to his wall, he says, "Thanks for checking the mail. I should have thought about doing that. Summer called and asked for our address and told me to look for her letters with specific instructions not to throw them away." He sheepishly rubs the back of his neck. "It probably sounds pretty pathetic, considering my age, but I've never lived alone. I think I've maybe checked the mail all of two times in the past decade. Somehow, over the years, it always ended up on the counter or my bed without me ever going to the box myself."

He picks up the paint roller and dips it in the pan, giving me his back, and I focus back on my own wall to see where I need to move the ladder. I could stay silent and continue to give him the cold shoulder, but in the end, that gets me nowhere, no matter how much he might deserve it. Plus, hearing stories about Summer will only help me better understand her personality and the things she might like to see in her new room. So I throw him a bone.

"Yeah, I didn't really think to do it myself. After all, I have no reason to. No one knows I'm here. But when I went for a jog this morning down to the end of the road, it was there."

"You like to jog?"

"It's the one exercise I do regularly. I was restless and needed to clear my head."

"Don't run up to the road. If you want to run, I'll take you. Don't go alone."

That pinches my brows in confusion. He's making it sound as though it's not safe, and that makes zero sense. "Why the hell not? I don't even have a set of keys to this house. The door is always unlocked, but now running down the road is unsafe?"

He dips the roller in the pan for more paint. "Are we talking, or are we painting?"

I understand what he's saying. Minutes ago, I asked him for a break to avoid discussing anything serious. The reason being I don't want to argue. "We're painting, but I want to come back to that." I slowly climb the ladder, and since I don't hear the roller on the wall, I know his eyes are glued to my every step. "When does Summer come home?"

"She's supposed to be gone for eight weeks."

Yep, he's definitely watching me. I can tell by the way his voice carried.

"Eight weeks? That seems really long for a summer camp," I question before lining up my brush with the crown molding base that runs the ceiling's length.

"The camp is only four weeks. She'll be with family on the East Coast for the other four weeks to finish the summer. One of her cousins is with her."

Once I've finished covering the last of the exposed white wall along the ceiling and my hands have returned to the ladder, I hear the roller hit the wall.

"I noticed she calls you Coach. Does that mean she's a tomboy? I imagine growing up on a baseball field leans into that."

"Maybe, if you're asking if she knows the game and plays. Hell yeah. I coach, and Holden, her godfather, though she calls him Uncle H, is a professional baseball player. It's hard for her not to soak it in, but she still plays with Barbies from time to time, and she likes to dress up. I will say she's wise beyond her years. She's an old soul, for sure. There's not a person she meets that doesn't instantly fall in love with her."

"She must get that last part from her mother." I couldn't help myself. The words came out before my brain had time to fully process them.

I turn around, ready to apologize, but he keeps rolling.

"I guess you would think that. I haven't given you any reason to think differently."

"Connor, I am—"

"Don't say sorry. I haven't earned it."

He keeps rolling, and I move my ladder to the next wall as I contemplate changing the subject. The thing is, I want to know about his ex. Part of me needs to know the story about Summer's mom. I clear my throat and climb my ladder. "Is Summer's mom in the picture?"

The rolling stops, and for a second, I think I pushed too far, but then I remember I'm currently standing at the top of the ladder, and he did the same thing when I finished the trim on the last wall. He's watching.

"Are you asking because you want to know if there's another woman in the picture, or…"

I turn around and find him staring, just as I knew he would be. "Ha-ha, very funny." I spin the brush in my hand. "I'm going to go out on a limb and say you're not a slimy asshole who sleeps with his fake wife while there's another woman in the picture."

He bites his lip, and his eyes drop to my bare legs. "There's no one else. I was never involved with Summer's mom, and no, she's not in the picture."

Well, that was a loaded response. I turn around and bring my brush to the wall to dissect his answer. On the one hand, I'm too happy to hear that no one else is in the picture. My heart practically flipped in my chest when he confirmed as much, but it was quickly just as sad for the little girl whose mom isn't around. I grew up without a dad, and while my mom was amazing, there was always that dull ache in the recess of my mind that hurt and told me I wasn't enough, I wasn't worthy, and that's why he didn't stay. As for the part about not being involved with Summer's mom, I take that to mean one of his hookups ended up pregnant. Which reminds me, I need to find a doctor. I'm not on the pill. I take birth control shots, and I'm about due.

"Do you have a family doctor?"

He stops rolling the wall and turns to me, his face full of concern. "Why do you need a doctor?"

I put my hand on my hip. "It's none of your concern. You don't need a full rundown of my medical history. I need to refill my prescription."

"Prescription for what?"

I lay my brush down on the paint can. "Just forget it. I can go to a clinic. It's probably easier, anyway. I won't need an appointment. I'm going to get cleaned up. I've had enough painting for one day."

I've barely made it two steps toward the door before he says again, "Prescription for what?" his voice firmer, demanding a response.

"Relax. It's not that serious, but if you must know, I need to get my birth control shot."

"That's an appointment that won't be happening. My wife doesn't need birth control."

I put little weight into his comment. There's no way it's literal. I roll my eyes and grab the door. "I'm taking a shower. Leave the paint can when you're finished, and I'll trim that wall tomorrow."

CHAPTER 20
CONNOR

I've been lying in my bed, staring at the ceiling for the past hour. I can't sleep. A million thoughts are running through my head. I'm mad I left my father's house early. I'd hoped to press my dad for more information about Mackenzie and what he knew. While I understand a little more why he so easily pushed me into an arranged marriage, considering that's how his marriage to my mother started, it doesn't explain everything. My parents and I needed to have that conversation last night, but I'm not so naïve that I didn't notice the timing. They've been divorced for two years, and suddenly, now was the right time to tell me. Holly's case, while not active, considering she's been serving out her sentence, has always been a priority, which means things with her case started changing, and they didn't tell me.

I will admit I underestimated my mother. I quickly made her a victim, but she's clearly just as ruthless as my father. I didn't miss the subtle glances they gave each other, saying a million things with zero words. I don't doubt their story. They have no reason to lie about it, and considering their charity work and how they've thrown our doors open to help people like Cameron and Evan over the years, it all aligns. My parents mean well. It's their methods I question.

Right before the call came through, I felt like I was on the cusp of getting things from my father. He said he handed Mackenzie a letter, one she didn't open, and the contents held her new name and job. What I can't piece together is why he won't just come out and say what he means. Last night, he was talking in riddles the same way Garrett did. It's not as though that is something new. They are lawyers. They've always done that to some extent. The problem is, this all impacts Summer, and I can't help but feel that's why my father is being so secretive, and it scares the shit out of me. The only reason I haven't flown off the handle is because when it comes to that little girl, I know he would never risk a hair on her head.

I should have returned right after getting my call from Cayden, but I couldn't. I had to get shit done here. The first was stopping by Holden's to get my gun out of his safe, something I'm glad he wasn't home for. I didn't care to answer questions on why I needed it. As soon as River was born, all our muzzleloaders, hunting rifles, and guns we used for fucking around shooting targets were locked up. We probably should have been doing it all along, but it's a small town. Deer hunting and duck hunting are hobby sports. It's not rare to see a rifle in the back of a truck. Aria put her foot down, breaking us of our bad habits. When she would find one of our guns left out, instead of locking it up, she'd change the safe code and lock us out. Holden got smart and bought a new gun when she refused to give him one of his guns. Let's just say that fight lasted all of two days when she put him in the doghouse and denied him sex.

Two things I was sure of after my call with Cayden. First: Garrett's theory that Holly wasn't innocent like we previously thought was accurate, something I started leaning into after our meeting a few weeks back. The theory shed new light on some of the things that had been happening with Holly in jail. My father and the Marion Federal Prison Camp Superintendent attend the same country club and have occasionally shared a few rounds at the golf course. He knew my father was one of the lawyers on Holly's case and told him that a request had come across his desk to have her moved from Marion to Greenville. When my father asked if she had listed a reason, he said medical. Holly claimed she needed to be moved to Greenville so that her mental health could improve. She explained she couldn't keep in touch with her daughter because the Marion facility was too far of a drive. My father immediately knew that was bullshit. He's aware that Holly specifically asked that I not speak about Summer on our visits, not to mention I've never brought Summer to any visits. She has no idea that her mother is in jail. My father told him if it wasn't too much of an ask to let the move happen. It didn't make a difference to us where she was kept. However, a few months after being transferred to Greenville, she had to be moved again. This time for a security threat. Another inmate went after her with a shank, which we found highly suspicious. Those types of attacks are somewhat rare for Federal Prison Camps, considering most people are serving time for nonviolent crimes, and their sentences are relatively short compared to a jail or penitentiary.

The second certainty is that Mackenzie is indeed important. Not only was Holly not innocent, she was a major player. My father and Garrett have only really considered the Trent piece as it relates to Mackenzie. They overlooked the scorned ex, Holly Barden. She ran straight home, and the first thing she did before she went dark was visit Sweetwater Senior Living to pay a visit to one Tish Mercer. I'm confident that Mackenzie's mother, Tish, has no idea where she is. Her name has changed, and she had specific orders not to contact anyone back home, but Cayden did tell me he saw Holly pass an envelope to one of the staff, which means Tish is being watched. After her visit, she went dark. Cayden thought he had eyes on her, but she gave him the slip, and that's not all. Apparently, Tish Mercer's missing daughter was somewhat of a big deal in her hometown. Billings, Montana, isn't exactly a small town, but there's a tight-knit community in the part she is from. While Cayden ordered his breakfast, sitting in a booth at the back of a local diner, he overheard some guys saying they sent a crew out for Mackenzie. I'm not surprised. I had a feeling a call I made earlier this week would set things in motion, but for that very reason, I'm lying wide awake with a gun on my fucking nightstand.

I'm done with not talking. Initially, I didn't want to talk because I hated that she was Trent's girl. In my eyes, the fact that she would even give a guy like Trent the time of day made her someone I couldn't ever take seriously, then add that she slept with him. No fucking way. It spoke volumes about her character that she would associate with a guy like that, let alone sleep with him. But somewhere, throughout this, I stopped caring about her past because all I wanted was her future.

After I finished painting the room—trim and all, because there was no way I would allow her to climb a damn ladder again without me present—I cleaned up and went downstairs. I assumed she would be ready to talk. For once, she didn't storm out of the room, determined to shut me out. Well, aside from the fact that she thought I was joking about her birth control. I'd be lying if I said those words didn't catch me by surprise. It's all I could think about the second she let me have her bare in the grotto. When she brought me to climax, riding my dick, I grabbed her hips hard and shot my cum deep. It was the first time I'd ever come and felt this innate desire to put a baby in someone. The second she rolled her eyes, I wanted to cross the room, slam the door, and fuck her bare just to prove a point. However, I realized how crazy my comment sounded, given the status of our relationship, so I let it go. For now, anyway. However, it doesn't change that even now, hours after I've had time to think on my words, nothing has changed. They still ring true. I wouldn't be mad if that woman told me she was pregnant with my child. It's one more way she'd forever be tied to me.

When I went downstairs, the house was quiet, but the door to her room was cracked. After I pushed it open, I found her wrapped in a towel, passed out in the middle of the bed. As much as I wanted to wake her, I couldn't. When I got home today, I could see it in her eyes: like me, she hadn't gotten any rest the night before. I hurt her. I promised I'd come home last night, and after what we shared, she trusted I'd keep my word. It doesn't matter if she doesn't want me. Our connection can't be helped. I know it because I feel the same way. She's the last complication I need, but she's all I want.

I'm rolling over to shut off the light beside my bed when I hear a thud. My body stiffens as I strain my ears to hear anything else. The noise definitely came from downstairs. I quickly grab my phone and pull up the security system. It's armed, and as I flip through the perimeter frames, I don't see any movement outside. Another bang happens, but this time, it's more distinct. It sounds like a knock on the wall. I throw my legs over the side of the bed and look for my shorts. However, when I hear it again, I forgo the search for my shorts and instead grab my gun. The chances of someone being in the house are slim, considering the alarm is armed. However, I don't care to risk that for the sake of the two seconds it takes me to grab shorts. An attacker isn't going to care that I'm in my underwear. Their focus will be on the barrel pointed at their head.

I stick close to the wall and try to keep the element of surprise on my side as I look over the open stairwell to the lower level. I can see into the living area and front entry from where I stand, but I take off when I hear a cry. Fuck surprise. I go barreling down the steps before hopping over the rail when I know I'm close enough to clear the jump and haul ass down the hallway toward Mackenzie's room. When I push open the door, I find her thrashing in the middle of the bed, tears rolling down her face. The headboard nudges the wall and explains the noise I heard upstairs. I rush to the bed, lift the cover I laid over her earlier, and pull her against my chest.

"Shhh, shhh, shhh, Mackenzie. It's okay. I'm here, baby. You're safe," I coo as I run my hands through her hair. I know from experience with night terrors that Summer had when she was younger, you're not supposed to wake someone. It can be jarring and, in most cases, makes the terror much harder to forget. I used to rock Summer through hers until it ended and gently coax her back to sleep, but she never cried or jerked around the bed like this. Waking her feels like the lesser evil.

"I'm sorry," she mumbles through tears, and I can tell the words aren't for me. She's not with me.

"Shhh." I pull her tighter so that we're skin-on-skin. She fell asleep naked, and I'm only in my boxers. I throw my leg over her body to help fight the tremors and continue running my fingers through her hair. "Wake up, baby. Let me take it from you," I speak softly. Her hand comes up to my chest, and her nails dig in almost enough to draw blood before her tremors slowly fade. Her breathing steadies, and her tears begin to dry. "That's it, baby, wake up. I promise I'll take care of you."

"Connor." Her voice is quiet and unsure, clearly confused.

"You had a bad dream. I came down and found you crying and thrashing on the bed."

Her pale blue eyes pull away from my chest, and she peers up at me, only to shake her head. "I'm sorry—"

"Don't be sorry…" I bite my tongue and try to adjust my tone. Those words trigger me. She said them in her dream state, but I try to remain calm. This isn't about me. However, I can't help but be invested. I want to know what upset her. I want to take it away. I want to make it better. "Can you tell me?"

She furrows her brow and pushes back to see me more clearly. "Can I tell you in the morning? Right now, I just want it to go away." She gives me her back, but doesn't move away. "Will you hold me?"

"Is that even a question?" I pull her flush against my chest into a spooning position. "I never intended on letting you go."

We lie in silence for long moments, and my mind reels over what scenario played out in her dream that upset her to that extent. *What trauma did she endure? Is it the one that brought her here?* God, I can't help but be pissed with my own stubbornness. I should have gone back last night to speak with my father. Even after my parents' confessions, I was still livid. Empathetic but livid. I know I'm being used, that they are feeding me pieces instead of giving me the whole damn story. It's why she and I need to talk, though it's hard to stay mad when their choice gave me her.

As I lightly drag my fingers over the bare skin on her shoulder, I feel her heart rate start to level out. The tension that had previously racked her body has loosened, and her clenched muscles are now soft against my front. Her skin pimples, and I feel a shiver run down her spine.

"Are you cold?" I pull the comforter I laid over her earlier up over our heads to trap in the warmth, and her breath catches. "I'm sorry, is this too much? Are you scared of the dark?"

"Not as long as you're in it with me."

Being this close to her is different than it was moments ago. Her nakedness wasn't affecting me the way it is now. My cock is fully aware of every inch of her exposed flesh, and I know I'm supposed to be here comforting her, not trying to fuck, but right now, my dick doesn't know that.

"Connor," she questions, her voice soft and sexy as hell.

I know she feels my hardness pressed up against her ass. I

wrap my arm around her chest, ensuring she doesn't try to pull away before I press my lips to her neck. "Who else would it be?"

Her breath hitches, and I can't be sure if that means she is just as affected by our state of undress as I am or if it means she wants me to leave, but fuck, I can't help myself.

"I'm sorry. I'm a man, and you're currently curled up naked in my arms. I've been trying to keep my hands from grabbing one of your tits for the past ten minutes."

Her head subtly shakes. "That's not… I mean…" she trails off somewhat sheepishly, and I can tell she's nervous. What I don't know is why.

"Tell me." I kiss her shoulder.

"I thought you said the bed was for lovers." She throws my words back at me, comments that may have garnered a different response yesterday, but not today. Today, I'm all in, so the words come easy.

"I know what I said." It's saying something without really saying anything at all. I know this, but she knows me well enough to read between the lines.

My hand slowly moves from her side and up her ribs until finally I reach the weight of her breast, and I can't help but squeeze it hard, remembering how perfect they were in my mouth as she rode my cock in the grotto. The tiniest of moans rumbles up, but when she presses her ass into my groin, I know she wants me just as much as I want her.

I let my fingers slowly rake down her body as I suck and nip at the skin on her neck. I know I'm not being gentle. These little bites will surely be visible tomorrow. We've been really good at putting off things we need to talk about today until tomorrow, but this is one she won't forget. She's letting me have her, and I'll be damned if I'm going to watch her forget it in the morning.

My hand leaves her breast, only to trail down her soft stomach until I reach the apex of her thighs. I don't immediately slide my fingers through her lips. Instead, I pump my hard cock into her ass while letting my hand cup her pussy. I know I'm teasing her. She did the same thing to me this afternoon while painting. I had to watch her ass play peek-a-boo with the hem of my shirt every time she extended her arm to paint, which reminds me: I need to find all her spandex shorts and burn them. There's no way I'm letting her leave the house in those.

She pushes her ass back against my length, and I can't help but let my middle finger glide through her folds. Fucking soaked and ready. I dip my finger in, and her tight pussy clenches around it, and I can't help but groan, wishing it were my cock.

"I love how responsive you are to me." I pump into her as she rocks her clit against my palm.

"I want more," she rasps as she presses back against my dick.

I throw the blanket off us, hot as hell and determined to see her face and every inch of her perfect body. "You want my cock?"

"You know I do." She reaches her hand between us and lowers the band of my boxer briefs. Her soft fingers wrap around my cock, and she strokes it hard. As a hiss escapes my lips, a bead of pre-cum drips from the tip.

Fuck. "I need to be inside you."

She presses her ass into my groin, aligning my tip with her entrance, and as much as I want to pound into her, I only push in enough to tease, but her greedy pussy clenches what little bit I give her.

"God damn," I groan against her neck. "I love when you take what you want."

I push in slowly as my hand moves back to her breast, where I pinch her nipples into hardened peaks. She is so damn tight that I have to push in a few times before I finally fully seat myself. I start pumping into her in long, slow strokes, taking my time to drag my tip over that spot I know she loves. Her breathing quickens as the sounds of our arousal pick up in crescendo, saying more than words ever could.

She's soaked and sucking me in because of how turned on she is from how I'm making her feel, and I know because I'm right there with her. This moment with her, in this house, as my wife, feels surreal. I can't help but feel like this was where we were always meant to be. Hooking my arm under hers and around her shoulder, I pull her down on me with each thrust.

"You're so deep." She pants. "I need more."

"This isn't deep. If you want deep, I'll give you deep." I pull out and flip her onto her back. Pushing the remaining blankets out of the way, I spread her legs wide with my knees before slamming back in hard, making her cry out. I only do it once before slowing my pace. Tonight, I want to feel her. I'm in her bed, somewhere I said I would never be, and now that I've come this far, there's no turning back. This is what I want. Now that I'm here, it's where I'll be every night.

I drop down to my forearms, caging her in. In this position, I can feel her nipples graze against my chest, a sensation that makes my back break out with goose pimples. The awareness of how much my body physically craves her is achingly present, but it's when she wraps her legs around my back that I catch myself falling. *Fuck.*

In an attempt not to lose it completely, I lean down and take her exposed breast into my mouth. She arches into me when I do, and I let go. I suck it hard before biting her nipple.

"Hey, that's going to leave a mark," she argues feebly as her eyes roll when my tip hits her spot, but fuck that. I'm done pretending.

"These are my tits. I'll mark them as much as I want."

"Yours?" She moans, and I can't tell if that's a question or an acknowledgment, but I respond all the same, ensuring there's no misunderstanding.

"Yeah, mine. I keep telling you that. I've just been waiting for you to believe it," I say as I hold her eyes and continue pumping into her slowly before trailing my tongue around her pert nipple and sucking it into my mouth. After giving it a little nip with my teeth, her pussy spasms and those perfect lips part with a gasp. "Then maybe I can be yours." Those words make her clench hard. "Fuck," I rasp out as I drop my head into the crook of her neck.

She's on the edge. I can feel it, but I want more. I slow my pace to rein in my need to come and slowly kiss my way up her neck until I reach her jaw, where I switch to open-mouth kisses, letting her feel my tongue and making my intent known. I want that mouth. When I reach her chin, I look up and find her eyes are on mine. I push in with more force, digging deep and teasing the spot I know drives her crazy.

"I want to kiss my wife."

"Connor." Her tone is a warning.

I place my forehead to hers. "I know your terms." My eyes search hers, hoping they convey that my heart echoes the same sentiment. I'm all in. Our mouths are mere inches apart as our breath mingles. Those perfect lips part once more as my tip drags over her G-spot.

"Con…" She closes her eyes, and I see her worry.

"Let me have this tonight and every day after that."

Her head shakes, and the smallest of tears escapes the corner of her eye. "But what about our sec—"

"No more secrets. Let me in. Let me keep you."

Those pale blue eyes open once more and steal my breath. She's so damn beautiful. I've been under her spell since day one, but it hits differently now that I'm done fighting. She doesn't say anything, but those eyes soften enough to look like home, and I hold in deep as I bring my lips closer to hers. My mouth barely grazes hers, seeking the permission I'm ninety-nine percent sure I have, but my heart races all the same. When she doesn't turn away from me, I try for more and tease her lips in mine. They are just as soft as I imagined they would be. I want to dive in and take more, but I don't.

Instead, I reposition myself so that my arms are cradling her head. I haven't ever given anyone this side of me, and I need her to see. I need her to see and feel what I can't bring myself to say. Brushing her damp hair, stuck to the side of her face from the pleasure she's letting me take from her body, my eyes search hers again, ensuring she sees my sincerity. I'm not going to take something just to take it. I know what she's giving me, and I'm not taking it for granted.

Her hand comes up and runs through the hair at the base of my neck before she gently pulls my mouth down to hers, and I swear my heart fucking soars. A groan of what can only be described as pure bliss leaves my chest without my consent, as if my body, my soul, has found its home. Words can't describe this moment or how I suddenly feel for the woman beneath me. When my tongue brushes against hers for the first time, I know there will be no one else. She's the only woman I want to kiss for forever. My cock twitches, and I know I'm not going to last.

Reluctantly, I pull my mouth mere centimeters away from hers to breathlessly pant. "You need to get there. I'm not going to last. You beneath me in this bed is too much."

Her fist tangles in my hair as she pulls my lips back to hers and locks her legs around my waist. *Fuck.* I pump into her hard, hitting her deep twice before her walls clench, and we come together. Chests heaving, hearts racing as we fade in and out of each other. As we both let go, our hearts are the only sound, and I don't want to leave this moment. I'm breathless, caught up in her, and she's mine. Only mine.

Movement beside me stirs me awake, and my eyes slowly open. As they adjust to the subtle glow of the morning light, the soft body tangled up in mine registers. I fell asleep wrapped around her. There was no way I was letting her go, just like now. She hasn't realized I'm awake as she slowly tries to peel herself away. My thigh is draped over hers, and my arm is wrapped around her torso as my hand cups her breast. Fucking perfect. She tucks her arms and tries to subtly shift her weight to wiggle free, but I only apply more pressure, and she notices.

"You're awake?" she questions softly.

"Yes," I answer, my voice groggy. "Is there a reason you're trying to sneak out of our bed?"

"Our bed?"

"Call it what you want. It doesn't change that this is where I will be from now on, preferably with you naked. I thought I made it clear last night…" I trail off to pull her closer. "I'm keeping you. The morning hasn't changed that."

She turns in my arms, our faces mere inches apart and eyes locked when. "Okay."

"Okay?" I question. That's all she gives me: an 'Okay.' She bites her bottom lip, and her brows furrow slightly. Raising my hand to her face, I brush my thumb over the place between her eyes. "What's this?"

"We should probably talk first." She pushes back and moves to sit up, pulling the cover around her.

The move upsets me but only because I know there's nothing she can say that will change things, and it frustrates me that she believes there is. That slow simmer that takes root only reminds me of what brought me to this bed last night.

"How about you start by telling me what that dream was about last night?"

Her eyes close, and the strain on her face and the tension

in her fists as she clenches the blankets tighter don't go unnoticed. My teeth grind of their own accord.

"Connor, that night is why I'm here, and it hurts. I've had a few dreams since then, but I didn't realize they were affecting me as you witnessed last night." She pulls her legs up and wraps her arms around them. "Though I suppose there would have been no one around to notice."

"Tell me so I can make it go away."

"How are you going to make it go away? It happened. It can't be undone."

"Tell me," I grind out, pissed that she's right, but I need to know all the same. It will only give me more reason to pull the trigger when I get the chance.

"It happened about two months ago. I showed up at an abandoned warehouse—there's another story behind that—and before you say anything, I realize that in itself was a dumb move. Me showing up at a sketchy warehouse on the wrong side of town is asking for problems, but I had a damn good reason. I'll admit I was tempted to turn around and go home when I got there. There were multiple signs telling me to hightail it, but I couldn't, not with what was on the line."

She tucks her hair behind her ear, and I rise to sit beside her with my back against the headboard. I already have one hundred questions, but I stay silent. I don't want to deter her from sharing. I can tell it's not easy.

"When I entered the warehouse, it was different from what I thought it would be. On the outside, it appeared as though no one was there, but looking back, that was the point. The first level was vacant and empty, but the farther I walked, I could hear the faintest of hums that sounded like base from music. That sound is what kept me pressing on. I knew I hadn't found what I was looking for. At the end of the corridor I was in, I heard a door open. However, it was locked by the time I reached it. I stood there pacing back and forth, trying to devise a plan when another side door opened. This time, I tucked myself into the shadows of the warehouse and waited for whoever it was to open the door. Once they did, I caught it with my foot before it could close and waited until they were far enough ahead that they would overlook the stowaway who came in behind them."

She takes a deep breath and shakes her head as she fidgets with her nails. "Maybe this makes me a prude, but I wasn't prepared to see the things I saw in there. I'm not a virgin. I've done—"

I grab her hands and cut her off. "Mackenzie, I don't want to hear about you with other men." She rolls her eyes, something I will have to correct her for later. My wife needs to start taking me seriously. "I mean it."

"My point is, women were walking around in nothing but thongs. Some were serving drinks. Others were busy doing nefarious acts right out in the open. It was obvious not all of those women were there by choice, and I stuck out like a sore thumb, seeing as I was the only woman wearing clothes, so I veered off out of the space and took the first open door I could find. Hearing stories about the type of scene I stumbled into and seeing one is very different. I instantly feared I wouldn't get out undetected and would be subjected to what I had just witnessed. The hallway I found was quiet, and I was trying to think of how to get out when I heard a familiar voice. A voice I trusted with my whole heart."

Her hands clench, and so does my chest. I hate knowing someone hurt her, but I think knowing someone had her heart first hurts more.

"I hurried down the hall, expecting to find help, and that's when things got ugly." She pauses, pulling in a stuttered breath.

Fuck, I hate this. I hate that she's in pain. I don't want to make her relive this, but I also need to know. I reach for her hand and interlace our fingers before gently rubbing my thumb across the top of hers in a manner meant to soothe. "You're safe with me, Mackenzie."

"I found a girl on her knees when I pushed open the door. She was dressed the same as the girls on the floor serving drinks, wearing nothing but a thong, but she wasn't on her knees for just anyone. She was on them for my boyfriend. His eyes met mine, and I knew I was in trouble. There was no remorse, only anger. He pulled her hair so she'd release his cock, and he cursed as he fumbled to tuck himself back in, and when he took a step toward me, I took one back. That's when he lunged and grabbed my hoodie. I was so dumbfounded. I couldn't wrap my mind around the fact that the guy I'd known and trusted for eight years was the same one standing before me, but my instincts kicked in, and I fought back. I bit his hand so he'd release my hoodie, and it worked until he slapped me hard across the face."

"Mackenzie, I've heard enough." My anger threatens to get the best of me. I know I asked, but this is only causing us both pain. I can't undo what's already been done. I can't take it back.

Her hand squeezes mine. "Just let me get this out." Those crystal blue eyes find mine, and I see it. Telling me is releasing something for her, and I'll be damned if I don't want to be the man who comforts her. The one who makes her feel safe. I nod and squeeze her hand for her to continue. "Looking back, it's possible he was in shock. After he hit me, neither of us moved. It wasn't until the girl beside him moved that I thought to move, and when I did, so did he. The fear I felt that he might hit me again made me stumble. I lost my footing and hit my head against a table. The next thing I knew, I woke up in the hospital. There was a police officer stationed outside my door, and once I was cleared, he took me down to the station for questioning. There, I saw Zane cuffed with a black eye and a busted lip. I immediately felt bad for him and told him I was sorry. When he hit me, I saw anger, but I think the act surprised him as much as it did me. I was clearly the last person he expected to see that night."

"Why the fuck would you tell him you were sorry? You had nothing to be sorry for, Mackenzie. He hurt you, not the other way around."

She nods in agreement. "Yeah, I know that. I think I knew that then, too, but my whole world had just been turned upside down. Plus, I did sustain a minor concussion. You have to understand. Zane was my first and only boyfriend. We'd been friends since we were twelve and started dating in high school. I trusted him. I never in a million years thought he would cheat on me or that I would catch him in a place like that. I know it doesn't make sense, but I blamed myself for putting him in jail and ruining us. If I hadn't shown up, none of that would have happened."

My mind is racing as I'm trying to listen to every word, but right now, I can only focus on the name. "Wait, you said your boyfriend's name was Zane?"

"Yeah, yeah, I know it's a trailer park name. Parker already filled me in."

"What?" I pinch the bridge of my nose, clearly perturbed. "No, I mean the guy you were with before you came here. His name was Zane, not Trent?"

She turns to look at me, and I can tell she's clearly trying to read my emotions and my sudden fascination with her ex-boyfriend's name. "Yes, Zane Barden," she answers slowly.

Many things suddenly start to come together, and it's almost too much to process. Holly's visit to Tish Mercer at Sweetwater, Mackenzie's mom, makes a hell of a lot more sense now. Zane Barden is Holly's younger brother. She was there trying to find out if Tish knew where he was.

Once I have my boxers pulled on, I ask, "What happened after you left the police station and returned home? How did you end up here?"

"Well, I never actually made it home. When I was walking

out of the police station, someone approached me, which initially scared the shit out of me, considering what I had just been through, but he threw his hands up and immediately told me he was there to help. He said he was…" Her pause has me stopping in my tracks to read her expression.

"Are you trying to remember or attempting to change your story?"

Her head snaps up, and her eyes go wide. "What?"

"People don't just forget significant details like that, Mackenzie. What aren't you telling me?"

She pinches her lips together and shakes her head. "I'm sorry that I'm not most people. I'm sorry that when I walked out of that police station, I still had a minor concussion, and things take me longer to recall because of it."

Damn it. Gathering the sheet around her, she moves to get off the bed, but I'm faster, and I slide up next to her, throwing my arms around her waist. "I'm sorry," I rush out. I wasn't thinking. I'm so quick to pit her against me like everyone else seems to be as of late, and that's not fair. "I'm sorry. It's just that the details are crucial, Mackenzie. I need them so I can keep you safe."

I kiss her shoulder, and she releases a breath.

"The man said he could help me, that I wasn't safe after what I witnessed, and that I couldn't go home. Apparently, there were people now after me, accusing me of being the reason the pop-up brothel got busted. I was the outsider who led the cops in. I stayed in different motels throughout the state for two weeks as I was moved around, ensuring I didn't have a tail until finally I ended up here." She shrugs. "And, well, you know the rest."

The fucked-up exploitation of women must run in the family. Something must have tipped Garrett off for him to justify watching Zane. My family loosely has a thumb on the heartbeat of the sex trafficking world, mainly through its efforts to find safe houses and rehabilitation centers that help victims reenter society. Still, over the past decade, a few lines were blurred when cases hit close to home. It was easy to stay distant, only providing legal services and donations, when it wasn't on your doorstep, but the second my uncles and my father heard of a few cases in the area, they couldn't help but do more. Knowing the full extent of my mother's story leans into that a bit more. My mother's abuser, Craig, never served any prison time himself, and I can't help but draw the conclusion that lines have been blurred to protect and help anyone they could because my father probably feels he failed my mother in some way by not seeing Craig behind bars before he met his end.

"Who is Trent?" she asks, turning her face slightly over her shoulder to look at me.

"No one you need to worry about." That's one silver lining in all this. When my father said she was important to him, I assumed he meant Trenton Wells. We've been looking for him for years, ever since Holly was put away. I thought Mackenzie was his ex, and I know damn well my father knew I was drawing that conclusion, which only further pisses me off. He could have saved me a hell of a lot of headaches by using a fucking name instead of being so damn vague.

Mackenzie stands while I'm caught up in my thoughts and turns to point at me, anger written all over her pretty face. "You said we were going to talk. You've told me nothing. I want to know why you said yes."

I close my eyes because fuck if I don't want to tell her. She deserves to know, especially considering that I have no plans of letting her go, but I can't. "Does why I said yes matter if I'd do it again in a heartbeat?"

"Connor," she says on a frustrated exhale, clearly upset with my response.

I crawl across the bed and grab her hands, bringing them to my lips, hoping to draw those eyes to mine. That pale blue ethereal gaze lands on mine, and my heart can't help but stumble. I don't want to hurt her. I'm tired of secrets. I promised her no more, and I meant it, but now I need more time.

"Look, my truth is a little more complicated. It doesn't belong to just me. Can you just trust that I promise I'll tell you when it's right?" I release one of her hands to caress her chin. "Trust in what I know you felt last night."

She pulls in a stuttered breath that makes my own catch in my throat. Those words are an admission that this is more. Sure, I've said things that have insinuated as much, but they were in front of other people and could easily have been misconstrued as her believing they were for appearances or in the heat of passion when I'm thinking with my dick and not my heart. This right here, right now, is none of those things.

"Okay, I'll let it go for now, but"—she drops the sheet covering her body, leaving her naked before me—"I'd like to revisit the topic of my safety and why I can't run alone."

I reach to pull her into me, but she steps back, and I can't help but bite my lip and smile. "Playing dirty now, are we?"

She cups her breasts, shielding herself from me. "I guess you don't have to tell me that either, but you won't be getting any more of this until you do."

"Oh, I'll tell you about your safety," I growl out before lunging at her and pulling her down on me, making her squeal. "The one person you need worry about is currently under you, and he's a prickly fucker with an insatiable sexual appetite." My hands glide down to her hips, holding her tight as I press my growing erection against her clit.

"Mmm." She moans before I flip her over and take her mouth. She tastes even better than last night. She's the dealer, and I'm the shameless fiend. Her tongue brushes against mine, deliciously exploring her new territory, and I can't help but revel in it. I'm hers for the taking. I lift her leg onto my hip, opening her up to press myself more firmly against her core, but then she pulls back. "We don't have time for this. We're going to be late for work."

"You asked me about your safety. I'm only trying to ensure it." I run the tip of my nose along her jaw until I reach her ear and suck her lobe into my mouth.

"And how does this ensure my safety?"

"Lesson number one: I mark what's mine, and you, Mackenzie Callahan, are mine."

CHAPTER 21
MACKENZIE

"I'm driving you to work and anywhere else you need to go for the foreseeable future, do you understand?"

"Yes, Connor. I'm not arguing. I just don't think this is all as serious as you do, that's all."

After rolling around in the bed for an hour we didn't have to spare and giving me three more orgasms, we're finally on our way into work. I couldn't say no. I haven't been able to say no since day one. Connor Callahan disarms all my defenses with one look, consequences be damned, and right now, the stakes have never felt so damn high.

"Can you explain again how your safety is not paramount right now? I just told you that your ex-boyfriend is not only out of jail but looking for you, and we both know the kind of shady shit he was put away for. Just because he was released doesn't make him innocent. It just means they don't yet have a solid case against him. They need more evidence. It happens all the time. People are released, and the cops will watch them, waiting for them to fuck up so they can lock them up for good."

I twist my fingers and look out the window. "I just think if he was going to—"

"Don't even say *hurt you*." He hits the wheel hard. "Mackenzie, he did hurt you. He gave you a damn concussion."

My stomach instantly knots, and I feel shame because he's right, and here I am making excuses. When did I become the girl who makes excuses for abuse? Sure, I pissed him off, but that never warrants a violent reaction that ends with me on the floor. It's so hard to let go of eight years because of one day. Before that day, he was never that man. If anything, Zane was overprotective, and the other part that I can't wrap my head around is, if Zane was indeed the bad guy and my brother Josh had been keeping tabs on me all this time, why would he let me stay? Why wouldn't he have forced my hand? Showing up to that warehouse was a choice. Josh said I could burn the letter and act like I never received it. Does that mean he would have let me continue to be with a man who was involved in heinous shit behind my back? I have so many questions, and after this morning, more than ever, I feel like I have even more secrets. But at least I now know why I'm here. I'm bait, and not just for one man.

Connor refused to tell me why he agreed to marry me, but he did give me something, and it's a big something, one that has me feeling sick. When I gave Connor my ex's name, he was shocked. I could see his wheels turning, though he was trying hard to hide it. It was obvious he thought Trent was my ex, but I'm not sure what gave him that impression, and what's more, I can't help but wonder if that's not one of the reasons he agreed to marry me. When we said our vows, he clearly thought my connection to Trent was very different, and when I pressed him for more just to be sure I wasn't reading into it wrong, his reaction only confirmed it. There's bad blood between Connor and Trent, and now I'm stuck in the middle because what Connor doesn't know is that Trenton Joshua Wells is my brother. Now I just have to figure out what caused this war because on either side is a man I don't want to lose.

"What do you plan on using that gun for?"

He does a double take, stealing his eyes away from the road to get a read on my reaction. "It's for protection, Mackenzie. Do you think the kind of men involved in what you witnessed don't carry weapons? I can fight my way through anything except the barrel of someone else's gun."

"Have you ever shot someone?"

His hand tightens around the steering wheel, and he looks toward me once. "No, but I've come close."

"Will you tell me?" I want to know. Scratch that. I need to know what behavior would warrant him pulling the trigger. I have no clue what my brother has in store, but I don't want either of them to get into a fight someone can't walk away from.

"If I tell you, will you start taking all this more seriously?"

"Connor, I do take this seriously. Earlier, my comment was flippant. It wasn't thought out, and I'm embarrassed I said it. I never expected to be this girl, yet here I am. I wasn't in an abusive relationship until suddenly I was. I don't expect you to understand, and it's not easy to talk about. I'm still trying to wrap my head around all of it myself. I hate myself for not seeing the bigger picture, and I hate him for doing that to me, for making me that girl."

"Hey, hey. You're not that girl." He reaches across the console and grabs my hand. "You can't blame yourself for what you didn't know, and people will have opinions no matter what, but I can promise you he's going to pay."

"What does that mean, though?"

"There is a lot of bad in this world, but there is also good. For every asshole like Zane, there's someone like me trying to make it go away, trying to seek retribution. You asked me if I ever killed anyone, and I said I came close. I only came close because karma is a bitch. My first introduction to some of the under-the-table dealings my family did behind the scenes was with Holden and Aria. Long story short, like you, she witnessed things that forever changed the trajectory of her life. Holden was and is my best friend, and I wasn't about to stand by and watch people I care about get hurt. Ultimately, the people after her were taken care of before Holden or I ever had to make a choice we couldn't come back from. Because you see, people like that have enemies. They might have hurt or wronged you somehow, but chances are you're not the only one."

His justification settles my inner turmoil enough to make me believe there's hope that things won't end badly when all truths are finally laid on the table. Maybe with time, I can be the reason this feud ends because I know that Josh would never hurt me. Therefore, Connor should have no reason to hurt him.

We pull into the parking lot at the Fields, and he says, "Can you do me a favor and not leave the concession stand today? If Cameron is here, don't run off with her. No gas station runs or fast food. Just promise me you'll stay put."

I nod in agreement, and he squeezes my hand before releasing it to get out of the truck. I open the door and hop out. At the same time, Parker walks out with trash. Our eyes lock momentarily before he scowls and walks around back. Big hands wrap around my waist, and Connor pulls me flush against his front.

"Are you good? You know you don't have to work here—"

"I'm good. I can handle Parker."

His head dips down and nuzzles into my neck. "Are we still good?" Those perfect lips start kissing my neck, making my entire body shiver.

"Why wouldn't we be good?" I manage before everything gets too hazy for me to focus. All logical thought goes out the window when his hands are on me.

He spins me in his arms, and his lips pepper my jaw with

kisses until my mouth is all that's left. Those dark, stormy eyes meet mine and make my heart beat double time. "Just checking. I was really only looking for an excuse to pull you close and put those lips back on mine."

His mouth covers mine, and I swear all the breath in my lungs disappears. I twist my hands into his shirt, needing something to hold on to, to ensure I don't fall as his kiss consumes me. A kiss has never felt like this. I cease to exist when his mouth is on mine. His big hand reaches down and grabs a handful of my ass, and I can't help but whimper at the reminder of him taking what he wanted this morning, wringing every ounce of ecstasy I didn't know I had from my body.

A voice clearing behind us has him releasing my mouth with a growl.

"Is there a reason you're interrupting me and my wife, Michaelson?"

"Well, if I were Parker or Elijah, I might be interrupting to tell you to take your hands off the staff."

I turn around, but Connor doesn't release me. Instead, he pulls me close to his front.

"Holden Hayes." He steps forward to shake my hand. "I don't think we've formally met."

I extend my hand. "Mackenzie. It's nice to meet you. I've heard a lot of things working down here, so it's nice to finally put a face to the gossip."

"Gossip." He crosses his arms. "All good, right?"

"Oh, yes, maybe I should have said 'legend.' People are always talking about the kid who made it pro."

"Yeah, well, that man behind you is quite the legend himself. You know Connor could have gone pro, too?"

Connor cuts in, "Yeah, yeah, yeah. I'm fine just where I am. The whole being on the road isn't for me."

Holden adjusts his hat. "I get that."

"Why are you down here this early anyway, Hayes?"

Holden looks between me and Connor and clears his throat. A telling sign that he's fishing. He probably has something he wants to speak with Connor about, but I'm here, and Connor clearly isn't letting me go.

"Well, I wanted to know if you and the family were coming out this weekend for the Fourth of July party we always throw at the house. I haven't had to ask if you'd be in attendance for the past eight years since you lived in my basement."

"You could have texted me for that."

He rolls his lips and rocks back on his heels. "Yep, but I was driving by and figured I'd stop in. Plus, I had something else I wanted to get your opinion on, if you have a minute."

Just like I suspected, guy talk.

"He's all yours. I need to get inside anyway." I try to slip out, but his hold only tightens.

"Can you give us a second?"

"Yeah, I'll be under the pavilion."

He pulls my chin up so my eyes are on his. "Remember, don't leave the concession stand for any reason. Text me if you need anything."

He kisses my forehead one more time and walks off, and I'm left looking after him, dumbfounded by the turn of events and how he went from cold, distant, and uncaring to the selfless, kind, fierce protector willing to burn down the world to defend my honor. This morning, he asked, "Does the why matter if I'd say yes again in a heartbeat?"

And all I've been able to think is, God, I hope he meant that.

"Girl, Parker's been cursing your name all morning. You're never late. What gives?" Cameron says, bumping my hip as I load the beverage fridge. "And don't even try to bullshit me. I'm not an idiot. After you left Friday night, shit went down."

"What do you mean, 'shit went down?'"

"After you left, Connor went inside with his parents, only to storm out an hour later on his phone and peel out of the driveway. We were all out back when we heard the tires burn out, so Parker and Elijah went inside to see what was happening. More yelling started inside, and the rest followed, but the second we walked into the house, Everett went upstairs, and Moira and Kipp left with Elijah and Parker following hot on their footsteps. This morning was the first time I saw Everett since Friday."

I don't say anything because I'm not sure what to say. I have no idea any of that went down apart from Connor speaking with his parents. He said as much when he asked me to go home. Because he knows Zane is out of jail and has reason to believe he's looking for me, it's obvious I was the topic of conversation. What I haven't been able to piece together is the rest.

"Hey." Cameron pulls me by the arm over to the corner and speaks lightly, "You know you can talk to me, right? I mean, I'm hoping you know that anyway."

I consider her words. It's not that I don't trust Cameron. It's just that I've never had anyone like her in my life. I've never had a best friend or anyone to lean on apart from Josh until he disappeared. Then, it was just me and my mom. Parker and Elijah are clearly not going to be of any help. They never were. Elijah seems to have his marching orders, and while Parker might have broken the rules for me, I'm no longer willing to pay his price. But I still need to tread lightly. There's too much on the line to put all my trust in any one person.

"How long have you known the Callahans again?"

"My whole life."

"Wait, what? I thought you said your dad worked for Everett, and he took you in after the crash."

"He did." She shrugs. "But not just because Everett worked with him. Everett was my dad's best friend. They grew up together and went to college together. Moira and my mother were even pregnant with Connor and my older brother Kelce at the same time."

My eyes widen with surprise. I didn't realize her history with the family ran that deep. "Why didn't you mention that before?"

"Because I didn't want to be judged. No one else sees it. You see it because you are new, and having someone to talk to about something I can tell no one else is refreshing."

Damn, she has me there. I've been in the same spot for the past two months. Zero people to talk to about what's going on with me. That's it. It's settled. I just found my new ally.

Before I can respond, Parker walks up behind us and says, "Seriously, if you guys don't start working, I will fire you. I don't care who you are. I need people who are actually going to help."

My head snaps around, and I see what I didn't see earlier. He looks tired, and I'm not here to cause any problems.

"Yeah, sorry," I say quietly.

He rubs the back of his neck and drops his gaze to the floor. "You know what? How about you guys grab a cart, collect the trash, and put new bags in? Be back here in thirty minutes to open."

The second he walks away, Cameron says, "Man, maybe you should piss him off more often. I don't care to do trash duty, but not having Parker hover around is nice. He is always so serious."

We head toward the back door, and Connor's words from earlier about not leaving the concession stand briefly cross my mind, but I quickly dismiss them. It's not like I'm leaving the premises, and I'm not alone. Plus, I'm just doing my job.

As we start down the hill to the shed to grab supplies and the side-by-side to collect trash, Cameron says "So, are you going to start talking or what?"

I have so much to ask, but I'm unsure where to start. However, I'm a pretty good judge of character, and I've always known there's more to Cameron than meets the eye. After what she revealed back at the concession stand about Everett, I'm certain that was her olive branch of sorts. She shared something she keeps close to her chest, hoping I'll do the same, but I'd be stupid to give it all away. At the end of the day, while Cameron may not be blood, she does live under the same roof as Everett, and if she has it her way, she'll never leave—but I also think she could be my ride or die if I just take the bait.

"I'm not sure where to start, but I'll start with asking, what do you really know about me? I know you're not stupid. You've been around long enough. You know Connor's personality. Does he strike you as the type of person who goes out and gets married on a whim to a girl who hasn't met his family?"

I'll learn a lot about the woman at my side by how she answers this question. People can be great at talking without actually saying anything at all. I know because I'm one of them. It's why even though I like Cameron, I've watched my Ps and Qs. I'm no stranger to my reflection. Like me, Cameron is bent and misunderstood.

She opens the barn door to the shed. "I was wondering if we were ever going to discuss the elephant in the room." Waving her arm, she says, "After you."

"I knew you knew more than you were letting on," I say as I walk in and head straight to the utility bench where the bags were the last time I came here with Parker.

"Well—" she starts, only to be cut off when a loud bang behind us has us practically jumping out of our skin. She grabs my shoulder and clenches her chest. "Connor Callahan, you scared the fucking shit out of me. What the hell are you doing down here?"

He points the end of an infield rake he grabbed off the wall straight at me. "I could ask my wife the same question."

"We're on trash duty." She releases my shoulder and moves her hands to her hips. "We came down here to grab bags and a side-by-side."

"Trash duty?" he questions, never taking his eyes off me, even though I'm not the one doing the talking. "I thought I told you not to leave the concession stand."

"Why can't she leave the concession stand?"

Connor slowly walks in my direction and ignores Cameron's question. "Cameron, do you mind giving me a minute with my wife?"

She looks at me and then at him. "Actually, I do. We are supposed to be on trash duty for the next thirty minutes, and there is no way in hell I'm about to do it by myself…" She draws off, shaking her finger between us. "So you can save whatever shit this is for later."

"I'll take trash duty with Mackenzie." He finally breaks his stare off with me to give Cameron a pointed look. One that she looks ready to challenge, but ultimately thinks better of, and honestly, I can't blame her. So would I if the situation were reversed. "Go make yourself scarce for the next thirty minutes."

She shakes her head. "Fine, you don't have to ask me twice. I don't do trash anyway. I only agreed because Mackenzie was doing it." Then she turns on her heel and exits.

No sooner she exits the shed than Connor starts laying into me.

"What the hell, Mackenzie? What is it going to take for you to take me seriously? I said don't leave the concession stand. Are you deliberately disobeying me for a reason?"

While a big part of me loves having this new side of

Connor, this right now is not one of the things I care for. I'm twenty-one years old, not sixteen. I've managed to get by just fine. Sure, it could be better, and before I left home, I was barely keeping my head above water between work, bills, and taking care of my mother. Still, outside of what happened at the warehouse, I've never been some timid little girl in need of rescuing, and I still don't see myself that way.

I give him my back, continuing my search for the trash bags. "I'm a big girl, Connor. Believe it or not, I can handle myself. If it makes you feel any better, I recalled your words before I left the concession stand and still chose to come down here. I wasn't alone, and I didn't leave the premises. Nothing happened."

"Mackenzie, don't turn your back on me. That's a childish move, and I think we're past the stages of running and avoiding each other. Nothing ever gets resolved that way."

I clench my fist at my side and pull in a deep breath to calm my nerves and school my face. I know he's right, but I don't want to give him the satisfaction of knowing. Turning around, I find him leaning against the side-by-side parked behind me, which suggests he's not as pissed as I initially thought.

"I had my reasons for asking you to stay put, and I should have laid them out. I'm not used to having to explain myself. I know about the flowers, Mackenzie."

His eyes hold mine, but where I thought I'd see anger or the over-the-top possessive alpha-hole I know he can be, I don't see anything but a budding curiosity. Which only serves to remind me of the secrets that still stand between us. I don't say anything and wait to see if he'll speak and offer me something I can use to spin my own tale to match whatever narrative he's decided fits.

"Were you planning on telling me your ex-boyfriend sent flowers to your work?"

My poor heart feels like it might give out at any moment

as it struggles to keep up with the constant whiplash. I thought for sure Trent's name was going to come up. I think quickly about the night Parker brought the flowers into the office. I go over my words and try to recall if I indeed mentioned they were from an ex, but I know I don't need to. No one here is supposed to know about my old life, and no one from my old life is supposed to know I'm here. I know I said nothing.

The first week I was in town, I asked Parker if there were cameras in the office, and he said no. It's those words that give me the confidence to lie. "They didn't come with a note. I searched for one and never found it. After the week we had, I assumed they were from you."

Those attentive, all-knowing eyes attempt to penetrate my defenses, but I don't let them. I'm not going to break. I can't, not on this. It's too important. Finally, he buys my bluff.

"Well, I did not send them, but can you at least see how that looks for me? The girl I'm married to, the one I am supposed to protect, my WIFE, is getting flowers out of the blue from someone that's not me." He leans the rake against the side-by-side and runs his hands through his hair. "I'm not trying to fight with you. I'm so damn tired of fighting, but fuck, Mackenzie, it's clear now more than ever that those flowers came from him. He's out of jail, and he knows where you work. He's clearly sending a message, and excuse me for not wanting to see you have another episode like the one you had last night."

His confessions make me feel like an ass. A lot of half-truths have been slung at me in a short amount of time, and it's hard to know who to trust and what to believe, especially if the words are coming from a man. Josh suddenly shows up back in my life after being gone for years. The boyfriend I've had since middle school cheated on me in the worst of ways, and my second impressions of Connor weren't stellar, not to mention he still has skeletons in his closet that he's keeping close. I've been burned, and because of that, I quickly wrote off his actions as high-handed and arbitrary. I didn't even think to consider his feelings.

I walk up behind him to where he stands with his hands tightly gripped on the tailgate of the side-by-side and wrap my arms around his waist. "I'm sorry. I didn't consider how you saw things, and I don't want to fight. I've never wanted to fight with you."

He turns around and grabs my face, his eyes piercing mine with an intensity that feels like love.

"I just want to keep you safe. You could be the one thing that shuts it all off for me, Mackenzie. I've already been walking a fine line when it comes to my humanity. Summer is the only thing keeping me on the right side of the line, but I know I need more. There has to be more. I want…" He closes his eyes and clenches his jaw, choosing to keep the words on the tip of his tongue to himself, and my heart can't help but beat out of sync from the confession I believe I was about to receive. "I just need you to help me. Please," he pleads, resting his forehead on mine.

"I promise. I just need you to let me in," I answer quietly.

"Why can't you see, I already have?"

It's those words that almost break me. This whole time, it's been too easy to make Connor my enemy, my jailor, instead of seeing this and him for what this really is: two souls held captive, chained together by an unpredictable fate. Connor didn't want this any more than I did.

Reaching up, I put my hands around his neck and pull his mouth to mine. Words don't always fill the cracks. They aren't always enough, and sometimes they are the last thing you need because that's all they'll ever be—words. But this moment speaks volumes. His hands frame my face, his forehead presses against mine, and I feel his heart. This is what I will remember when I reflect on this day years from now: the man who showed me his vulnerability through his eyes and touch. His tongue caresses mine, and butterflies dance through my insides the way they have from day one. My mom, being the true hippie she was, always had peace, love, and butterflies around the house. She used to tell me that only butterflies knew the true beauty of change, and I can't help but think the butterflies I feel every time this man kisses me are just that. He's changing me.

He pulls back on a groan. "We need to stop." His words catch me off guard, and I can't help but feel a little disheartened. "Don't look at me like that. I'm serious. It dawned on me while speaking to Holden that I haven't taken you on a proper date."

My eyebrows practically rise off my forehead in surprise. Those were not the words I was expecting out of his mouth. "Really? After everything, that's what you're thinking about in your free time?" I query as I push out of his arms and grab the bags I was after.

"Well, yeah," he says, somewhat exasperated. "I can't change how we met or how we got to where we are now, but I thought I should at least date my wife." I toss the bags into the back of the side-by-side and climb in as I try to hide the goofy smile on my face. He slides into the driver's seat. "Does that smile mean you like the idea or…"

"It depends. What did you have in mind?"

"Easy. Ikea or the shooting range."

"What's Ikea?"

He side-eyes me as he throws the utility vehicle in drive. "Really, I list a shooting range as a potential option, and you ask, 'What's Ikea?'"

"Well, I know how to shoot a gun. I don't know what Ikea is."

He throws on the brakes. "Wait a minute, what? You know how to shoot a gun?"

Damn. I really wish I knew what Ikea was so I could have kept my mouth shut. I don't want to ruin a good moment by bringing up my ex.

"Zane taught me how to shoot."

"Of course he did," he mumbles under his breath. "Well, considering the shady shit he was involved in, that's the least the asshole should have done for you. Regardless, that's our first stop. I want to see for myself what exactly you know."

As he steps on the gas, I say, "You never explained what Ikea was."

"It's a huge furniture store. They have everything you could possibly need for a house there."

"You want to take me to a furniture store? Your house is already furnished."

"I thought you could help me pick out some items to finish Summer's room," he says, a little unsure.

"I'd love that. I have a lot of ideas."

I peek over and see him trying to hold back his own smile. From everything I've gathered about Connor so far, I know he doesn't do relationships. One-night stands have been his M.O. I think this is his first real date, and my heart can't help but swell. Under that rough exterior is a bleeding heart, one I'm starting to think bleeds for me.

CHAPTER 22
CONNOR

I'm not sure why she thought a summer dress was acceptable attire for the shooting range. Maybe she didn't believe I'd actually take her there, but either way, I had to watch her hit the fucking target like a badass the entire time. She wasn't lying when she said she knew how to shoot. This woman never ceases to amaze me. I've never seen her as weak, though I believe she sees herself that way after what happened back home. Her reasons for not liking Parker as more than a friend support that theory. I also think that's why she's quiet and borderline submissive occasionally. From everything I know about her, she didn't grow up with the best of anything. Mackenzie lived in a trailer park in a small town. Her dad left when she was young, she had no siblings, and from what Cayden says, she was a loner. It's been her and her mom. Now she doesn't even have her.

After finding out about her desire to keep the truck after our arrangement, I looked into her finances. She had less than two hundred dollars to her name when she came here. She worked at a local hardware store, one that it appears she worked at since age sixteen, and all of her paychecks went toward helping pay for her mom's bills. Over the past six months, she turned off the cable and internet and canceled her phone to get a pre-paid one. The car she was driving was her mother's, and a few months after she went into the assisted living home, Mackenzie sold it to pay for the next four months of her care. After learning all this, I drove straight home and took that piece of shit truck.

I was so fucking pissed, not at her but at all of it. The cards she'd been dealt, my father's decisions, everything. I tore out down the road dead set on righting wrongs. That day, I put things in motion, and one of the first things I took care of was ensuring that piece of shit truck was gone. Crashing it hadn't been in the plans. It happened as I reflected on why I was getting rid of it. I was getting rid of that truck so she would have a safe car to drive home, visit her mom, and drive to work. The more I thought about those reasons, the angrier I got. I was ensuring her needs were met back home, a home that didn't include me. That's when I got reckless and stupid and floored the gas, heading straight for the river bank. At the last minute, I jumped out the door and watched as the truck went over the bank. It was a satisfying release, even though I knew it would make her mad.

Sometimes, we need help seeing what's good for us. Mackenzie is anything but weak. I know she can more than handle herself. I'm not trying to take her control. I want to give it back, and as I follow her through Ikea now, I can't help but feel like this afternoon brought back some of the confidence her ex stole the second he hurt her.

"I can't believe how big this place is. There are so many floors. Don't we still have an entire level to go?" she asks as she picks up a dark purple fuzzy pillow, only to flip it over, look at the price tag, and place it back on the shelf.

"Will you stop doing that?"

"Doing what?" She looks at me, confusion written all over her pretty face.

"Putting stuff back when you think it's too expensive. If you like it, put it in the cart."

She balks. "Connor, they want forty dollars for that pillow. It's cute, but I'm sure I can find something just as cute for less."

"I asked you to help me decorate Summer's room. I never gave you a budget. If your design likes that damn fuzzy pillow, then that's the one we get."

"But—"

"But nothing. I have money, and I asked you to spend it. Fucking spend it."

She gives me a look that says she is not impressed but proceeds to grab two of the damn pillows and throw them in the cart. Good. I don't want her to settle for second best. When she wants something, I want her to take it. I need to know she's capable of demanding what she deserves.

As I follow her down the next aisle, she says, "Didn't she have a favorite color before purple? I thought she mentioned it in one of her letters. Maybe I could use that as an accent color to ensure she likes some of the design. You know, just in case purple was a flippant comment. What if this week's postcard says 'never mind, I changed my mind to blue.'"

"Green."

"Green?" she questions, her eyes narrowing on mine as if I chose a color out of thin air.

"Yes, green. Sage, to be exact."

"Sage? And how would you know all that?" She turns back to the wall of lampshades.

"Well, as you know, we lived with Aria and Holden. Last year, Aria upgraded their son River to what she calls a 'big boy' room, which meant a toddler bed and a whole new aesthetic: trees and mountains. Aria hung decals on the wall, and I painted them one weekend while Holden was out of town with River. Summer, of course, was helping and said her favorite color trees were the light green ones, to which Aria said, 'That color is sage.' After that, she wanted sage everything."

Her chin rests on her fist as she stares at the options before her. "That's actually a very sweet story. One I wasn't expecting from you, but helpful all the same. Sage is a great accent color for purple."

"You don't think I can be sweet?" I question, her remark a little offending.

"I didn't say that. It's just not the side you choose to show me or…" She trails off and starts down the aisle. "If you do, it's usually canceled out with some overbearing, primitive— Oh, this is perfect."

She stops mid-sentence to outstretch her arm for a lamp that is clearly out of her reach, which makes her already short dress rise dangerously high. I rush to her side and grab the lamp she was after.

Handing it to her, I say, "That dress is getting burned when I get home. It's way too short."

She smirks. "See? Sweet then barbaric."

"I'll show you barbaric." I pull her against my growing erection. "This is what you in that dress does to me." I grab a heady handful of her cheek and squeeze hard. "As long as my name is attached to yours, this ass is mine."

Her eyes are locked on my mouth, mere inches away from hers, and I'm about to take it when she says, "Did you know I want to be a designer?"

"What?" I mutter, unsure if I should be offended that she's clearly changing the subject during an intimate moment.

She clears her throat and gently pushes me back before licking her lips, dropping her gaze, and collecting her thoughts. Good, I didn't read that wrong. I do the same thing with her when I can't think straight. I have to look away, or she'll consume me.

"Yeah, I painted a few murals back home for customers who frequented the hardware store. It happened organically while discussing paint colors. One thing led to another, and I was doing a side job. Word got out, and I did another. I really enjoy painting. I enrolled in college, but then…"

She trails off, and her forehead creases. I know what happens next. I did my research. That's when her mom fell, and things got bad. She only did one semester before she dropped out. Her subject change during our intimate moment now makes sense. I see this for what it is. She's trying for more, for something real. We already know the attraction exists, but what about the real stuff?

My hand finds the side of her face, and my thumb brushes her cheek. "You know you can tell me, right? I want to know."

It's not a lie. I want to know everything, but most importantly, I want her to want to tell me. Not because I demanded it or it was forced out of her due to our circumstances, but because she found me to be a worthy confidant.

She leans into my hand and closes her eyes. "It's not that. I just don't want to visit that memory right now. Maybe another time." Turning away from me, she puts the lamp into the shopping cart. "I think a few sage accents will balance out the shades of purple."

I don't push even though I'm a little disheartened. It's a start, a genuine moment in this fake marriage, and that's something I'm grateful for.

Turning the corner, we enter the bedding section. I watch as she runs her hands over bedspread after bedspread, feeling their softness before finally settling on a white quilt.

I rub the back of my neck, a little uneasy because I don't want to tell her no, but I have to. "Summer really loves soft blankets. I'm not sure she's going to—"

"Oh, this isn't for Summer's room. I wanted this for our room."

I can't help but bite my lip as I try to stifle the huge grin that is threatening to take over my face. She sees my reaction, and her cheeks heat once she realizes her chosen words.

"I-I mean, I didn't mean it like that. I was only saying that because—hey, look, a teepee." She drops the quilt in the cart and beelines to the corner where there's a quaint teepee set up, complete with twinkle lights and throw pillows.

When she drops to her knees and pulls back the flap door to peek inside, I pounce. I can't take it anymore. I've already been sporting a semi for the past three hours, and her slip just now referring to her room as 'ours' has me rock-hard. I've called her mine on more than one occasion, but she has yet to claim me, and I'll be damned if her accidental slip doesn't do just that. Her subconscious mind has already decided and is fully committed to a path. It's why she said those words without actively thinking about them. She's thought about us, a real us. Otherwise, she wouldn't have said, "our." I drop down behind her as though I'm interested in taking a look myself.

"Connor, oh my God, how sweet is this? Do you think Summer would like this, or is she getting too old for things like this?" she says, admiring the tent's interior that is jam-packed with tons of throw pillows.

"I think she'll love it, but maybe we should make sure it's big enough for sleepovers," I say as I push her through.

"Connor, what are—" she starts, but I throw my hand over her mouth.

Bringing my lips to her ear, I say, "Shh, I'm about to fuck my wife, who thought to tease me all afternoon by wearing a tiny dress that barely covers her ass." I suck her dainty lobe into my mouth as I grind my erection into her ass. "Can you be quiet for me?"

I release her mouth, and she whisper yells, "There are cameras. We're going to get caught."

"There are no cameras in this tent. We'll only get caught

if you can't keep quiet while I bury my cock inside that tight pussy."

I know I'm being vulgar, but her face flushes whenever I am, and I know it's because she likes it. Mackenzie has never told me to stop. Her body lights up under my touch. With that in mind, I run my hand up her front and cup her breast to find she's wearing no bra. Fuck. With ease, I pull the front down and delicately tug her nipple. I know she fucking loves when I play with her nipples. Her pussy always clenches me hard when I do.

"Does your silence mean yes?" I ask as I run my tongue from the base of her ear down the curve of her neck to her shoulder.

She presses her ass back into my groin. "Do I have a choice?"

"You always have a choice with me."

The next thing I know, she is lifting her dress, dropping to her elbows, and baring her thong-clad ass to me. I want to slap it hard, but I don't, remembering where we are.

I pull her red thong to the side and immediately run a thick digit through her center. Already finding her semi-wet, I slip my finger into her pussy to get her ready. As much as I'm prepared to slam in, she's not wet enough. I've yet to take her once where she hasn't had to acclimate to my size. My cock strains against the zipper at the mere thought of how she feels wrapped around me, rocking back and forth to fit me. With my free hand, I make quick work of freeing my dick.

She pushes back on my hand, seeking more, and those cheeks spread just enough to give me a view of that tight pink hole. I add another digit, and she lets out a delicious moan that's borderline too loud as her juices thoroughly coat my fingers.

I pull them out and bring them to my lips, fiending for a taste. There's something so sexy about tasting her juices on my tongue, knowing I'm the reason they exist. "Fuck, you taste good. You'll take my cock now, but later I want that pussy to sit on my face."

With a hand on either cheek, I squeeze and spread, letting my cock run through her folds before slightly dipping my crown inside and repeating the move until my cock glistens. This woman has me in a trance. Her warm lips teasing my bare cock have me in a chokehold. I don't go bare. I wasn't even bare when Summer happened. That thought has me lining up to push inside. She said she needed to go to the doctor for more birth control, and I'll be damned if I don't want to put a baby inside her before she gets the chance.

I can't stop the hiss that falls from my lips as I feel her warmth wrap around the first half of my cock. My hands move up to grip her hips so that I can better control the pace, but as I slowly start to pull back only to push in once more, she shoves back hard.

"God, yes," she purrs. "You're not going to hurt me. Not when it feels this good. I want it hard, Connor."

"You have no idea what you're asking for," I say as I pull back, debating on whether I will give her what she wants. On the one hand, we haven't fucked hard yet. Mackenzie isn't a screamer, but it's obvious she's never been stretched properly. I'm not sure fucking her hard for the first time inside a teepee at Ikea is the best place to find out if my style of hard doesn't turn her into one. However, we aren't in here to make love. We're in here to fuck.

"You want me to go hard?" I pull back and slam in, bottoming out, and she yelps. "You better bury that pretty face in a pillow while I bury my cock in your pussy."

She nods adamantly and then reaches for a pillow. Damn. I slam in hard again and hear her muffled cry as I bottom out. "You better tell me if it's too much. I'm not messing around, Mackenzie."

When she says nothing, I squeeze her hips and find my rhythm of pulling her onto me and bottoming out with every thrust. Sweat starts to bead on my forehead from the adrenaline coursing through my veins as I fuck my fake wife, who happens to be the woman of my dreams, inside a teepee at Ikea. I want to draw this moment out. I don't want it to end, and not just because it's hot as fuck, but because she knew the risk and allowed it. She wants this just as much as I do, consequences be damned.

"Fuck, I forgot how wet this pussy gets for me."

I considered her sexy moans but overlooked how wet she gets. The sound of our arousal is more likely to get us caught than her stifled cries. I slow my pace so my balls don't slap against her wet pussy.

"Don't stop. I don't care if we get caught. I need this, Connor. I need this with you."

"Damn it, wife. What are you doing to me?"

There's no way in hell I'll deny her request. I don't particularly care to go to jail tonight, but hey, I have a family full of lawyers, so fuck it. I pound into her mercilessly. Anyone passing by would know precisely what the hell is going on in this teepee. If I'm going to be Clyde, there's no one else I'd want as my Bonnie. It can only be her. My fingers grip her hips so hard I'm sure there will be marks tomorrow serving to remind her of what she asked for. I feel the second her orgasm starts to hit, and I come hard as she milks me.

I hold in deep until every last drop has coated her womb. I'm completely spent. All I want to do is fall back onto these damn pillows with her wrapped in my arms, but I can't. Reluctantly, I pull out, readjusting her thong and pulling down her dress to cover her ass before tucking myself back in.

She moves into a seated position, her cheeks rosy as hell with that just-fucked afterglow that makes me want to go again. Right now, she's completely satisfied and full of my cum. *How could I not want to make her look like that all the time?* That thought has me asking another.

"What did you mean when you said you needed this with me?"

"It's never been that good. I've only been with one person, and he told me he loved me." She pauses and pulls at her necklace before closing her eyes. "I don't know how people can fake whole relationships. You are my lesson learned. Love and good sex aren't exclusive."

Is she fucking kidding me right now? I'm unsure where her words are coming from. The ones she gave me earlier meant something entirely different to me. Maybe my confessions haven't been enough, and she still believes we are fake, that what we are has an expiration date, and there's no chance for a real us after everything is said and done. Or maybe, like me, what we shared just now felt like more, and she's unsure how to deal with it. I drop my gaze and try not to take her words personally. Our experiences shape us, and we grew up very differently. She's never had a man in her life worth a shit. I want to be that man, but this is new for me, too.

"I don't think you have to choose. When it's right, you'll have both." Without giving her another glance, one I can't stomach, I pull open the flap on the teepee. "You, me, and this teepee, that's real. That was more than just sex for me."

I'm not sure how she doesn't see it. I told her I wanted to keep her. Is it love? I'm not sure I've ever felt it, but I'd imagine it looks a lot like a future you don't want without them in it, and that's how I feel every time my eyes collide with hers. Regardless of what I want or think I feel, I'm not discussing forever with her inside a tent at Ikea.

CHAPTER 23
MACKENZIE

I know what I did at the store. I hurt him. However, I'm still unsure if it was intentional. Did I know what I was saying? Yes and no. I threw my walls up without thinking about the fallout because I was scared. I gave him words and didn't consider their meaning. When I asked him not to stop, it was because I didn't care. All that mattered was him. We lost ourselves. For a moment, the outside world disappeared, and it was everything. I knew the second I let him kiss me on the mouth I was done for. I've fallen hard, and things are moving at warp speed. We've been forced into an impossible situation, and I can't help but wonder, if circumstances weren't different, would what we have still exist? The day at the ball field, before we knew what was to come, I was the last person he wanted to see. I'm clueless as to how successful relationships work. My mother never had any, and the one I had ended dismally. Connor makes me feel everything, and it's so easy to get caught up in him and the thought of there actually being an us when this is all said and done.

Therein lies the problem, though. I didn't come here for an us. I came here for my family, and at the end of the day, he can give me all the words he wants. It doesn't change that we both still have secrets, ones we don't trust the other with, and that says something. After we climbed out of the tent, no more words were exchanged. He silently followed me through the rest of the store, and when we got home, he took everything up to Summer's room before walking down to the lake at the bottom of the hill.

We got home late. It was pitch-dark outside. At first, I thought he was leaving. It's what he's been good at, but after half a bottle of wine and walking around the house in circles, I realized his truck was still in the driveway. I peered out every window in the house, trying to see if I could find him in the dark. There are no lights out here. It makes for some epic stargazing, but if you're not looking up, everything is drenched in utter darkness. So I was surprised when movement caught my eye. The light from the moon reflecting off the water allowed me to capture his shadow as he skipped a few rocks across the water before finally taking a seat on the edge of the dock. He spent hours down there.

The adult thing to do would have been to go down there and tell him everything I was feeling. Lay all my cards on the table and let the chips fall where they may. After half a bottle of wine, I had convinced myself that was what needed to happen. But as I walked to the bedroom to grab a pair of shoes, a text came through. It was as though the world was sending me a sign. Don't cave. Not yet.

Parker: You have three paychecks in the office. Should I mail them to the house?

I immediately fell to my knees in the middle of the hallway. With everything going on between the marriage, the letters, and my feelings, I forgot about my mother and the pile of bills back home that needed to get paid. Shortly before I left home, I sold her car, which paid for a few months of care, but that would only get us so far. Everett was clear on one thing: no contact with anyone back home. But I need to help her. She has no one else. These were the thoughts that crippled me and left me on the floor.

Somewhere in the night, Connor picked up the pieces of me I threw on the floor. He turned on the bathroom light and left water on the nightstand along with Ibuprofen. *Why does he have to be good to me even when I don't deserve it?* As he pulled the blankets over me, my mind drifting in and out of consciousness, I heard him say, "If what we are is fake, I don't want to be real. I think I could pretend with you forever." He may not be in bed with me now, but I know he was last night, at least for a little while. His warmth didn't immediately leave me after he gave me those words, though it's more than gone now.

Sitting in bed, I reach for the pills and the water Connor left before looking for my phone to find the time. Connor changed my schedule to align with his. The other day, after Parker put me on trash duty, I was supposed to go back and work the window for another two hours with Cameron, which I wasn't mad about. Connor interrupted our girl talk, and I was looking forward to finding out more information about the past between my brother and Connor. Now, I no longer work during peak hours unless Connor has a game at the same time, and Cameron basically only works during peak hours when she does decide to come in. But today, I need to devise a game plan to see her, so I need my phone, which is nowhere in sight.

Reluctantly, I throw the covers off and realize I'm still wearing my dress from yesterday and feel disgusting. My head is still pounding as the pills haven't begun to work their magic, so I prioritize bathing before searching for my phone. I'm hopeful that since Connor and I now have the same schedule, he won't allow me to be late for work. Turning on the shower, I reach for my toothbrush, which is oddly nowhere to be found. I check the shower, thinking maybe I walked in with it the last time I was in here, but nothing. *What the hell?*

I can't forego brushing my teeth, so I check the drawers, thinking I must have thrown it in one while I was getting ready yesterday. After Connor mentioned sleeping in the master bedroom from here on out, I felt the need to tidy up the bathroom instead of leaving all my things on the vanity. When I pull open the top drawer, I find my toothbrush, but that's not all I find. There's another letter.

Closing my eyes, I pull it close to my chest. Finding these letters in this house means he's close. Like maybe he's here just waiting for the right moment to come out. "Please," I murmur out loud, wishing resolve into this letter, hoping it's the letter that gives me a place to meet him.

M,

Do you remember the summer Mom took us up to Swan Lake to camp? Do you remember the sunset the night we rented a canoe? I need you to remember that night, M. Remember that night this weekend.

Josh

I let out a sigh of frustration and shove the letter back into the envelope a little forcefully, pissed that all it offered me was more damn riddles. *Fucking Josh.* What the hell am I doing here? I take the letter and place it in my cosmetic bag before grabbing my toothbrush and entering the shower. I'm about at the end of my rope here. I want to help my brother. I knew there would be a price to pay. He said as much in his first letter. He warned of the risks. I just hadn't prepared for my heart to become collateral damage along the way.

"I've given you space, but now it's time to talk about last night."

"Connor, I'm sorry about what I said. I know it hurt you, and I can't say I'd take it back if I could because I think it needed to be said. How I feel doesn't matter. I didn't say 'I do' for you, Connor…" I draw off breathlessly because while it hurts, it is true, and I know it's true for him. "And neither did you."

He presses his lips together, never taking his eyes off the road as his fingers flex around the steering wheel. "That's not what I was referring to, but yeah, let's start there."

Damn, how could I be so stupid? I should have realized he was referring to finding me on the floor and not our time in the tent. My words might have stung, but he's a guy. He probably woke up this morning and gave it zero additional thought. Only women stew over details for days on end.

We arrive at the Fields, and as he pulls into a parking spot, he says, "So just to be clear, this fake marriage is just that fake? There's no alternate ending where you and I are endgame?"

"Does what I want matter?"

He slams both of his hands on the steering wheel, and I flinch. "Yes, it fucking matters."

I reach for the handle to get out, determined to put space between us before giving him my parting words. "If that were true, there wouldn't be any secrets between us."

"I swear to fuck, you better not get out of this truck Mackenzie. You don't get to run away from this. I told you what I want, but sitting on the dock last night, I realized you've never once told me what you want. Sometimes I look at you, and I see everything. I see our truth, this irrevocable bond that doesn't give a fuck about how we exist, only that we do because it's what's meant to be. But then it all goes black, and I see nothing. Help me understand it, Mackenzie, because this"—he gestures between us—"you and me, it's all I want, and if you don't feel the same—"

I cut him off, climbing over the center console to straddle his lap. Taking his face in my hands, my eyes search his. He's so damn beautiful, his words didn't only steal my heart but my ability to think, find reason, or objection—but in the end, no words are needed because I feel the same damn way. Leaning in, I prepare to take his mouth and show him that everything he said is all I want, but before our lips can connect, he turns his head.

"I need your words, Mackenzie."

"I'm scared, Connor. I'm so damn scared. It feels too good to be true. How does a story with a beginning like ours stand a chance? Two strangers thrown together by some twist of fate, not once but twice, and then there's still…"

"Don't say secrets. It's not something I'm choosing to keep from you. I'll lay all my truths down at your feet."

"I'm scared of getting my heart broken but equally scared of walking away from this, from us, and living a life without you in it, not knowing if you could have really been my person because…" I close my eyes and point to my heart. I won't say love. I can't. Not yet. "This space right here feels like it belongs to you."

Pushing a strand of hair behind my ear, he lays his forehead against mine. "I've been in the dark so long I didn't know my heart still existed until you. I'm scared, too, Mackenzie. But the truth is, you had the power to break my heart since you walked into my life. You might break it, but even broken, you'd still own the pieces. So, you see, either way, it's yours. It's always been yours."

My mouth crashes to his, my tongue diving deep, claiming him as mine. He has echoed the sentiments of love to me on more than one occasion, and the other night, he said he's only been waiting for me to believe. I'm done not allowing myself to take something I want. I can't tell you why he hates my brother. I don't know why Josh wanted me here, but I'm done believing that any of those reasons can overshadow what we have. The spark that's always been there is now a full-fledged flame that no amount of deception can snuff out, not when the flame is eternal.

His hands move to grip my ass, and a delicious moan escapes his sexy mouth, one that I swallow down and answer with my own. Those big, calloused hands slowly make their way up to the waistband of my shorts, and I feel them dip under the band. He wants to take them off, and fuck if that's not what I want, but we can't.

Reluctantly, I pull back. "Connor, we can't do that—"

"Sure we can. No one will see us, but if you're that worried about it, I'll throw this shit in reverse, and we can go home right now."

I bite my lip at his playful banter. I love that he wants me just as much as I want him. I shake my head and smile. "It's not that. We can't because I started my period this morning."

He grabs my chin, catching it between his thumb and forefinger. "That changes nothing for me. I love every part of your body." My cheeks heat for multiple reasons, and he notices. "Don't do that. You have nothing to be embarrassed about." His hand trails up my neck, and his fingers weave through the hair at the base of my neck, making my skin pebble as though my body knows its master is pulling the strings. Then, pulling me forward until my lips are a hairsbreadth away from his, he says, "If anything, you should be scared." My brow furrows for the briefest of seconds before he answers by pushing his erection against my clit. "It just means I'll have to try harder to make them disappear."

His lips find mine once more, and I let him take them. I'll give him this for now because damn if I don't crave the sentiment, and fuck if letting him try won't be fun, but kids are not something I want right now. I'm still young. I have things I want to do, goals I want to accomplish, places I want to see, and lastly, but most importantly, I want to have time to get to know my man. Time that's just ours.

A hand hitting the hood breaks our kiss.

"Loverboy, let's go. It's the holiday. We all want to clock in and clock out."

He presses his head back into the seat rest as I turn to see who our visitor is. It's Bret, his assistant coach.

"I should have just called practice off today."

I turn back to him. "Why aren't they playing this weekend, anyway? I know there's a big 7U tournament here tomorrow, but why not your team?"

"Holden and I had a big discussion about this when planning the calendar for this year. Many teams play holiday weekends, but last year, we had fewer scouts when we held our major tri-state tournament on the fourth. You have to remember, it's a holiday for them too. That's why I changed it this year, and we held the tournament last weekend. The whole point of this organization is keeping the guys loose in the off-season while getting them exposure. By changing the weekend, I had seven more recruiters attend than last year, so that's a win. We only have two more games, but I need to set an example. I need them to take this seriously, to take the organization seriously. They wouldn't throw in the towel if this were the major leagues, and I don't want them to do it here. Perception is reality. You want to be big, you need to think big."

"That last part was very insightful, but I was wondering, does that mean we will be leaving early?"

Those big hands grab my ass, and he smiles. "Depends. Are you going to let me put it in?"

I swat his chest and reach for the door handle. "No, you might be fine with it, but I'm not."

"Wait." He stops me.

"Connor—"

"No, it's not that, but we will be revisiting this topic. I have something for you."

Then, opening the center console, he pulls out a strap.

"What's that for?"

His hands find the hem of my shirt as his thumbs gently brush over my hip before he takes the strap and fastens it around my waist.

"It's a gun holster. Why did you think I wanted to take you shooting?"

I smile. "To get emasculated by a girl who's a better shot than you."

He smacks my ass. "Watch it. I took you to determine if you are ready for this." Reaching back into the console, he pulls out a small Glock.

"Connor, I can't carry that. I don't have a permit."

"You think the people coming after you have permits? Do you want me to show you the safety? After watching you with the guns, I'm confident you know your way around one, but I don't want to assume anything. This is important, Mackenzie."

I pinch my lips together and shake my head.

"Words, please."

"I'm good," I say as he tightens the strap around my waist and slips the gun into the holster on my back.

"It should be out of the way here. It's loaded, but the chamber is empty."

Once he's happy with its placement and the tightness, his eyes meet mine, and I know he sees it. I'm nervous. Sure, I'm comfortable around a gun, but I never expected to be wearing one for my own safety.

"I don't plan on letting you out of my sight. Therefore, this gun should never need to be pulled. If any gun is pulled, it would be mine."

"Then why give me this?"

"Because you seem to be very good at not following

directions. You have deliberately done the opposite of what I've asked on more than one occasion." He tugs my strap. "Consider this peace of mind." His hands leave my waist. One grabs the handle on the door, and the other his keys. "Let's get to work so we can get out of here."

I do so without question because, somehow, I'm getting out of this car without having to answer for last night, and right now, that's a major win. We may want forever, but we both still have loose ends to tie up. I plan on keeping him, but first, I must take care of my mom.

"Hey, thanks for meeting me here. I know your shift isn't until this evening, but I could use your help. The other day, you said you hoped we could be allies, and I'm really hoping you meant that because I have a big ask. This must stay between me and you."

Crossing her arms over her chest, Cameron says, "If I say yes, does that mean we can get out of this freezer?"

"No, this is the only place I'm certain has no cameras or microphones."

"What?" she questions, looking around.

"Look, are you in or not?"

"Duh, girl. You had me at 'can you keep a secret' from your text this morning."

"Okay." I release a breath and blow it on my cold hands. I forgot to put on the damn coat hanging beside the door before I walked in. I've been in here for at least ten minutes since I got anxious about meeting with her. I pull my three paychecks out of my back pocket. "I need you to take me to the bank so I can cash these, and then I need you to wire the money into an account for my mom."

Her eyes narrow briefly in bemusement from what I just

threw at her, but without missing a beat, she says, "Done, but you're giving me the details in the car."

She turns to walk out, and that's when I say, "Yeah, about that. I'm going to need you to sneak me out to the car."

If my comment surprises her, I wouldn't know because without missing a beat, she turns back to me and asks, "How flexible are you?"

Fuck. What did I just get myself into?

"So tell me, why am I sneaking you to the bank to wire money to your mother?"

God, I don't even know where to start with this story. It's so convoluted. I want to tell Cameron. I need someone to talk to about everything, not just to learn more about my brother, but just for an ear to bend. Sometimes, we need someone else to tell us we are not crazy to validate our feelings, and I believe if anyone could understand my current dilemma, it would be the girl who has a crush on her godfather. However, I can't spill the full details of why I'm not asking for Connor's help as it relates to my mother, for the same reason I'm not asking him for help. No one here knows that Trenton Wells is my brother. I'm certain Connor has looked into my past, but it's clear he hasn't dug deep. Otherwise, he would have made the connection, and since he hasn't, I don't want to give him any more reason to go digging. Not yet, not until I'm ready.

"Connor and I have an arranged marriage," I blurt out.

She casually glances over at me as though my words didn't surprise her before returning her eyes to the road. "Tell me something I don't know."

"What? You knew that?" My voice squeaks with shock.

She purses her lips and taps her thumb on the wheel. "Okay, technically, I didn't know, but I suspected it. I was at the pool the day the movers carried stuff out of the house.

Everett never told me what was in the boxes, and I didn't know who they belonged to, but you did go out to the pool house to change that afternoon, so I suspected they might be yours, and then when I came to the house to help you uncover the furniture, I saw the boxes collapsed outside by the trash. But the better question might be, why was Connor's wife staying in Everett's pool house?"

I look out the car's side window as I try to find my words. I've already committed to sharing my secrets but can't give away everything, so I steal a play from Connor's handbook. "The Callahans are helping me. Taking Connor's last name achieves that, but there's more to it, and I am still trying to work out how everything fits together. All I have are pieces and some things I can't tell you. At least not yet."

She's quiet as she considers my words, and I can't help but wonder if she's upset I'm not telling her everything. But then she says, "I want to help you, but I need to know that you're not going to hurt Connor." She pauses, her eyes finding mine. "Because I can promise you nothing about the way that man looks at you is fake."

"Hurting Connor is the last thing I want to do. I plan on keeping him, but the road to hell is paved with good intentions, so I get it if you want to wash your hands of all of this. You won't hurt my feelings."

Pulling into the bank's parking lot, she asks, "So tell me, what's the plan again?"

"I'm just going to cash my checks and give them to you. I need to pay some of my mother's bills. She's in a home, but I can't have any contact with her. It risks giving away my location."

"That sucks. I'm sorry. I can't imagine it's easy being away from your mom."

I nod and grab the door handle. "It's not, but I'm doing this for her, for my family. That's what I try to remind myself when it gets hard." I pause momentarily. "I guess you don't need to come in. I'll cash the checks and come back out, and we can make the call."

She pulls out her cell phone. "I'll be right here."

After cashing the checks, I take the two thousand dollars and hand it to Cameron. She will wire the money to Sweetwater to pay for my mother's stay. In total, my checks added up to roughly twenty-two hundred dollars, but I kept two hundred for myself. I haven't had to pay for much since I arrived, only buying hygiene products. I'm sure Connor would buy what I needed if I asked, but I don't want to ask him for money. I don't care who you are. No one wants to feel like they need someone for money, and I don't want him to think I'm sticking around for his. On the next check, I'll be able to hold back a little more and pad my little savings.

"Okay, so when they answer, all you need to say is, 'I'd like to make a payment on Tish Mercer's account.' They don't typically ask any other questions. All they care about is getting their money."

Clearing her throat, she says, "Got it. Tish Mercer. I like that name, Tish. She sounds like a hoot."

"She was definitely something." Before she presses call, I say, "Hey, thank you for doing this for me. It means a lot."

"Are you kidding? I'm happy I can help, but more than that, I'm glad you trusted me with this." She pulls in a deep breath. "Ready?"

"Yep, make the call."

This idea came to me in the shower this morning. Everett was clear that I couldn't contact anyone back home, and now that I know Zane is out of jail, I understand a little more of the why. Whatever fucked-up shit Zane was involved in is nothing I want any part of, and I'm sure he isn't happy with me. I was the outsider at the pop-up club that night. I'm the one who got everyone busted. I'm the one who got him arrested.

"Yes, I'm calling to make a payment on Tish Mercer's

account. Yes, no problem." She covers the phone with her hand and whispers, "They're pulling up the account." I nod and watch as she traces her red-manicured nail over the BMW emblem on her steering wheel.

"Yep, I'm still here. Yes, the name is Tish Mercer." Her fingers stop trailing the steering wheel. "Are you positive?" She snaps her fingers at me before covering the phone once more. "She's saying the account looks like it's been paid for the next year, and you can't make any further payments until you come in and sign an updated contract for the next billing cycle and term."

What? How is that possible? Josh said he would help, but he was clear that he could only help after I helped him.

"See if they'll tell you who made the payment."

She nods in agreement. "Are you able to tell me who paid her bill?"

Pulling the phone away from her ear, she presses the speakerphone button as the person on the other end of the line says, "Connor Callahan."

Connor paid the bill? Quickly, I pick up my phone, point to the date underneath the time, and whisper, "Ask her when it was paid."

"I'm sorry, does it show when the bill was paid? My husband must have made the payment and forgot to tell me. I just want to make sure it cleared."

"Oh sure, it says here it was posted two weeks ago, hon," the woman on the line adds kindly.

"Thanks for all your help," she says before clicking off the phone. "I guess we didn't need to sneak you off in a crate after all. Looks like lover boy knows more than you think."

"It would appear that way." I turn my focus out the window.

"Ready to head back, then?"

"Yeah, I'm ready."

"You want to talk about whatever is going through that head of yours? I might be able to help you work it out."

I'm quiet as I try to think through what all this means. Connor knows who my mom is. Honestly, I'd expected as much. A simple search would give him that information, but I don't think he knows that I'm related to Trenton Wells, and the more I think about it, the more I'm convinced it's by design. The night of our vows, Everett made a comment to me that has stuck with me since I arrived. He said, "We both know you haven't been transparent in coming here." It didn't dawn on me then that he could have been referring to Trent. It didn't make sense. How could Everett have any idea that Trent reached out to me, that he was the reason I was at the club the night of the bust? Regardless, I'm positive he knows that Trent is my brother, but I don't understand why he would keep that from Connor. For that reason, I won't flat-out share my relation, not until I know more.

"The other day before Connor interrupted us at the shed, I was going to ask, do you know who Trenton Wells is?"

She purses her lips as she pulls out of the bank parking lot. "The name sounds familiar. Is he one of Connor's friends?"

"I think so. The other day, when Connor and I were talking, his name came up, and I'm pretty sure he believed that I dated him at one time." I leave off the other details and see if my words spark any recognition.

"I want to say I recall him being around years ago, but you have to remember, Connor and I have a six-year age gap, so I was still in middle school and high school when he was in his college party days. Not to mention, I technically didn't live with the Callahans back then. I was only around on holidays."

Dang, I was really hoping she could give me something, anything.

"You know who would know, though? Aria. We can ask her tonight at the party."

"No, Cam, we can't do that. I've already told you too

much. I can't tell Connor's best friend. That's just asking for problems."

"No shit, Sherlock. I could subtly slip it into a conversation. I'll come up with something. Don't worry about it. We'll get your answers."

Maybe, but right now, all I can think about is the wrath awaiting me back at the concession stand. Our trip to the bank took longer than expected, and I'm sure Connor has realized I'm not there by now.

"Great." I sigh as we turn down the drive leading to the Fields. I can see Connor standing under the pavilion with his hands on his hips. Just like I suspected. I've been caught.

"Hey, at least I don't have to stuff you inside a crate to get back into the concession stand, and this might be a good thing."

"How could this possibly be a good thing?"

"He obviously knows more about you than you think, and he's still all in."

"I suppose that's one way of looking at it, but right now, I'm about to get chewed out."

"Fights are a way of communicating that only strengthens relationships, if you ask me. You learn each other's boundaries. Typically, they start because you care. Plus, there's the added bonus of make-up sex."

As she pulls into the parking space, I expect Connor to rush the car in his typical imperious fashion, but he doesn't. Instead, those dark coal-black eyes pierce mine through the window that separates us. *He's definitely mad.*

Before we exit the car, Cameron says, "Good luck. I'll see you tonight."

I can't help but feel like a kid who just got caught sneaking out of their bedroom window as I walk up to the concession stand. I'm almost halfway up the path, and he still hasn't moved toward me, worsening my anxiety. I've learned how to deal with his overbearing, domineering, alpha-male tantrums, but this right now is new. His hands are tucked into the pockets of his faded light blue jeans as he leans against one of the pavilion posts. The dark blue Bulldogs hat he's wearing is doing a fine job covering the fury I know is there.

When I get within a few feet, I chicken out and drop my gaze. "Look, I know you're mad—"

I don't even get out all of my apology before he cuts me off. "That's what you think this is right now. You think I'm mad?"

My eyes snap up to his. "You're not mad at me?"

He heatedly adjusts his cap. "We're not doing this here. Let's go."

Without another word, he walks past, leaving me dumbfounded. *How the hell is he not mad?* He specifically asked me not to leave, and I did.

I follow him toward the truck. "I know you asked me to stay here. I get it, but I wouldn't have left if it weren't important."

He stops dead in his tracks, and I almost run into him. "Are you saying how I feel isn't important?" I look at him perplexed, and the second he sees the question in my eyes, he gives me his back. "Forget it. I don't even know why I asked."

"Stop saying that. I'm not mad."

I round the truck to climb in, but when I open the door, a box of M&M's is in my seat with a note:

M+M's for my M+M. You may have taken my last name, but you, Mackenzie Marie, are still my M+M. You make my days sweeter.

He remembered the conversation I had with Cameron in the kitchen. Damn it, he's not mad. He's hurt. How could I be so stupid?

Glancing over at me, his jaw ticks. He clearly put these in

here before he realized what I had done. Taking his hat off, he rubs his forehead. "I thought I could do this, Mackenzie, but I can't. Not right now. I don't want to say stuff I don't mean, so just leave it alone."

I find my words as he pulls out of the space to drive us home.

"You may not want to talk, so I will. You don't have to say anything." I pause to see if he'll argue with me, but he doesn't. Instead, he keeps his eyes pinned on the road with his jaw firmly clenched. "Last night, when you found me on the floor, I was there because I had a panic attack. It's not easy being here, Connor. I don't have anyone to miss me back home, but I do have my mom, and she's sick. I don't know how much time I have left with her where she remembers me even a little."

I glance in his direction to see if my words affected him, only to see that they haven't. I should have expected as much. He paid for her stay through the year. He knows she is sick, so I try to give him more. Something he doesn't know.

"Cameron sneaking me out wasn't premeditated. It only came to me this morning while I was doing inventory."

Movement out of my peripheral catches my eyes as he rubs his jaw in annoyance. Clearly, my words did little to tame his rage.

"Your talking isn't helping," he says, not trying to temper his irritation, but I keep going anyway.

"I needed someone to take me to the bank so that I could cash my checks. My mother is in a nursing home, and I needed to make a payment on her account." I pause to see if he'll own up to what he did. After the initial shock wore off that he knew about my mother and paid the bills, I was able to start sorting through timelines. The timelines and recent events, like Connor telling me Zane is out of jail and taking me to shooting lessons, suddenly have me seeing this from a different perspective. When Connor asked me for a name the night he found out my ex hit me at the bar, I refused to give him one. Driving to Montana in search of a guy with no name would have been like looking for a needle in a haystack, but finding my mother was easy. I was told not to contact anyone, but Connor did it anyway. He did it to lure Zane out and bring him to our doorstep. In hindsight, what I asked of Cameron would have done the same thing. I clearly hadn't thought that plan through, but now I'm a little peeved knowing he knew the risk and did it anyway.

When he stays quiet, I ask, "Why didn't you tell me you paid my mother's bills?"

With his eyes glued to the road in front of us, he still refuses to glance my way, and for a second, I believe he's going to keep his silence until he says, "Why didn't you tell me you had bills that needed to be paid?"

I should have known I wouldn't get a straight answer.

"Just forget I said anything. I told you where I went and what I was doing. I thought we could have an honest conversation for once, but it's clear you just want to keep playing games."

The truck wheels hit the gravel drive and he speeds up.

"That's rich coming from you. You asked me if I was mad, and I can promise you I wasn't, but I am now. You want honesty, you want trust, and you say you want me, but then you go and pull shit like you did this afternoon. Did it cross your mind what your stunt did to me? How worried I was or how I would feel when I played back the security footage of my wife being rolled out in a crate to escape me? After everything we shared this morning, I thought maybe I would finally be the guy you trusted or, hell, respected. You couldn't even spare me the fucking decency of a text message."

Tears well in my eyes as my frustration builds. He's right. I didn't consider any of that. I didn't think about how this might look from his perspective. I honestly hadn't thought of anything more than helping my mom, which was incredibly selfish. But he's been selfish, too. Like it or not, he strapped this gun to me because he put me in danger, and I refuse to let him think I don't see that. I wipe a stray tear off my cheek and give him a piece of my mind because while everything he said hurts, he hurt me, too.

"You want to talk about respect or hurt. Where was your honesty when you strapped this gun to me? I didn't hear you saying 'I want you to carry this because I paid for your mother's medical bills, and now your ex is on his way to town.'"

"Zane was always going to come here. I just sped up the timeline so that it's on my terms. For some reason, you keep making me out to be the bad guy in this equation, and I can't figure out why that is, but I can't do more than I've already done." He hits the brakes harder than necessary as he pulls up in front of the house to park the car, throwing me forward against my seat belt. "Let's not get it twisted. You're right. You're in danger, but I'm not the one who made you a target. I put that gun on your hip so you could protect yourself. Believe it or not, every time I said forever, every time I said I wanted to keep you, that you were mine, I meant it."

Without another word, he exits the truck and slams the door. My heart is pounding because I know I fucked up.

Jumping out of the truck, I close the door. "Then tell me."

He stops dead in his tracks but doesn't turn.

"I meant all of it too, Connor. You fucking know I did. Let's do this. You said you had truths. You said you'd lay them at my feet. Tell me, tell me so I can do the same."

His shoulders slump in defeat, and for a second, I believe he's ready, but then he says, "There's a little girl tied to the end of my truths. If you can't handle that, forever is not in our cards."

My heart clenches in my chest from the ache of guilt those words deliver, and I say nothing as I watch him walk into the house. I got truths. They may not have been the ones I sought, but I got them all the same. The truth is, I haven't considered him or his little girl. Somewhere in my selflessness, I've become selfish. I've been so hyper-focused on helping my family that I haven't considered his. How's that saying go? 'It takes two people to have a relationship, but only one to screw it up.' My intentions may have been well and good, but everyone knows it's our actions that we will be judged by. Now, I can only pray he believes in forgiveness because I never meant to hurt him today.

CHAPTER 24
MACKENZIE

He hasn't said more than one sentence to me since our argument on the way home from the Fields this morning. After the way we left things, I assumed we would not be attending the Fourth of July party at Holden and Aria's. Not knowing what to do with myself, when I walked inside, I went straight up to Summer's room and started decorating with the items we had purchased the other day. However, ten minutes ago, he came upstairs and told me we would be leaving in fifteen minutes. By that time, I was sweaty and looked like a hot mess after deciding to rearrange the room. The only thing that has changed between fifteen minutes ago and now is that at least I'm no longer sweaty. Now, I'm just bloated and wet from the shower.

With the towel wrapped around me, I hurry to the closet to find something to wear. I was tempted to tell Connor to go without me tonight, but then I remembered the conversation Cameron and I had this afternoon. I'm no longer looking at this as my problem but our problem. Yes, I still want to help my brother, but I also want to find out what Connor thinks he can't share with me. I'm starting to feel like whatever it is, it's not something he doesn't want to tell me. It's something he can't, so if I figure it out on my own, maybe I can bridge this space between us. I want to let it go and trust that he'll tell me when the time is right, but I know that, like me, whatever secret he's carrying is draining him. These secrets are wearing on us, and if we continue down this road, they might break us. Just because he's been honest that a secret exists doesn't mean it's not still a lie. At the end of the day, he can't be his true self, and neither can I—not when we are guarding something so deep, so precious.

I spy a red strapless sundress cinched through the bodice and flowy from the belly button to right above my knee. It's perfect for the occasion and my bloating. Just as I drop the towel to put on my dress, a voice behind me has me covering my breasts.

"Are you ready…" Connor trails off when he notices I'm not ready but stark naked.

"A knock would have been nice." I quickly pull the dress off the hanger and use it to shield my nakedness. "I need ten more minutes."

His lips thin, and he turns his head away, utterly uncharacteristic of the man I've become accustomed to. This morning, he would have let his eyes wander. He would have stalked over and pulled me close hungrily, but now it's as though the sight of me naked repulses him, and it hurts.

"Ten minutes," he repeats and walks away.

The second he walks away, my fingers instinctively pull at the silver necklace I wear around my neck. I have yet to take it off since Josh vanished. He wasn't the one who gave it to me, but I received it the day he disappeared, and I haven't taken it off ever since. Somehow, I've become superstitious about it. I realize it's irrational, but wearing it reminds me of him. It makes me feel like he's with me. Touching the charm grounds me, and I'm reminded of his letters. He told me this is where I am meant to be. It's those words I've held onto for the past few hours as I've replayed Connor's parting words. In my heart, without Josh's letters, Connor is worth the fight. I've had to dig deep and really take stock of what I want when all this is said and done, and I think what I'm learning is, love is worth the grief because there is no outcome I will be happy with if it doesn't end with him by my side. I messed up today. Now, it's time to make it right.

We've just pulled up to Holden and Aria's place, and we haven't even made it inside, but I can tell the place is incredible. The house sits on over fifty acres and is not too far from Connor's house, which means the river is nearby. That's why they have some trees in this otherwise semi-barren state. I'm convinced between the two of them, they bought all the land in the state with wooded areas. Connor has been silent the entire way here, and I can't help but feel like it's because he left the proverbial ball in my court this afternoon.

"Connor, can we talk before we go inside?"

"No," easily comes from his mouth, but before I have time to be upset, he says, "I think seeing this will help." I look away from the house and turn to him in question, unsure of where he's going with that statement. He must see the perplexed look on my face because his lips pull up into the smallest of knowing smiles. "There's a side of me you haven't seen. You haven't met the girl who holds my heart. She's not real to you. None of her things are in my house. You've only read her letters and heard the few stories I've shared, but here, she has lived. Here, she exists. Maybe seeing this will help you understand why I can't give you the parts of me that belong to her."

Before I can even bring myself to speak, he's out of the truck and coming around to my side to open the door. I hastily remove my seat belt and throw myself into his arms when he opens the door.

"I'm so sorry. I've been so selfish and narrow-minded. I would never ask you to do anything that jeopardizes her safety or wellbeing. You have to know that."

He holds me tight against his front, and his tense muscles loosen as though the past few hours have worn on his nerves as much as they have mine.

"I haven't been without fault either, Mackenzie, and it was unfair of me to put that all on you. Nothing about us or the situation we have been forced into has been normal. I'm not sure why I expected it to be. I'm hopeful there won't be any more surprises, that all the big stuff is out of the way, but I can't promise that—at least, not yet." Pulling back, he tips my chin up so that my eyes meet his. "But I'm trying."

I nod in agreement before pressing up on my tippy-toes to go in for a kiss. "I'm trying, too." He meets me halfway, his lips pressing to mine, sweetly and unhurried as his hand reaches up to wrap around the back of my neck, sliding into my hair so that he can position me just how he wants me, and I revel in it. His touch has become a drug, and I need it as much as I need air. His tongue dips in but only enough to tease before he pulls back and nips my bottom lip.

"I could stand here and kiss you all night, but I want to take you inside. Holden and Aria are family to me. I've called this place home for far too long, more than overstaying my welcome, but first…" He trails off, stepping around me and reaching into the glove compartment. "I need to know which strap you want to wear. Thigh or waist?"

Rolling my eyes, I say, "Really? Do you think I need that here tonight? I thought this was just friends and family?"

He drops to his knees. "I don't think you need it here. I want you to get used to not leaving without it. I want this on your person anytime you leave the house." His fingers graze my ankle as he taps for me to lift my leg.

"I thought I had a choice in which holster I wear?" I

question as he slides the thigh strap up, tantalizingly slow, letting his fingertips gently caress my skin.

"You did until I decided I wanted to put this one on," he says as he moves it into place, ensuring it's snug and level around my upper thigh. Once in place, his hand trails higher, and I let it. His touch feels too good, and when his thumb presses against my silk panties as he rubs my clit, I close my eyes with a groan, forgetting myself until his fingers skim the hem of my panties, preparing to pull them to the side.

My hand immediately flies down, and I grab his wrist. "Connor, we can't. I told you I'm on my period."

His lips are partially parted, his eyes hooded with lust. "And I told you I don't care about that."

I step back and pull away, and because he's on the ground, there's not much he can do to stop me. "We are going to have to agree to disagree on this one. Come on. You said you wanted to show me inside. Let's go."

His lips press together, and he curls his finger, gesturing for me to come back.

"Connor," I warn.

"Come here so I can put the gun in the holster."

"You can hand it to me, and I will put the gun in the holster."

He quirks a brow. "Fine, but I want to watch."

I stick my hand out for the gun, half believing he won't, but the second he does, I take it and start walking toward the house. I could give him a show, but teasing him teases me, and there's nothing I can do about it right now.

The truck door closes, and seconds later, I'm squealing as he swoops me into his arms.

"Shh, I'm sneaking you in the back door."

"Connor, please, I'm serious—"

"Not for sex, but you better believe you'll pay for that little stunt. I want to show you the basement, and we may never make it that far if we go through the front door. Everyone will try to steal you away from me."

When we reach the back door, he sets me on my feet and keys in a code on the French doors.

The basement is enormous. I don't know why, but whenever I heard mention of Connor living in a basement, I envisioned some college frat house situation, but that isn't the case at all. The space is wide open. The walls are covered in what looks like a heather gray fabric wallpaper, and the floors are a dark walnut. Large wooden beams that match the floor run across the room's length. There's a full kitchen, a sitting area, and a workout room that looks like a professional gym. It's bigger than my trailer back home.

"Wow, this place is nice. I can see why you haven't left."

He gives me a soft smile and pulls me by my hand. "Come on. I want you to see Summer's room."

When he opens the door, I see he was right. Her favorite color was definitely sage. The walls are sage, the bedspread is sage, she even has a few sage mountain pillows, but there are also pinks and purples. She's not all tomboy as I suspected. There's a little reading corner with cushions of every shape, hearts and rainbows set atop a big, fluffy rug. You can see her personality through the things she has out. A handful of chapter books are placed on her shelf that look above her reading age. Her room is spotless, and while I'm sure Holden and Aria have people who come clean the house, it's apparent this space was tidied by a child, not an adult. You can tell by the way her pillows are lined up and how her blankets are laid out on the bed rather than folded. If I were to bet, she cleaned it before she left and told Connor he better not touch it.

He was right. Being in Summer's room makes her feel real. But the best part is seeing him in her room. Seeing his dad side does funny things to my heart.

"Where's your room?"

He gives me that sexy smile and bites his lip before pulling me by the hand. When we finally get to his room, it's dark. I didn't envision light colors, but I also didn't expect it to be so colorless. Everything is gray: the walls, the bed. The only other color in the room is the black furniture.

"Why is everything so dark? Do you have an emo side I don't know about?"

He smiles as he walks over to his bed and throws himself onto it as I continue perusing the space, looking at the cologne on top of his dresser and what I assume is a picture of him and Summer sitting on a dock. Her hair is nearly as blond as mine, hanging halfway down her front in pigtails. The smile she's wearing lights up her whole face. You can tell she's a happy kid.

"Is this Summer?" I ask as I pick up the frame.

He tucks his hands behind his head. "Yeah, that was taken last summer at Lake Kinkaid. I like to fish when I have leisure time, and surprisingly, she likes it too."

"She's so pretty. You're going to be in trouble the older she gets."

Who would have thought seeing this space would fill in the blanks? Being here with Connor's things in the space he called home makes me feel more connected to him. Add in that he wanted to show it to me—priceless. You can tell Summer wants for nothing, but I can also tell by how she keeps her room that she's an intelligent girl, which means Connor has done an excellent job keeping her grounded. I didn't think it was possible that I could like him more, but I was wrong.

When I turn around, he pats the bed. "Come sit."

I eye him suspiciously.

"I promise, I won't make a move unless you want me to."

The problem is, I more than want him to. I always want him. *Stupid period.* I walk toward the bed and circle around to the left side before letting myself fall back.

"This bed feels amazing. Now I see why you threw yourself on it the minute we walked in." I lie there for a few seconds, enjoying the room's darkness. The longer I do, the more I understand the aesthetic. It's peaceful, it's cold, it quiets the mind. Instinctively, I roll over and scoot across the bed before tucking myself into his side. "Thank you for showing me."

He gives me no words as he turns his face toward mine on the pillow. Our faces are mere inches apart. Those soul-piercing dark eyes feel as though they're pleading with mine for more. He told me he wouldn't make a move, and he's keeping his word, but damn it if I'm not weak. I close the distance and press my mouth to his. His lips mirror the slow tease of mine, only giving what they receive, making me want more. My hand runs up his chest before my fingers fist in his shirt, and I hungrily deepen our kiss. The fervor of my movement draws out a heady moan as his tongue tangles with mine. His hand skims over my hip, squeezing me hard, sending my already piqued libido into overdrive. I'm already sensitive, and with everything he's given me tonight, his touch melts me. My hips intuitively rock against him, searching for more of what my body craves, and that's all it takes for his arms to wrap around me in one swift movement, pulling me on top of him.

His lips never leave mine as they explore new depths. In the last twenty minutes, we shared things not out of need but want. Tonight was as organic as two people dating and discovering their chemistry naturally. For us, however, the chemistry has been there from the start. It's the rest we've had to slowly fill in, and with every new morsel of information, the depth of our connection grows. His hands move to my hips, and he positions me right where he wants me before pressing his hard length up into me, hitting me in just the right spot that momentarily has my breath catching in my throat.

I pull back with a gasp as his lips chase mine. "Let me have this. I want to make you feel good. Ride me."

"You know I want that, but—"

"I'm not asking you to take your clothes off. I want you to grind that pretty pussy against my dick and make yourself come." His teeth graze my jaw as he kisses his way down my neck, slowly pressing himself into me, and I let him. Everything feels too right: him, this room, us. He gently moves my hips, and I can't help but meet his thrusts. I'm already sensitive down there, and he feels so good. "That's it, baby. Let it happen. Take it."

His hands leave my hips to slide up my sides until he reaches the top of my strapless dress, easily pulling it down with one tug, exposing both of my breasts. He wastes no time pulling me close and suctioning his mouth to one of my nipples.

"Why does that feel so good…" I draw out as my pussy clenches.

Zane sucked on my nipples but never with the same level of hunger that Connor does. Connor feasts, sucking, nipping, and biting, and damn if I don't love the sensation of his five o'clock shadow rubbing against my sensitive skin as he alternates between breasts. He sucks hard, and I can already feel my orgasm taking root. Damn it, I don't want this to end, but fuck if I don't want to come.

"Sit up, baby, let me see you." His hands glide up my thighs, his right stopping when it comes to the holster. My hand immediately meets his to remove the gun, but he stops me, "Leave it," he says, eyes locked on mine as his fingers lightly trail over the top of mine before moving to my hips, where he squeezes me hard as he pulls me down onto him, deliciously grinding his length against my throbbing center. "Do you know how sexy you look right now? Your pretty face is flushed, those pale blue eyes are lidded with ecstasy, and these perfect nipples are hard and marked by my teeth. You're the sexiest woman I've ever been with, Mackenzie." I throw my head back as his words send me spiraling. "Fuck, I can feel your tight pussy spasm through your panties."

I fall forward in search of his mouth as I rock through the aftershocks of my orgasm, and his tongue meets mine, thrust for thrust, alternating between devouring me and whispering words of praise. "You're perfect, you're so beautiful," and my favorite, "I'm going to keep you." It's that last one that has me pulling away from his mouth and kissing my way down his neck, exploring him for the first time. I slide my hands under the hem of his polo, taking his undershirt with me, letting my hands memorize every muscle. "Mackenzie, what are you—"

"Shhh." I push his shirt up to his chin and kiss his chest. "It's my turn to return the favor."

His hand winds through my hair, and a moan escapes his lips as I leave a trail of open-mouthed kisses down his chest. When I reach his belt, he pulls my hair, forcing my eyes to his. "You don't need to do that."

"I know, but I want to."

His grip loosens, and my hands make quick work of unfastening his belt, pulling down his briefs, and freeing his cock. Pulling him out, it's clear he, too, enjoyed my ride because his tip is already glistening with pre-cum.

I greedily take it in my mouth, desperate to finally taste him, and he groans loudly as his cock twitches in my hand.

"You look sexy as fuck with those lips wrapped around my cock." I take him down to his base on the first try, determined to make this good for him, only to choke. I've sucked dick before, but he is bigger. "Relax your throat, baby."

When I go back for more, intent on giving him the best fucking blow job of his life, I do as he said. My eyes can't help but water as I do, but I don't care. I want him to wreck me. I want to feel, and with him, I feel everything. My long hair cascades around my head, blocking his view, blocking my view, and pissing me off. I don't want him to miss one second, so I release him. His heavy dick smacks against his perfect stomach, and his eyes find mine in question.

I flip my hair to the side. "Mind helping a girl out? I want to ensure my husband has a clear view of his wife sucking his cock for the first time."

His eyes are so lidded with desire they're barely open as his hand wraps around my hair, ensuring his view is unobstructed when I reach for his base and teasingly lick the tip.

"My God, you're driving me crazy, woman." With his eyes locked on my every move, I flatten my tongue against his length and lick him from root to tip, making the hair on his thighs stand with awareness. It's then I take him deep. His grip on my hair immediately tightens before I feel his fingers splay against my scalp as he matches each bob of my head with a thrust. "Fuck, fuck, fuck. My wife's mouth wrapped around my cock feels incredible. I'm not going to last." I don't relent. If anything, I suck harder. I want him to come fast. I want him to lose himself. I want him to lose control. But even more than that, I want to be the one to take it from him. I want him to fall apart. "You going to swallow me down, wife?"

I don't answer him. He's taunted me with that nickname from the start. The term once felt condescending, but not now. Even with the mocking tone, I know he's using it to further solidify the fact that I'm his, and that's exactly what I want to be, so I taunt him right back, showing no mercy as I go harder until his hand stills my head and he lets go.

"My God…" he growls as the hot ropes of cum hit the back of my throat. His hand loosens, but I don't pull off. I suck him until the last jerk subsides, ensuring I don't miss a drop. Now I understand how he must have felt the night we met. I want to taste him in my mouth all night to serve as a reminder of this moment when he came undone because of my touch.

No sooner my mouth releases his cock than he sits up and gathers me against his chest before pulling my mouth to his. His tongue trails over the seam of my lips as his eyes stay glued to mine. "I'm never fucking letting you go. Do you hear me?" I nod in agreement and his tongue pushes into my mouth.

I didn't know dry humping my husband and giving him a blow job could be a turn-on. If we were at home, I'd totally let him have his way with me, insecurities be damned. When he stands up, my cheeks heat for another reason. His pants have a wet spot on them from where I rode his cock. Clearing my throat, I say, "I'm not sure you can leave the room just yet."

His eyes narrow on mine, and for a second, I think he believes I'm asking for round two. I roll my lips and drop my eyes to his crotch. Those hooded eyes follow my line of sight, and that sexy dimple makes an appearance. "It's about time my wife claimed me. The pants are staying on."

"Connor, you can't be serious?"

"Like hell I'm not." He pounces back onto the bed, crawls to me, grabs my chin, and takes my mouth. His tongue dives deep and he groan from the taste of himself that I know still lingers. He pulls back, pecking my lips. "Let's get out of here before I can't."

"Aria, I'd like you to officially meet my wife, Mackenzie. Mackenzie, this is Aria Hayes, Holden's wife and one of my best friends."

Aria extends her hand to me with a massive smile on her face. If she has one negative thought one way or the other regarding our marriage, it doesn't show. You know when someone is being fake to your face, and I can tell her smile is authentic.

"So you're the girl who's been driving Con crazy," she says with a playful smile that tells me that comment was just as double-edged as it sounded.

When I look at Connor, I can't help the cheesy smile that splays across my face at her assessment. I know he and Aria are close, so if his best friend tells me he's crazy about me, double-edged or not, it must be true. I realize he's told me more than once what he wants, but it hits differently when you hear it from someone else, someone who you know is a confidante. His cheeks are slightly piqued with the faintest blush before he schools his expression and kisses my forehead.

"You already know I more than like you." He squeezes my ass. "I'm going to grab a drink. Are you good here?"

"Shoo, Con, she's mine now," Aria says with a wave of her hand.

"You don't have to tell me twice." He walks down the hall, and I hear the guys start hollering and heckling him as he turns the corner.

She loops her arm through mine like we've been friends for years. "Walk with me. I need to find my son. I'm pretty sure he ran out back with his cousin, but I need to check."

As she pulls me through the house, I can't help but comment on how beautiful it is. You can tell she's thought of every detail. "Your house is gorgeous. Did you design it yourself?" A sweet smile pulls at her face as she glances at me, and I can't help but think maybe I overstepped. Perhaps that question is distastefully suggestive, and she thinks I'm implying she couldn't have made it look this great on her own. "I didn't mean to suggest that you couldn't—"

"No, no, stop it. I just haven't been asked that question in a long time. You're new to town, which means you don't know Holden's and my story. There was nothing unseemly about your question at all.

"This house, the property, and every minute detail hold so much meaning for me. This is the only house I will ever live in. You see, when Holden and I met—"

The screen door opens, and in rushes a little brown-haired boy with blue eyes. He's a dead ringer for his dad. "Mommy, I need a Band-Aid. I got a splinter."

Aria swoops him up. "Let me see."

He sticks out his little hand, all his fingers splayed as he tries to show her his pointer finger.

His chubby cheeks are streaked with tears. "Can I have a Band-Aid now?"

"Well, we need to get the splinter out first, and then we can get a Band-Aid." She looks at me and says, "I guess we found him."

Walking up behind us, Cameron interrupts, "I've been looking for you. I saw Connor's truck parked out front almost an hour ago. Where have you been?"

I do my best to play it cool and not give away that I spent the first half hour of my time here giving Connor a blow job. "I've been around. Connor showed me downstairs and introduced me to a few people."

Lucky for me, she quickly loses interest in what I have to say the second she sees River's face. "Buddy, what's wrong?"

"I have a splinter," he says as he holds his hand out for her to see.

"You want me to get it out? You know I'm the best at removing splinters. I even have some magic fairy dust I can sprinkle on it."

Those blue eyes widen. "Really?"

"Yep, let's go get that splinter pulled out." She throws me a wink. Now I see what's going on. Cameron might be good with kids, but she's killing two birds with one stone.

Once we're in the bathroom, Aria sets River on the counter and gets to work. She lays out the tweezers, Band-Aid, and first aid spray.

"So what did I miss? What were you girls talking about before I found you?" she asks as she takes River's tiny finger, angling it to find the right spot to grab for the splinter.

"Aria was just telling me how special this house is to her…"

"I bet. I know Summer has lots of fond memories here.

Well, all her memories are here or at Everett's. I remember the first time I heard about you was from Summer."

"Really?" Aria questions, seemingly intrigued. "I guess that would make sense. I always forget how old I am. Our paths wouldn't have crossed when Holden and I first met. You would have been fourteen." She runs her hand soothingly through River's hair as Cameron works on the splinter. "So what was Summer's first memory of me, anyway?"

"When is Summer coming home?" River asks, looking up at his mom.

"Soon. I think she comes back in a week, if I remember correctly. Next Tuesday?" She looks at me in question, and my eyes go wide.

Where has this summer gone?

"I think you're right," I answer because, honestly, she probably knows better than I do. Connor and I have yet to discuss what date Summer is coming home, and lately, I haven't wanted to. When we got married, he wasn't too happy about the possibility of me still being here when she returned. In my mind, it's always felt as though her return was the expiration date on us.

"I'm sure she'll keep you on the edge of your seat for days with stories when she gets home. She loves to tell them. Her enthusiasm is contagious. You can't help but get wholly invested."

"That reminds me of my brother Josh. He could take something that I knew firsthand sucked and make it sound great. By the end of one of his reenactments, I'd be unsure if we really just went on the same adventure because looking at it through his eyes was so completely different. I remember one time my mother took us to the lake. It was our first camping trip, and Josh was excited to rent a canoe. All he could talk about for weeks after the trip was canoeing on the lake and how he couldn't wait to return. We fought for weeks afterward because I never wanted to go back. The day we rented that canoe, I followed him around the lake for a damn mile trying to find a good place to put the canoe in the water. You had to walk through tall weeds to get down to the shoreline where we were. After walking for what felt like forever, we finally decided to traipse through the tall grass, only to get our shoes stuck in the mud and get eaten alive by mosquitos. Then, when we tried to get into the canoe, we flipped it. I remembered all the bad parts. All he remembered was floating in the middle of the lake, watching the sunset."

"Sounds like Summer. The first time she met Aria, Aria had come over for a party. It was Holden's signing party. From her perspective, Aria saved the day because she helped Summer get her Barbies' clothes on. Apparently, her Barbies needed to be dressed for the party too. She told me after her Barbies were dressed, it was the best night ever. However, from what I heard, Holden punched a hole in the wall and threw everyone out after Aria left on the arm of another guy. I think his name was Trent."

Great segue, Cam!

"Ouch!" River cries.

"All done. Time for the fairy dust," Cameron says as she sprays his finger, only to blow it dry.

"No, I never dated Trent. God, Holden would have killed him before he let that happen."

"Who's Trent?" I ask casually while inside I'm on pins and needles, waiting for her response.

"Oh, he was this guy who was around for a little while a long time ago. None of the guys liked him. He always seemed to rub people the wrong way. I only interacted with him myself a few times. One of Holden's first requests of me was to stay away from him. After what happened to Holly, I see why. The guy was bad news."

"Thanks for fixing my finger," River says as he hops off the counter and runs toward the bathroom door.

"Hey," Aria calls out after him, and he turns back around,

running toward her and hugging her around her legs. "Where are you going?"

"Out back with Dad. He was getting the sparklers ready when I got the splinter."

As she kisses his head, I try to find my words. I'm married to Connor. I know Cameron is aware of the arrangement, and I'm betting since Aria is Connor's best friend, she's knowledgeable, too, so I risk my next question.

"Can you tell me the story about Holly? Connor doesn't really talk about it much."

Aria's eyes soften, letting me know my question must not be as outlandish as it sounds. I feel like I should know about my husband's ex.

"I only know the story because of Holden. Connor doesn't like to talk about it with anyone, so don't feel terribly left out. The story is all sorts of convoluted, and the truth lies somewhere between Holly, Trent, and Connor. I never met Holly. She was never Connor's girlfriend. It's no secret that he's not the girlfriend-keeping type, until now." She throws me a smile. "Anyway, that summer when I first met Holden, Connor sat with me on the bleachers to watch some of Holden's games, and I remember on one occasion seeing him take off into the parking lot to talk to a girl. I remember thinking she was stunning but nowhere near Connor's type, not that I knew what his type was. It just didn't feel like her. They were clearly arguing, and he never came back to the bleachers that night. In hindsight, I'm pretty sure that was the day she showed up to deliver the news that she was pregnant. I don't think Connor believed it was his. They had hooked up once after a party when she first showed up in town, and that was it. By the end of the summer, she was running around with Trent Wells. Everyone knew they were a couple, and that's where things started to get hazy."

I cut her off as I move to the bathtub and sit on the ledge, suddenly feeling lightheaded. *How could I not have put this together?* "I'm sorry. Do you remember what Holly's last name was?"

She snaps her fingers. "Yeah, it was… It was Barden. Holly Barden. Do you know her?"

Do I know her? Yes, I fucking know her. Do I admit that? No. I lie. "It sounds familiar, but no, I can't place it."

"Well, where was I? Oh yeah, by the end of that summer. I left for California, and Holden got drafted, so I can't be certain about all the details. However, I'm not sure they matter. All I can tell you is that Connor blames Trent for getting Holly locked up. He's the reason Summer has grown up without her mom."

Oh my God. How did I not see this? I'm going over every damn conversation I've heard from the start, trying to remember if anyone has ever mentioned her name, and I don't think they did. *Why didn't I ask what her name was?* Holly Barden is Zane's sister. Now I see how I fell on Everett's radar. Zane was on his radar because he's Holly's brother, which automatically put me there too. However, things still aren't adding up. I don't remember my brother being in a relationship with Holly back home, so the fact that he would have up and left without a word to follow her here seems off. But the bigger question is, why would Trent want me here? I'll admit I understand Connor's hatred for my brother, but I can't help but think this has to be one big misunderstanding.

I have to find Connor. We need to talk. There's no way he hasn't already connected the dots between me and Zane. It's time for me to give him the rest of my story so I can clear my brother's name. That has to be why Josh wanted me here.

"Knock, knock. I assumed you were all decent with the chatter going on in here. Do you mind if I steal my wife?"

Both Aria and Cameron swoon, "Awww…" at his term of endearment for me, making his dimple pop and his cheeks flush.

Entering the bathroom, he takes the two steps and holds

out his hand. "Come on, I have something I want to show you."

"Oh my God, this is breathtaking. Do they do it like this every year?" I ask as Connor pulls me out the back door onto the wraparound deck that overlooks the yard. Meteor lights hang from every tree with tiny white twinkle lights sprinkled in, making the trees look like fireworks. In the middle of the yard is a huge stone firepit with what has to be one of the most giant bonfires I've ever seen. Beyond that, there's a huge pavilion wrapped in more lights with picnic tables, food, and a band.

"Yeah, Holden likes fireworks. I usually help him wire the fireworks out in the field for the show."

I'm just about to ask him if we can talk. I want to talk about Zane and Holly. I want to put everything on the table so he and I can finally move forward. I'm more confident than ever that Josh wanted me to help clear his name. It's the only thing that makes sense. Holly wasn't innocent. Now that I know the truth about the shady shit Zane was doing behind my back, it's more obvious than ever that Holly screwed Josh over, not the other way around. "Hey…"

"Hey," he says as his hand circles my waist from behind, and he kisses my bare shoulder. "Did I tell you how incredible you look tonight?" The band starts with their next song before I can respond, and he says, "Dance with me."

I look around and shrink a little from his request. "No one else is dancing."

"It doesn't matter. Everyone and everything fade away when I'm touching you." He pulls me closer and puts his forehead against mine, melting me from the inside out as we start to sway. "Do you know this song?"

I listen to the lyrics, and they sound familiar. "Isn't this a sad song?"

"Some would say that, but others will argue it's one of the most iconic love songs of all time. An achingly romantic song about being consumed by it."

His words make my chest tight. Once again, they dance around the sentiment of love, just like this song. I know how I feel about him, and I'm pretty sure he feels the same, but I would never push anyone into saying it. When and if he ever says it, I want it to be on his terms because he's ready. I was irresponsible with those words. I gave them away easily once before, and the next time I say them, they will be for my person, for my forever.

His eyes are intense as they study mine, making me nervous, so I attempt to ease my anxiety and ask, "Is that how you see it? It's a love song?"

His thumb lazily strokes the curve of my lower spine. "Unrequited love, yes, but now that I'm standing here listening to it with you in my arms, I'm not sure, because now, when I hear it, all I see is you. Whenever you're near, I can't help but be consumed as I cease to exist, and I *fade into you*."

My mouth instantly covers his because there is no question in my heart how I feel. I love him. I love him with my whole damn heart. His arms hold me tight as he kisses me back with what feels like the same unspoken sentiment, and all I can think is, the only reason we aren't saying the words that are clearly there is because of this stupid arrangement. I push back reluctantly because I don't want this moment to end, but I want what's on the other side more.

"Connor, can we talk?"

His brow furrows in concern as his eyes search mine, but before I can offer him reassurance, Aria calls out behind him, "Con, can you help me inside really quick? I promise it will only take two seconds."

"Yeah, I'll be right there," he says as his hand caresses my cheek. "Don't move. I'll be right back."

I nod and give him a small smile. "I'll be right here."

Once the back door closes behind him, I walk toward the railing and look out over the yard, but as the sun starts to set, a different view catches my eyes. Holden and Aria have a lake in their backyard with a familiar view. A strange sense of déjà vu settles over me as I try to place it. A man at the edge of the yard wearing a ballcap with his hands in his pockets steals my attention, and I pull in a stuttered breath as my heart starts to beat rapidly.

Josh's last letter practically begged me to remember our night on Swan Lake, and this view right here bears an uncanny resemblance to the one he and I shared on that canoe. "Josh," I mutter in a barely audible tone. It's too dark, and the distance between us too great for me to be sure, but I know it's him. It has to be. He hasn't moved. He's looking straight at me, unmoving. I know I told Connor I wouldn't move, but it's my brother, who I haven't seen in over eight years. When I head toward the steps, he follows my movement. It isn't until I reach the bottom that he turns, giving me one last glance over his shoulder before he heads down a path toward the lake, and I follow.

CHAPTER 25
MACKENZIE

I didn't feel like I was that far behind him, but the farther I walk down this path, the more I question whether I even saw him. Where the hell did he go? I know it's him. It had to be. The letter, the scenery, the fact that he was standing there looking at me on the porch. I felt it in my bones. I know it was him.

I'm just rounding the corner when the dock comes into view. There's no one on it, but I walk out onto it nonetheless. It's beautiful down here. The view is magical as the last sliver of sunlight breaks behind the trees. I take one last look around before deciding I better head back up to the party. Connor will be looking for me, and the last thing I want to do is upset him after the dance we shared on the deck. He's my forever, and I don't want to keep him waiting.

No sooner I turn to walk off the dock than my heart rate spikes once more as a shadowy figure appears. My palms begin to sweat as I clench my fist to rein in my fear when my visitor's face comes into view.

"Hey, Mac. It's been a while. I missed you."

My heart is beating so fast it feels like it might run straight out of my chest. It wants to run, just like me.

"Zane, what are you doing here?"

I hadn't thought much about seeing Zane again because I hoped I wouldn't. I don't trust my emotions, and I don't trust him. It's hard to look at him now and not feel anything when he used to be everything. No part of me wants him back, but he's been by my side since middle school. He was my only friend until high school, when we became more. Zane knows me better than anyone. That's when it hits me.

"Oh my God, have you been the one sending me the letters?"

How else would he have known I'd be here? I thought I saw Josh, but maybe I saw what my mind wanted me to see. Zane knows me. He knows everything about…

"What letters? Who is sending you letters, Mac?"

The surprise on his face and the question in his voice tells me he didn't. He takes a step toward me when he sees my distress. "Don't!" That is all I manage to get out as I try to calm my racing heart and get a grip on my emotions.

"Mac, you need to tell me. I'm here for you. I came to get my girl back."

Is he on drugs? How the hell could he possibly think I'm still his girl?

"The last thing I am is your girl, Zane. You lost that privilege the night I…" I trail off, unable to bring myself to say the words out loud, not only because they hurt but because they disgust me. He takes a step toward me, and I instinctively take one back. "Don't. Don't touch me."

He runs his hand down his face with a growl of annoyance. "Mac, you have to let me explain. It's not what you think."

"It's not what I think? Are you kidding me? I saw you. I saw you in that place with one of them. I caught you red-handed."

He closes his eyes and shakes his head. "I was there undercover, Mac."

My eyebrows shoot up in surprise as my eyes feel like they're about to pop out of their sockets from his absurdity.

"You must really think I'm an idiot if that's the best you got. You went to jail, Zane. They don't fucking lock up innocent people."

"They do when they don't want their cover blown."

"You're a forklift driver in a lumber yard, Zane! You really expect me to buy this undercover crap? Why would they hire you to go undercover?"

He pulls in a visible breath and takes a look around. "Look, I'll tell you everything you want to know, but not here."

I shake my head in disbelief. "I'm not leaving with you."

His eyes hold mine as if he's searching for some little shred of hope that I'll change my mind. "If I tell you here, will you reconsider?" I cross my arms but give him no words. "It's all because of Holly. This entire mess is her fault. I went to visit her a few months ago. That's when all this started. It had been a few years since my last visit, and after I heard she was attacked, I wanted to check on her. When I was going through checkpoints to get in, I got pulled to the side. It was a new facility, and I thought maybe it was standard procedure, like when you go to the airport, and they pull every tenth person who enters through an extra checkpoint, but I was wrong. An agent pulled me aside and asked if I'd be willing to wear a wire and ask Holly some curated questions. Alarm bells immediately went off, but I was curious. How could I not be? Holly was in jail for fraud charges, and from the letters we received from her, she was getting out early for good behavior. Plus, you know we were young when she got locked up." He shrugs and puts his hands in his pockets, and my heart pangs with empathy.

We were in middle school when our siblings disappeared. Well, Holly didn't exactly disappear, but either way, one day, they were part of our lives, and the next, they were gone.

When you're young, you don't understand things the same way you do as you get older, and I'm sure part of Zane wondered if the stories he was being told about Holly weren't being censored for his young mind. He knows I have a soft spot in my heart for him because of Holly. It's why we bonded back then. We both lost someone we cared about, and part of me can't help but wonder if he's exploiting that now.

"Get to the point, Zane. How did that visit land you in the warehouse?"

His chest deflates, letting me know I was right. He was trying to manipulate my emotions. "Ever since we were little, Holly was a storyteller. Spinning stories became an obsession for her, and the older she got, the more she used it to her advantage. Turns out she was, and is, a big player in a significant crime ring back home. The cops saw an opportunity to use me to get to her, and so far, it's worked. I led them to the warehouse that night from one of Holly's tips. I was able to help three guys get put away that night. They'll be serving life sentences for crimes related to trafficking."

My brain is overloaded with all this new information. A big part of me wants to believe him. Trusting him is familiar. It's what I've done for as long as I've known him. I drop my head, feeling somewhat defeated. Events from that night are still hazy.

"Being a part of my world automatically made you a target in hers. Come on, Mac. You know me. I did this to protect you."

My mind goes back to that night as I try to sort through the things I remember clearly. His story sounds credible, but isn't there an element of believability in every lie? Not to mention, he's had eight years by my side to learn what makes me tick. He knows my vulnerabilities.

"Was getting your dick sucked to protect me? Was that part of the job as well? I can't trust you. I don't trust you. Not after that."

He frustratedly runs his hands through his hair. "She wasn't one of them. Fuck, Mackenzie, I'm not one of those men. I fucking swear it. You know me, Mac." His eyes plead with mine, begging for me to believe him. When he sees nothing, he drops his gaze. "She was undercover with me. Her name is Shannon. We'd been working together for three months. I never once thought of her in that type of way. I never once thought of her as anything more than the girl I was undercover with, but that night when she showed up wearing one of those outfits to blend in with the others, I—"

"Just stop. I know the rest. I was there, remember? Go home, Zane. There is nothing here for you anymore," I say as I give myself a wide berth away from him to exit the dock.

"We're not done," he says as he takes three large steps and grabs my wrist. "You're still wearing the necklace."

My eyes snap up to his, and he instantly sees my fear. His face softens as he says, "I'm sorry—" and I scream as a right hook catches him in the jaw and takes him to the ground.

CHAPTER 26
CONNOR

"Oh my God, Connor, stop. You're going to kill him," Mackenzie screams from behind me as I pound my fists into the face of the asshole she used to call her boyfriend.

"Good, he deserves it."

Her hands hit my back as her fingers clench around my shirt, and she attempts to pull me off. "He's not worth it, and Summer needs her father. She can't have two parents in jail."

Those words, coupled with her hands on my body, have me pulling back. The last thing I need is her getting caught in the crossfire.

Zane gets to his feet and wipes the blood from his busted lip. "Who the fuck are you?"

"I'm her husband." I turn around and yank the damn necklace she has around her neck off to make my point clear. "She's mine." I'm livid.

As I raise my hand to toss it into the lake, she screams, "No!" but it's too late.

"You've been living under my roof, sleeping in my bed, and telling me you want forever, all the while wearing a necklace from another man." I watch as tears stream down her face like I somehow crushed her heart by removing his necklace, which pisses me off. "You'll have to excuse me for giving zero fucks about your tears now."

"This is your guy, Mac? You can't be serious. He clearly doesn't know you."

My fist connects with his jaw once more before I have time to process that I consciously decided to hit him. I'm furious for more reasons than I can count. I need something to take out all my pent-up aggression on. Why not him? Why not the asshole who hurt Mackenzie? The one who is clearly still lying through his teeth. But no sooner he attempts to take his shot at me than the sound of a bullet loading in a chamber snaps both our heads away from each other and toward the sound.

"Stop it!" she yells. "Stop fighting. I'm done with all of this shit." She points the gun toward Zane, her hand trembling as she blinks back tears. "I'm not sure why you came down here, Zane. If you truly thought I'd buy your lies, then you never really knew me at all."

He slowly raises his hands. "I'm not lying. I can prove every word, Mackenzie. I swear it."

"You are!" she screams, making us both slightly jump because she is clearly upset and holding a loaded gun. "You came here tonight and gave me half-truths, thinking they would be enough. You knew where to find me, Zane, which means you knew my new name—"

"Fine, okay, fine. I fucked up, Mackenzie, and I know that, but I swear I never meant to hurt you—"

"Stop, just fucking stop." She shakes the gun at him. "I don't care anymore, that's what you don't seem to understand."

Those words have me taking a risk and stepping toward her. As much as I'd love for her to shoot this asshole, I don't want her living with the scars.

"Mackenzie, baby… please," I say as I inch closer.

"No, I'm just as mad at you. You have no idea what you just threw away," she says, turning the gun toward me.

My heartrate kicks up a notch from the adrenaline that comes from having a gun pointed at me but also from her words. I'm so fucking lost right now. *Why the hell is a necklace that he gave her so damn important? How is it more important than everything we've shared?* I clench my jaw and bear through it.

"Then tell me, help me understand—"

She shakes her head. "No, I've given you multiple chances. I've tried to talk to you from the beginning. I wanted to share this burden with you, but you told me no."

"Baby, I told you why—"

"Don't call me that. That term is for lovers—"

"Don't you dare finish that sentence, Mackenzie. You're hurt. I get that. So am I, but don't say things you don't mean. You know damn well I was ready to give you everything. You walked off that porch, not me. If you want to give me those words, fine, but only say them because you believe them."

"I wasn't walking away from you. I thought I saw my brother and—"

"Wait, Josh is here?" Zane asks, pulling Mackenzie's attention away from me and back to him.

That's when I pounce, stepping in, putting my hand around the gun, and pulling her into my arms. My heart is pounding every bit as fast as hers when I spin her so that her back is to Zane. His presence is affecting her. The last time she saw him, he fucking gave her a concussion, and now all this bullshit. I aim the gun at him.

"You have ten seconds to get the fuck off this dock and never come back before I take away your choice."

He shakes his head and rolls his lips. "I'm going to prove I was here to help, and when I do, she'll be mine again. We have history."

I fire a shot into the water right past him. "That was your ten seconds. The next shot won't miss."

I didn't want to fire that shot, nor did I want to let him go, but my girl needs me. Plus, if he came here for her, chances are he's not leaving. He'll be back, and I'll be waiting. He walks off the dock without another word, and I lift her into my arms.

"I'm taking you home."

Even if she's mad, she needs me, and I know this because fuck if I don't need her. Everyone at the party is now going to be on their way down here to see what the hell is going on, and we need to leave before we have to explain anything. The last thing we need right now is an audience.

As I take the long way back to the front of the house to avoid family and friends with her wrapped tightly in my arms, I can tell she is in shock. She holds me tight and keeps her head buried in my chest, and fuck if it isn't tearing me up. After I was through with helping Aria take s'mores platters out to the bonfire, I returned to the porch, ready to give her everything. Every truth I own. When she said she wanted to talk, I only thought the worst for a moment, allowing my tortured soul to play tricks with my heart. There was no way, after everything we've shared thus far and after our dance on the porch, that I read her wrong, read us wrong. I felt it in my soul. Like me, she physically couldn't take the secrecy anymore. Our arrangement is the only thing left standing in the damn way of us stepping into forever.

Initially, when I couldn't find her, I assumed she'd gone to the bathroom, believing there was no way she wouldn't be waiting for me in the exact spot I had left her, but when I checked the house and the yard, I knew something was off. That's when a guy wearing a baseball cap caught my eye. He looked so out of place. Everyone at the party knows each other. This is a small town. I watched him walk up the path from the lake with his head down and his hands in his pockets, only to stop dead in his tracks and look at me. It was as though he could feel my eyes on him. I couldn't make out who he was. It was too dark, but he knew I saw him. Looking back, I think he wanted me to see him. He dropped my gaze and continued up the path, walking the yard's perimeter. I wanted to follow him, but he was alone. He wasn't posing any threat, and I still had not found Mackenzie. Were it not for that shady fucker walking up the path, I may not have thought to check the lake. I may have been too late.

Running down to the lake, worst-case scenarios were cycling through my head. That shady fucker hurt her, and I'm about to find a body. Knowing I didn't know everything about her made my thoughts that much worse. My anxiety eased just a little when I heard her voice—but then I heard another. I stayed back, letting the tall grass surrounding the lake conceal me as I eavesdropped on their conversation. I needed to know who and what was more important than the talk we were about to have. But then he touched her, and I saw red.

Pulling open the door to my truck, I quickly place her inside. Then, reaching across her body, I click her seat belt into place and glance at her eyes. They're pinned straight out the window with a faraway look telling me her mind is anywhere but with me.

"Mackenzie, baby…" I trail off, putting my hand on her face and gently nudging it, forcing her eyes to meet mine. "I need you, baby. Tell me what to do so I can make it better."

Her eyes barely search mine before they close, and a single tear falls. "I just want my brother back. I thought he was here." Her hand reaches to her chest for the necklace that's no longer there, and her face pinches in pain.

"Connor," Holden's voice calls out.

Closing the door, I run around to the driver's side and climb in so that we can get out before I have to answer for anything. I'll send him a text once I'm on the road.

On the way home, she says zero words, which leaves me with my thoughts. Something triggered her back at Holden's place. A lot of things happened in a short amount of time, so it's hard to pinpoint exactly which one set her off. All I know is that she's here with me. She trusted me to care for her, and I'll be damned if I let any intrusive thoughts take that from me. I had no idea Mackenzie had a brother. One would think that would have naturally come up in conversation over the past few weeks or, hell, when I investigated her, and the fact that it didn't has me feeling unsettled.

Pulling into the driveway, I hurriedly park the truck and jump out to come around to her side and help her down. Holden was pissed when I sent a voice text on the way home. I know he isn't buying my story about betting Mackenzie I could shoot a fish. He knows about our visit to the shooting range a few days ago. He was the one who brought over one of Aria's smaller guns for me to strap to Mackenzie while we got all this shit sorted. I'll eventually own up to what happened tonight, but I was trying to salvage what was left of their holiday while getting her out of there. Right now, my priority is getting her inside where there are guaranteed to be no further distractions. Where it can finally just be us.

Walking through the front door, I lead her over to the couch. "Baby, lie down." I take her purse and throw it on the chair opposite the sofa before stacking a few throw pillows for her to lie back on. She does as I ask, and I pull her wedges off. "I'll be right back."

We were occupied doing other things at the party. She probably hasn't eaten since lunch, so I head to the kitchen for some coconut water that I know she loves and snacks. The other day she was in here, chopping up fresh vegetables to go with the homemade hummus she made. I quickly grab the Tupperware container and two cans of water before returning to the living room. After I set the containers on the table, I sit on the end of the couch by her feet and drop my head into my hands. She hasn't said two words to me since we left Holden's, but I'm hoping that giving her some of mine will get us back to where we were just a few hours ago.

"Mackenzie, you are the last thing I expected to find this summer. There's a reason I don't do relationships, and it's not just because of Summer. It's because I don't know how to do them. I feel like I care too much or not enough. It doesn't seem like there's any in-between. Whenever I thought I was doing something for you, you thought I was doing the opposite." I run my nails across my scalp and pull at my hair. "I don't even know where to start. I want to apologize, but I'm unsure what I did wrong. I'm going out on a limb here, Mackenzie. I'm trusting you with my heart and secrets, but most importantly, my little girl."

"It was the necklace, Connor," she says, her voice small and strained. "I didn't mean to freak out. I'm sorry."

When I look up, she's reaching for the satchel I tossed on the chair.

"Let me get it." I grab the bag and hand it to her so she doesn't move. Her nerves are clearly still getting the best of her, as her hand shook when she outstretched her arm.

"Zane gave me that necklace, but I never thought of him when I wore it. It reminded me of my brother. He went missing eight years ago."

The annoyance I've felt since the second I ripped that chain from her neck slowly starts to ebb. I've watched her lazily play with it or reach for it from time to time, and given that she never took it off, it was clear it meant something to her. However, on the way home, I couldn't feel remorse for my actions. All I could hear was him saying, "We're not done… you're still wearing it." How else was I supposed to take that?

"Why didn't you tell me you had a brother?"

"Because he's the reason I'm here. A few months ago, I got a letter from him out of the blue. Connor, I was so damn happy. He was twenty when he disappeared. At that age, the cops don't do much. They had no reason to suspect foul play. One day, he was there, and the next, he was gone without a trace. It didn't make sense that he would just up and leave me and Mom without a word. We were close. After eight years, I started to believe that maybe I was wrong. Maybe he really did leave on his own, but then I got a letter. That letter was why I went to the warehouse that night." She pauses and reaches for one of the coconut waters, and all I can think is I already don't like this guy. Who sends their little sister into a place like that? "He explained that he missed me and had kept tabs on me all these years but needed my help. The letter had a location, date, and time for me to show up. He made it clear that I by no means needed to go, and that he understood if I didn't. However, he had to know there was no way I wouldn't go, Connor."

I place the vegetable platter on the seat between us. "Can you please eat while you talk?"

She nods and dips a carrot stick in hummus. "You know what happened after I showed up at the warehouse, but the part you didn't know was I got another letter while I was in the hospital getting checked out for my concussion. It was vague as hell and made zero sense when I opened it. It read: *Take the help, M*. That was it. It wasn't until one of your father's men showed up and offered to help me that I understood what it meant, and even then, I wasn't convinced. Everything has been one big fucking riddle."

I'm trying hard to follow everything she's saying, but nothing is adding up. I feel like I'm missing something big. She says she came here because of her brother and the letters he's been sending. That's when my father's words from when we got married come rushing back. He said, "We both know you haven't been completely transparent in coming here." My father must have known then about the letters. He knew she wasn't just taking his help for refuge.

"Mackenzie, who is your brother?"

Her eyes soften, and her bottom lip trembles as she looks down. Opening her satchel, she pulls out three envelopes. "Will you read these first? I need you to have all the pieces I have before I give you a name."

"Why can't you give me a name?"

"Because I'm scared you'll push me away when you find out. That his name will cancel out all the rest…"

My phone rings in my pocket as a truck starts honking its horn barreling down the driveway.

"You have got to be fucking kidding me," I say as I stand and pull my phone out of my jeans and head toward the front window.

When I see it's Cayden calling me, I answer. "The world better be on fire."

"It might be. Trent and Holly are on the move, and so is her brother. Shit is about to go down. Get the fuck outside. It's me pulling down your driveway."

"Damn it," I say as I end the call, stuffing the phone back in my pocket and rushing back toward the couch.

"Baby, I have to go. I wouldn't leave if this wasn't important. I need you to stay here." I reach for her gun I tucked in the back of my belt when we left the party. Laying it on the couch beside her, I say, "When I walk out that door, I want you to turn the alarm on. I will have Elijah come get you and take you to my dad's. I don't want you here alone. Not tonight."

"Connor—"

I take her face in my hands, lay my forehead to hers, and say, "I know," before pressing my lips against hers. Leaving is the last thing I want to do right now. "This is the last time. I fucking swear on my life. When I get back later, you're mine. We're not leaving this house until it's all out, do you hear me?"

She nods, and I kiss her one more time before pulling away.

"Lock this door, Mackenzie. Don't open it for anyone but Elijah."

CHAPTER 27
MACKENZIE

We'd been home for no more than ten minutes before Connor and I were epically interrupted once again. I was too shaken up and distraught on the car ride home to give him anything, and I fucking hate myself for it right now. Seeing Zane hurt. His visit brought back memories, and hearing his words shook me. I was already reeling from all the revelations, and then Connor had to take the damn necklace. *Why did he have to take the necklace?* My heart still fucking hurts. I felt like he took a part of me and threw it in the lake. I know it's not all his fault. He didn't know, but I was so angry. It was my last piece of Josh.

I know it's stupid. Josh technically didn't give me the necklace. Zane gave it to me, but he gave me that necklace on the same damn day Josh disappeared. It brought me comfort. It filled this emotional void that my brother's disappearance had brought on. When things felt hard, I would rub my necklace. When I was happy, I would grasp it hard as if I were hugging him. It's just a silly silver necklace with the letter M on it for Mackenzie, but that's why I connected with it even more. That was his nickname for me, and for it to show up on the day he disappeared… I don't know. It just felt like a sign. It gave me hope, and Connor threw it all away in two seconds.

He was right on the dock. If I had said the words he knew were coming, it would have been in anger, not because they were how I truly felt. But I couldn't help myself. I wanted to hurt him the same way he had just hurt me. Now, all I have is an empty house to comfort me because, once again, I failed at using my mouth to communicate the words in my heart. I look at the letters I laid on the table from Josh, and I leave them. I've kept them close since I started getting them again, but we are done hiding. The truth can only set me free, but first, I think it might piss me off.

Closing the front door, I lock it before arming the security system. I don't know where Connor had to go or why, but I know it was important. He wouldn't have left otherwise. If tonight proved anything, it's that we are both ready to take the next step so that there's no longer anything fake about our marriage. Connor said he would send Elijah to pick me up, so with that in mind, I head down the hall to grab a change of clothes. I'd love to shower, but I doubt I have time.

As I push open the door to my room, I head straight for the closet to grab some comfy clothes and fresh underwear. I'll shower at Everett's house. Lord knows he has more than enough bathrooms. I grab a pair of sweats and forgo one of my shirts in favor of one of Connor's. He said he liked me wearing them, and if by chance he doesn't pick me up before I fall asleep, at least I'll still have part of him with me. Exiting the closet, I throw the clothes on the bed in search of a bag when another damn envelope catches my eye. It has the same M scrolled across the front as all the others.

"What the hell, Josh?" I murmur out loud as I go over to the bed to read the letter. In all the chaos that unfolded tonight, I haven't even had a chance to wrap my head around the fact that it was his last letter that had me leaving the porch in search of the lake. Why the hell would he send me that letter and not show up?

M,

I'm so sorry. I've been saying that a lot lately. I didn't know Zane would be there. It was me. You saw me. I wanted to hug you so bad. I wanted to come out. You have no idea how tired I am of hiding. But I couldn't risk it after Zane showed up. There's too much at stake. I know your heart, M. In the end, you'll understand. I'll see you soon. I promise.

"I knew it." I fucking knew it was him. God, at least I know I'm not totally losing my shit, and my instincts are still intact. Standing on the dock, I questioned a lot of shit when Zane appeared instead of Josh. My emotions have had me in a fucking chokehold all damn day. I may have lost a piece of my past tonight, but a part of me was living there. I see that now. I couldn't move forward with Connor if I kept putting Josh first. Holding this secret held me back. Connor did me a favor by taking the necklace off. We can't heal our pasts, but we don't have to keep living in them either.

As I angrily shove clothes into my bag, preparing for Elijah's arrival, I can't help but go over all the words I plan on giving Connor the second I see him. I won't allow there to be any more distractions. There will be no more hiding, no matter the cost.

"I don't understand why we can't get a hold of him, Everett. Why aren't you doing more to find him?" I grind out as I make breakfast for Summer in the kitchen. It's been three days since Connor left in the middle of the night, destination unknown, and in that time, Summer came home a week early with a sprained ankle. I know he'd be here in a heartbeat if he knew she was home, and that's what has me worried now. I feel like something has happened, and Everett is keeping it from me.

"I said we couldn't get a hold of him. I never said I didn't know exactly where he was."

I can't help but slam the butter knife on the counter.

"You know where he is? Why wouldn't you tell me that?"

Before he can answer, Summer returns. "Can we go down to the Fields tonight? I know the Bulldogs have a game, and I don't want to miss it even if Coach isn't back in time."

"I'll check my schedule and see if I can take you there. What time do they play?" Everett asks as he leans against the countertop and sips his coffee.

"The game starts at five fifteen p.m. Can Mac take me if you have to work? Please, please, please." She adds a pouty lip to go with her prayer hands like she knows exactly which strings to pull when it comes to him.

He looks at me over his mug. "I'll clear my schedule if Connor isn't home."

I can't help but roll my eyes. Everett hasn't let me leave the property since I showed up, but it hasn't been all bad. The first night was me and Cameron staying up and talking about all that's happened. She literally knows all the details now, and I mean everything. Letting go has felt cathartic. I can breathe, and having someone to confide in has been eye-opening.

Cameron doesn't think after everything that Connor will hate me because of who my brother is, and after talking it through with her, if anything, I feel stupid. *Doesn't every couple have someone in the family their significant other doesn't care for?* We've all got that one uncle who always crosses the line or that parent who is too extra. At the end of the day, we aren't building a life with those people. We are building a life with each other, or in our case, the three of us will be creating a life together.

On the second night of captivity, Summer came home. I'll admit when she first walked through the door, I was nervous as hell. I knew who she was, but she had no idea who I was. I didn't know what to say or how to introduce myself. I felt like I was on the biggest job interview of my life. Summer is one person I need to like me. It was naïve to think I only had one heart to earn, one heart to worry about. Connor doesn't come by himself. He comes with an adorable sidekick.

While I was standing in the foyer with Cameron and Everett, feeling largely out of place and underprepared for this family reunion, Everett took the guesswork out of my title and introduced me as Connor's wife. I wanted to shrivel up and die right there. I don't know much about children, but I was sure that was not the right way to handle the situation. I think telling Connor's daughter that her father married while she was away at summer camp should have been eased into, maybe not even shared at all until Connor returned to do it the way he saw fit. After all, it's his daughter. But it just goes to show how much I don't really know about him or this family because other than her eyes going wide for about ten seconds, she was unfazed and said, "It's about time."

Connor wasn't exaggerating when he said she was wise beyond her years. The girl is an old soul and funny as shit for a kid. She entertained Cameron and me for hours with stories about camp and her time at her cousin's house. We stayed up watching movies, painting each other's nails, and eating our weight in snacks.

"Well, if you guys are going, so am I," Cameron says, entering the kitchen and stealing a piece of bacon from the platter I've yet to set out for everyone to eat. "We can make it a family night." She sits on the stool.

"Sounds like fun." I carry the bacon and eggs over to the island and place them close to Summer, ensuring she gets first dibs.

Everett stays quiet in his corner as he looks at the three of us dishing out our breakfast onto our plates, and I slowly start to lose what little appetite I had. All I've been able to get out of Everett is that Connor had to handle things with Holly, but Everett is well aware that I know it's more than that. I told him what happened at the lake the night of the Fourth of July party and the events that took place after we got home and Connor left in a rush. I've been worried sick that something happened, and I've had zero opportunities to drill Everett with Summer around. The only thing holding me back from going off the deep end now is that Everett doesn't seem worried. I have to believe that if something awful happened, Everett wouldn't be so damn calm. I'm choosing to let that be enough for now.

"Evi, I need your card. I want some popcorn."

Everett reaches into his back pocket to grab his wallet. "Take Cameron with you."

"Ugh, I'm eight years old. I can go by myself. Plus, I know everyone here."

She reaches to snatch the card out of his hand, but he's quicker. "I don't want you going alone. Not tonight."

"Fine," she huffs. "I'll take Mac," she says with a shit-eating grin. The little girl is quick. I can tell you that much. She hasn't missed that Everett hasn't suggested my name once for anything or that he's told her no every time she's asked to leave with me over the past two days.

I stand. "I'll take her. It's not a problem."

His eyes narrow on mine as though I've somehow challenged him. What I don't understand is why he introduced me as Connor's wife, which would infer that I am her stepmother, someone who would take care of her and have her best interests at heart, given I'm married to her father, only to treat me like I can't be trusted.

He doesn't give us any words and instead hands over the card.

"Thanks, Evi," Summer says, snatching the card before he has time to change his mind and pulling me by my hand down the bleachers. "You've met Parker and Elijah?"

"Yep, I've met them. Why?"

"Just making sure I don't get in trouble for bringing a stranger with me into the concession stand when we skip the line and go through the side door."

"I like how your mind works, but we will be fine. I worked down here all summer with your dad." I pull open the side door and gesture for her to enter. "After you, Sunshine."

She pauses in her tracks, and it's then that I realize what I said. "Summer, I'm sorry. It just came out. I didn't mean to overstep." I drop down to one knee so I'm at eye level with her. "I know that's what your dad calls you. I'm not trying to take that. I won't say it again. I promise."

I didn't mean to say it or take his words, but after spending time with her, the nickname is more than fitting. She's a breath of fresh air. She keeps you on your toes, there's never a dull moment, and with those platinum blond ringlets and blue eyes, she looks like summer. She looks like sunshine.

"It's not that. It doesn't bother me that you called me Sunshine. I just wish Coach were here. I miss him."

I pull her into me and give her a hug. "Me too."

"Wow! You two could pass for mother and daughter," Elijah says, stopping dead when he sees us by the door.

"Well, she is kind of my mom. Right?" Summer says as I pull away to stand.

My heart squeezes so damn tight in my chest. God, I wish Connor were here. "I'll be whatever you need me to be, Summer."

"Well, the resemblance between the two of you is uncanny." He looks between us more.

I suppose she does look like me. I hadn't really put too much thought into it. My mind has been pulled in a million different directions over the past few days. Summer shrugs and runs over to the popcorn machine, and I take a second to see if Elijah will tell me anything.

"Do you know where Connor is?"

His brow furrows as if he's confused. "He's not out there coaching the game?"

"No," I say, but don't offer any more. Given how close he is to Everett and my situation, I thought maybe he would have an idea of what's going on, but it's obvious he doesn't.

"Elijah, do we have any more Swedish fish back in storage? We're out up front," Summer says as she returns with her popcorn.

"No, I just sold the last box a few minutes ago. Sorry, squirt."

"It's okay. What about blue Gatorade?"

"Come on, I'll give you one on the house. I was just coming to get more out of the back refrigerator."

"Yes," she exclaims as she pumps her fist in the air.

While I wait for her to get back with Elijah, I check my phone to see if I have any missed calls or texts from Connor. Still nothing. My thumb hovers over the call button. I've sent a few texts and called countless times. I'm sure he'd call me back if he had his phone, but it doesn't stop me from hitting the call button anyway. Bringing the phone to my ear, I send up a silent prayer, hoping it goes through, but it doesn't. Instead, I get the generic 'this inbox is full' message.

"Ready to go?" Summer says, sneaking up behind me.

"You know, you're pretty stealthy for someone with a sprained ankle."

"Fast healer. Plus, I've always been good at being sneaky. I need to use the restroom before we head back to the bleachers. Can you hold my stuff?" she asks as I push open the door to the concession stand.

"No problem," I say as I take her snacks and watch her go around the cement wall into the bathroom. God forbid I lose sight of her for one second. Everett would have my head.

A finger taps my shoulder as soon as she's in the bathroom. When I turn around to see who my surprise visitor is, my heart stumbles. His hair is darker, he's taller, his shoulders are broader, and he has facial hair that definitely wasn't there the last time I saw him, but it's him. I'd know those pale blue eyes anywhere because they match mine.

"Oh my God, Josh. You're here," I say as I throw myself around his waist. The popcorn spills out of the bucket. I forgot it was in my hand as my head snuggles into his chest and tears well in my eyes. I can't believe this is real. That he's here. "Is it really you? Tell me I'm not dreaming this."

"It's me, M. God, I missed you so much." He wraps his arms around me just as tightly.

"Mac, I'm… Oh, hi, I'm Summer. Are you one of Mac's friends?"

Josh releases me and looks between the two of us. "She looks just like you," he says as his features soften. "I'm Josh, Mackenzie's brother."

She eyes him from head to toe, sizing him up. "Josh, is that short for Joshua?"

He smiles and laughs. "Why yes, as a matter of fact, it is."

"Well, Joshua, I have a bone to pick with you."

His brows shoot up, and he adjusts his ball cap. "Yeah, and what's that?"

"It would appear that you bought the last box of Swedish fish, and you may not know this, but it happens to be a tradition that at every Bulldogs game, I get a tub of popcorn and a box of fish, which guarantees a win. So you see, I'm going to need that box of Swedish fish unless you want to explain to my boys back there why they didn't bring home a win tonight."

His face contorts into a huge smile that he quickly bites back once he realizes she is not joking. Pulling the box out of the front pocket of his flannel shirt, he hands it to her. "When I was up there buying my gum, I noticed there was only one box left, and something told me to buy it. It must have been my second sight knowing a little girl would rob them from me to save the fate of a game."

I can't help but cover my mouth and laugh. A guy walking behind us curses loudly as he drops his beer, ending our stolen moment of happiness because in the next breath, Josh's face sobers, and he says, "I have to go."

"What? Why? You just got here. Let me take Summer back to her grandfather, and I'll—"

He shakes his head. "This isn't bye forever. It's bye for now. I'll see you soon."

I'm about to argue again when I see Everett walking our way. Before I can utter another word, Josh is walking past me as though he never stopped at all, and I let him because at least I got one of the men in my life back tonight, and I'm hopeful that means the other one isn't far behind him.

"Hey, do we have marshmallows inside?" Summer asks as we sit around the firepit in the backyard.

After the Bulldogs won their second-to-last game of the season, everyone was high on the rush of the win. We were winning by one run the entire game. Every time we'd score, they'd score, and finally, in the bottom of the ninth, they tied it up. The game went into extra innings, but our lineup started from the top. The boys were fucking hungry. We ended up getting three more runners home while it was our turn at bat, and when Chavez took the field for his last inning, he dug deep and delivered an immaculate inning, striking all three batters out. Needless to say, everyone was excited, even me, and that's saying something. I've never watched or followed sports as a fan or enthusiast, and I was thoroughly entertained.

Moira came back to join us as well. I've only ever lived with my mother and whatever boyfriend she would allow to stay over from time to time, so I'm not sure what divorced couples or blended families should look like, but I suppose it's good that Moira and Everett still get along. Summer is thrilled she is here. Cameron, on the other hand, not so much.

"I'll help you find the marshmallows. We can grab the skewers while we're in there, too," Cameron says as she gets up to follow her in.

As soon as the back door closes, the privacy gate to the back yard opens, and it's a good thing I'm sitting because the person who enters has my whole body feeling like mush as my emotions threaten to get the best of me. His eyes crash into mine and steal my breath. My heart literally fucking hurts. I missed him so much, but with one blink, the affection that was there is instantly gone, and the longing is replaced with ire as a scowl takes over his face.

I quickly look away to hide my hurt, only to catch Everett and Moira sharing a knowing look. It's clear I'm the only one who is surprised to see him. I am the only one who has yet to learn where he's been or what he's been up to.

"Connor, come sit down. We were just about to do s'mores."

He approaches the fire, but I don't look at him. I can't. It hurts just knowing he's here and not excited to see me. I thought I'd be one of the first people he'd want to see. At least, that's how he made me feel before he left.

"I'm not staying. I came to get Summer."

I try hard to keep my eyes pinned to the fire and not let the sound of my heartbreaking show.

"Connor…" Everett's voice is a warning.

Same as me, he heard Connor's dismissal loud and clear. I saw my brother for the first time in eight years today, and now Connor's back. The writing on the wall is loud and clear. Our arrangement has come to an end. I got my brother back, and I'm assuming whatever secret he held close to his heart has also found its resolution. I open my mouth, ready to fight my battles and leave this arrangement with whatever remaining pride and self-worth I can scrounge up, because I don't care who you are, getting your heart broken fucking sucks. You can't help but feel low and unworthy. It doesn't matter that I know I did nothing wrong. It doesn't matter that I know I'll find someone else eventually. Heartbreak is nothing new for me. You're a fool if you believe that hearts weren't made to be broken. I just really thought this time I had found the person who makes it beat, the person who makes it whole.

"No, not this time. The two of you royally fucked up. I'm your fucking son!" he yells.

Everett stands. "Connor, calm down."

"No, you knew all along. You knew exactly what you were doing. You knew I would love her."

I can't help but look up from the fire when he uses that word in reference to me, and when I do, his eyes meet mine, and I see his pain when he says, "All of you played me like this wasn't real, like I didn't matter…" He pounds his chest. "This is my life! All of you knew what was at stake, and none of you thought I was important enough to clue in."

The hurt in his eyes helps me find my words. I want to make it better. I want to take it away. It doesn't matter that I'm hurting. We fought this whole time, endured the pain, made the sacrifices, and I'll be damned if I'm not going to fight now, so I ask, "What do you think I know?"

He shakes his head and rubs his jaw. "This entire time, you used me. You used me to get to her."

"Connor, I have no idea what you're talking about," I say as I stand up and step toward him. "Can you please calm down—"

"I read the letters, Mackenzie! All of them." Okay, that gives me something to work with. He finally figured out that Trent, the same one he hates, the same one who was responsible for getting Holly locked up, is my brother. "You knew who I was and what I had. You let me believe that this was more, but you were here doing his bidding the entire time. 'You're right where you need to be… I'm sorry, but I need you to get close to Callahan.'" He parrots Josh's letters. "And to think I actually thought you loved me." He turns to his parents and adds, "Any of you!"

Walking toward the house, he asks, "Where is she? We are leaving."

Everett's by his side, instantly stopping him from going into the house. "You are not going inside like this. You need to calm the fuck down. Go walk it off, Connor." Connor pushes his dad back, but Everett doesn't budge. "You want to fight. Let's go, take your hurt out on me. I'll gladly take it from you, but you're not setting foot inside that house until you get your shit together."

Connor rubs his thumb over his lip and shakes his head. "I'm not going to fight you. I don't even care to fight. You're not worth it. You turned my own family against me."

"What the hell are you talking about?"

"Cayden! You knew I'd ask for his help."

"I gave Cayden nothing. Did I know what he'd find? Yes, but whatever he chose not to tell you was based solely on whatever vibes you gave him in conversation. Apparently, everyone else can see what you refuse to accept. You're the only one standing in your way."

Without another word, Connor walks off toward the front yard, and I follow after him.

When he hears the gate close, his eyes flash to mine, and all I see is hate, but it doesn't stop me from approaching him. I can't help but feel if I could touch him just once, he would settle down the same way I did on the Fourth of July. I was so mad at him, but the second he held me in his arms, the anger started to recede.

"Go home, Mackenzie. Go back to your fucking double-wide trailer and have a nice life. There's nothing left for you here."

I slap him hard across the face without thought. It wasn't the kind of touch I was planning on giving him, but it's the kind he deserves.

"Are you fucking kidding me right now?" I yell.

The rise and fall of his chest is more pronounced as he pulls air through his flared nostrils to rein in his anger. Those dark eyes that once talked of forever now bore into mine with an almost palpable hate, but I'm not scared. I refuse to back down. I don't care how mad he is. That comment was below the belt.

"Coach!" Summer's voice breaks our stare-off as she runs out the front door and leaps into his arms. He holds her tight, so damn tight. The way I thought he'd hold me when I saw him again.

"Ready to go, Sunshine?"

She nods, and before she can say another word, he puts her in the back of his truck and closes the door.

"Please don't do this," I say as he rounds the truck.

"You played me." He points his finger at me. "But she's mine. I'll fight you tooth and nail."

"I don't understand—"

"Bullshit." He hits the hood of the truck. "You knew she wasn't my blood. It's why you're here. To get close to me, to take her. You knew I didn't like Trent, and I told you why I couldn't give you my secrets. Never once did you say Trenton Joshua Wells is my brother. Because you were never here for me. You were here for him. I get it. He's your family, but she's mine. Blood doesn't make it so."

I offer him no further words as he climbs up into the truck. I can't because I'm fucking speechless. Summer Callahan looks like me because she's my family. She's my niece.

"It's not a big deal. I don't need my clothes. They were never really mine to begin with. I came here with the clothes on my back, and I can leave the same way. I just need a ride to the bus station," I say as I pack my satchel with the few items I brought.

"I just think you're giving up too easy. Connor is hurt, Mac. People have the right to feel hurt."

She's not wrong. The problem is, I can't fix this. He saw the letters from Josh that I left on the table and he made his choice. There are no secrets left between us. He has everything, and he's still choosing a future without me in it.

"I'm not saying he isn't entitled to his feelings, Cameron, but I have mine too. From the beginning, I've tried to talk to him. Things kept getting in the way: our insecurities, our fear, and life, but isn't that fate? Everything is destined to happen a certain way regardless of what we want."

She throws a suitcase onto the bed. "You're not wrong. Fate is a preordained destiny. We can't control who or what comes into our lives, but we can choose who we keep. I've been by your side the last few days. I've watched you worry, and I've watched you hope. I think you dreamed of a future with him in it. You wanted it with your whole heart. I'm a dreamer, Mac. Dreams give us hope, and I believe they have the power to change our fate if we let them. You just have to have the courage to fight for it. I don't want you to leave. This is where you are meant to be."

Her words have power. She's not wrong, and I want to have faith, but I'm hurt too.

"Cameron, I know you mean well, but Connor isn't the only one in pain. I was used too. Everett has known all along that Josh was my brother. He kept that from Connor, and he kept Summer's paternity from me. He sat back and pulled the strings. You can't tell me that he didn't see this happening. I can't stay here. I need to check in on my mother anyway."

"Well, I'm not letting you leave without more clothes," she says, opening her drawers and throwing her stuff into the suitcase.

"That's not necessary—" I start, only to be interrupted.

"You're right, it's not because you won't be leaving. At least not tonight, anyway," Everett says as he pushes open the door to Cameron's room.

"Everett, I have nothing to say to you, and you can't keep me here. It's over."

He rubs his short beard and briefly considers my words. "Is it over if you haven't heard my side of the story? Before you cast me as the villain, I think it's only fair that I get to share my piece. It's late. You can stay here for the night, and if you still wish to leave in the morning, I won't stop you, but first, I'd like to tell you about my son."

"Would you care for a drink?" Everett asks from where he stands at the bar cart, pouring his usual glass of cognac.

"No, thank you. I'd rather you just get to the point so I can get out of here. I don't see how anything you could possibly have to say would change things."

He walks to his desk as though my words didn't faze him. I

hate feeling like he doesn't care how deeply he hurt his son and me. As he takes his seat, he takes a drink and closes his eyes. "I did this because I love my son."

I roll my lips and try to bite back my irreverent response but don't. "Your definition of love is fucked-up if you believe the pain you caused is justified."

"You can't know love without pain. Can you sit there and tell me that it didn't hurt to hold onto your secret? That you didn't endure its pain out of love for your brother and for the love of my son?"

His eyes study me as I think about his words. He's not wrong, but at the same time, he was the cause.

"You pulled the strings, Everett. You interfered. You could have saved us all this grief by being honest from the start."

"I didn't keep secrets to hurt you. I kept them because I knew of you. I've always known exactly who you are. What I didn't know is if you knew anything about my family or that little girl I consider my granddaughter. I knew you didn't stumble upon that warehouse. Your medical reports from the hospital revealed as much."

"What is that supposed to mean?"

He takes a quick pull off his drink. "A nurse asked why you were there, and you told her your brother sent you. I was already going to help you because of who you were and what your ex did that night, but those words changed things. Trent knew I was watching Zane because I'd been watching Holly. Bringing you here helped me accomplish two things: First, I couldn't leave you in good conscience after what happened. I wouldn't be able to sleep at night, but secondly, I had something important to Trent, and having you close helped me deduce what you did and didn't know and get a better idea of his intentions. That letter you never opened was a test. The fact that you didn't immediately open it, hungry for whatever details it could possibly hold, told me that while you may have come here with ulterior motives, you weren't clear on your mission. Which would make sense with everything that's recently been brought to light where Trent is concerned. Regardless, I was leery. I had to be."

"If the letter was a test and I passed, why go through with all the rest?"

He swirls his drink as he thinks over his next words. "Because it didn't change that Trent was still on the other end using you. We haven't been able to find him since he left town eight years ago, and suddenly, he was back, making moves that included sending you here. You have to understand that while Summer isn't blood, we raised her. I couldn't let you come in here and do Trent's bidding. Elijah told me about the night he picked you up at the bar. There was clearly an attraction between you and Connor before you ever knew who the other was."

I can't help but roll my lips in irritation. "So you thought exploiting us was the answer?"

"Exploitation feels a little strong. I more or less stacked the deck. I couldn't make the two of you have feelings for each other. I couldn't make him love you. That happened all on its own. I merely got him out of his own way. I won't lie and tell you that I didn't have my own motives. Clearly, I did. You're Summer's blood. Of course I wanted things to work out. The two of you falling in love and staying married ensured we didn't lose her."

He's right. I want to be mad, but arguing his logic is hard. It doesn't make it okay or change that this has turned into one big mess that feels insurmountable, but knowing his intent was never malicious takes the sting out of the wound. If I can find forgiveness in my heart for Everett, maybe the same can be said for Connor, but I'm not ready to visit that hurt.

So, instead, I ask, "What can you tell me about my brother?"

He smirks, seemingly satisfied that he's cleared his name. "You ready for that drink?"

CHAPTER 28
MACKENZIE

It's just after midnight when I finally make it out to the pool house. I had planned on sleeping with Cameron, but she had fallen asleep by the time Everett and I were done talking. I'm glad I didn't leave. Running would have been easy, and I wouldn't have found closure. Even if things between Connor and me don't work out, I have truths. Opening the door to the pool house, I flip on the switch—only to jump out of my skin when I find Josh sitting on the sofa.

"What the hell, Josh? You scared the living shit out of me. Why are you sitting in the dark?"

"I said I'll see you soon," he says as he stands with a smirk and throws his arms out. I hesitate for the briefest of seconds before running into his arms.

I hold him tight and don't let him go. I have my big brother back, my best friend. I let his big arms wrap around me and bask in their warmth. After the day I had, I need someone who truly cares about me to hold me. I need my family. When he left, I was twelve years old. His muscles are more defined, he's taller, and his dirty-blond hair is darker, but he's somehow still the same Josh, and it's almost as though no time has passed at all. It's that last thought that has me pulling back and punching him in the stomach.

"Ow, that hurt."

"Yeah, well, you deserve it. You have some explaining to do."

His face softens as he tosses his ballcap on the sofa behind him. "God, M. I don't even know where to start."

"Well, I have a list. For starters, why did you leave to begin with? Or how about, where have you been all this time? And most importantly, why didn't you tell me you had a daughter?"

He falls back onto the couch behind him and leans his head against the back, staring up at the ceiling. "The summer I left, I never planned on leaving, and I definitely didn't plan on staying gone, but Holly Barden asked me for a ride, and I went for one I couldn't get off."

I curl onto the oversized chair. "What do you mean, 'she asked you for a ride?' I don't even remember the two of you being friends."

He runs his fingers over his forehead. "That's because we weren't, but I'm a guy, M. Holly Barden was hot. I ran into her outside of the gas station. She was sitting on the curb smoking a cigarette and asked me if I could give her a ride to the bus station. The next thing I knew, the bus station turned into Waterloo, Illinois."

"Why did she need to come here?"

Sitting up, he looks at me. "The story was, she was trying to visit one of her friends who went away for college, but after we arrived, I realized that was a lie. She wasn't here to visit a friend. She came here for a job. Holly was grooming girls online, giving them tips on how to make easy money in exchange for services." He pauses and reaches for the bottle of water on the table.

So far, his story aligns with everything Everett and I discussed this evening. I picked Everett's brain for hours. Regardless of whether I stayed or left, I needed to know what he knew about my brother to know if I could trust him when I heard his truth. I'd like to think he wouldn't hurt me, but I never thought he'd leave, and people change. Which begs the question: why did he stay?

"Why didn't you turn her in and come home?"

"Well, she turned an eighteen-hour car ride into a week. By the time I arrived, we were more than acquaintances. I think I already mentioned the part about how hot she was..." He trails off, breaking eye contact and scratching his head. He's telling me without telling me that eighteen hours turned into a week because of the hookups that took place along the way. She laid the bait, and he took it. "I'm a guy, M. I liked her, and in the beginning, I wasn't positive that I was right about everything I began to suspect. Once I knew for sure, I thought maybe I could make her stop. I believed we had something, but I was wrong. Once I had enough evidence to do something about it, she blackmailed me. I was suddenly an accomplice, and you were back home hours away from me, an easy target for the crew she ran with to pick up."

I pull a blanket off the back of the chair to cover my legs and get cozy because we are nowhere near done with this conversation. "Okay, that explains the how but not the why. Why didn't you ever call, or better yet, why didn't you come home after she was locked up?"

"You don't miss anything, do you?" He sighs. None of this is easy to talk about. I get that. I'm over here selfishly thinking about its effect on me, but he lived it. "On the way down here, I lost my phone, or at least at the time, I thought that's what happened, but looking back now, I wouldn't have put it past Holly to have thrown it out at a truck stop just to isolate me. That's why I never called to check in or say 'hey, I'll be home in a few days.' Then, after we got here and I started suspecting things, I thought better of having any communication back home. I didn't need you on her radar any more than you already were just by being my sister. I wanted her to forget you existed. As for why I didn't come home after she was locked up, that's a little more complicated. No one in this town liked me, which, believe it or not, was part of my plan. I didn't want people to like me. Liking me put them in Holly's orbit. Needless to say, once she went to jail, I had a target on my back. Everyone so easily bought her tale of being set up when, in reality, she was the ringleader. I didn't know the Callahans were even looking for me when I left. They weren't my concern. Holly's crew was, and as for Summer, I never even knew Holly was pregnant. I didn't find out she had a daughter until a year ago when one of my father's guys told me."

I move up to the edge of my seat in disbelief. Josh hates his father. He was named after him, which is why anyone close to him calls him Josh instead of Trent. "Wait a minute. Are you talking to Trenton now? After all these years and what he put Mom through?"

He sits forward and puts his elbows on his knees. "M, I went to him out of desperation. I needed protection, and I got it. I paid a price, but I got it."

Trenton Wells, Josh's father, was our mother's first love. She said it would have been him if she had ever married, but he was also the exact reason she never married. Men couldn't be trusted. Trenton Wells lived a double life, and Josh was a product of that. Trenton was very married when he was sleeping around with my mother. He was a smooth talker with deep pockets, and after he found out my mother was pregnant with Josh, he gave her an ultimatum. She could live in one of his houses as his girlfriend, or he would cut her off and give her no support. Of course she chose the latter. Who wouldn't? But she didn't know that he would make her life hell as he tried to force her hand and bend her to his will. It's why she was limited to working jobs for people who knew her before she ever met Trenton Wells and why we never left the trailer park.

Knowing the kind of deals Trenton Wells makes, I ask, "What was the price, Josh?"

His eyes lock on mine, and I see the apology in them before he ever speaks a word, and then he says, "You."

"What the hell is that supposed to mean?"

"Turns out we aren't half-siblings. Even after Trenton did her dirty, she fucked around with him again and got pregnant with you. When Mom found out she was pregnant with you, she cut him off for good. She didn't want him to know about you. She was convinced things would just get worse. For a while, he didn't think anything of her silence. They went back and forth for years, going for extended amounts of time without contact. When he found out she had a daughter, she lied and told him you were Bobby's because that's who she happened to be dating at the time. But he suspected she was lying, and honestly, I'm not sure how she thought he'd buy it. We look alike." He finishes his water bottle and gets up, heading straight for the kitchenette. "Want something?"

"Yeah, I'll take a sparkling water," I say as he grabs a Coke and a snack-size bag of chips from the counter. "So Trenton Wells is my father?" I've never known who my father is, and I'm unsure how I feel about finding out it's him. I have a lot of preconceived notions about him because of Josh and the little bit I'd heard my mother complain about him over the years. But other than being a two-timing prick who couldn't keep his dick in his pants, I know nothing.

"M, I'm sorry. I'm sorry I put you in this position, but I was rocked to my core once I found out about Summer. I planned on coming out of hiding to clear my name. Trenton had the resources to help me do that, but finding out about Summer changed the game. I acted out of haste and made a deal without thinking it through. Trenton isn't as bad as Mom made him out to be."

"So he didn't cheat?"

"No, he cheated..." His eyebrows rise as he opens his bag

of chips. "But he had his reasons. Those will be his to share. I don't want to fill your head with the colors I've chosen. I've already put you through enough. Including the mess you're in now."

"Yes, please do fill me in on how you saw all this playing out," I say as I open my water, trying to come off less affected than I am. However, I know my voice failed me.

"M…" He sets his chips down before rising off the couch and dropping to one knee before me. "God, I wish I could go back and do things differently. I started sending you those letters for selfish reasons. I needed you to get close to the Callahans, but I also knew they'd protect you. I had no idea that Everett would force your hand in marriage, but I'd be lying if I said I wasn't somewhat happy that he did. Taking Callahan's last name protects you from Trenton if you don't want to speak with him. I told him I would bring you to him. He wants to meet you, but you carrying the Callahan surname gives you the choice. Everett Callahan is one of Trenton Wells's biggest rivals. Callahan defends the good guys, but someone has to defend the guilty. Right now, Callahan has him by the balls for a certain deal he may have cut corners on with a high-profile client." He moves to get off the floor. "It's another reason the timing felt right to bring you into the fold. Trenton doesn't want to make waves."

"What?" feebly falls out of my mouth, as I'm at a loss for words. That was a lot of information to absorb. Defender of the guilty or not, it sounds like dear ol' Dad has his shit together. I always assumed he was a lowlife, the way our mother talked about him. I never would have thought he was a successful lawyer.

"Yeah, I'm guessing Everett left that out of your little chat tonight. To his credit, Everett never connected the dots between Trenton Wells and me because he had no reason to. Trenton has been married to the same woman for over twenty years and has no known children. That last part is another reason Trenton went after Mom. He wanted his family."

"Everett knows you're here? In town, I mean." If he does, it makes sense why Everett was so paranoid about me leaving anywhere with Summer over the past few days. He either thought I'd take her and run, or Josh would intercept me.

He quirks a brow. "You seriously think he doesn't know exactly where I am right now?"

I hadn't considered that Everett might know he was here, but it doesn't surprise me after talking with him and getting his version of why he played his hand the way he did. The truth about Summer's paternity would eventually come to light, and he doesn't want to lose her. He's trying to do what's best for his family, even if his tactics are questionable.

"Yeah, well, you disappeared for eight years. I'm pretty sure that means you know a thing or two about going undetected."

Josh smirks before taking a pull off his Coke. "Don't get me wrong. I don't think he's happy I'm here, but he knows the truth. Like it or not, I wasn't the bad guy, and Summer is my daughter." His face pinches, and I can tell those words are still foreign to him.

"She's great, Josh. I know there's bad blood between you and Connor, but he did a good job."

"Yeah?" he questions, genuinely curious, and I want to offer him more, but I can't. Instead, I get choked up because I didn't just fall in love with Connor. I fell in love with her, too, and it hurts that I'm now on the outside. I close my eyes, determined not to cry, but Josh sees my pain.

"M, this is my fault. I got you into this mess and promise I will get you out. I'm here now, and I don't plan on going anywhere. Summer is here, so this is where I'll be. If you want to stay, you can stay with me. Now that I don't have to hide, I plan on getting a place here."

I play with the blanket on my lap, folding and unfolding

the corner as I ponder his words. I don't want to leave him. I just got him back, and now that I know Summer is his blood, I want to stay for her, but there's still my mom. "What about Mom?"

"We can bring her here. We can find a nice place for her to stay. I have money, M. I can take care of us."

I bite my lip, unsure of what to say. He's offering me everything I wanted, everything I hoped would come out of all this, so why does 'yes' feel hard? My eyes close as my heart answers the question for me: because Connor isn't here. He fills all the cracks.

"Let me handle Connor—and not for you, for me. I messed this up. I'll fix it. I asked you to get close, but I was vague with the reason. I didn't expect you to fall for him…" He pinches the bridge of his nose. "I may have said some things, and that's on me."

"What do you mean, you 'said some things?'"

He stands up and grabs his hat like he's getting ready to leave.

"Trenton Joshua Wells, you tell me what you said. What did you do?" I demand as I fly out of my chair, blocking his path.

He shakes his head. "I was mad, Mackenzie. I'm still mad, and he was an easy target. I lost years with my daughter that I can never get back because these assholes helped put a target on my back. I understand they had good intentions, and if the roles were reversed, I'm not sure I wouldn't have done the same things they did to protect a little girl and her mom, but unfortunately, that's not this story. This time, they got it wrong. I'll get over it, but it's going to take time. The wounds aren't going to heal themselves overnight. Just let me handle it."

"Where are you going now? It's midnight."

"To fix it."

CHAPTER 29
CONNOR

The last three days have been a total mind fuck, gaslighting, and psychological manipulation all rolled into one. A masterfully constructed play with me, the unsuspecting star of the show. Eight years ago, a girl I had a one-night stand with told me she was pregnant, and it changed the course of my life. Initially, I didn't believe Holly when she came to me. I knew I had wrapped it up the one night I was with her after a house party in town. I was drunk off my ass that night. She was not the type of girl I typically go for. Don't get me wrong. Holly was a beautiful woman. Every guy in town took notice of her. Her sun-kissed olive complexion, long brown hair, and chocolate eyes were the talk in the locker rooms. Then, add that she was the new girl in town, untouched by anyone I knew. Hooking up was a no-brainer. Fast forward two months later, and that dream was an instant nightmare. She handed me an ultrasound picture that showed she was indeed eight weeks along, which fit the timeline of our hookup. I don't care who you are. No guy in their early twenties wants to find out his drunken one-night stand is pregnant.

Trent Wells wasn't in the picture when she first came to

town. He was around, but to my knowledge, they weren't an item. Had she been seeing someone else then, I would have questioned it. If I had known she was sleeping with Trent when she first came to town, it would have made sense that she was trying to pin me with her baby. Trent was a loner who rubbed everyone the wrong way. He was not father material. That's probably why she chose to pin me with the baby. It ensured her baby had a decent future. *Fuck.* I pour myself another drink as I sit alone at the island in my kitchen, where I've been since I tucked Summer in for the night.

I've always known some version of what's happening now was in my future. There would be a day when I would tell Summer I wasn't her biological father, but I thought it would be on my terms, and not because someone was trying to take her from me. Holly voluntarily gave up her parental rights forty-eight hours after Summer was born, which gave me sole custody. It was my name listed on the birth certificate, not Trent's. When Summer was six months old, I went to visit Holly. It was something I had done monthly since she got locked up. Initially, we worked hard to clear her name, and I would show up with updates on her case and Summer.

That six-month visit changed things. She asked me to stop giving her updates about Summer. I was immediately caught off guard. Why wouldn't a mother want to hear about her daughter? The confusion written all over my face pissed her off. She knew how that request looked, and that's when she told me I shouldn't care so much. Summer wasn't mine. I didn't argue with her. I didn't say anything. I simply got up and left. At the time, it felt like she was looking for a fight. I thought she was hurt. It was the only thing that made sense. She was in jail, and I was on the outside raising our daughter. But on the drive home, I couldn't help but have this sinking suspicion that she wasn't lying. Summer didn't look like my baby pictures, and while I know a baby's eye color can change up to a year after birth, she had the bluest of blue eyes, and Holly and I both had dark brown eyes.

Within a week of that visit, I was sitting in the doctor's office getting a DNA test done, but even as I was getting it done, I knew it wouldn't change anything. I may not have been her biological father, but I would protect her. Holly was in jail, an unfit mother who couldn't care for her, and while she didn't tell me who the bio dad was, I put it together on my own. That's what sealed the deal for me. There was no way I would let a guy I knew was shady as fuck have her. She became my job. The older Summer got, the more obvious it was that Trent Wells was her biological father, but no one questioned it. Trent left town when Holly got locked up. People's memories of them and their appearance faded over the years. No one remembered the color of Holly's eyes, and they had no reason to believe Summer wasn't mine. But now that will all change, and I'm not ready, and he's the last person I'd ever thought would be in the picture.

The sound of the motion detector chimes on my phone, and I see a man in a ballcap walking up the front steps. "You've got to be fucking kidding me," I say before slamming my drink down and heading to the front door. We said all that needed to be said when shit went down the other night. Throwing open the front door, I say, "Get the hell off my property, Wells. You have no business being here. Summer is legally mine, and your mole is gone."

I go to shut the front door, and he stops it. "We'll have to agree to disagree on both fronts, because that mole and little girl are both reasons for me to never leave your front porch. You don't have to like me. I'm not asking you to, but I'm going to be in that little girl's life. I have money to fight you for her, Callahan, but I'm not here for a fight."

God, I fucking hate him. I hate him so much, but my hate isn't going to solve anything, and over the past few days, I've realized why it's grown so deep. Everything I want in this world is his: the little girl I raised and the woman I thought I'd keep forever. My fear is the root of my hate, and it will destroy me if I don't face it.

"Wait here," I say as I shut the door and head toward the kitchen in search of the bottle of whiskey I've been drinking for the past hour. If I sit down and have a conversation with Trenton Wells, I know I will need a drink.

Exiting the front door, I find him under the gazebo on the side of the porch. After pouring my glass, I set the bottle and extra glass I brought for him on the rail before taking a seat on the built-in bench.

"I'm assuming you're here to talk about seeing Summer."

He turns to me and rubs his jaw. I can tell the topic affects him as much as it does me. I'm not happy about sharing her as much as he hates that I have her.

"She's on the list, but first, I wanted to show you this." He pulls a letter out of his back pocket. One that I don't take. I'll be damned if he's going to serve me papers. He doesn't miss the tic in my jaw and quickly realizes the direction of my thoughts. "It's not what you're thinking. Just read it."

He steps toward the bench I'm sitting on and tosses the letter next to me. Now that it's lying beside me, I can see it's a folded-up piece of notebook paper. As I unfold the note, I expect to see Mackenzie's writing, and when I don't, my lungs deflate with a breath I didn't know I was holding, only to get punched in the chest when I read the signature scrolled across the bottom.

"Is this…" I can't even bring myself to say it.

"A suicide note? That's debatable. In typical Holly fashion, she doesn't fail to spin a story."

We all have a role to play. I played mine. There are two sides to every story. Some will tell you one is a lie and one is the truth, but who gets to decide? Right and wrong, good or bad, neither exists until someone defines it. That's what I did. For every wrongdoer, enemy, and foe, there will always be a victim. I merely bridged the gap. They were both going to exist anyway. They say nothing good comes out of a lie. I wonder if my daughter would agree. Cast me the villain all you want. I saved her, and it will save me.

Holly

"She was a narcissist, through and through, painting herself the victim, offended by the truth. But you don't get to be a victim of a problem you created," I say before asking, "Where did you get this?"

He shrugs. "I stuck around after you left and didn't put it past her to fake her own death. A cyanide pill felt too easy. When the paramedics showed up, I spotted it tucked into the jacket they removed when they attempted to resuscitate her. The cops were busy with the two guys she had with her, and Zane was focused on her. I easily picked it up and walked off."

This note answers nothing. If anything, it should deepen my anger, but it doesn't even do that. I should be mad that I don't have solid answers regarding her choices, like why she chose me over Trent to raise Summer. I should be bothered that this note isn't for her daughter, one she never got to know. But I can't because that would mean I never had Summer.

I hand it back. "Don't ever show that to Summer. She doesn't know much about Holly other than that she existed. She doesn't need to read a fucked-up note from a villain who tried to paint themselves a hero."

Taking the letter, he sticks it into the back pocket of his jeans, and as I watch him, I can see his nerves. It's clear talking about Summer isn't easy. I get the impression bringing her up isn't either, so I ask, "Are you ready to talk about Summer?"

With his eyes cast down, he shakes his head and puts his hands into the front pockets of his jeans. "No, I can wait. I've waited eight years. What's a few more minutes? I'd like to talk about a girl I've known since the day she was born. A selfless girl with big dreams and an even bigger heart."

I can't help the discontentment that washes over me. Somehow, talking about Summer felt easier than talking about Mackenzie.

"I think we have more important things to discuss than your sister."

"You're not wrong, but I need you to hear me out," he says as he leans against the spindled rail. "I let you believe I used her more than I did because I was mad, just like you. I realize you have this perception of a person you believed me to be for the past eight years, and that doesn't just disappear overnight, but you have to understand I've had my own bias toward you. Your family was quick to make me the bad guy and put the cops on my tail. I couldn't prove my innocence, and in some ways, I wasn't. I knew and saw things I'll forever have to live with, but I did it to protect Mackenzie. Holly used her as blackmail against me. Then fast forward to finding out the guy who helped force me into hiding raised my fucking kid, a child I had no idea even existed. Yeah, I was a little fucking pissed off."

He crosses the gazebo, grabs the bottle of whiskey I brought out, and pours his glass. "I didn't use Mackenzie in the way you think I did. I just didn't correct you when you let yourself believe that I did. When I sent her here, I did so for selfish reasons. Did I want her to get close to you? Yes. But I also knew your family could protect her in ways I couldn't until the Holly shit was cleared up. She had no idea Summer was mine. I couldn't risk it. Zane was good to her for a long time until he wasn't—"

I stop him there because while I might be sensitive to the fact that he missed years with Summer he'll never get back, he put his sister in danger. "I should fucking punch you right now for that shit. You put her in danger, and now you expect me to trust you with Summer—"

He holds his hand up. "I sent Mackenzie in there, knowing Zane was inside. He lied about not cheating on her. Zane was messing around with that undercover cop for months. I wanted her to see the truth and know what was going on, and I needed her to see the ugly that was happening all around her to protect herself. Mackenzie is tougher than you think. I had no idea Zane would react the way he did. It took everything I had not to blow my cover when I found her in the hospital hours later. That's why I sent her the letter to 'take the help.' I knew your dad was watching Zane. I knew he'd protect her."

As much as I hate it, I buy his crap about Zane, even if I don't like it. I would have bet money that everything he said to Mackenzie on the dock was a lie, but I would have been wrong. It was easy to call into question his character because of his relation to Holly. She was a pathological liar, a master manipulator of the worst kind. But he was indeed working with the Feds to get his sister locked up for good, even if that's not what happened in the end.

I take a long drink, remembering the events that transpired a few nights ago. That night hasn't left me and undoubtedly clouded my judgment in everything. It's not easy to let go of what you thought to be true. Accepting that your perception of reality was false is hard to swallow, but then toss in that it was that false belief you held onto that informed your decisions. While I may not trust Trent, I also don't trust myself. How could I? I spent the past eight years believing in the wrong person. It's made me call into question everything. That's why I returned to the house after everything went down and didn't leave. I didn't trust myself to be around anyone. Today was the first time in the past three days that I felt like I had a lid on my emotions. It wasn't until I got to my dad's house and saw the family that I was once again triggered.

"I realize I can't make you forgive her. At the end of the day, she kept my secret, but you kept one too. Mackenzie was truly innocent in all of this. Whatever happened between the two of you was not my doing. She didn't know about our past. She didn't know about Summer. All she knew was her brother asked her to come here, and if she's anything, it's loyal. If she gave you any piece of her heart, which I think we both know she did, you'd be a fool to let it go."

Fuck. I hate that he's right. I'm a masochist. I drew the line. I pushed her away, and now I'm upset she's gone. I inflicted my own pain, thinking it would somehow make me feel better. Even if she knew about Summer, my heart knows there's no way she faked falling. I threw my walls up out of fear. I was already losing so much. At least losing her would be my choice. I clear my throat, expecting to find my next words, but nothing comes. They won't, not unless she comes back. Doesn't everyone know the tallest walls are built to protect the most profound love? I may have laid the bricks, but she was the mortar binding every brick, filling every crack, and now I'm afraid I may have let the best thing I ever had slip away.

Mackenzie's car pulls down the long gravel drive, but I don't allow myself to move. I can't. It's been one week. One week since my world was turned upside down and one week since I broke her heart and mine. We started out fake. We always had an expiration date. I drew my lines, and she drew hers, but somewhere along the way, those lines faded into one beautiful smear. It's why I'm sitting outside this house on this cursed ground—for inside holds all her memories.

I pick up a rock from the pile I brought out here when I decided that this is where I will be for yet another day, and skip it across the lake, watching it fly across the smooth water, gliding with grace. Its path distracts me from my own. I don't know why she's here. Maybe it's to collect her things. I can't be sure, but I refuse to move. Moving risks feeling, and feeling is the last thing I want to do. I came out here to escape and quiet the noise. It doesn't matter that I need her sound more than I need my next breath, but the silence is better, for it holds answers too.

The car door slamming has me wanting to turn my head just to catch a glimpse, but I don't. Not even the sound of her feet walking down the gravel path to the lake is enough to make me turn my head and risk the hurt. But when she steps onto the dock and doesn't say a word, I chance using my own. She's here for a reason. May as well get all the breaking done at once.

"What are you doing here, Mackenzie?" I ask, not sparing her the irritation laced in my tone.

"Well, for starters, we're still married," she says without missing a beat, but where I thought I'd hear disdain and derision for still being saddled to me, I hear an impish taunt. "Why do you have to be so damn stubborn?" Her voice now hints at irritation.

"What the hell are you talking about?" I demand as I finally give in and turn from my spot on the blanket, only to quickly regret my choice. Even pissed off, she's more beautiful than I remember, but I'll be damned if she didn't come here to spite me. She's wearing that same blue dress she wore the night we met, the same one she wore when we said our vows. Mackenzie knew that dress would affect me. It's written all over her face.

"Did you mean it?" she huffs out as she puts her hand on her hip.

"Mean what?"

"Did you mean it when you told Everett, 'You knew I'd love her?'" Her voice softens just enough to show her vulnerability. She's nervous, too, and fuck if that doesn't give my heart hope.

"Every word," I grind out optimistically, unsure of where she's going with this line of questioning but refusing to give her anything but honesty. I'd rather leave my heart on the line to be shredded into pieces than not give her everything and question later if I didn't give her enough.

Her lips press together, and she furrows her brow as her eyes narrow in confusion before she asks, "Then what are you doing sitting here on this dock?"

My heart starts pounding as I stand, my chest tightening in anticipation of her reaction to my self-induced isolation and silence. My words would only fill her mind. I needed her to feel my silence so she could hear my soul. It's why I haven't left this place. If I was destined to live without her, so be it, but I'd live with her memories all the same. I'd let them tear my heart open just to feel. Her memories were here, and while painful, they were ours. Every word, every fight, every feeling, they were ours. Sitting in my silence, I was able to hear her. It's how I knew I had to let her go. I couldn't be the one to go after her, even if she deserved an apology.

"Waiting for forever to come back to me."

"What?" breathlessly falls from her pretty mouth before she drops her gaze.

"Your hand was forced the first time. I wasn't going to force it again. It was the only way. I'll lay my whole world at your feet, but you have to want to be a part of it because it's your world, too."

Before I can utter another word or have a chance to assess her reaction, she's running into my arms, sending us crashing back onto the blanket. I hold her tighter than I ever have, determined to love her harder than I ever did because that is what this is. It's what it's been all along. Sure, we were forced together, but our choices were always there. We didn't have to sleep together. She didn't have to give me her mouth or her heart. Pulling back, her eyes search mine, and my hand cups the side of her face as those crystal blue eyes steal my breath. "I'm so damn sorry…" I pull in a ragged breath. "For everything, all of it."

"I'm sorry, too." Her eyes fall to my mouth, and then her lips are on mine.

There's nothing gentle or sweet about her kiss. Her mouth devours mine in an all-consuming kiss that tells me this past week was as hard on her as it was on me. She takes what she wants, and I let her. As her hands slide around my neck and pull me close, threatening to never let me go, I wrap my arms around her just as tight with the promise to do the same. Her nails drag over my scalp, making every hair on my body stand on end, and I can't help but get hard.

I reluctantly pull out of her kiss. "Mackenzie, I don't want to ruin this. I don't want to mess it up, but if you keep kissing me like that, I'm going to want more." I know she can already feel the evidence of what more is springing to life in my jeans.

She's currently straddling my lap, as this is how we landed after she crashed us to the ground. Grinding herself against my dick, she asks, "Are we alone?"

I can't help but groan from her feel and the inference. I want what she's offering, but I begrudgingly unwrap myself from her and lean back on my palms. A frown instantly takes over her face. "Don't do that. You can feel how much I want you, but I want to do things right. You deserve to be swept off your feet, wooed, romanced—"

I'm instantly silenced as she pulls her dress over her head. She's completely naked. Her full tits that I love hang heavy as her nipples instantly pebble from the cool air. "What if I don't want that?"

I struggle to find any words. My dick has the woman of his dreams sitting naked on his lap with nothing but a zipper separating him from heaven. But somehow, I manage to feebly reply, "Why wouldn't you want that?"

"Because it's not our story. Nothing about us started out normal. I'm not a princess. This isn't a fairy tale. I want us." Fuck if those weren't all the right words. Those words steal mine, and she knows it. If she's the painter, I'll gladly be her muse. She adds color to my world by just existing. My eyes stay locked on hers as I try to hold onto the sliver of corporeality that remains as my brain settles into an ineffable fog that is nothing but her.

Her hands find the hem of my shirt only to slip underneath as her delicate fingers trail up my stomach, sending tendrils of need straight to my groin. As she glides her hands up my chest, she pulls my shirt with them until all that's left is removing it, and I gladly let her take it off. Once it's off, her eyes connect with mine, and I fall into a diamond-blue abyss I hope never to climb out of. Her perfect mouth covers mine once more, but this time, her kiss is slow and unhurried like she has all the time in the world—and she does because there's nowhere she can go that I will not be by her side. My hands leave the dock to run up her thighs and slide up her waist, but I barely have time to savor the feel of her soft skin under my hands before she breaks our kiss.

My mouth can't help but chase hers, and she playfully smiles before pressing her hand to my chest and saying, "Lie back," and I go without pause.

Looking at her straddle me stark naked with the backdrop of a gray sky behind her is breathtaking. I'll remember this day for as long as I live. I came down here with the biggest bottle of whiskey I own to drown out the memories of her, and it still wasn't enough. It could never be enough. Not when she's the breath in my lungs and the blood that runs through my veins.

Her hot mouth trails warm kisses down my stomach that instantly make my skin prickle as the crisp air from the storm rolling in cools my heated skin. When her lips meet my jeans, she doesn't pull them down as expected. Instead, she keeps her lust-filled eyes on mine as she licks the outline of my erection through my pants. My cock twitches and a bead of pre-cum leaks from the tip.

"Fuuuck," I hiss out as I close my eyes and try to pull back my desire. At the rate things are going, I'm going to come before she ever pulls my dick out.

Before the thought has left my mind, she's unbuttoning my jeans and pulling my boxers down. "Looks like your cock missed my mouth as much as my tongue missed its taste."

I bite my lip hard as she uses the same damn line I gave her the night in the shower when I took her for the first time. Her tongue runs up the underside of my cock once before she sucks my tip clean, and I stop her. That night was more for her, just like it was for me, but it's her hand currently wrapped around the base of my cock wearing the ring I put on her finger that tells me everything. She's all in. This isn't a game. She's mine.

"Get up here." Her big eyes are marred with confusion when they land on mine. "I need you up here with me so I can swallow every moan and savor every kiss." Releasing my cock, she slowly crawls up my body, letting her full breasts skim my stomach and chest. She's teasing me, and I'm here for it. Those lips I requested find the crook of my neck at the same time her wet pussy glides over my length. An untamable groan rumbles from deep in my chest. "I need to be inside my wife."

"Wife?" She pulls back and quirks a brow but doesn't stop her ministrations, letting my cock slowly glide between her warm lips. I could force it in. I could make my tip slip in easily, but I won't. I'll play her game, especially when I know exactly what she's after. Her left hand is firmly planted against my chest as she uses it for balance while she rocks slowly against my dick. I take it away, catching her off guard and bringing her down to me.

Once her lips are a hairsbreadth away from mine, I spin the ring on her finger. "You're still wearing my ring."

"Should I have taken it off?"

"No. It's exactly where it needs to be."

Her eyes flutter between mine and my mouth. "Does that mean you're officially keeping me?"

"I may have let you go, but you stole my heart. I plan on letting you keep it." I let my tip nudge her entrance, making her pouty lips part with a gasp. Her lidded gaze lands on mine, and I can't help myself. I push in more.

"Mmm," she draws out, and I close the distance, desperate to feel her ecstasy vibrate through my soul. Our mouths connect, and she pushes back on my cock, fully seating herself in one go, only deepening her throaty moan. She's fucking ready. Like me, this past week wore on her mentally and physically. I could tell the moment she took her dress off that she hadn't been eating every meal. The curves I love to grab aren't as prominent, but I'll be damned if I'm not going to spend every day of the rest of my life trying to make her happy.

"Ride me, baby," I say as I pull back on a breathless pant.

She pushes up onto her hands just enough to find the angle she wants, which puts her perfect tits right in my face. I immediately palm one and suck her nipple hard into my mouth.

"Oh God," she cries as she picks up her pace. My mouth leaves one, only to nip and suck my way over to the other, but before I pull her other nipple into my mouth, I lose myself and bite her a little too hard. "Ow," she growls, but before I can apologize, she says, "Fuck, do it again."

"Yeah?" is all that slips from my lips. She's riding my cock hard, and her juices are dripping down my balls when I pinch her nipple between my teeth before sucking it into my mouth. "Yes," she hisses, slowing her stride to let my cock drag over that spot she loves deep inside. "You feel so good. I don't want to come. I don't want this to end."

"It's not going to end. We're going to finish this here, and then I'm taking you back inside the house and not letting you leave until I've rediscovered every inch of this body." My hands glide down her hips, and when they slip farther down her back to grip her cheeks, a bandage catches my attention. I hold her still and ask, "What happened? What is this?" I let my finger run over the edges.

"I'm fine. It's nothing. I just got my shot," she says as she wiggles her hips to keep going, but I stop her.

"That's not nothing, Mackenzie. I want a baby with you." My eyes search hers, and I know she sees it. Without words, I know she hears what I'm saying. I love Summer with my whole heart, but I want biological children. I want a piece of me and her. "I want to start a family with you. I want everything."

Her eyes soften, and the smallest amount of regret bubbles inside me when the truth behind my ask registers. I don't want her sympathy. I want her to want what I want. I want her to want a family with me.

Leaning down, she gently kisses my lips. "I plan on having them all."

"All?" I quirk a brow before confirming, "As in, more than one?"

She smiles. "Yes, more than one. Just not today. Right now, all I want is you. Can you be happy with that?"

I hear her ask. She's nine years younger than me, and I understand wanting to take the time to be just her and me. Pushing her hair back behind her ear, I say, "As long as I have you, I have everything I want." But it doesn't stop me from taunting her anyway. I can't help myself. "How accurate is that shot?" My hands return to her hips, and I pump up into her.

"Ninety-nine percent," she answers as she bites her lip.

I quickly flip her over, pinning her beneath me and push in hard. "I won't be held responsible for the one percent." Her legs wrap around me, and it feels like home. It is home. I have the girl of my dreams wrapped around me. As much as I want to go hard, I don't. Even as the rain starts to gently fall, I don't hurry this moment because you can't rush something you want to last forever.

"Connor." Her hand cups the side of my face. "I haven't said it yet, but I know you felt it because it's been there all along." Her thumb runs over my bottom lip, and her eyes pour sentiment behind the words I know she's about to say. "I love you. I love you with my whole damn heart."

"My heart has loved you from the start, even with broken pieces and missing parts." I lay my forehead to hers and push in slowly one more time because I know that's all it will take. We've been on the edge from the start, willing this moment to last forever. "Come with me, baby." Those words are all it takes for us to let go.

As we catch our breath and come back down, the rain really starts to fall. I use my body to shield her, and as I hover on top of her, I say, "You were wrong, you know?"

"About what?" She bats her eyes as raindrops blow in and find her lashes.

"Us. This is a fairy tale. The virtuous protagonist forced into marrying a malevolent villain. Their journey is twisted and messy. They both blur the lines until suddenly they fade into one happily ever after. I'm pretty sure that's a love story."

A slow smile spreads across her face. "I love our story."

CHAPTER 30
MACKENZIE

EIGHT MONTHS LATER

"Connor," I call out as I walk through the first floor of the new house we are building opposite the lake. I couldn't find him anywhere, and he told me to meet him at the house. After searching every room back at the main house, I gave up and came down here, assuming I got it wrong. As I stand in the middle of the foyer with my hands on my hips, voices sound like they are coming from upstairs. "What the hell? I know he heard me," I mumble as I walk up the steps to the second floor.

After the dust settled and Connor and Josh realized that neither of them would ever escape each other, I came up with the idea to build a house for Josh on Connor's property. Connor and I have no plans of getting divorced, and Josh is not only my brother, but Summer's father. Josh was looking at buying houses in the area anyway, so why not build? It's the perfect setup for Summer. She gets the best of both worlds. She can come and go between houses as she pleases. Plus, it was the ideal opportunity for me to try my hand at a custom build from start to finish. My floor plans, my designs, everything. I've been vlogging and posting updates regularly as I try to build my brand, and so far, it's been great. I hadn't planned on becoming a social media influencer in the process, but I can't complain. The further along in the project I got, the more people started following to watch the progress, which led to some brand collaborations. Those followers and this new status are what's allowing me to gain a following, find projects and paying customers. It's how I'm turning my dream into a reality. That last part is what sold Connor. While the appeal of having Summer close was a top contender, supporting me in the pursuit of my dream was bigger.

When my foot hits the top step, I hear what sounds like sniffles, and I stop. "I just don't want you to feel like I don't love you," Summer stutters out between sobs. I should go back down the steps and leave them to whatever private moment this is, but any movement I make would be a distraction. The floors are still unfinished. If I move, my footsteps will be heard.

"Summer, you will always be mine. A name doesn't change that. If you want to call Trent 'Dad,' I promise I'll be okay. I know what we have is special."

Tears instantly well in my eyes, and now I'm the one trying not to sniffle. It hadn't escaped me that once Summer was living with us, I never once heard her call Connor dad. She always called him Coach. He said he never pushed her to call him dad when she was little like most parents do. When you have babies, one of the first words you try to teach them is 'mama' or 'dada.' He explained he never did that because it didn't seem fair. It would only make the day she found out the truth that much harder because he knew in his heart there would always be a truth. Connor never planned on keeping her paternity a secret. He just didn't expect Josh to be in the picture. But the events that transpired over the past few months forced his hand, and now he's coparenting with my brother. I think they've discovered they don't hate each other as much as they thought they did. However, neither is ready to own up to that truth.

"You promise you won't look at me any different? What if I want to change my name?"

I can hear Connor pull in a stuttered breath. He's being so fucking strong. I know every damn word is gutting him. While we agreed to wait on starting our own family, I know the day I tell him I'm pregnant can't come soon enough, and I'd be lying if I said overhearing this conversation now doesn't make me want to give him exactly what he wants just to help heal his hurt.

"Sunshine, you forget I've always known exactly who you were, and I loved you anyway. The universe conspired against me and brought you into my world. It's because of you that I got to learn what love is. If you choose to become Summer Wells, that doesn't change anything."

I hear her say, "Okay," her voice more assured as her snivels subside. His words made it all better. "I didn't mean to ruin the surprise."

"You didn't ruin the—"

No, no, no, no. What surprise? Crap, the last thing I want to do is ruin a surprise. I stomp my foot on the landing and call, "Connor, are you up here?" acting as though I haven't been standing here for the past five minutes.

"Yeah, we're in Summer's new room."

I walk down the hall and pinch my cheeks so that, hopefully, my face isn't splotchy from being choked up. I wear my emotions on my sleeve. I always have, and I hate it. Everyone always knows exactly how I'm feeling.

When I turn the corner, I find them in the room sitting on buckets. "What are you guys doing up here?"

"Summer is thinking she wants one of those hanging beds in her room, and I couldn't remember if you vaulted the ceilings up here."

My eyes shoot toward the ceiling to look at the beam

placement to see where we would have to put the bed if this is really what she wants.

"We'd have to move the bed over four feet." I look at the wall, throwing my arms out wide, and add, "It wouldn't be centered."

Looking over, I see immediate disappointment written all over Summer's face. I think quick and try to come up with a new spot. "What if we put it in front of the window? That could be nice."

Her face lights up, and she instantly clasps her hands together. "That would be perfect." She runs over, throws her arms around my waist, and hugs me. "Thank you, thank you, thank you. I'm going to go tell my dad right now."

I immediately look at Connor, but he drops his gaze, not wanting to meet my eye. I know this is hard for him, and I don't want to make this a bigger deal than I know it is. So I leave it alone because her other comment warrants my attention as well.

"I thought Josh was out of town until Friday?"

"Oops." She covers her mouth and turns toward Connor. "Sorry, Coach."

That's when I notice their outfits. They're both dressed nicer than usual. Summer is wearing a dress with a wool shawl that matches the jacket Connor is wearing. His coat is unzipped, revealing the attire underneath is just as nice. He's wearing a long-sleeved white polo, light blue heathered slacks, and light brown wingtips. The man looks fucking edible. I love it when he wears dress pants. They stretch across his thighs and ass perfectly. They are my weakness. While we have no issues in the sex department, he knows dress pants are a guaranteed, 'I'll take you here, and it doesn't matter who sees.' But what doesn't make sense is he told me we were staying home tonight. We usually go out to eat on Friday nights.

"What gives? Did Josh come home early and you guys changed your minds on dinner? Why are you dressed up?"

Connor's hands are in his pockets as he stares at the ground. I'm about to walk over and give him a hug I know he needs after hearing Summer refer to Josh as 'dad' when his lips purse before quirking up into the softest of smiles.

"Summer, can you give me a minute alone with Mackenzie?"

She smiles real big and says, "Yep," before scurrying off down the hall.

I bite my lip as I try to control my face. I don't want to smile before I have a reason to, but these two are clearly up to something. He waltzes across the room with a little extra swagger in his step as those dark brown eyes meld into mine. This man makes me weak in the knees, and he knows it. I keep waiting for the day I'm not so wholly smitten, but it has yet to come. Every day with him is better than the last.

Grabbing me around the waist, he pulls me close. "You know I love you, right?"

My eyes search his, looking for some clue as to where he's going with this line of questioning, but I come up short. "I think you love me about as much as I love you. Endlessly."

He presses his forehead to mine and steals my breath. It's his signature move. I know he's serious when he does it. At this distance, there's no mistaking his intent. The man doesn't just want my attention. His heart does.

"I hope you mean that because I have a surprise for you."

"What—" He steals my words by taking my mouth, his tongue instantly demanding access that I grant without reservation as he pulls me tight, letting it brush up against mine in one long, slow, tantalizing stroke, only to let me go with a growl.

"Come on. I can't kiss you right now. If I stand here a second longer, I won't leave this room, and I have something to show you." He pulls me by the hand and leads me out.

"Connor, where are we going? What is this?" I ask as he pulls me down the hallway toward the stairs at the back of the house. He doesn't answer me, and I start to get nervous. *What could possibly have him this worked up?*

He stops at the back door but doesn't give me his eyes. "Almost a year ago, a very important question was taken away from me. Tonight, I wanted to rectify that." Before I even have time to process his words, he's pulling the back door open, only to face me and drop to one knee. "Mackenzie Marie Callahan, will you do me the honor of being my wife again?"

My eyes instantly dart from him to the back yard, where all our friends and family are watching, waiting on bated breath for my reply. Some of them know our story, and others know a half-truth version. The majority of this town believes we eloped. That wasn't too far of a stretch. Our ceremony was private and secret.

When I take too long to respond, he says, "This is how it should have always been."

My eyes return to him, and when they do, I see he's pulled out a pear-shaped diamond ring. Neither of us has ever removed the rings Everett presented us on the day we officially became married, and I never asked for more. I didn't need it. I don't need this now. Connor is everything I want. I don't need a ceremony or diamond to make it any more authentic, but if I've learned anything about my husband, it's that he's traditional. Connor is doing this because it's important to him. He wants to experience everything with me, and this is part of that. My heart can't help but melt as I get choked up and frantically nod because there is no way I could make my lips work and hold back the river of tears pooling behind my eyes. I hold out my hand, and he easily slips the ring on, sliding it next to my band before sweeping me into his arms and twirling me around.

"Because of you, I get to be the man I've always dreamed of being. My heart will forever be yours." My tears can't help but fall, and he sets me down. Pulling my face into his hands, he says, "Don't cry, baby."

I shake my head. "These are happy tears. I love you so much it hurts."

His lips cover mine, and everyone cheers, but the sound quickly fades like it always has when it's him and me. When I have him like this, the world falls away. His strong arms wrap around me, and it's home. His hand quickly snakes down and grabs my cheek hard before he pulls out of our kiss and yells, "In case you missed it, she said yes!" I can't help it. I smile so big my face hurts. His excitement is contagious. That's when my eyes connect with my mother's, and my heart stumbles. Connor immediately notices when my hand tightens around his, and says, "I thought she should be here." He kisses my forehead. "Meet me at the altar in twenty minutes, wife."

"What?" I question, wholly confused.

He points to one of the guests standing by the bar, and I see that it's Morgan, the same old white-haired man who married us the first time. "I'm not waiting a second longer to make you mine in every way, in front of all our friends and family, the way it should have always been." I nod, and he lets me go. "Go see your mom."

As I walk down the back steps, I take in the backyard. It's decorated beautifully, simple, rustic, and timeless. Tall gas heaters are strategically placed throughout the yard as well as small firepits to keep guests warm. It's nothing over-the-top, but it's perfect. There's a bar and a canopy of gold lights with a table running down the center set for all our guests, and at the very end, I can see an altar. God, I love this man. He has the biggest fucking heart of anyone I know. It's hard to look back and find a time when it wasn't so, and that's because, in the end, tough love is still love. It might not be easy, but it's worth it.

When I finally reach my mom, I see recognition. Having her here has been great. Josh brought her down and found a facility here in town for her to stay. The place is a lot nicer than the one back home, but they've also worked with her in ways the other place didn't. More money has truly translated into better care. When I found out how much her care was costing, I worried that Josh would go broke within a year. Turns out, he spent the past five years getting his law degree in Munich and working for my father. However, it's not his money paying for Tish's care. It's my father's.

It took me a while to care to meet my father. I had always assumed I would never meet him. I never cared about finding him. Why would I, when it appeared he didn't care to find me? I didn't think I was missing out on anything. Little did I know my mom was keeping us from him, but I understand why she did it, and that's why I had to let meeting with him marinate. In some ways, meeting him felt like I was betraying my mother after all she sacrificed to live without him. But on one of her days of clarity, I asked if she would tell me about him, and she said, "Letting him go was an act of love. It was my sacrifice. It doesn't need to be yours. The love between a parent and their children differs from that shared between lovers. I was wrong to keep you from him. He can and will love you the way he couldn't love me."

I hadn't realized how much I needed those words until she said them. My whole life I believed that my mother didn't believe in the concept of love or the sanctity of marriage. Her beliefs molded my own and heavily influenced what I allowed myself to feel. Looking back, I know it's what kept me from trusting Connor with my secrets, even though I felt it in the depths of my soul that he was always meant to be mine. Hearing her words freed me, and next week, I'm meeting with my dad.

"You're a lucky girl, Mackenzie. That man loves you with everything he is, and it shows," my mother says from her seated spot on one of the haybales beside a firepit.

"Thanks, Mom, that means a lot coming from you. I'm so glad you got to make it out tonight. I know you don't like to leave the Magnolia House."

She waves her hand in dismissal. "I wouldn't miss this. Plus, Josh said he wanted to show me the new house I'd be living in."

Before I can question her, Josh walks up behind me and squeezes my shoulders. "Mom, I told you to let me tell her first." He sits beside our mom and takes her hand. "I want Mom to stay in the first-floor master. I'll take a room upstairs. I want Summer to get to know her grandmother while she can." My mouth opens to argue, but he stops me. "Before you say she needs the treatments and assistance, I don't want you to worry. I've already handled all that. I have an in-home care nurse who will start working with her at Magnolia House next week to make her transition from there to here easier."

"That sounds amazing," I say as I kiss my mother's forehead before taking Josh's hand and adding, "Mom, I'll be right back. I have something I need to talk with Josh about." She smiles, and I can see her moment of clarity is fading.

"Josh, I don't think you know what you're getting yourself into. I know Mom is doing better, but there isn't a cure for this. I just worry about the impact it could have on Summer. When Mom isn't present, it can be jarring. It's why I made the decision to get her help even though it drained everything I had."

His gaze drops to the ground. "I'm doing this for Summer. I know it won't be easy, but you have to understand, Summer's world has done a complete one-eighty over the past few months." He runs his hand through his hair, and his eyes meet mine. "We found each other, and our instant connection has been more than I ever could have hoped for, but lately, she's been asking more about Holly, and I've been having a hard time finding anything to say." His eyes break away, and I see his pain.

Summer knows Holly passed away. The story we've told her is a half-truth that fits her age and isn't exactly a lie. Her mother was sick. Holly was a narcissistic psychopath. She would manipulate, charm, and exploit people and feel no remorse for the harm she inflicted. I read the letter Holly wrote before Josh decided to burn it. The woman thought she was doing society a favor. She thought people should thank her for the heinous crimes she committed. Holly was rotten to the core, and I understand how Summer asking questions can be triggering when you have nothing nice to say. Josh is processing, too. It's easy to overlook his pain when there's a little girl involved.

"Look, M, I know moving Mom in is a little selfish. It will be a transition for her. It won't be all rainbows, but I want her close. Not just for me, but for Summer, too. I want her to know her family. She's already lost her mom, and you and I have yet to discuss Zane. Don't get me wrong. I'm not ready to cross that bridge, but this is something I can give her. And I want it for myself too. I lost time, too."

Zane doesn't know about Summer. The week after everything went down with Holly, he stayed in town to handle getting her transported to Montana for burial. During that time, he came looking for me at the Fields and once again tried to argue his innocence, claiming what he did was to keep me safe and what happened at the club was an accident, that he never meant to hurt me. However, as much as I wanted to believe him, if not for any other reason than to erase the stain his actions caused and look to the future—one where he's part of my life because of Summer—I couldn't, because our definitions of an accident are vastly different. An accident is falling down, spilling mustard on your white shirt, or writing the wrong date while filling out a form. That night at the club, he made a decision. Though sudden, it was thought out, and it had consequences. It's only an "accident" or "just this once" until it happens again. What you allow, you become.

That day, I had to explain it was too little too late. I would never be able to trust him after everything he put me through. Maybe things could have been different if he had come out and been honest with me from the start. It's possible if I'd known all along, I never would have shown up at that address, but then I never would have ended up here. Zane wasn't my person. It would only be a matter of time before we figured it out. It was clear during his visit that he had no idea Holly was a mom. Summer never came up, and I wasn't about to tell him. I'm still unsure how I feel about telling Zane. I don't trust him. That one misstep was big and erased any good that existed. It called into question every truth he ever told me. The night it happened, I didn't see remorse on his face for his actions. I saw anger. He wasn't sorry. He was angry he got caught. Now, I understand the pressure Josh is feeling. He wants to give his daughter something. He wants to fill her world with the people he can give her while he can.

"Okay, we'll figure this out. Instead of having a first-floor laundry room, I'll move it to the basement, and we can convert that space into a maid's quarters so that the nurse can be close."

His eyes light up when he sees I'm on board. Pulling me into his arms, he hugs me. "Thank you, M. I promise it's all going to work out. Also, I feel weird saying this—it doesn't feel natural, but that's just because I'm still adjusting to this new normal—but I wanted to say I'm happy for you. Connor is a good guy."

I smile and look over my shoulder in search of him, only to find him standing across the yard, talking to Holden and his uncles. His eyes flash to mine, and he smiles. "Yeah, he's pretty great."

"You should go. I have a surprise for Summer I need to go get out of my truck."

"Oh, yeah? What's that?" I say, my eyes narrowing on him as I try to determine what else he's plotting.

"It's a surprise. You'll see it soon enough."

"Fine," I say as I turn on my heel and look out over the crowd of people who have come to celebrate with us tonight.

That's when I spot Everett on the back deck alone, drink in hand, with a scowl on his face that doesn't fit the evening. When I follow his line of sight, I see why. Cameron is sitting at the bar, her head thrown back, laughing at something Parker has said. The laughing doesn't help, but it's not the root of his impassioned glare. No, I have no doubt that's from the sight of Parker's arm wrapped around her waist. *That's new.*

When I reach the bar to grab my own glass of wine, Parker drops his arm and whispers something in her ear. She nods in agreement, and he walks off. I immediately fill his vacated space and ask, "What was that?"

Cameron smiles. "I'm not sure what you mean."

"Bullshit. Spill it. Are you and Parker a thing now? When did this happen?"

She rolls her eyes. "We're having fun. It's not a big deal."

"Cam, we both know Parker is not a 'just having fun' type of guy. You're going to break his damn heart."

She looks around before leaning in. "No, I'm not. He knows the deal. Tell me, have you noticed anything else tonight?"

My eyes narrow on hers, and I know immediately what she's asking. "You mean the scowl that's been plastered on Everett's face. Yeah, it's hard to miss." That's when it hits me what this is. "No, Cam. Tell me you are not using Parker to make Everett jealous."

She shrugs nonchalantly like it's no big deal. "Parker knows exactly what I'm looking for, and he's happy to oblige."

"You're telling me you told him you wanted him to pretend to be into you so that you could make Everett jealous?"

"Not exactly. I told him I needed a fake boyfriend. I didn't tell him why. He asked if that came with any benefits, and I didn't say no."

She pulls a compact and red lip gloss out of her purse to reapply, and I say, "I don't know. I don't think this is a good idea. Everett considers Parker family. If anything, that might make things harder for you."

Snapping her mirror closed, she says, "Sometimes men need an extra push to get them out of their own way. I'm sure what I have with Everett looks like a girl crush, but I promise it's more than that. It might have started out that way, but Everett isn't an unsuspecting victim. He plays into my hand, he knows what I want, and I'm done watching him pretend he doesn't want the same damn thing."

"Hey," Connor's big hands wrap around my waist from behind. "I'm going to need to steal my girl back. I owe her some words."

Cameron twists up her face. "You two are too cute. You make me sick, but I'm happy for you guys, especially because not only did I get a best friend out of the deal but"—she punches Connor in the arm in jest—"we got Con back."

"Come on." He pulls me by my hand. "I'm done waiting to make you mine."

"You do remember I already have your last name, right?"

He gives me a shy smile before pulling me into his chest. "Yeah, you might have my name, all my days, and all my nights, but now it's time to give you the rest of my life." He leans down and gently presses his lips to mine before nodding toward the altar. "Ready?"

"I've never been more ready," I say as I let him pull me by the hand, letting the past and its pain fade away and fall apart so that all that's left is falling into forever.

THE END

BONUS EPILOGUE

Did the story end too soon? Do you want more of Connor and Mackenzie? Hear their vows, find out what Summer's surprise was, and get ready to swoon over Connor's grand gesture as something old makes a reappearance.

Click here to read now or scan below.

ALSO BY L.A. FERRO

Want Holden & Aria's Story? Read about it now in DIG.

DIG: A Second Chance Romance

Trope list: Sports Romance, College Romance, Dark Secrets, Emotional Scars, Second Chance, Redemption.

The Delicate Vows Duet - A Billionaire Romance

Trope list: Billionaire Romance, Off-limits, Age-gap, Secret Virgin, Different Worlds, He Falls First.

Wicked Beautiful Lies: A Taboo Romance

Trope list: Taboo/forbidden, Mistaken Identity, Enemies to Lovers, Dark Secrets.

Sweet Venom: A Why Choose Romance

Trope List: Taboo, Enemies to Lovers, Friends to Lovers, Dark Secrets, Different Worlds, Unrequited Love.

ACKNOWLEDGMENTS

I can't write an acknowledgments section without first mentioning TL Swan. Were it not for her selfless decision to share her trade secrets with the world and inspire writers with a dream in their hearts to put pen to paper, this journey never would have begun.

AK Landow, you're not just an author bestie. You're a confidant. I value your input and appreciate your friendship more than you know. You've pushed me outside of my comfort zone more than I'm willing to admit. First, it was the book signings and then the beta readers. All the good stuff is always outside of our comfort zone. Thank you for helping me grow.

My author besties, Jade Dollston, Carolina Jax, and Kay Cove: Our daily conversations, whether they be author-related or not, fuel me. I love the support we all give each other. On my hardest days, I know one of you will always come through with words of affirmation or jokes that make whatever weight I was carrying less heavy. Your friendships on this journey have been invaluable.

To my first ARC reader turned Beta Lakshmi, thank you for taking the time to be one of the first sets of eyes on my heart. Yes, I said heart, not book, because that's what every book is to me. It's my heart spilled onto these pages. I pour my soul into these characters, and sharing that with someone for feedback isn't easy. I appreciate you so damn much. Thank you for pumping me up and helping me sparkle. I'm truly grateful.

To my ARC & Street Teams: So many of you have been with me from the beginning, and that seems so crazy to me. I can't tell you how much it fills my heart that so many of you come back time and time again. I want you to know that I see you! Your support gives me the strength to go out there and promote my books with confidence for every launch and every day after. Below are a few of the incredible people that came with me on this journey.

Allison Thommen, Brandy Wine, Ren Somers-Day, Dorothy Yvonne, Jennie Cathcart, Kat Sheree, Kailey D, Kayla Price, Leah Edwards, Taylor Nobles, Kate Schaeffer, Autumn Kiger, Sayward Callaghan, Jayde Skillington, Kimmy Diaz, Nicole Kincaid, Elizabeth Satala, Serena Dolce, Ashlyn Romero, Stephanie DeWaide, Aliyah Smith, Tiffany Kinchen, Kat Schumacher, Breana Molina, Jessica Johnson, Tanya Fenner, Kass Baker, Heather Williams, Brittany, Kelani, Maizie Love, Mara Gregory, Emily Cherry, Layla, Jessica Lee, Court Anne, Wendy Kairschner, Becky Jaegle, Amanda G, Terry Wilson, Melanie Darrow Sweeney, Kassandra Lopez, Carla Dionne, Meredith Denese, Heather Douglas,Olivia Pace, NaToshya Reed, Stephanie DeWaide, Martha, Tracie Mattingly, Hottopicreads, Olivia Rose, Kolleen Irene, Stephanie Vicente , Victoria Shelton, Ashley Townsley, Kelly Streeter, Savannah C, Kim Lewis, Anna Pendergast, Shannon Walsh, Nancy A Pasquale, Stormy Porter, Keli Moore Bruce, Nichole Demello, Doni Smith, Samantha, Maggie Marrero, Kat Wood, Kayla P, Brittany Morrow.

Your kindness is everything. THANK YOU!

ABOUT THE AUTHOR

L.A. Ferro has had a love for storytelling her entire life. For as long as she can remember, she put herself to sleep, plotting stories in her head. That thirst for a good tale led her to books, where she became an avid reader.

The unapologetically dramatic characters, steamy scenes, and happily ever afters found inside the pages of romance novels irrevocably transformed her. The world of romance ran away with her heart, and she knew her passion for love would be her craft.

When she's not trailing after one of her three crazy kids, she loves to construct messy 'happily ever afters' that take her readers on a journey full of angst, lust, and obsession with page-turning enchantment.

Made in United States
Troutdale, OR
11/17/2023

14665133R00221